Whistling Past the Graveyard

And Other Tales

By
Jonathan Maberry

JournalStone

JOURNALSTONE
YOUR LINK TO ARTISTIC TALENT

JournalStone books may be ordered through booksellers or by contacting:

JournalStone

www.journalstone.com

The views expressed in this work are solely those of the authors and do not necessarily reflect the views of the publisher, and the publisher hereby disclaims any responsibility for them.

ISBN: 978-1-942712-67-1   (sc)
ISBN: 978-1-942712-68-8   (ebook)
ISBN: 978-1-942712-69-5   (hc)

JournalStone rev. date: July 22, 2016

Library of Congress Control Number: 2016941827

Printed in the United States of America

Cover Art & Design: Robert Grom
Image Credits: Grave Stone: Stuart Monk/Shutterstock, Crow: Marcin Perkowski/Shutterstock, Blood: Suzi Nelson/Shutterstock

Edited by: Aaron J. French

Dedication

This is for William F. Nolan.

Bill's story, "And Miles to Go Before I Sleep," was the first piece of short fiction I ever fell in love with. It was suggested to me by Ray Bradbury, who gave me Bill's wonderful collection, *Impact 20*, on a snowy February evening in 1971. Ray had written the introduction to the book and said I would love all of the stories, but that one in particular. He was right. It also ignited within me a love of short form fiction.

Thanks Ray, and especially thanks to you, Bill!

And, as always, for Sara Jo

Table of Contents

Introduction

By

Scott Sigler

May 9, 2016

Delve deep into the history of American entertainment, and you'll find yourself in an idyllic little town where the sheriff enforced the law with nothing more than down-home common sense, an aw-shucks grin, and a brook-no-bullshit attitude caked in casual calmness. Of course, that sheriff would have never used the word "bullshit," because there just weren't no need to curse when you visited Mayberry.

From 1960 to 1968, Mayberry was the setting for "The Andy Griffith Show." Andy Griffith was the sheriff of a small town that epitomized the projected values of Main Street, USA. He was famous for not carrying a gun. His erstwhile, bumbling deputy Barney Fife *did* carry a gun, yet had only one bullet.

Yeah. That was 1960. This is 2016, and there's a new sheriff in town. This one most certainly does carry a gun. More accurately, *guns*. Lots of them. He also lives in a "Mayberry," of sorts, but it's spelled a bit differently—"Maberry," as in, the mind of author Jonathan Maberry.

People are all different, but there are tells that let you instinctively group them by nation, by region, and if you're *from* that region, sometimes even by a specific town or city block. People talk a certain way, act a certain way. Their values, both the ones they openly espouse in the light of day and the ones they hide away in the dark, they can be fingerprints that thumb-down on a particular zip code. That's what Jonathan's stories are like—no matter where the kids wind up in the big bad world, no matter if they succeed or fail, they all graduated from the same high school—within a few sentences, you can just *tell* these stories came from the same place.

Let's call this place "Maberryland." It's a small town set somewhere in America's mountains, where maps aren't all that accurate, where families have lived for ten generations, where cell phones rarely get service and where outsiders simply *do not* go. Which is good, actually, because while outsiders may walk in vertical, they usually leave horizontal. If they leave at all.

Jump in a time machine with me. We travel from 1960-68, the era of The Andy Griffith Show's eight seasons, to 2006-2016, the first ten years of Jonathan's writing career. In the 45-odd years between the two, the Hollywood image of American law enforcement has shifted, to say the least. We leap from Andy Griffith—an unflappable pacifist—to the signature creation of Jonathan's mind, Joe Ledger, a man who embraces both his justified rage and the face-shearing violence that comes with it.

A man who has his Maberryland High School varsity jacket hanging up in the back of his closet.

Mayberry was clean and polished, a fresh-baked apple pie of a town where the only real fugitive was Old Sam, a legendary lunker of a carp that escaped Andy, Barnie, Opie, Goober and Floyd the Barber. Ha-ha! That crazy fish got away *again*!

Maberryland is dirty, sweaty, unapologetic. There's fishing here, sure, it's just that your boat is a Navy SEAL SOC-R, your tackle box is eight feet long and contains a mini-gun, a Remington 870, a rapid responder folder knife and some C4. "Old Sam" is a genetically engineered monster grizzly-squid with one tentacle holding the dead man's switch of a low-yield nuke poised to wipe out NYC. Sure, you can bring Opie along for a day of dappled sunlight, because *this* Opie went to Maberryland Junior High—he knows fifteen ways to kill you with his bare hands, has an AR-15 strapped across his back and is carrying that blowgun he made in shop class.

Mayberry's entire law enforcement complement had one bullet. In Maberryland, one bullet doesn't even cover the high-caliber Jonathan sprinkles on his morning Cheerios. We're talking at least an eight-round mag before the day even begins, with slices of C4 spread on yummy MREs (if you don't know where your mom hid the C4, there's extra in the SOC-R's tackle box).

If we had to focus on just one point where Mayberry, USA and Maberryland differ, it is this: the former is a place without killing—the latter is a landscape of carnage, a Megadeth opera of bullets, brain matter, bravery and brawn. Are there smart people in Jonathan's stories? Of course there are, Jonathan's work makes it clear he does not brook stupidity in life or in his characters. But does intelligence ensure the win? Rarely. Even for the brightest of characters, in Maberryland the simple argument over a parking spot often devolves into a gnashing, spit-splattered, knife-slashing battle of who wants to live more.

When it comes to Jonathan's fiction, the small town metaphor works in another way as well. Small towns are the home of regular folk. Jonathan doesn't do his wet-work in the land of generals, politicians or super-powered heroes. You come to Maberryland to read about the people on the front lines, death-dealers soaked in the blood of their enemies.

Some people write about the decision-makers. Jonathan writes about *operatives*, those that do the up-close nasty work, as in the tale "Death Song of Dwar Guntha." Who writes a story about the world of John Carter from Mars that doesn't feature John Carter? Jonathan Maberry does. John Carter is untouchable, bulletproof and godlike—not so the men that serve under him. Those poor bastards can die, which makes them permanent residents of Maberryland.

Take the story "Clean Sweeps," for example, where far-future grunts have the same dirt-eating job as the grunts of this century and centuries long past—killing and being killed on the front lines, because of the decisions of others.

Or in the story "Chokepoint," where the zombie apocalypse begins. Are we in the tent of some high-ranking colonel? Or the CDC lab where the brightest and best puzzle out this strange infection spreading across the land? No. We're with four grunts, guarding a bridge, with no support, no communication and no explanations.

Oh, I didn't mention that zombies live in Maberryland? Sorry about that. Because they do. Hordes of them. So do vampires. Vamps *love* Maberryland. In short: Andy Griffith's down-home charm wouldn't be worth two wet farts in this place, and One-Bullet Barney Fife would be a vamp's blood-doll bitch in ten seconds flat.

Jonathan even manages to make the unstoppable force that is GI Joe more grounded and realistic in "Flint & Steel," perhaps the only story in that particular universe that made me think, "You know maybe it *wouldn't* be all that fun to be a Joe..."

Yes, Maberryland is the place where grunts live, but don't think you're safe because you're not in the armed forces. In this town, the word "grunt" doesn't apply to just soldiers. It applies to everyday Americans, the workers, the toilers, the luckless, those that never had a chance—the very bones of the nation. It's the fog rolling through the peaks of Appalachia, where a young man seeking his family past unfortunately finds it in "Calling Death." It's a sociopathic little girl whose pretty pony fun-time doesn't involve ponies at all, but rather her hapless sister and a lovely man known as "Doctor Nine." It is the plague of meth and hopeless children in "Crooked." It's an inner city tattoo parlor where black and white take on different meanings in "Ink." It's even Sherlock Holmes, who gets a taste of West Virginia justice in "The Adventure of the Greenbrier Ghost."

But this collection isn't *just* about Maberryland. Up the road a piece, a little higher in the mountains, there's a little town called Pine Deep. Sure, you've heard of it, you've heard of the "Most Haunted Town in America." This is where Jonathan's fiction career began. His first three novels were the Pine Deep Trilogy, consisting of Bram Stoker Award-winning GHOST ROAD BLUES, DEAD MAN'S SONG, and BAD MOON RISING. If you've been itching to come back to this place, you're in luck—here there be *four* stories that baste you in the horror gravy of this tiny Pennsylvania town: "Long Way Home," "Mister Pockets," "Property Condemned," and the titular "Whistlin' Past the Graveyard."

This collection documents Jonathan's love affair with the short story. Novels are his bread and butter, but short fiction is his delicious dessert. I know how he feels, as I've been lucky enough to pen four short stories for Maberry-edited anthologies. I hope to write many more for him, and I sure as hell hope he keeps writing them himself.

I want him to write more because Maberryland is just *begging* for a new cul-de-sac full of slightly sagging homes and suspicious mounds of fresh dirt. As you read through these pages, allow the zombies to roll out the welcome wagon, the vamps to invite you to the PTA meetings, the grunts to fire up the VFW barbecue and the unabashedly American chamber of commerce to take you fishing.

There's a new sheriff in town. And this one has a *lot* of bullets.

-Scott Sigler-

Whistling Past the

Graveyard

And Other Tales

Author's Note on "Doctor Nine"

This story is the very first of a loose cycle of tales told about a place called 'The Fire Zone,' which doesn't quite exist in the real world, but which exists in the private worlds of every person. Down the hill from the bright lights of the Fire Zone is a darker place called Boundary Street. Bad things happen there. Worse things live there. I created the Fire Zone for an experimental play I wrote in the early 1980s, and elements of it have begun to appear in my fiction. "Doctor Nine" is not set in the heart of either the Zone or Boundary Street, but the influence of the latter informs this story.

Oh, and 'Doctor Nine' was the name I gave to my personal boogeyman when I was a troubled little kid.

Doctor Nine

-1-

They blew into town on a Halloween wind.

The Mulatto drove the big roadster, and the Sage sat beside him, snickering into his yellow beard. Telephone poles whipped by, one after the other, and Zasha made a joke about their looking like crosses waiting for saviors. They all laughed and laughed, except for Doctor Nine who always smiled but never, ever laughed.

The car tore through the veils of shadow that draped like sackcloth between the distant lampposts. The night was in no way larger than the car, though it tried—and failed—to loom around the vehicle. The car was really the darkness of that night; it was far more a part of the night than the shadows. You couldn't imagine what that car would look like in daylight. It wasn't that kind of car.

Flocks of shapeless nightbirds flew on before the car and whenever the roadster would stop the birds would wheel and circle beneath the hungry stars. Against the fierce glow of the sneering moon the birds were tatters of feather and bone. Their call was more mocking than plaintive. The birds were always there; as long as Doctor Nine was there, they were there. It was in the manner of things and both the birds and Doctor Nine accepted the arrangement. It suited them all.

The Mulatto never spoke when he drove. He never spoke at all. He could, but he chose not to, and his throat had gone dry and dusty over the years. When he laughed it was the whisper of rat feet over old floorboards. Knuckly hands clutched the wheel and his bare feet pressed gas and brakes and sometimes clawed the carpeted floor. Around his neck he wore a medicine pouch, which he'd taken from a Navajo crystal gazer, and some parts of the crystal gazer were in there, too. He wore jeans and a faded Dead Kennedys t-shirt, a stolen wristwatch, and seven wedding rings, one on almost every finger. He was working on a complete set. Little sparks of light flickered from his fingers as he wheeled hand-over-hand around bends in the highway.

Beside him, the Sage ate chicken from a metal bucket. The bucket was smeared with chicken blood, and feathers drifted lazily to the floor. He offered a wing to Zasha, who declined with a wicked smile, but Spike bent forward from the back seat and plucked the wing out of the Sage's fingers. In the brief exchange their hands were contrasted in a display-counter spill of light from a passing streetlamp: the yellow, faintly reptilian mottling on the Sage's fingers, the thin webbing which had begun to grow between his thumb and index finger; and the overly-long, startlingly delicate fingers of Spike, dusted now with a haze of brown hairs, nails as long as a fashion model's though much sharper. The wing vanished into the back and Spike bent forward to eat it. He shot a quick, inquiring glance at Doctor Nine, who nodded permission and looked away out into the night. Spike ate with as little noise as he could manage, the bones crunching softly between his serrated teeth.

Doctor Nine looked dreamily at the passing cars, imagining lives and hearts and souls contained within those fragile metal shells like tins of caviar. In the hum of the car's engine he could hear the hum of life itself, the palpable field of human energy. As subtle as *chi*, as definite as arterial pumping. In the whisk of cars passing one another he heard gasps and soft cries, the stuff of nighttime encounters, expected and unexpected.

"Take the next exit," he said to the Mulatto and the big roadster followed a line of cars angling toward a big city that glowed like embers under a cloud of carbon smutch.

Doctor Nine smiled and smiled, knowing that something wonderful was about to happen.

-2-

Bethy sat awake nearly all night watching Millie die. She thought it was quite beautiful. In the way spiders are beautiful. The way a mantis is beautiful when it mates, and feeds. If her sister thought it was something else…well, so what? Bethy and Millie had never seen eye-to-eye, not once unless Bethy was lying about it. Bethy was a very good liar. All it took was practice. It was a game they had started playing just a couple of hours after they all got home from camping. Mom and Dad were already asleep in their room, and Bethy had convinced Millie that it would be fun to stay up and pretend that they were still camping, still lost in the big, dark woods.

Millie thought that would be fun, too. Millie was easy to lead, though she truly had a completely different sense of what was fun.

Millie thought Pokémon was fun. Millie liked her Barbies unscarred and her Ken dolls unmelted. Millie liked *live* puppies. Millie was blind to the sound of blood, the song of blood.

Bethy said that they could pretend that Doctor Nine was going to come and tell them spooky campfire stories. Dad's big flashlight was their campfire.

Millie, sweet and pretty in her flannel robe with the cornflower pattern, her fuzzy slippers, agreed to the game even though she thought that Doctor Nine was a dumb name for an imaginary friend. Well, to be fair, she truly did think that Doctor Nine *was* imaginary, and that Bethy had no actual friends.

The clock on the wall was a big black cartoon cat with eyes that moved back and forth and a tail that swished in time. Millie loved that, too. She called it Mr. Whiskers and would tell time according to what the cat said. "Mr. Whiskers says it's half-past six!"

Mr. Whiskers was counting out the remaining minutes of Millie's life, and wasn't that fun, too.

Bethy looked at the clock and saw that nearly an hour had gone by since Millie had drunk her warm milk. Plenty of time for the Vicodin to enter her bloodstream through the lining of her stomach wall. If Millie was going to get sick and throw them up it would have happened already, but...nothing, and that was good. It kept this tidy. Getting her to take the pills had been so easy. Once mashed with a hammer from the cellar the powder was easy to dissolve. It was no matter if it made the milk a little lumpy, as Bethy had brought big cookies upstairs as well. Cookies to dunk in the warm milk. Just perfect. Millie had swallowed all of it. Bethy only pretended to drink hers.

Now it was time to watch and learn. Bethy took out her diary and her pen and sat cross-legged on the floor, and watched.

-3-

Doctor Nine smiled as the car whisked down the ramp and entered the city. He stretched out with his senses, with perceptions grown old and precise and indefatigable with long, good use. Hearts pumped for him alone, of all the creatures on the window—black streets; minds thought for him, stomachs ached and rumbled with hunger for him, hands groped with lust for him. Eyes searched the shadows for delicious glimpses of him. Tongues tasted waiting lips and flesh ached to be touched. All by him, for him, with him. He knew that; just as he knew that these hearts and minds were few— fewer than in years before, but still there. Still strong and waiting and wanting.

Doctor Nine knew all of this, knew it without the dizzying rush of ego that might taint another creature of less cultured understanding. He licked his lips with a pink tongue-tip.

An SUV came abreast of their car and Doctor Nine turned in his seat to examine it. The Mulatto sensed his desire and shifted lanes occasionally so that Doctor Nine could see each passenger in turn. It was a family car burdened with a roof rack heavy with suitcases and camping tents. Each window of the car was like a picture frame that contained a separate portrait. One showed a wife, a pale creature defined by that label. Just wife. If there had ever been a more definite and individual personality it had either been leeched out of her along with the color of her skin, or she had put it away in some forgotten closet, perhaps with some thought that a life spent in sacrifice and servitude was a life well spent. Doctor Nine fought the urge to yawn.

The driver's window framed the father. Haggard, bored, distracted, and bitter. A jock-type with a soft jaw and receding hairline. Of no interest at all to Doctor Nine. This one wouldn't even have fantasies dark enough to be interesting.

The window behind the driver showed the profile of a pretty little girl with pigtails and pink cheeks who was bent over the piss-colored glow of a Game Boy screen, her face screwed up in concentration and her mind distressingly empty.

But then, as the Mulatto slowed the car just a little, Doctor Nine came abreast with the rear window, back where the luggage was usually stored, and there, with her face and hands pressed against the smoked glass, was a pale figure that stirred something old and deep in the Doctor's heart. She was the same age as the other girl, perhaps nine; but as unlike her twin as two creatures can be, born in same spill of shared blood. Dark unkempt hair and luminous brown eyes, large in the small, pale mask of her face.

Doctor Nine looked at her, totally aware of her. He could feel the intensity of her mind, the sharpness of it, the need of it. Just as he could feel the ache and the pain as she rode through the night surrounded by these meat sacks that pretended to love her and pretended to care for her when in reality they probably feared her.

As they should. He smiled at the thought and tested his senses against the razor sharpness of her need, knowing that she could and would cut, given the chance, given some direction.

Doctor Nine moved his consciousness deeper into the young mind and found that, though young in years, the hunger he encountered was every bit as old as that which coiled and waited within his own soul. Her darkness was too lovely, too profound to be trapped in the cage of meaningless flesh which contained it. Her soul was a screaming thing, locked by circumstance in the fragile shell of the human form. It shrieked for release.

Doctor Nine felt her fear and her need, and measured them against each other. He would not come to her to relieve her fears; nor would he come to satisfy her needs. He might come, however, if her need was strongest of all, stronger than all of the other splintered and badly formed emotions, because to him, need was the only true emotion.

He exerted a fraction more of his will and the little girl lifted her sad eyes toward his window. He made her see him through the dark glass, and as she turned toward him she saw him and she knew him.

From dreams she knew him. From dreams that her parents and her sister would have called nightmares; dreams that, had she been unlucky enough to share them, would have sent them shuddering and screeching into the nearest patch of light. As if light could protect them. He knew—could feel and sense and taste—that this little girl had dreamed of him, that she knew his name as well as she knew her own pain. As well as she knew her own need. Doctor Nine looked into her mind and knew that there were no gods in her dreaming world, just as there were none in her waking hell. When she looked into darkness, whether behind closed eyes or under the bed or into the moonless sky she saw only him. He was always there for her kind. Always.

Doctor Nine smiled at her.

The little girl looked at him for a long time with her owl-brown eyes. When she finally smiled it was a real smile. A smile as hot as blood and as sweet as pain. Her small mouth opened and she spoke a single, silent word, shaping it with her need and her love for him.

"Please."

The SUV veered suddenly and turned onto a boulevard and headed south toward the smutch and gloom that was clamped down around the heart of this city. It vanished from sight in a moment and the Mulatto rolled to a slow stop at the next corner. Everyone in the car stopped and quietly turned toward Doctor Nine.

Above them the nightbirds wheeled in the sky. Then one by one they peeled off and followed the SUV down the boulevard. Soon only the big roadster was left, alone and waiting.

Without haste Doctor Nine reached forward and touched the Mulatto's shoulder.

"Follow," he murmured.

The Mulatto nodded and turned the car around and then turned again to enter the boulevard. Spike and Zasha exchanged a glance.

"Something...?" Zasha asked casually, hiding the interest that brightened her eyes.

Doctor Nine nodded.

"What?" Spike asked. "That car we just passed?"

Another nod.

"Too late, Boss," muttered the Sage. "We'll never find it again."

Zasha jabbed his shoulder with a long fingernail. "Of course we will," she said, looking to Doctor Nine for approval.

They all looked at Doctor Nine, and he endured their stares mildly. After a long while he said, "We've been invited to a coming-out party."

He smiled at them.

Soon, all of the others laughed.

The night followed them like a pack of dogs.

-4-

Bethy wondered how it felt for Millie to die. It was something she tended to think about, even when she was killing a cat, or a dog. Poison sometimes hurt and so she stopped using it. Not because she wanted to spare pain—that was just a silly thought—no, it was because pain was such a distraction. Medicine was so much easier. No pain, just a fuzziness and a sleepy feeling that was warm and a little fluttery, like moth wings in the head. Bethy knew because she had tried the pills herself. First one of them, then two. The most she'd ever taken at once was six.

According to the Internet four was supposed to be fatal. She tried six just to confirm a theory...a suspicion, or a hope. The moths had fluttered around in her head for a deliciously long time, during which Bethy had so many strange thoughts. Almost feelings, but not quite. Close enough so that she guessed that anyone else taking the drug would have had true feelings. It gave her perspective on what Millie's reaction might be.

Millie was probably having such feelings now. And thoughts, too—Millie wasn't completely incapable, Bethy had to remind herself of that and to be fair to her sister. Millie's expression kept changing as if she'd had a sudden idea but when she spoke, which was less and less often now, her words were a junk-drawer jumble of nonsense, half-sentences and wrong word choices. Bethy found it interesting and she wished she could read minds. She bet that a mind-reader could make sense of what Millie was trying to say. Mind-readers didn't need actual language, she was sure of that. Then she wondered if a mind-reader could read an animal's mind, and if so, could they translate the thoughts into human words? Would an animal's thoughts change as they died, especially if they realized that they were dying? She hoped she would find out one day.

Maybe she could ask Doctor Nine. She was sure that he was coming tonight. She was sure that she had seen him out there, driving in a big car that was the color of night. When she looked at the window she could see that there were dark birds lined up on the sill and on the power lines across the street. The birds belonged to *him*, she had no doubts.

"B...Bethy...?"

Hearing Millie speak now—very clearly except for a purely understandable hitch—broke Bethy's reverie.

"Yes?" Bethy asked, utterly fascinated by anything Millie would say at this point. She pulled her diary onto her lap and picked up her pen.

"I don't feel..." Millie lapsed back into silence, her eyelids flittered closed.

Hm. What did that mean? *I don't feel.* Feel what? Bethy wondered. Was Millie losing her emotions? Did they die first before the rest of the body?

No, she didn't think so. She'd read about dying confessions, which was guilt; and about dying people saying nice things to comfort the people sitting around a death bed, which was compassion. Weird, but there it was.

Then she got it. Millie was trying to say that she didn't feel good. Or maybe that she didn't feel quite right. How...ordinary.

"It's okay, Mils," Bethy said. "It's just the medicine."

Millie's eyelids trembled, opened. There was a spark of something there. Confusion? Bethy could recognize emotions even if she didn't have any. Or, at least she could recognize emotions that she didn't share. She saw fear there, and though she didn't understand it she enjoyed seeing it.

"I'm...not sick." With a furrow of her brows, Millie whispered, "Am I?"

"Sick?" Bethy replied with a comforting laugh. "Oh no, honey! You're not sick." She patted her hand the way Aunt Annie sometimes did. "No need to worry."

She saw relief in Millie's eyes and Bethy took a taste of it.

"Not...sick...?"

"No, sweetie...you're just dying," Bethy said, and wondered if teasing this way was being greedy, and...was that okay?

Millie's eyes snapped wide and she tried to move. Bethy estimated that it took every ounce of her strength to move as much as she did, but all she could manage was a flap of one hand and a slight arch of her body. Then she collapsed back onto the pillows they'd brought down from the bed.

Bethy wrote a quick description of it in her diary.

The clock ticked, Mr. Whiskers' eyes flicking one way, his tail swishing the other. Bethy counted seconds. She got to one-hundred and sixteen before Millie's eyes opened again.

"Why?"

Just the one word, and it was clear that it cost her to get it out. Bethy wondered how many words Millie had left to spend.

"Because, Mils. It's for me. And for him."

Millie looked confused. Her lips formed the word 'who,' but she could not afford the breath to say it aloud.

"For *him*. For Doctor Nine."

There was another flare of expression—mingled confusion *and* fear. Nice. Again Bethy wished she could read minds, though she was pretty sure she knew what Millie was thinking, how she would be sorting it out. Doctor Nine was the boogeyman. Bethy's imaginary friend. Something she and everyone else laughed about behind her back. A dream, a nothing.

Even before Bethy had started experimenting with Aunt Annie's pills she had wanted to kill Millie for that—though strangely, and appropriately, that's not why she was killing her now. It wasn't revenge because revenge was soft. Revenge would disappoint Doctor Nine the same way rage would. There was no beauty in a lack of control.

Besides, this was not about punishment...it was about rewards.

Bethy thought about that as Millie's eyes focused and unfocused over and over again. 'Rewards' wasn't exactly the right word either. She chewed her lip and thought about it as her sister died, bit by bit.

There was a sound and then blades of light cut into the room between the half-closed blinds, and Bethy got up, excited, knowing who was outside. She started to run to the window and then in the space of two steps slowed to a walk and then stopped, still yards away. Running was silly. Running to check if he was out there was bad. It wouldn't show faith, like that Bible story about Moses tapping the rock and then not being allowed into the Promised Land. After everything he did right, he was reminded that *everything* had to be done right, and so Bethy turned around and sat back down, picked up her diary and pen, and continued making notes until Millie stopped breathing. It took nearly forty minutes, and she would have been lying if she didn't feel the tug of that window and the image she would see through the blinds. But feeling a thing and becoming its slave were different. Doctor Nine had told her that in her dreams.

When Mr. Whiskers said that it was two-thirty in the morning, Bethy put down her diary, set her pen neatly on top of it, and took a couple of slow breaths just to make sure she was calm. She reached over and touched Millie's cheek. The skin was still soft but it was already cooling. Bethy sat back, leaning on both palms, and watched for a little while longer. There had been no more words from her sister. No additional emotions had crossed Millie's face. After that last outburst she had simply gone to sleep, and in sleeping had settled down into a deeper rest. Her body had not visibly changed except that her chest no longer rose and fell. While she watched now, though, Millie seemed to shrink in on herself, to become less solid, and it took Bethy a while before she realized that it was just the blood draining from Millie's flesh and veins to the lowest possible point in her body. She'd read about that on the Internet, too.

When she had surfed the Net, Millie had read a lot about killing. About the laws of it, the history of it. The art of it. There were so many killers that she felt happy that she would always have new brothers and sisters. Some of them even killed in the name of God, which was a funny thing. She'd have to ask Doctor Nine about that, but she already knew what he would probably say—the essence of it, at least. If God is All then God is killing, too. And really, God kills everything, from microscopic life forms to whole worlds. Maybe that was why so many have worked so hard to make killing a ritual and an art: it was their only way to try and connect with God. Even at nine Bethy understood that. If God made man in His image then man reflects the killing nature of God. To kill is to be godlike. That should be obvious to everyone.

And yet they didn't call killers 'gods' or even 'godlike.' They called them monsters.

Bethy got up and walked across the bedroom and stood in front of the mirror that hung on the door of their shared wardrobe. She still wasn't letting herself look out of the window. Instead she looked at the monster in the mirror.

It still looked like her. The *her* she had always seen.

"Monster..." she murmured. Not for the first time she wondered if every one of the godlike monsters she'd read about on the Net had stood in their rooms, just as she now stood, and looked at themselves and announced who and what they were.

She hoped so. It felt like a family thing to do.

Finally Bethy turned away from the mirror and walked past the cooling meat. Millie was gone now; the body was nothing to her. She paused for just a moment, bending to pick up her diary and trying not to feel disappointed. Millie had been her first, but she hadn't learned as much from her as Bethy had hoped. Maybe next time she would use less of the Vicodin. Or maybe she'd re-visit pain. Perhaps she'd been too hasty in deciding that it had no place in the process.

Doctor Nine would be able to advise. Bethy was sure he would have something interesting to say about that.

Bethy changed into jeans and a t-shirt, put on her sneakers and brushed her hair. She put her diary and a change of clothes into her backpack.

When she was ready she took her pen and tested its point against the ball of her thumb. It seemed sharp enough. She held out her left arm and held the pen tightly in her right fist. She wasn't afraid of pain and so there was no hesitation at all as she abruptly jammed the point into the soft flesh of her inner forearm. The pen bit deep as she knew it would and blood—so rich that it looked more black than red—welled out of the puncture. Bethy licked the pen clean and put it in her bag and then she walked around the room and dribbled blood here and there. Then she put a Band-Aid over the puncture and put the wrapper in her pocket. Then she picked up a pair of bedroom slippers and used the sole of one to scuff some of the blood, drawing the line in the direction of the window. She left the slipper lying on the floor by the wall a few feet from the window, just where the hem of the long shears would brush against it. She put the other slipper in her backpack. The effect was pretty good.

Satisfied, Bethy finally stood in front of the window. She grasped the cord and pulled the blinds all the way up. The line of nightbirds scattered from the sill, their caws sounding old and rusty as they flew to join their brothers on the power line. The window was already raised a few inches and she raised it the rest of the way and for a moment she looked out and down at the street.

The big black roadster was there, idling quietly, parked across the street in the glow of the sodium vapor lamp. Just as she always knew it would be. There was almost no traffic, not this late. No pedestrians. And just for a moment—for a single jagged second Bethy stared at the roadster and saw that it cast no reflection, that the fall of lamplight did not paint its shadow on the street. Doubt flickered like a candle in her heart.

What if it wasn't real?

That voice—sounding more like Millie than Bethy—whispered in her ear. What if Doctor Nine wasn't down there at all? What if Doctor Nine was never down there?

Millie's voice seemed to chuckle in her mind.

What if...

What if Doctor Nine was not real?

"But I'm a monster," Bethy said aloud. Millie's voice laughed, mocking her.

Then the roadster pulled away from the curb...very slowly...and moved into the center of the boulevard on which they lived. Bethy watched, suddenly terrified. Was Doctor Nine a ghost of her mind? Was he leaving now that she had started to believe that he was only part of whatever made her a monster?

Bethy's stomach started to churn.

"No!" she said firmly. "No...he's here for me."

Another car came down the street and Bethy realized that it would have to either veer around the roadster or pass through it. If it was real, the car would veer. If Doctor Nine lived only in her head the oncoming car would just pass through it, reality passing through fantasy.

"No," she said again. She felt that her feet were riveted to the floor, held fast by nails of doubt driven through her flesh and bone. All she had to do was wait there, to see the car and how it reacted, or didn't react. Just five more seconds and then she would know whether she was a godlike monster or a mad little girl.

"Doctor Nine..." she breathed.

The car was almost there. Moses doubted, he tapped the rock.

The cartoon cat on the wall mocked her with its swishing tail.

"No," she said once more.

And Bethy turned away from the window before the car reached the roadster. Her decision was made. Without proof either way. She picked up her backpack, slung it over one shoulder, and left the bedroom. Left Millie and the blood and the fiction that she had constructed. She left her room and her parents and her Aunt Annie. She left her life.

She never looked back.

In the end she did not need to look to see if the car veered or drove straight through. She walked quietly down the stairs, placing her feet where she knew there were no squeaks and headed to the front door, flitting out into the night.

To the roadster. And to Doctor Nine, and to the other monsters he had collected along the way.

She knew they would be there.

She had no doubts at all.

Author's Note on "The Adventure of the Greenbrier Ghost"

This was the third short story I ever wrote. I was approached by editor Michael Knost to write a story for *Legends of the Mountain State Volume 2*, which continued his series of anthologies featuring folklore and urban (or rural) legends from West Virginia. He asked me to tackle the very real legend of the Greenbrier Ghost. Since the story was set in the late 19th century I took it as a chance to write a dream project—a story of Sherlock Holmes and Dr. John Watson. The story was written in April of 2008 and the book published in October of that year. I have since written other tales of Sherlock, and am even co-editing (with Michael Ventrella) a Sherlock Holmes anthology of my own. But my relationship with the Great Detective began here.

The Adventure of the Greenbrier Ghost

-1-

In late November of 1896 I had the pleasure of accompanying my good friend Mr. Sherlock Holmes on a cruise to America. Rather discretely he had been approached by a representative of the American government to help with a matter concerning a suspected forgery of the Declaration of Independence. Although this was a very grave matter, and one that could easily have shaken the foundations of the young and mighty nation, it took Holmes less than a single afternoon to put the matter right and to hand over the notorious Canadian forger DesBarnes to the authorities.

It was all hushed up and I allude to it now only to establish that Holmes and I were indeed in America at the end of that year, and we decided to take the opportunity to enjoy a rail trip from Washington D.C. throughout the southern states, which were enjoying fine weather despite the time of year.

Our plan was to return to Norfolk in Virginia in late February and from there take ship back to England. The weather and relaxation had done Holmes a world of good and he was more animated and less laconic than he had been in recent months. It did nothing but raise his spirits to discover that crime was rife in the American south—and indeed throughout much of this vast country. As states were being settled and industry introduced to all quarters there was as much room for corruption, treachery, theft and murder as there was for the more placid and commonplace pursuits of growth and settlement.

On the sixteenth day of February we found ourselves in the shipping office at Norfolk making arrangements for several large trunks of chemicals, specimens and books to be shipped back to our lodgings at 221-B Baker Street when a young man in the livery of a telegraph employee came running across the wharf calling Holmes' name. The young fellow skidded to a stop, knuckled his cap and thrust out a message.

Holmes took it with a bemused expression. It was neither the first nor the tenth such urgent communiqué he had received during our journey. As he tipped the boy and unfolded the message I murmured, "Holmes, our ship sails with the dawn tide. We don't have time for any—"

He cut me off with this singular question, "Do you believe in ghosts, Watson?"

I hesitated, for Holmes had tricked me more than once with such a question only to trounce any credulity I had with some fact or scientific proof. "Many do," I said vaguely.

"You are getting careful in your dotage, Watson." There was mischief in his eyes as he handed me the note. "Read this and then decide if you want to catch our boat or wait for another tide."

I stepped into a patch of sunlight to read the letter, which was short and enigmatic.

Dear Mr. Holmes

My daughter was murdered. Her ghost has told me the name of her killer. For the love of God and justice please help.

Mrs. Mary Jane Robinson Heaster

Richlands, Greenbrier County, WV

I looked up and saw that Holmes was staring, not at me but at the shadows clustered under the eaves of the shipping office, his lips pursed, eyes narrowed to slits.

"Her daughter's ghost has revealed the identity of her killer?" I said with half a laugh. "Surely this is the rant of a distressed and overly credulous woman, Holmes. We've heard this sort of rubbish before."

"And yet, Watson," he said as he took back the letter, "and yet..."

Holmes let it hang there and turned on his heel and marched across the shipping yard to the rail transport office. With a resigned sigh and weary shake of my head I followed.

-2-

America is a railroad nation, perhaps as much as England though its scope was Olympian. We took three connecting trains and within two days we were rattling down a country lane in a wagon pulled by a pair of brown horses. The driver chewed tobacco and every few minutes would spit across to the verge with great accuracy and velocity.

"Tell me, my good man," said Holmes, pitching his voice above the rumble of the wheels, "do you know Mrs. Heaster very well?"

He turned and looked at us for a moment, chewing silently. "You fellers are here about what happened to her daughter, aintcha?"

"Perhaps."

"Mrs. Heaster been saying that young Zona was kilt deliberate," said the man, "but the doctor and the sheriff said it were an accident."

"And what do you think?" asked Holmes.

The man smiled. "I think it were all done too fast."

"What was?" I asked.

"The burial, that inquest, all of it. It were done fast like there was something to hide."

"Is it your belief that there was some mischief?" Holmes asked.

"Miss Zona were a country girl, you understand? 'Round here even girls with breeding like Miss Zona grow up climbing trees and hiking them hills." He made a face. "You can't tell me no country girl just up and tripped down some steps and died."

"You don't believe that it was an accident?" Holmes prompted.

"I were born at night, sir, but it weren't last night." With that he spit another plug, turned around and drove the rest of the way in silence.

-3-

He deposited us at a lovely if rustic country house with a rail fence, chickens in the yard and a view of green hills. In London there would be a foot of snow but here in Greenbrier Country it was like a spring paradise.

Mrs. Mary Jane Heaster met us at her gate, and at once we could see that she was much troubled by recent events. She was a strong-featured woman, and her face was lined with grief. "Mr. Holmes," she cried, rushing to take his hand as he alit from the wagon. "God bless you for coming! Now I know that my Zona will find justice."

I saw Holmes' face take on the reserve he often showed with effusive displays of emotion, particularly from women, and he took his hand back as quickly as good manners would allow. He introduced me.

"Heavens above, Doctor," she exclaimed, "I have read each of the wonderful accounts of your adventures with Mr. Holmes. My cousin is married to a London banker and she sends me every issue of *The Strand*. You are a marvelous writer, Dr. Watson, and you make each detail of Mr. Holmes' brilliant cases come alive."

Holmes barely hid a smile that was halfway to a sneer. His opinion of my literary qualities was well known and he often berated me for favoring the excitement of the storytelling format instead of a straight scientific presentation of case facts. I'd long ago given up any hopes of explaining to him that the public would never read straight case reportage. I also thought it tactless to mention that many of our most interesting cases came about because of the notoriety Holmes had achieved with the publication of my stories.

"But I am a dreadful hostess," cried Mrs. Heaster, "making my guests stand chattering in the yard. Please come into the parlor."

When we were settled in comfortable chairs with teacups and saucers perched on our knees Mrs. Heaster leaned forward, hands clasped together. "Can you help me, Mr. Holmes? Can you help me find justice so that my daughter can rest easy in her grave? For I tell you truly, my dear sirs, that she is not resting now. She walks abroad crying out for justice."

There was a heavy silence in the room and her words seemed to drift around us like specters. Mrs. Heaster sat back, and in her eyes I could see that she was aware of how her own words must have sounded. "Of course you gentlemen have no reason to believe such a tale. But I assure you it is the truth."

Holmes held up a finger. "I will be the judge of what is the truth," he said curtly. "Now, Mrs. Heaster, I want you to tell us everything that has happened. Leave nothing out, however minor a detail it may seem to you. Be complete or we cannot hope to help you."

With that he set his teacup down, sank back in his chair, laced his long fingers together and closed his eyes. Mrs. Heaster glanced at me and I gave her an encouraging nod.

"My daughter was Elva Zona Heaster and she was born here in Greenbrier County in 1873. She was a good girl, Mr. Holmes. Bright and quick, good at letters and sewing. But..." and she faltered, "she got into trouble a few years ago. She had a child."

She let it hang there, expecting rebuke, but Holmes gave an irritable wave of his fingers. "I am a detective, madam, not a moral critic."

Mrs. Heaster cleared her throat and plunged ahead. "As you can appreciate, an unmarried woman with a child cannot expect much in the way of a good marriage. She resigned herself to living alone, but then in October of 1896 she met a man named Erasmus Stribbling Trout Shue. Most folks around these parts called him Edward, though I've always thought of him as 'Trout:' cold and slippery. He was a drifter who came here to Greenbrier to work as a blacksmith, saying that he wanted to start a new life. He alluded to a hard past but never gave any details. He went to work in the shop of James Crookshanks, which is located just off of the old Midland Trail. Trout had talent as a farrier and in farm country there is considerable work for a man skilled at shoeing horses and cows. Shortly after Trout came to town my daughter met him when she went to arrange for shoes for our bull, which we let out to stud at local farms." Mrs. Heaster sighed. "It was love at first sight, Mr. Holmes. You've heard the expression that 'sparks flew,' well it was true enough when Zona went into the blacksmiths and saw Trout hammering away at his anvil. He is a very big and muscular man, powerful as you'd expect of a blacksmith; but handsome in his way. Perhaps more charming than handsome, if you take my meaning. He had a smile that could turn his hard face into that of a storybook prince; and the attention he lavished on Zona made her feel like a princess. He asked me for her hand in marriage and though I had my misgivings—it seems I am too old to be taken in by a handsome smile and thick biceps—I agreed. My daughter, after all, had such limited prospects."

"Of course," I said.

"From the outset I felt that Trout was hiding something, but he never let on and I found no evidence to confirm my suspicions. I began to think I was just becoming that proverbial 'old woman,' yielding to fears and interfering with my daughter's happiness...but my fears were justified," she said and as I watched I saw all the color drain from her face. "Worse than justified, for how could I know of the terrible events to come?"

Holmes opened his eyes and watched her like a cat.

"Zona and Trout lived together as man and wife for the next several months. Then, on January 23 of this year—on that terrible, terrible day, Andy Jones—a young colored boy who had been sent to their house by Trout on some contrived errand—came tearing into town, screaming that he had found my Zona lying dead at the foot of the stairs. He said that he saw her lying stretched out, with her feet together and one hand on her abdomen and the other lying next to her. Her head was turned slightly to one side. Her eyes were wide open and staring. Even though Andy is a small child he knew that she must be dead. Andy ran to town and told his mother and she summoned Dr. George Knapp, who is both our local doctor and coroner. Dr. Knapp was out at one of the more distant farms and it took him nearly an hour to arrive."

Mrs. Heaster took a breath to brace herself for the next part. "By the time Dr. Knapp arrived Trout had come home from Mr. Crookshanks' shop and he had taken Zona's body upstairs and laid her out on the bed. Normally town women tend to the dead, washing them and dressing them for the funeral; but by the time Dr. Knapp had arrived Trout has washed Zona and dressed her in her best dress, a long gown with a high collar, with a veil covering her face."

Holmes leaned forward. "Describe the veil and collar."

"It was a white veil recut from her wedding gown so she could wear it to church."

"And the collar?"

"Very high and stiff-necked."

Holmes pursed his lips and considered. "Pray continue," he said after a moment. "Tell me about the findings of Dr. Knapp's examination of your daughter."

"That's just it, Mr. Holmes, there wasn't much of an examination. Dr. Knapp tried, of course, but Trout clung to Zona throughout, wailing in grief and agony, abusing the doctor for disturbing his poor dear wife's remains."

"Were you there, Mrs. Heaster?" I asked.

"Yes, I stood in the doorway, shocked into silence by what had happened, feeling my heart break in my chest."

"Where was Trout Shue while the doctor was examining your daughter?"

"Excellent, Watson," Holmes said quietly.

"He sat at the top of the bed, cradling her head and sobbing," said Mrs. Heaster.

"Did he order Dr. Knapp to stop the examination?" Holmes asked.

"No, but he was so demonstrably overcome with grief the doctor relented out of pity and gave Zona's body only the most cursory of examinations. Barely enough to assure himself that she was in fact dead. However," she said slowly, "he did notice that there were bruises around Zona's throat."

"Bruises? What did he make of them?"

"Nothing, Mr. Holmes."

"Nothing?"

"Nothing."

After a moment's pause Holmes asked, "What did Dr. Knapp determine was the cause of your daughter's death?"

Mrs. Heaster sneered. "At first he called it an everlasting faint. I ask you!"

"That's preposterous," I cried. "All that says is that he had no idea of the cause of death."

"There was a lot of such criticism," agreed Mrs. Heaster, "and so when he filed his official report Dr. Knapp changed it to 'female trouble,' which shut every mouth in the county. No one will talk of such things." She made a face. "People are so old fashioned."

"Was there any history of gynecological distress," I asked, but she shook her head.

"Nor were there any complications during the birth of her son. She was a healthy girl. Strong and fit."

I shot a covert glance at Holmes, who was as likely as anyone to steer well clear of such delicate matters, and indeed his face had a pinched quality, but his eyes sparkled with interest. "In your letter you allude to murder," he said.

"Murder it is, Mr. Holmes. Brutal murder of the boldest kind."

"And the murderer? You believe it to be Trout Shue?"

"I know it to be him!"

"How is it that you are so certain?"

"My daughter told me." She said it without the slightest pause.

"Your...dead daughter?"

"Yes, Mr. Holmes. For several nights she has come to me in dreams and told me that she was murdered by Trout Shue. She is caught between worlds, trapped and bound here to this world because of the evil that was done to her. Until justice is served upon her killer my daughter will wander the earth as a ghost. That, gentlemen, is why I implore you to help me with this matter."

Holmes sat still and studied Mrs. Heaster's face, looking—as indeed I looked—for the spark of madness, or the dodgy eye-shift of guile—and he, like I, saw none. She was composed, clear and compelling, which neither of us had expected considering the wild nature of her telegram. Holmes sat back and steepled his fingers. The long seconds of his silent deliberation were counted out by an ornately carved grandfather clock and it was not until an entire legion of seconds lay spent upon the floor that he spoke.

"I will help you," he said.

Mrs. Heaster closed her eyes and bowed her head. After a moment her shoulders began to tremble with silent tears.

-4-

"Surely you don't believe her, Holmes," I said as we cantered along a byroad on a pair of horses the good lady had lent us. Holmes, astride a chestnut gelding, did not answer me as we made our way through sun-dappled lanes.

It was only after we had reached our Lewisburg inn and handed the horses off to a stable lad that Holmes stopped and looked first up at the darkening late afternoon blue of the American sky and then at me.

"Do you not?" he replied as if I had just asked my question this minute instead of an hour past.

I opened my mouth to reply, but Holmes would say no more.

-5-

The very next morning found us in the telegraph office where Holmes dictated a dozen telegrams and left me to pay the operator. We then went to municipal offices where Holmes demanded to speak to the county prosecutor, one Mr. John A. Preston. Upon presenting his credentials Mr. Preston first raised bushy eyebrows in surprise and then shot to his feet.

"Dear me!" he said.

Holmes gave him a rueful smile. "I perceive that I am not entirely unknown even this far from London."

"Unknown! Good heavens, Mr. Holmes, but there is not a lawman in these United States who has not heard of the great Consulting Detective. Why, not eight months ago I attended a lecture in Norfolk on modern police procedure in which the lecturer thrice quoted from your monographs. I believe it's fair to say that the future of police and legal investigation will owe you a debt, sir."

Preston's words penetrated even Holmes' unusually unflappable cool and for a moment he was at a loss for words. "Why thank you, sir. If only Scotland Yard were as progressive in their thinking."

"Give them time, Mr. Holmes, give them time. A prophet is never accepted in his own country." Preston laughed at his own witticism and waved us to chairs. "What can I do for the great Mr. Sherlock Holmes?"

"I will get right to it, then," said Holmes, and he told Preston everything Mrs. Heaster had told us, even to the point of handing him her letter for examination. Preston chewed the fringe of his walrus mustache as he handed the letter back.

"Mrs. Heaster has already been to see me," he admitted.

"And have you done nothing?"

Preston cleared his throat. "To be honest, Mr. Holmes, superstition abounds in these parts. Though we are fairly modern here in Lewisburg, much of West Virginia is still wild and a good many of my fellow citizens are deeply superstitious. Everyone has a tale of a ghost or goblin, and this would not be the first time I'd had someone sitting in that very chair there telling me of knowledge shared with them from a friend or relative months or years in the grave. Wild-eyed kooks, Mr. Holmes; superstitious country bumpkins."

"And is it your opinion, Mr. Preston, that Mrs. Heaster is another wild-eyed kook?" Holmes' tone was icy, for indeed the woman had impressed my friend with her calm clarity.

"Well," Preston said cautiously, "after all, her daughter's ghost...?"

"You are not a believer?"

"I go to church," Preston said but would venture no further.

"You have, I hope, had at least the courtesy to read the transcript of the case, including the remarks of the county coroner?"

"No sir...I confess that I did not take the case seriously enough to care to investigate further."

"I do take it seriously," said Holmes with asperity.

They sat there on opposite sides of Preston's broad oak desk, and as I watched the prosecutor I realized that it was possible for a seated man to give the impression of coming to full attention and even saluting without so much as moving his hands.

"If you will do me the courtesy of coming back tomorrow at ten o'clock," he said, "I will by then be fully familiar with this case."

Holmes stood. "Then we have no more to talk about until then, Mr. Preston. Good day." We left and outside Holmes gave me a wink. "I believe we have lit a fire there, Watson."

-6-

Preston was better than his word and not only read the case but officially re-opened it. At Holmes' urging he sought approval from the judge to exhume the body of Zona Heaster-Shue. Holmes and I attended the autopsy, which was held in an empty schoolhouse, the children having been sent home for the day. It was the custom of West Virginia, perhaps of this part of America, for family members, witnesses, and the accused to all be present during the post mortem. I found this deeply unsettling, but Holmes was delighted by the opportunity to study Trout Shue in person for we had not yet met the gentleman in question.

He entered with a pair of burly constables behind him but Shue was so massive a man that he dwarfed the policemen. He had the huge shoulders and knotted muscles of a blacksmith. His hair and eyes were dark, and there was a cruel sensuality to his mouth. His jaw was thrust forward in resentment and he made many a protestation of his innocence and expressed deep outrage at this unnecessary violation of his wife.

"I'll see you all in court for this!" he bellowed as we gathered around the body that lay exposed and defenseless on the makeshift table.

"I hope you shall," replied Holmes and the two men stared at each other for a long moment. I could feel electricity wash back and forth between them as if their spirits dueled with lightning bolts, parrying and thrusting on a metaphysical level while we watchers waited in the physical world.

Finally Shue curled his lip and turned away, the first to break eye-contact. He flapped an arm in apparent disgust. "Do what you must and be damned to you. You will never prove anything."

I broke the ensuing silence by stepping to the coroner's side. "I am entirely at your disposal," I said. He nodded in evident relief, throwing worried looks at Shue.

We set about the dissection. Zona Heaster-Shue had been in the ground for weeks now but her body was not nearly as decomposed as I had expected in this temperate climate. The flesh yielded to our blades if the skin were yet infused with moisture. It was unnerving, and dare I say it—unnatural; but we plowed ahead.

We examined her all over but as we proceeded Holmes quietly said, "The throat, doctors. The throat."

We cut through the tissue to examine the tendons, cartilage and bone. The coroner gasped, but when he dictated his findings to the clerk his voice was steady.

-7-

"...the discovery was made that the neck was broken and the windpipe smashed," said the coroner from the witness box in the courtroom. "On the throat were the marks of fingers indicating that she had been choked. The neck was dislocated between the first and second vertebrae. The ligaments were torn and ruptured. The windpipe had been crushed at a point in front of the neck."

From the spectators' gallery I watched as the findings struck home to each of the twelve jurors, and I saw several pairs of eyes flick toward Trout Shue, who sat behind the defense table, his face a study in cold contempt.

In was hot in the courtroom as a June sun beat down upon Lewisburg. Following the arrest of Trout Shue, Holmes and I had returned to England, but a summons from Mr. Preston had entreated us to return and so we had. Despite the autopsy findings it was by no means a certain victory for the prosecution. Shue at no time recanted his claim of innocence and the burden of proof in American law is entirely on the prosecution to establish without reasonable doubt that the accused was the murderer. The evidence as it currently stood was largely circumstantial. Overwhelming, it seemed to me, but in the eyes of the law things stood upon a knife-edge.

During a break in the trial Mrs. Heaster accosted Mr. Preston. "You must let me testify," she implored.

"To what end, madam? You were not a witness to the crime."

"But my daughter—"

Preston cut her off with some irritation, for in truth this was an argument they had revisited many times. "You claim your daughter came to you in a dream. A dream, madam."

"It was her ghost, sir. Her spirit cries out for justice."

Holmes gently interjected, "Mrs. Heaster, at very best this is hearsay and the laws of this country do not allow it as testimony. You cannot prove what you claim."

She wheeled on Holmes while pointing a finger at Preston. "Are you defending him? Are you saying that I should just be quiet and let my daughter's murderer glide through this trial like the oiled snake that he is?"

"Indeed not. In fact I have provided some evidence to Mr. Preston that he may find useful."

"What evidence?" Mrs. Heaster and I said as one.

"Watson, do you remember that I sent a number of telegrams when we first arrived in Lewisburg?"

"Of course."

"I cabled various postmasters in this region in a search for forwarding addresses for anyone of the name Erasmus Stribbling Trout Shue, or any variation thereof, and I struck gold! It turns out our Trout Shue has quite a checkered past. He has already served time in jail on a previous occasion, being convicted of stealing a horse."

"That hardly bears on—"

Holmes brushed past my interruption. "Zona Heaster was not his first wife, Watson. Not even his second! Shue has been married twice before, and in both cases there were reports..."

"...unofficial reports," Preston interjected.

"Reports nevertheless," snapped Holmes, "that each of his previous wives suffered from the effects of his violent temper. His first wife divorced him after he had thrown all of her possessions into the street following an argument. She, of the three Mrs. Shues, survived this man; her successor was not so lucky."

"What do you mean?" demanded Mrs. Heaster.

"Lucy Ann Tritt, his second wife, died under mysterious circumstances of a blow to the head, ostensibly from a fall— according to Shue, who was the only witness. The investigation in that case was as lax as it was here," Holmes said and gave Preston a harsh glare. "No charges were filed and Shue quickly moved away."

"And came here and found my Zona." She shivered and gripped Preston's sleeve. "You must secure a conviction, sir. This man is evil. Evil. Please for the love of God let me testify. Let me tell the jury about my daughter, about what she told me. Let me tell the truth!"

But Preston just shook his head. "Madam, I will try to introduce the evidence Mr. Holmes was clever enough to find, but it, too, is circumstantial. This man has not been convicted of harming any woman. I cannot even bring in his previous conviction for horse theft because it might prejudice the jury, and on those grounds the defense would declare a mistrial. I am bound by the law. And," he said tiredly, "I cannot in good conscience put you in the witness chair and have you give legal testimony that a ghost revealed to you in a dream that she was murdered. We would lose any credibility that we have, and already we are losing this jury. I thank my lucky stars that the defense has not learned of your claims, because then he would use it to tear our case apart."

"But the autopsy report—"

"Shows that she was murdered, but it does not establish the identity of the killer. I'm sorry, but please remember, the jury have to agree that there is no doubt, no doubt at all, that Shue is the killer; and I do not know if we possess sufficient evidence to establish that." He began to pull her hand from his sleeve but held it for a moment and even gave it a gentle squeeze. "I will do everything that the law allows, madam. Everything."

She pulled her hand away. "The law! Where is justice in the law if it allows a girl to be murdered and her killer to walk free?" She looked at Preston, and at Holmes, and at me. "How many more women will he marry and then murder? How will the law protect them?"

I opened my mouth to mutter some meaningless words of comfort, but Mrs. Heaster whirled away and ran from us into a side room, her sobs echoing like accusations in the still air of the hallway.

Preston gave us a wretched look. "I can only do what the law allows," he pleaded.

Holmes smiled and clapped him on the shoulder. "We must trust that justice will find a way," he said. Then he consulted his watch. "Dear me, I'm late for luncheon."

And with that enigmatic statement he left us.

-8-

The trial ground on and true to Preston's fears the evidence became thinner and thinner, and the defense attorney, a wily man named Grimby, seemed now to have taken possession of the jury's sympathies. Had I not looked into Shue's face during the autopsy and saw the cold calculation there I might also have felt myself swayed into the region of reasonable doubt.

Again and again Mrs. Heaster begged Preston to let her testify, but each time the prosecutor denied her entreaties and I could see his patience eroding as quickly as his optimism.

Then calamity struck.

When the judge asked Mr. Grimby if he had any additional witnesses, the defense attorney turned toward the prosecution table and with as wicked a smile as I'd ever seen on a man's face, said, "I call Mrs. Mary Jane Robinson Heaster."

The entire courtroom was struck into stunned silence. Preston closed his eyes, looking sick and defeated. He murmured, "Dear God, we are lost."

I wheeled toward Holmes, but my friend did not look at all discomfited. Instead he maintained what the Americans call a poker face—showing no trace of emotions, no hint of what thoughts were running through his brain during this disaster.

"Mrs. Heaster?" prompted the bailiff, offering his hand to her.

The good lady rose with great dignity though I could see her clenched fists trembling with dread. To have been denied the opportunity to speak against this evil man and now to become the tool of his advocate! It was unthinkably cruel.

"Holmes," I whispered. "Do something!"

Very calmly he said, "We have done all that can be done, Watson. We must trust to the spirit of justice."

Mrs. Heaster took the oath and sat in the witness chair, and immediately Grimby set about her, gainsaying niceties to close in for a quick kill. "Tell me, madam, do you believe that Mr. Shue had anything at all to do with your daughter's death?"

"I do, sir," she said quietly.

"Did you witness her death?"

"No sir."

"Did you speak to anyone who witnessed her death?"

"No sir."

"So you have no personal knowledge of the manner of your daughter's death?"

She paused.

"Come now, Mrs. Heaster, it's a simple question. Do you have any personal knowledge of how your daughter died?"

"Yes," she said at length. "I do."

Grimby's eyes were alight and he fought to keep a smile off of his face. "And how do you come by this knowledge?"

"I was told."

"Told? By whom, madam?" His voice dripped with condescension.

"By my daughter, sir."

Grimby smiled openly now. "Your...dead daughter?"

"Yes sir."

"Are we to understand that your dead daughter somehow imparted this information to you?"

"Yes, my daughter told me how she died."

The jury gasped. Preston could have objected here, but he had lost his nerve, clearly believing the case to be already lost.

"Pray, how did she tell you?"

Mrs. Heaster raised her eyes to meet Grimby's. "Her ghost came to me in a dream, sir."

"Her ghost?" Grimby cried. "In a dream?"

There was a ripple of laughter from the gallery and even a few smiles from the jury. Preston's fists were clutched so tight that his knuckles were bloodless; while to my other side Holmes sat composed, his eyes fixed on the side of Mrs. Heaster's face.

Grimby opened his mouth to say something to the judge, but Mrs. Heaster cut him off. "You may laugh, sir. You may all laugh, for perhaps to you it is funny. A young woman dies a horrible death, the life choked out of her, the very bones of her neck crushed in the fingers of a strong man. That may be funny to some." The laughter in the room died away. "My daughter was a good girl who had endured a hard life. Yes, she made mistakes. Mr. Grimby has been kind enough to detail each and every one of them. Yes, she had a child out of wedlock, and as we all know such things are unthinkable, such things never happen."

Her bitterness was like a pall of smoke.

"Mr. Grimby did his job very well and dismantled the good name of my daughter while at the same time destroying each separate bit of evidence. Perhaps most of you have already made up your minds and are planning to set Trout Shue free." She paused and flicked a glance at Holmes, and did I catch just the slightest incline of his head? "The law prevents me from telling what I know of Mr. Shue's life and dealings before he came to Greenbrier. So I will not talk of him. Mr. Grimby has asked me to tell you how I came by my personal knowledge of the death of my daughter, and so I will tell you. I will tell you of how my dear Zona came to me over the course of four dark nights. As a spirit of the dead she came into my room and stood at my bedside, the way a frightened child will do, coming to the one person who loves her unconditionally and forever. For four nights she came to me and she brought with her the chill of the grave. The very air around me seemed to freeze and the ghost of each of my frightened breaths haunted the air for, yes, I was afraid. Terribly afraid. I am not a fanciful woman. I am not one to knock wood or throw salt in the devil's eye over my left shoulder. I am a mountain woman of Greenbrier County. A farm woman with a practical mind. And yet there I lay in my bed with the air turned to winter around me and the shade of my murdered daughter standing beside me."

The room was silent as the grave as she spoke.

"Each night she would awaken me and then she would tell me, over and over again, how she died. And how she lived. How she endured life in those last months as the wife of Edward Trout Shue. She told me of the endless fights over the smallest matters. Of his insane jealousy if she so much as curtsied in reply to a gentleman tipping his hat. Of the beatings that he laid upon her, and how he cleverly chose where and how to hit so that he left no marks that would show above collar or below sleeve. My daughter lived in hell. Constant fear, constant dread of offending this offensive man. And then she told me what happened on that terrible day. Trout Shue had come home from the blacksmiths, expecting his dinner, and when he found that she had not yet prepared it—even though he was two hours earlier than his usual time—he flew into a rage and grabbed her by the throat. His eyes flared like a monster's and she said his hands were as hard and unyielding as the iron with which he plied his trade. He did not just throttle my daughter—he shattered her neck. When I dared speak, when I dared to ask her to show me what his hands had done, Zona turned her head to one side. At first I thought she was turning away in shame and horror for what had happened...but as she turned her head went far to the left—and too far. Much too far and with a grinding of broken bones Zona turned her head all the way around. If anything could be more horrible, more unnatural, more dreadful to a human heart, let alone the broken heart of a grieving mother, then I do not want to know what it could be."

She paused. Her eyes glistened with tears but her voice never disintegrated into hysterics or even raised above a normal speaking tone. The effect was to make her words a hundredfold more potent. Any ranting would have painted her as overly distraught if not mad; but now everyone in the courtroom hung on her words. Even Grimby seemed caught up in it. I hazarded a glance at Shue, who looked—for the very first time—uncertain.

"I screamed," said Mrs. Heaster. "Of course I did. Who would not? Nothing in my life had prepared me for so ghastly a sight as this. After that first night I convinced myself that it had all been an hysterical dream, that such things as phantoms did not exist and that my Zona was not haunting me; but on that second night she returned. Once more she begged me to hear the truth about what happened, and once more she told me of the awful attack. I only thank God that I was not again subjected to the demonstration of the extent of damage to her poor, dear neck." She paused and gave the jury a small, sad smile. "I pleaded with Mr. Preston to let me tell my tale during this trial and he refused. I fear he was afraid that my words would make you laugh at me. I believe Mr. Grimby placed me on the stand for those very reasons. And yet I hear no laughter, I see no smiles. Perhaps it is that you, like I, do not find the terrible and painful death of an innocent girl to be a source of merriment. In any case, I have had my say, and for that I thank Mr. Grimby and this court. At least now, no matter what you each decide, my daughter has been heard. For me that will have to be enough."

She looked at Grimby, who in turn looked at the jury. He saw what I saw: twelve faces whose eyes were moist but whose mouths had become tight and bitter lines and whose outthrust jaws bespoke their fury.

Then the silence was shattered as Shue himself leapt to his feet and cried, "Tell whatever fairytales you want, woman, but you will never be able to prove that I did it!"

The guards shoved him down in his seat and Holmes leaned his head toward Preston and me. "Do you not find it an interesting choice of phrase that he said that we will never 'prove' that he did it? Does that sound like the plea of an innocent man or the challenge of a guilty one?" And though he said this quietly he pitched it just loud enough to be heard by everyone in that small and crowded room.

-9-

That was very nearly the end of the Greenbrier affair and Holmes and I left West Virginia and America very shortly thereafter. Erasmus Stribbling Trout Shue was found guilty by the jury, which returned its verdict with astonishing swiftness. The judge, with fury and revulsion in his eyes, sentenced Shue to life imprisonment in the State Penitentiary in Moundsville, where Shue died some three years later of a disease that was never adequately diagnosed. Mr. Preston sent Holmes a newspaper account from Lewisburg after Shue's death in which the reporter recounted a rumor that Shue complained that a ghost visited him nightly and as a result he was unable to sleep. His health deteriorated and when he died he was buried in an unmarked grave. No one that I knew of attended the burial or mourned his passing.

But before Holmes and I had even set out from Lewisburg, as we shared a late dinner in our rooms at the hotel, I said, "There is one thing that confounds me, Holmes."

"Only one thing? And pray what is that?"

"How did Mr. Grimby know to ask Mrs. Heaster about her story? It was not commonly known as far as I could tell, especially not here in Lewisburg. Certainly neither she nor Mr. Preston shared that information."

Holmes ate a bit of roast duck and washed it down with wine before he answered. "Does it matter how he found out? Perhaps he learned of it from a ghost in his dreams."

I opened my mouth to reply that it surely did matter when an odd thought struck me dumb. I gaped accusingly at Holmes and set my knife and fork down with a crash.

"If it was someone on this physical plane who tipped him off then it was criminal to do so! The risk was abominable. What if she had raved?"

"We have not once seen Mrs. Heaster rave," he observed calmly. "Rather the reverse."

"What if the jury did not believe her? What if Grimby had managed her better on the stand? What if—?"

Holmes cut me off. "What if once in a while, Watson, justice was more important in a court of law than the law itself?" He sipped his wine.

Once more I opened my mouth to protest, but then a chill wind seemed to blow through the room, making the curtains dance and causing the candle flames to flicker, and in that moment I could feel the heat of my outrage and anger leak out of me. Holmes cut another slice of duck and ate it, his glittering dark eyes dancing with a strange humor. I followed the line of his gaze and saw that he was looking at the curtains, watching as they settled back into place; and then the chill of the room seemed to touch my chest like the cold hand of a dead child over my heart. Though the day had been a hot one the night had been cool, and the maid had shut the window against the breeze. The curtains hung now, as still as if they had never moved, for indeed they could not have.

When I turned back to Holmes he was looking at me now, half a smile on his mouth.

Was it a breeze that had found its way through the window frame, or perhaps through an unseen crack in the wall? Or had some voiceless mouth whispered thank you to Holmes in the language of the grave? I will not say what I think nor commit it to paper.

We said nothing for the rest of that evening, and in the morning we took ship for England, leaving Greenbrier and the ghosts of West Virginia far behind.

Author's Note on "Calling Death"

A few years ago editors Eugene Johnson and Jason Sizemore contacted me about writing for an anthology they were putting together called *Appalachian Undead*. All zombie stories set in that strange and storied mountain range that stretches from Georgia to Maine. There were two big draws for me. First, I've traveled those mountains from end to end a couple of times. I spent a lot of time on the road and on foot and there is magic in them thar hills.

The second draw was that so many of my friends were involved. John Skipp, Gary A. Braunbeck, Tim Lebbon, Maurice Broaddus, Lucy Snyder, Bev Vincent, Tim Waggoner, John Everson...well, nearly everyone in the book! So, sure, I was in. And besides, I already had a story in mind about those mountains.

Calling Death

"It weren't the wind," said Granny Adkins.

The young man perched on the edge of the other rocker, head tilted to lift one ear like a startled bird, listening to the sound. He was stick thin and beaky nosed, and Granny thought he looked like a heron—the way they looked when they were ready to take sudden flight. "Are you sure?"

"Sure as maybe," said Granny, nodding out to the darkness. "The wind fair howls when it comes 'cross the top of Balder Rise. Howls like the Devil himself."

"Sounds like a howl to me," said the young man. "What else could you call it?"

Granny sucked in a lungful of smoke from her Pall Mall, held it inside for a five count, and then stuck out her lower lip to exhale in a vertical line up past her face. She didn't like to blow smoke on guests and there was a breeze blowing toward the house. A chime made from old bent forks and chicken bones stirred and tinkled.

She squinted with her one good eye—the blue one, not the one that had gone milky white when a wasp stung her there forty years back—and considered how she wanted to answer the young man.

Before she spoke, the sound came again. Low, distant, plaintive.

She left her initial response unspoken for a moment as they sat in the dark and listened.

"There," she said softly. "You hear it?"

"Yes, but it still sounds like a—"

"No, son. That ain't what I meant. Can you *hear* the sound? The moan?"

"Yes," he said, leaning into the wind, tilting one ear directly into its path.

"Now," said Granny, "can you hear the wind, too?"

"I..." he began, but let his voice trail off. Granny waited, watching his face by starlight, looking for the moment when he *did* hear it. His head lifted like a bird dog's. "Yes...I hear it."

They listened to the moan. It was there, but the wind was dying off again and the sound was fainter, thinner.

"That, um, 'moan,'" the young man said tentatively, "it's *not* the wind. You're right."

She nodded, satisfied.

"It's a separate sound," continued the young man. "I—I think it's being carried *on* the wind." He looked to her for approval.

She gave him another nod. "That's another thing about living up here in the hills," she said, tying this to their previous conversation. "When you live simple and close to the land, you don't get as blunt as folks in the cities do. You hear things, see things the way they are, not the way you s'pose them to be. You notice that there are more things around you, and that they're there all the time."

The young man nodded, but he was half distracted by the moans, so Granny let him listen for a spell.

His name was Joshua Tharp. A good name. Biblical first name, solid last name. A practical name, which Granny always appreciated because she thought that a name said a lot about a person. She would never have come out onto the porch if he'd had a foreign-sounding name, or a two first-name name, like Simon Thomas. Everyone Granny knew with two Christian names was a scoundrel, and half in the Devil's bag already. However, this boy had a good name. There had been Tharps in this country going back more generations than Granny could count, and she knew family lines four decades past the War of Northern Aggression. Her own people had been here since before America was America.

So, Joshua Tharp was a decent name, and well worth a little bit of civility. He was a college boy from Pittsburgh who was willing to pay attention and treat older folks with respect. Wasn't pushy, neither, and that went a long way down the road with Granny. When he'd shown up on her doorstep, he took off his hat and said 'ma'am,' and told her that he was writing a book about the coal miners in Pennsylvania and North Carolina, and was using his own family as the thread that sewed the two states together.

Now they were deep into their third porch sitting, and the conversation wandered a crooked mile through late afternoon and on into the full dark of night. Talking about Granny and her kin, and about the Tharps here and the Tharps that had gone on. Joshua was a Whiskey Holler Tharp, though, but there was no one left around here closer than a third cousin with a couple of removes, so everyone told him to go see Granny Adkins.

"Hell, son," said Mr. Sputters at the post office, "Granny's so old, she remembers when God bought these mountains from the Devil, and I do believe the Good Lord might have been short-changed on the deal. You want to know about your forebears—and about what happened when the mine caved in—well you go call on ol' Granny. But mind you bring your full set of manners with you, 'cause she won't have no truck with anyone who gives her half a spoonful of sass."

Granny knew that Sputters said that because the old coot phoned and told her. Wrigley Sputters was a fool, but not a damn fool.

Come calling is exactly what young Joshua did. He came asking about his kin. That was the first day, and even now they'd only put a light coat of paint on that subject. Granny was old and she was never one to be in a hurry to get to the end of anything, least of all a conversation.

Joshua's people, the true Whiskey Holler Tharps, were a hard working bunch. Worked all their lives in the mines, boy to old man. Honest folk who didn't mind coming home tired and dirty, and weren't too proud to get down on their knees to thank the good Lord for all His blessings.

Shame so many of them died in that cave-in. Lost a lot of good and decent folks that day. Forty-two grown men and seven boys. The Devil was in a rare mood that day, and no mistake. Guess he didn't like them digging so deep.

Granny cut a look at the young man as he sat there studying on the sounds the night brought to him. He was making a real effort to do it right, and that was another good sign. He came from good stock, and it's nice to know that living in a big city hadn't bred the country out of him.

"I can't figure it out," said Joshua, shaking his head. "What is it?"

Granny crushed out her cigarette and lit another one, closing her eyes to keep the flare of the match from stealing away her night vision. She lit the cigarette by touch and habit, shook the match out, and dropped it into an empty coffee tin that had an inch of rain water in it.

She said, "What's it sound like?"

That was a test. If the boy still had too much city in him, then there would be impatience on his face or in his voice. But not in Joshua's. He nodded at the question and once more tilted his head to listen.

Granny liked that. And she liked this boy. But after a few moments, Joshua shook his head. "I don't know. It's almost like there are two sounds. The, um, *moan*, and something else. Link a faint clinking sound."

"Do tell?" she said dryly, but with just enough lift to make it a question.

"Like...maybe the wind is blowing through something. A metal fence, or...I don't know. I hear the clink and the moan, but I can't hear either of them really well." He gave a nervous half laugh. "I've never heard anything like it."

"Never?"

"Well, I—don't spend a lot of time out of doors," he confessed. "I guess I haven't learned how to listen yet. Not properly, anyhow. I know Granddad used to talk about that. About shaking off the city so you could hear properly, but until now I don't think I ever really understood what he was saying."

Another soft moan floated over the trees. Strange and sad it was, and Granny sighed. She watched Joshua staring at the darkness, his face screwed up in concentration.

Granny gestured with her cigarette. "What do you think it *might* be?"

"Is it...some kind of animal?"

"What kind of animal would make a sound like that, do you suppose?"

They sat for almost two minutes, waiting between silences for the wind to blow. Joshua shook his head.

"Some kind of cat?"

That surprised Granny and now she listened, trying to hear it through his ears. "It do sound a might like a cat," she conceded, then chuckled. "But not a healthy one. Had a broke-leg bobcat get his leg caught in a bear trap once and hollered for a day and a night."

"So—is that what it is? A wounded bobcat? Is that clinking sound a bear trap?"

Granny exhaled more smoke before she answered. "No, son, that ain't what it is."

"Then...?"

She chuckled. "It'll keep. You interrupted your ownself, son. You was asking me a question before we heard yonder call."

He nodded, but it was clear that he was reluctant to leave the other topic unfinished. Granny felt how false her smile was. The mysteries out in the dark would keep. Might have to keep without the other shoe ever dropping.

"I..." Joshua began, fishing for the thread of where they'd been. "Right...we were talking about the day Granddad left for Pittsburgh. He said it was because there was no work, but he never really talked about that. And when he moved to Pittsburgh, he always worked in a foundry. He never wanted to go back to the mines."

"No...I daresay old Hack Tharp would never set foot in a mine again. 'Specially not in these hills, and probably nowhere. Lot of folks around here with the same thought. Those that stayed here gave up mining. I know men who wouldn't lift a pickaxe to go ten feet into a gold mine, not after what happened. Hack was one of 'em."

"Tell me about him. He died when I was ten, so I never had a grown-up conversation with him. Never got to really know him. What was he like?"

Granny smiled, and this time the smile was real. "Hack was a bull of a man, with shoulders from here to there and hands like iron. A good man to know and a handsome man to look at. Hack worked himself up to foreman down in the Hangood Mine. Swung a pickaxe for twenty long years down in the dark before he was promoted, and still sucked coal gas for twenty more as the foreman. The men liked him, no one crossed him, and his word was good on anything he put it to. Can't say as much about a lot of people, and can't say half as much about most."

Joshua nodded encouragingly.

"But Hack up and moved," said Granny. "He was the first, and over the years more'n sixty families have left the holler. Ain't no more than a hundred people left on this whole mountain, and I know of four families that are fixin' to leave before long. Might be that I'll be the last one here come next year, if *I'm* even here a'tall."

"People started leaving because the mine closed?"

"They started leaving *after* the mine closed. This place went bad on us that day, and it ain't ever goin' to get better."

The moaning wind and the soft metallic *clank* drifted past the end of her statements almost as if it were a statement itself.

Joshua cleared his throat. "Do you remember when Granddad left? I got the impression it was pretty soon after the disaster."

"It were on the third Sunday after the cave-in. Hack packed up only what would fit into that old rattle-rust Ford pick-up of his and drove off. Never came back, never called, never wrote. But...before he left, though, he came to say goodbye to ol' Granny." She sighed. "'Course I wasn't Granny back then. Just a young, unmarried gal who thought the sun rose in the morning 'cause it wanted to see Hack Tharp."

"Pardon me if this is rude, but...were you and Granddad sweethearts?"

Granny blew out some smoke. "There was no official understanding between us, you understand. Every girl in five counties wanted to catch Hack's eye, but for a while there I had some hopes. Maybe Hack did, too, 'cause I was the only one he lingered long enough to say farewell to. And—I blush to say it to a young feller like you—but I was something back then. You wouldn't know it now, lookin' at this big pile o' wrinkles, but I could turn a few heads of my own. Thought for a while that Hack might have been charmed enough to stay 'cause I asked him, but the cave-in plumb took all those thoughts out of his mind. He was set on leaving and he knew that I never would."

"Even if he'd asked?"

She sighed. "There are some things more important than love, strange as it sounds. At least…I thought so back then. You see…I had a talent for the old ways. With a talent for dowsing and a collection of aunts who were teaching me the way things worked in the world. Herbs and healing and luck charms and suchlike. Some folks call us witches. Even seen it in books. Mr. Sputters at the post office showed me a book onest called *Appalachian Granny Magic*. And I guess it's fair enough. Witch comes from some older word that means 'wise,' and that's all it is. Women who know such and such about things. My Aunt Tess was a fire witch. She could conjure a spark out of green wood with no matches and a word. My own mammy was the most famous healer in the holler. People'd come from all over with a sickness, or send a car for her to deliver a baby."

"I heard about that. Granddad told me a little. He said you could find water. He called you a *dowser*."

She nodded. "I been known to do that now and again. Mostly I make charms to ward off badness and evil. Half the rabbits in these hills walk with a limp since I started selling they's feet to ward off ill luck. And you can walk for two days and not find a soul who ain't wearing one of my snakeskin bags on their belts. Real toad's eyes in 'em, too, because fake charms don't stop nuthin'." She smiled. "Does that scare you, young Joshua? All this talk about witches?"

"Not as much as that sound does," he said, nodding to the night. "It's really creeping me out."

Granny puffed her cigarette.

"But the witches thing?" Joshua said. "No, I read up on that when I started researching this area for my book." He cleared his throat. "You were telling me about how Granddad came to say goodbye."

"So I was. Well...Hack Tharp stood foursquare in my yard, not two paces from where I sit right now. 'Mary Ruth,' he said, 'I'm gone. I can't live here no more, not with all the dead hauntin' me. My brothers, they never had a chance. They was so obsessed with earning that bonus that they went crazy, picking and digging like the Devil was whipping them, and then that whole mountain just up and *fell.* And it went down fast, too. Killed 'em before they could git with God. I was right outside taking a smoke when the mouth of Hell opened up and swallowed those boys. I haven't had a night's sleep since it happened. And I won't ever sleep a night if I stay here.'

"'Weren't your fault,' I told him. But Hack shook his head. 'I ain't saying it is. And I ain't losing sleep 'cause I feel guilty about being on *this* side of the grave when all my family was taken by death. No—the bosses killed all those men—killed my own brothers, two of my cousins. Killed 'em sure as if they blew the mountain down with dynamite. Killed 'em by digging too deep in a played-out mine. Killed 'em by greed, and that's an evil thing. Greed's one of the bad sins, Mary Ruth, one of them seven deadly sins, and it made my brothers sell their souls to old Scratch himself.'"

"I didn't know Granddad was so religious. He never went to church when I was a kid. Not even on Easter and Christmas."

"I suppose," said Granny, "that he lost the knack. Seen a lot of it after the collapse, just like I seen a lot of folks suddenly hear the preacher's call before the dust even settled. Since then, though...well ain't no one in this holler don't believe in the Devil anymore, so the unbelievers have started believing in God by default."

"Was there an investigation?" asked Joshua. "Did the authorities ever determine that the mining company was at fault?"

"Investigation?" Granny laughed. "You got a city boy's sense of humor, son. No, there weren't no investigation. And even if someone wanted to investigate, there weren't no way to do it."

"Why not? I've read a lot about mining, and a structural engineer could do a walk-through look at the shoring systems, the drill angles, the geologist's assessment of the load bearing walls of the mountain, and—"

"No one's ever going to do any of that."

"Why not?"

"'Cause they'd have to cut through a million tons of rock to take that look."

"They could just examine the areas dug out when the bodies were removed."

Granny studied him for a moment. "Your granddad didn't tell you?"

"Tell me what?"

She sighed. "Those dead men are still there, son. The company never dug them out. *Nobody* ever dug them out. That whole mountain's a tomb for all those good men."

Joshua stood up and stared at the darkness again, looking toward Balder Rise. The wind blew from that direction, carrying with it the soft moan. "God," he said softly.

"Oh, God didn't have nuthin' to do with what happened that day," said Granny. "Your granddad spoke true when he said that it were the evil greed of the mining company that brought the ceiling down. They dug too deep."

"That's something Granddad said a couple of times, and now you've said it twice. What's that mean, exactly?"

"The mining company was fair desperate to stay in business even though most of the coal had already been took from old Balder. They kept pushing and pushing to find another vein. Pushed and pushed the men, too, tempting 'em with promises of bonuses if they found that vein. Understand, boy, miners are always poor. It's really no kind of life. Working down there in the dark, bad air and coal dust, it's like you're digging your own grave."

The moan on the wind came again, louder, more insistent. The black trees seemed to bend under the weight of it.

"The company kept the pressure on. Everybody needed that vein, too, because the company *owned* everything. They owned the bank, which means they held the mortgage on ever'body's house and that's the same like holding the mortgage on ever'body's souls." She shook her head. "No, a lot of folks thought the Devil himself was whispering in the ear of ever'body, from the executives all the way down to the teenage boys pushing the lunch trolleys. Infecting them good-hearted and God fearing men with their own greed. Spreading sin like a plague. Makin' 'em dig too hard and too deep, with too much greed and hunger."

"Digging too deep, though—you keep saying that. Do you mean that they over-mined the walls, or—?"

"No, son," she said, "that ain't what Hack meant, and it ain't what I mean."

"Then what—?"

The moan came again, even louder. So loud that Joshua stood up and placed his palms on the rail so he could lean head and shoulders out into the night. Granny saw him shiver.

"You cold?" she asked, though it was a warm night.

"No," he said, without turning. "That sound…"

Granny waited.

"…it sounds almost like a person," Joshua continued. "It sounds like someone's hurt out there."

"Hurt? Is that really what it sounds like to you?"

"Well, it's something like that. I can *hear* the pain." He shot her a quick look. "Does that sound silly? Am I being a stupid city boy here, or—?"

"You don't sound stupid at all, son. That's one of the smartest things you've said. You know what's happening?" she asked. "The city's falling clean off you."

He studied her.

"It's true," she said. "Your daddy might have been born in the city and you might have been born and raised there, too, but you still got the country in you. You still got some of the hills in you. You get that from ol' Hack, and I bet he was always country no matter how many years he lived in the city—am I right or am I right?"

"You're right, Granny," said Joshua. "No one would ever have mistaken Granddad for anything except what he was. He…loved these mountains. He talked about how beautiful they were. How they smelled on a spring morning. How the birds would have conversations in the trees. How folks were simple—less complicated—but they weren't stupid. How he wished he could have stayed."

Granny closed her eyes for a moment, remembering Hack. Remembering pain. Remembering the horror of that collapse, and all the things that died that day. Those men, her love, this town.

"Is something wrong?" asked Joshua.

She opened her eyes and rocked back so she could look up at him. "Wrong?"

The moan cut through the air again. Louder still.

"I suppose you could say that nuthin's been *right* since that mine collapsed," she said, and Granny could hear the pain in her own voice. Almost as dreadful as the pain in that moan. "Close your eyes again and listen to that sound. Don't tell me what it ain't. Listen until you can tell me what it is."

Joshua closed his eyes and leaned once more on the rail, his head raised to lift his ears into the wind.

After a full minute, he said, "It sounds like a person...and that clinking sound...that's definitely something metal."

She waited.

Joshua laughed. "If it was Christmas, I'd say it was Old Marley and his chain."

When Granny did not laugh, Joshua opened his eyes and turned to her.

"That's from the—"

"I know what it's from, son. And it ain't all that far from the mark." She sucked in some smoke. "Not a chain, though. Listen and tell me I'm wrong."

He listened.

"No, you're right. It's, um...sharper than that. But the echoes are making it hard to figure it out. Almost sounds like a bunch of little clinks, almost at once. That's why I thought it was a chain; you know, the links clinking as it blew in the wind."

"But it ain't a chain," she said, "and it ain't blowing in the wind. Ain't echoes, either."

There was a stronger gust of wind and the moan was much louder now.

Joshua pushed off the rail and walked down into the yard. He stood with his hands cupped around his ears to catch every nuance of the sound. Granny dropped her cigarette butt into the empty coffee tin and lit another.

The moaning was so loud now that anyone could hear it. So loud that anyone could understand it, and Granny watched for the moment when Joshua understood. She'd seen it so many times. With friends, with her own daughter—who screamed and then ran inside the house to begin packing up her clothes and her babies. She hadn't come back.

Granny had seen a parade of people come through, stopping as Hack had stopped, wanting to say goodbye. Only one of them ever came back. Norm McPhee wandered back to the mountains after spending the last fourteen years in a bottle somewhere in Georgia. He came back to the holler, back to Balder, back to Granny's yard, and he stood there for an hour, his eyes filled with ghosts.

Then Norm had walked into the woods, found himself a quiet log to sit on, drank the rest of his bottle of who-hit-John, took the pistol from his pocket, and blew his brains all over the new blossoms on a dogwood tree.

Granny smoked her cigarette and wondered what Hack Tharp's grandson would do, because she could see his body language changing. He was slowly standing straighter. His hands fell slowly from behind his ears. His eyes were wide, and his mouth formed soundless words as he sought to speak the thoughts that his senses were planting in his head.

He turned to her. Sharp and quick, but his mouth wasn't ready to put voice to the thought that Granny could now *see* in the young man's eyes.

"I can hear them," he said at last.

Them.

"Yes," she said.

"It's not just one sound, and it's not an animal. There are a *lot* of them."

"Yes," Granny said again.

Something glistened on Joshua's face. Was it sweat?

"Granddad said that forty-nine people died that day. Mostly men, a few kids."

"Yes," she said once more.

"All of them digging down in the earth," said Joshua, and his voice sounded different. Distant, like he was talking to himself. Distant, like the wind. "All of them, digging like crazy." His eyes glistened. "What did Granddad say? You just told me... That those men were so obsessed with earning that bonus that they went crazy, picking and digging like the Devil was whipping them."

"And then that whole mountain just up and fell," agreed Granny softly.

"It killed them fast. Killed them before they could get with God."

She nodded.

"Like the mouth of Hell opened up and swallowed those boys," Joshua said, his voice thick, his eyes filled with bad, bad pictures. "God."

"I already said it," whispered Granny. "God didn't have nuthin' to do with what happened."

The moans were constant now. The voices clear and terrible. The metallic clinks distinct.

Joshua laughed. Too quick and too loud. "Oh...come *on*! This is ridiculous. Granny, I don't mean any disrespect, but...come on. You can't expect me to believe any of this."

"I didn't ask you to."

That wiped the smile off his face.

"Granddad left because of this sound, didn't he?"

Granny didn't bother to answer that.

The moans answered it.

The clank of metal on rock answered it.

"No," said Joshua. "You want me to believe that they're still there, still down there in the dark, still...digging?"

Granny smoked her cigarette.

"That's insane," he said, anger in his voice now. "They're dead! They've been dead for years. Come on, Granny, it's insane. It's stupid."

"Son," she said, "I ain't told you none of that. I ain't told you nuthin' but to listen to the wind and tell me what *you* think that is."

The voices on the wind were filled with such anger, such pain.

Such hunger.

The incessant clanks of pickaxes against rock were like punches, and Joshua actually yielded a step backward with each ripple of strikes. As if those pickaxes were hitting him. More wetness glistened on his face.

"Granny," he said in a hollow voice. "Come on..."

Granny rocked in her rocker and smoked her cigarette.

"All these years?" asked Joshua, and she could hear how fragile his voice was. It had taken three weeks of the sound before Hack had up and left. A lot of folks played their TV or radio loud and late to try and hide the sound.

One by one, people left the mountain. Took some only months; took others years.

Joshua Tharp stood in the yard and winced each time the wind blew.

He won't last the night, she thought. *He'll be in his car and heading back to the city before moonrise.*

"All these years...digging..."

His eyes were suddenly wild.

"Has...has...the sound been getting *louder* all these years?"

Granny nodded. "Every night."

"'Every night,'" echoed Joshua. He stood his ground, not knocked back by the ring of the pickaxes this time. Granny thought that either he had found his nerve or he had lost it entirely.

"I 'spect one of these days they'll dig theyselves out of that hole." She paused. "Out of Hell."

The picks rang in the night.

Again and again.

Then there was a cracking sound. Rock breaking off. Or breaking open.

Joshua and Granny listened.

No more sounds of pickaxes.

There were just the moans.

Louder now. Clearer.

So much clearer.

"God..." whispered Joshua.

"God had nuthin' to do with the collapse," said Granny. "And I expect he's got nuthin' to do with this."

The moans rode the night breeze.

So loud and clear.

Author's Note on "Flint and Steel"

Max Brooks wrote one of the landmark zombie novels of all time, *World War Z*. I know Max and he's a cool cat and a talented writer. When he reached out and asked if I wanted to write a story for an anthology he was editing, I said sure before I even asked what it was. Turns out he was not editing a zombie book. Max was editing an anthology of novellas set in the world of GI Joe. Yeah, *that* GI Joe.

Understand, when I was a kid (I'm older than Max) GI Joe was twelve inches high, fought in World War II, and hadn't even gotten his legendary kung-fu grip. I'd never played with the smaller and more sci-fi Joe characters. So I wound up getting a ton of toys and comics in the mail, and sat like a happy, overgrown kid playing with them and learning about the world of the Joes, while binge-watching the cartoons. I had a blast…and it was work related so, you know, it wasn't me having a second childhood. Ahem.

Max did not want kid stories, though. He wanted edgy, weird-science action thrillers. So that's what I wrote.

Flint and Steel: A Story of GI Joe

-1-

"The Island"

High Security R&D Facility
Near Area 51, Nevada

It was all coming apart. Gunfire tore holes in the night. There were screams and the constant rattle of automatic gunfire. Fires burst through the roofs of a dozen buildings sending showers of sparks into the sky so that it looked like the stars themselves were dying and falling.

Flint ran fast and low, using hard cover instead of shadows, moving from tree to rock to wall, his pattern random and unsymmetrical. He was hurt, he knew that much. The warmth running down the inside of his clothes wasn't all sweat. He could smell the sharp copper tang of his own blood.

His blood and the blood of others.

Doc. Law. Scarlett, too. God knew how many others. In his mind all he could see was blood.

Blood...and those *things.*

He ran and ran, his breath burning in his lungs.

He stumbled and went down, hitting chest-first and sliding, tasting sand in his mouth. He came to rest in the middle of the east parade ground. Exposed, vulnerable.

The screams began to die away. They did not fade like volume turned down on an iPod. They were cut off. Sharply, abruptly, in time with new bursts of gunfire.

Flint felt his consciousness begin to fade as fatigue or damage took hold of him.

"No," he mumbled, spitting sand out of his mouth. "No!"

If he passed out now, he knew that he would never wake up. Not in this world. *They* would find him. Find him and tear him apart.

He tried to get to his hands and knees, but weakness and nausea swept through him.

"No!" he growled, louder this time, and the harshness in his own voice put steel into his muscles. He rose, inch by agonizing inch until he was upright on his knees.

In the distance he could hear one of *them* coming.

A metallic clang, the squeak of treads.

How far? A hundred yards? Less?

Flint set his teeth and tried to get to his feet. No way he was going to die like this. If this was his last firefight, then by God he was not going out on his knees.

Pain flared in his side. He couldn't remember what had hit him. Bullets? Shrapnel?

It didn't matter; he forced one leg up, thumped his right foot on the ground, jammed the stock of his M5 on the ground, and pushed.

It was like jacking up a tank.

He rose slowly, slowly.

The squeak of the treads was closer. All of the screams had stopped.

Even the gunfire seemed to have died away.

"No!" he snarled and heaved.

He got to his feet and the whole world spun around him. He almost fell. It nearly ended right there, but Flint took an awkward sideways step and caught his balance.

The world steadied.

The squeak of treads was close. So close. Too close.

Flint turned.

It was there. Massive, indomitable against the firelit columns of smoke. It rolled to a stop ten feet away and with a hiss of hydraulics the black mouths of twin 7.62 caliber miniguns swung toward him. He raised his own gun.

The miniguns could fire more than four thousand rounds per minute, per gun.

He wasn't sure he could even pull the trigger.

Flint bared his bloody teeth in a grin that defied the machine, defied logic, and defied the certainty of death that towered over him.

"Go Joe!" he yelled.

And fired.

-2-

"The Island"—Conference Room #3

Three Hours Ago

"I'm not comfortable with this."

Dr. Allyn Prospero tossed the sheet of paper onto the table with a dismissive flick of his hand. The others at the table watched as the paper spun on a vagary of air and then slid halfway across the polished hardwood surface, coming to a stop almost perfectly equidistant between Prospero and the soldier. Then everyone looked from the paper to Chief Warrant Officer Dashiell Faireborn like spectators at a chess match.

Faireborn—known as Flint among his fellow Joes—had a face like a stone. His jaw was square and set, his nose straight, his eyes as uncompromising as those of a hunting hawk. Flint did not look at the paper, but he tapped the table in front of it.

"That's an Executive Order," he said quietly. "'Comfort isn't part of the standard phrasing."

"This is my project."

"That's not what it says on the pink slip. The U.S. government pays for two thirds of this, and the rest of the light bill is paid for by NATO. You're an employee," said Flint, "not a stockholder."

Prospero was as resolute as Flint. "This project would not even exist without me. I *am* the project."

Flint almost smiled. Almost. "Well, that means you must have the same tattoo on your ass that I have on mine."

Prospero frowned.

"'Property of Uncle Sam,'" explained Doc Greer, who sat to Flint's right. He grimaced. "A little military humor."

"I'm not a soldier. I don't work for the Army, I don't work for GI Joe, and I certainly don't work for General Hawk." He loaded that last name with enough acid to melt tank armor.

"That's true," admitted Flint slowly. General Hawk had warned him that he and Prospero were old political sparring partners with a relationship closely resembling a mongoose and a cobra. "However," he said, "you work for the DOD."

"I'm a private contractor," replied Prospero sharply. "I am *not* a rah-rah supporter of the military machine. My work is designed to save American lives, not find new wars in which to discard them."

"You're building war machines—" began Greer, but Prospero wheeled on him.

"What I'm building will ultimately take humans *out* of the combat equation. Does *anyone* in Washington actually read my reports?" When no one spoke, Prospero turned back to Flint. "Perhaps the real issue here is resistance in some quarters to projects that would deny certain persons the opportunity to pull triggers."

Flint said nothing for a moment. The small muscles at the corners of his jaw bunched and flexed. Before he could speak, Doc spoke. His voice was gentle, conciliatory.

"This kind of debate isn't productive, gentlemen," he said. "Politics, ethics, and philosophy aside, the real truth is that we all answer to the man in the Oval Office. With the military budget coming under fire in the press and in Congress, the President needs to be able to justify the kinds of expenditures that have been allotted for Project Caliban."

"My reports are—"

"Yes," cut in Flint, "your reports are fine. Detailed, exhaustive, and to most of Congress, incomprehensible. There are no scientists in either the House or Senate, and what they don't understand they won't support. Sure, back in the Reagan years they'd line up to throw money at a project with a cool nickname, but nowadays everyone's pinching pennies, and Department of Defense research projects are the first on the chopping block."

He bent forward and placed his forearms on the table.

"Dr. Prospero, you're not facing enemies here. I'm an advocate of your program. Hell, I'm an advocate of *any* program that will reduce the risk to men in the field. Cutting-edge drone programs like yours will save lives. American and Allied lives. Civilian lives, too. We all know that. But we need to have a clear evaluation statement that will convince Congress of that, or this program is going into mothballs. This isn't a debate. The decision has been made by the President. NATO follows America's lead when it comes to funding."

Prospero said nothing, but he pursed his lips, clearly thinking it through.

"And more to the point, Doctor," said Flint, "there is a long list of other projects begging for the kind of dollars you've been given. If there is any hint of resistance or obstruction on your part, the money train is going to get switched to a different track and within six months the only thing that will be in development out here will be tumbleweeds and cacti."

Flint knew that this had hit home with Prospero. This facility, codenamed 'The Island,' was really a bunch of buildings built into the unforgiving Nevada desert. Twenty years ago there were more than fifty active projects in development out here. Now there was Prospero's team and a few ancillary projects. It was an enormously expensive facility to maintain and only results could keep the lab open.

The doctor looked at the others seated around the table. There were three members of the Joe team present—Flint, team medical officer Dr. Carl 'Doc' Greer, and flame-haired Shana O'Hara whose call sign 'Scarlett' was hardly a 'covert' choice. None of them had shared their real names with the team here at the Island. Even though this was not a combat mission, General Hawk had ordered that only rank and call-signs be used. Part his policy of professional detachment.

The others at the table were members of Prospero's staff here at the Island. To his immediate left was Professor Elsbeth Miranda, once his most promising grad student during his days at MIT, then his protégé, and now the most valuable senior researcher on staff. Her knowledge of unmanned combat systems was only slightly less profound than his own. She was tall, slim, and had that blend of pale skin and foamy dark hair that usually made Flint's heart flutter like a jazz drum solo. She wore a lipstick that was a shade too bold a red for this kind of meeting, and her blouse was unbuttoned one button too low to have been anything but a deliberate move to attract attention. At first Flint thought that she was a hot-blooded woman who was taking a rare chance to attract something other than lab-coated geeks; but as the meeting progressed he changed his view. Her attention was clearly—and entirely—focused on Prospero; and it was at once possessive and protective.

Office romance, he wondered. *A May-December thing...or a female predator laying claim to the alpha in her environment. Had to be something like that.*

And yet he knew that the lipstick and the abundant cleavage she had on display was for his benefit—his and the other Joes.

A distraction? Sure. But to distract them from what?

He quietly studied the other scientists. Like Miranda they were lions in their fields—microsystems, software integration, computer engineering, nanotechnology, artificial intelligence, and tactical weapons sciences. None of them, however, were on Prospero's level, and probably not on Miranda's either. They were strong members of a pack. And, like Miranda and Prospero, they resented outside intrusion of any kind, and evaluations in particular.

However no one spoke. Everyone was aware of who the true alpha—at least in terms of scientific genius—was. Allyn Prospero had graduated from high school at age fourteen, college at sixteen, and had earned his first PhD at nineteen. Since then he had lost track of the many degrees, awards, and accolades he had collected in fifty years as the leading light in cybernetic combat. He had pioneered more new fields of study than anyone alive, and was named on over six hundred patents. He had four times been senior researcher on teams that won the Nobel Prize.

Flint knew all of this. He had Prospero's resume memorized. It was in the scary realm somewhere between 'impressive' and 'freaky,' though Flint tended toward the latter category.

Prospero sighed.

"Very well," he said heavily. "When do you want to begin?"

Flint kept a smile off of his face. "Now would be good. Our weapons and equipment have all been off-loaded and should be set up out on the sand."

"What kind of equipment?"

Flint spread his hands. "It would make a more effective and convincing test if you didn't know ahead of time. And, let's face it, the best way to guarantee the biggest slice of the pie from the budget committee would be for me to be able to tell them that I saw the system in full operation."

Professor Miranda shot Prospero a sharp look. "We're weeks away from a practical test—"

The scientist narrowed his eyes. There was some murmuring among his staff. None of them spoke directly to Prospero, though one or two bent close to whisper to Professor Miranda. After a moment's consideration she and Prospero leaned their heads together and hid their mouths behind their hands to exchange a few covert words.

Flint, Scarlett, and Doc exchanged quick looks, but did not comment.

Prospero held up a placating hand. "If that's what will get this over with and allow us to get back to work, Chief, then I think we can provide a demonstration that will satisfy *any* Doubting Thomases."

Miranda furrowed her brow at him. "You mean...*Caliban?*"

Prospero smiled. "Yes," he drawled. "I think Caliban would provide a very adequate demonstration of our potential."

Miranda studied him for a moment, and then she, too, smiled.

-3-

"What was all *that* about?" asked Scarlett once the team of scientists had filed out of the conference room.

Flint leaned back in his chair and blew out his cheeks.

"Hell if I know. Spooky bunch, every last one of them."

Doc said, "Prospero's oddly aggressive for someone whose ultimate goal is the end of war."

Scarlett closed the door and parked a shapely haunch on the corner of the table. "Prospero would make a wonderful mad scientist. Give him a white cat and a hollowed-out volcano and he's all set."

Flint grunted. "When you're that far out on the cutting edge a little eccentricity is expected."

"Scary smart," agreed Scarlett.

"Speaking of scary," said Doc. "Did you catch the mood dynamics of that team? There's a weird pecking order there. Prospero almost never looks at them. He looks at Professor Miranda, and she relays Prospero's moods through her own expressions and body language to the rest of the team. They in turn make quiet comments to her, and she conveys *some* of the comments to Prospero. Like a filtering process."

"He doesn't deign to speak to the little people?" suggested Scarlett.

"So it seems."

Flint shrugged. "Runaway ego is also pretty common with guys in his class. I'm not really worried about whether he rules his staff with an iron fist. It's an extension of the university model, so he probably picked that up at MIT. He was top dog there, too." He glanced at the closed door. "No, what concerns me is how possessive he is about this."

"Surely that's pretty common too among top researchers," said Doc. "Especially guys pioneering their own fields."

"Maybe," Flint said dubiously, "but it comes off more as arrogant and secretive. I could accept that a bit easier with an egghead running a software lab—you know, fear that someone else will copy the idea and rush another version to market. Happens all the time in the gaming industry. Can't say I'm fond of seeing it in a weapons designer working for us."

Scarlett stood up. "I know what you're saying, Flint. Prospero's attitude has been *noticed*. Duke said as much during our briefing. It's not just the viability of the program that's under the microscope."

"No joke," nodded Doc. "Last thing we need is an *actual* mad scientist going off the rails with forty billion dollars' worth of automated killing machines that only he knows how to control."

It wasn't meant as a joke, and no one laughed.

Flint got to his feet. "Okay…we asked for a demonstration. Let's go see what he has."

-4-

"The Island"—Dead Lake Testing Area

Dr. Prospero stood in the middle of the empty desert, surrounded by red flares that burst above him like fireworks and drifted down to encircle him like one of the rings of hell. As each new flare burst the scientist could see the clouds of white phosphorous smoke hanging in the sky, and then as the flares drifted down on their tiny chutes the sky above him faded again to utter blackness.

The desert at night was usually so quiet. He loved coming out here to think, to work things through. To consider the past and plan for the future. The emptiness and vastness of the Nevada desert was his sanctum, his cloister for years.

Now it burned with red fire and the silence was torn by the hollow, steady crack of automatic gunfire and the occasional deep-throated boom of missiles. Hellfire missiles, which Prospero thought was a fine irony.

He waited. Dragonflies flitted around him. They always made him smile. They swirled around him, buzzing on green wings that gave off a faint electric hum. Anyone unfamiliar with the tiny biomimetic machines would think they were really insects. Prospero extended a hand and one of them landed on it, antennae twitching, miniature legs bending and walking in an almost perfect imitation of life.

"Go play," he said and shook it off. The words sounded playful, but they keyed the search and observe protocols in their microchips. The dragonflies turned and flew into the darkness, hunting the monsters that hunted him, their beating wings recharging their batteries as they flew. Not quite a perpetual motion machine, but as close as he had been able to manage so far.

Prospero had also launched a half dozen of the larger but still man-portable SkyLite observation drones. The lithium-polymer batteries on the stealth drones only held a four-hour charge, but it took only a few minutes for them to reach thirty-six thousand feet. The Joes had satellites which could be targeted and destroyed by any number of air-to-space or space-to-space weapons; but Prospero had swarms of tiny machines that were harder to see, harder to catch, disposal and replaceable.

"Fly, fly, fly," he said in an almost dreamy voice.

There were gunships in the blackness above him, running silent and dark; and even though he could not see the wicked mouths of the miniguns pointing at him, he could *feel* them. At least a dozen of them, each capable of firing six thousand rounds per minute through their rotating six-inch barrels. Enough firepower to wipe out a company.

Because there was no possibility of escape, Prospero did not care about them.

There were other monsters in the dark, and he turned his head slowly from side to side, trying to decide the approach vector for the drones. He knew that at least two of the unarmed combat air vehicles would be zeroing him. There was a Phantom Ray II up there, the newest of Boeing's Phantom Works craft. Armed with the Hellfires and other goodies, some as experimental as the drone that carried them.

And if that psychopath Hawk had anything to do with planning this attack, then there would be a General Atomics Avenger up there, too, laboring under the weight of Paveway bombs. Hawk's personal favorite.

Prospero could try to run, but where could he go? They were drawing a circle around him, closing it tight like the neck of a drawstring bag. With him inside.

He smiled.

On his way out here he had carried two large metal cases that looked like dog carriers. Each case had a spring flap keyed to a pedometer built into his exosuit. Every fifty yards the flaps opened and dropped half a dozen Sprawlers. These small hexapedal devices dropped like spiders onto the sand, immediately activated ground sensors, and scuttled off into the dark. They were unarmed, but they were fast and long before the Joes found *him* he would know where *they* were.

Professor Miranda's soft voice whispered in his ear.

"They're coming."

"And about time, too," he replied.

"Are you ready?"

He hit a keypad and a hologram of a topographical map appeared in his visor. The map sparkled with blue dots that identified his Sprawlers and Dragonflies and SkyLites, and glowed with larger yellow dots that showed what his mechanical friends had found. "Completely."

"Be careful," she cautioned. "I don't trust them. I think they're determined to take you down."

Prospero laughed. "They're welcome to try."

"Then watch your back, because they're going to try right *now!*"

The world of darkness turned to blinding noonday brightness as missiles punched into the desert floor and burst. Twin fireballs curled upward and the concussive crossways blast of the shockwave hit the man with bone-crushing force, lifting him, throwing him like a doll into a sandstone wall sixty yards behind him. The force of the impact was enough to splinter bone and rupture muscle tissue, bend steels and shatter hardened polymers.

Except that none of this happened to the scientist.

He slammed into the wall and slid down, but only into a crouch. Fire and hot dust swirled around him, but he was safe and whole. And smiling.

He pushed off the wall and stood, turning left and right to watch for the next attack.

"Gunships!" cautioned Miranda's voice, but Prospero did not need the warning as fifty-caliber rounds pounded into his chest, driving him backward against the wall. Hundreds of hits. Thousands.

Then another salvo of rockets turned the sandstone wall into a rain of jagged debris, knocking him over, burying him to the waist. In the nearly constant muzzle-flash he saw the Blackhawks hovering ten feet above the desert floor, side doors open, miniguns swung out on electric turrets and opened up, their roar louder than thunder.

The guns hammered him until they fired themselves dry, then they rose slowly, moving upward and sideways, turning to bring their rocket pods to bear.

Prospero fought his way out of the waist-deep rubble. He grabbed a rock the size of a mailbox, lifted it with a grunt, and threw it to one side. Then he straightened, rising to his full height of nine feet.

"Night vision," he said and instantly the world transformed from black and red to green and black and white.

"SkyLites," he said, "talk to me."

One side of his vision was suddenly filled with images taken from the drones that circled like buzzards over the desert.

"Thermal overlay." Dots appeared on the image. He counted four Blackhawks and three fixed-wing drones. Hawk had sent *two* Avengers to back-up the Phantom Ray. All of the military drones were circling back toward him, their systems apparently ignoring the smaller UAC's that Prospero had launched. Other signatures showed a phalanx of fast-moving desert patrol vehicles converging.

It was anyone's definition of a worst-case scenario. A pair of Abrams tanks couldn't fight their way out of this. Which is why he'd sold his General Dynamics stock last month. The Caliban exosuit he wore was about to put the tank manufacturer in the antiques business.

"Are you all right?" asked Professor Miranda, her voice twitchy with stress.

"I'm perfect," he said and then laughed. "They've shown us what they can do. Now let's show them what *we* can do."

"Prospero...Allyn...please," she said urgently, "don't take any unnecessary risks. You—"

"Hush, darling. Hush. This is what we wanted. This is what we *needed.* We've been wracking our brains trying to figure a way to give a practical demonstration to our overseas friends. This was *handed* to us on a silver platter. A full system demonstration, and the government is not only paying for it, but mandating it. What could be more perfect?"

"I know, but these people, these Joes...just because they're military don't fool yourself into thinking their collar size is bigger than their I.Q."

He laughed again, and there was a wild quality to it. He even heard it, and didn't care. It was a time to be wild, to be fully alive!

"They're dinosaurs, my dear; they just don't yet know that they're extinct. Besides, the Joes will see only what we want them to see."

"Don't underestimate them—"

"Miranda, hush. Just make sure everything is fed to the secure uplink. I want our *friends* to see the Joes throw everything they have against us."

"Be careful, my love. The Joes are coming in for another run."

"Let them come," said Prospero. Then he switched from external to internal voice mode. "Caliban combat systems to voice control."

"*System on.*" Caliban's computer voice was the only part of this he didn't like. It was an older computer voice system that manufactured words instead of compiling them from a programmed library. The new voice software package had not been installed yet. He was sorry about that. The voice choices included Morgan Freeman, Mark Hamill, or Joseph Gordon-Levitt. Hamill would have been fun. Luke Skywalker guiding him through this would be fitting. It all seemed like science fiction anyway. Even to him.

"Laser targeting."

"*On line.*"

"Uplink to enemy tactical satellite."

"*Uplink established.*"

He stepped forward. The servos attached to his boot straps lifted the forty-pound foot as easily as if he wore a pair of flip-flops.

"Skyjack on line," he said.

"*Booting,*" said the computer voice. "*Skyjack system on line.*"

The whine of the chopper rotors increased as the Blackhawks tilted for a strafing run. They'd hammer him again, allowing the laser-sighting system of the drones to acquire him for another rocket attack.

"Initiate Skyjack protocol Prospero One-nineteen."

"*Initiating.*"

The satellite display board flashed and cleared, removing all of the identified combat craft. Then one by one they popped back on, but this time each dot was surrounded by a white circle. Before they had all re-appeared the circles were overlaid by white crosses.

Caliban's dispassionate computer voice began counting it off.

"Blackhawk one acquired."
"Blackhawk two acquired."
"Blackhawk three acquired."
"Blackhawk four acquired."
"General Atomics Avenger one acquired."

And on and on until all of the vehicles and aircraft surrounding him were logged.

Prospero smiled. "Prepare to accept command code."

"Ready."

"'Tempest,'" he said. Instantly the computer voice rattled off a stream of command codes.

"Destroy all enemy warcraft," said Prospero. He did not need to give that command, and in truth it did nothing to increase the lethality of the Skyjack program. The virus software would now be rerouting the systems of every automated vehicle, on land or in the air. In seconds the machines sent to *test* him would obliterate each other. All of that was written into the code...but it felt good to speak the order; when the destruction began it would be at his command.

Pleased, the old scientist sat down on the rock he had thrown and waited.

There were three seconds of silent darkness.

All around him the skies blossomed with white light. Gunfire roared. Rockets fired one after the other. Bombs fell.

The whole desert seemed to explode.

None of the bullets struck him. None of the missiles flew in his direction.

He smiled.

"Destroy them all," he murmured. "Burn them out of my sky."

On his helmet's monitor the blips indicating the Blackhawks and the drones and the fast attack vehicles flickered and vanished until only one craft was left. Then, it too burst into flame and fell like a meteor through the night. It struck the sandstone eighty feet from where he sat. Prospero didn't even bother to raise an arm to protect himself from the flaming debris.

-5-

The Ice House

Kaffeklubben Island, 440 miles from the North Pole

The man sat alone, draped in soft shadows, his shoulder and face etched by yellow firelight. Pine logs hissed and popped in the stone hearth. The air around him was troubled by the almost maniacal complexity of Rachmaninoff's *Piano Concerto No. 3 in D minor, Op. 30*, and yet the man in the chair found the music deeply soothing. It was like sailing through the eye of a hurricane—chaos all around and yet deep inside there was perfect stillness. And with stillness came clarity.

A glass of wine sat forgotten on the table beside his chair.

The man reclined in the chair, fingers steepled, eyes narrowed, lips pursed as he studied the images that played out on the flatscreen monitor that filled most of one wall. He watched with professional interest as a Phantom Ray veered off course and slammed its eighteen and a half tons into a General Atomics Avenger. Both drones exploded in a massive fireball and fell onto the desert floor far below. Unmanned tanks swung their turrets and laid down continuous fire at fast attack vehicles. Machine guns in remote controlled Black Hawks turned their guns on other helos flying in attack formation. All of it within seconds, all of it in a beautifully coordinated ballet of self-immolation and mutual destruction.

When the last of the guns fell silent, the man in the chair took a deep breath and let it out through his nostrils, puffing like a contented dragon. In the upper left corner of the screen a smaller pop-up screen showed the face of a beautiful woman with long brunette hair and glasses that hung around her neck on a silver chain.

"This completes our demonstration, sir," she said. Her voice trembled and she was clearly nervous. No, almost certainly afraid. Although she did not know the name, or even the code name of the man to whom she spoke, she knew enough about who he was and what he represented to be properly terrified. That pleased the man; it was as it should be.

The woman stared at him—or at the screen saver of a coiled snake, which was all that she would ever see of him—with expectation in her eyes. Was she waiting for praise?

Probably. He smiled. The next ice age would come and go before he would spoon out praise to a *vendor*. And a potential vendor at that.

"What is your asking price?" he said. There was at least a fragment of tacit approval in that question. Let that be enough for her. Let her suck what juice there was out of that.

But she was undeterred. She leaned toward the camera, double vertical lines forming between her brows. "Price is secondary," she said. "Your assurance is paramount."

"Of course," he replied with only the barest hesitation, "and you have it. I respect and endorse your ideals. Ending global conflict is our shared goal. How did Prospero himself phrase it? 'When no human hand touches a weapon of war, then war will not touch human hearts.' Elegantly phrased. Much better than my own clumsy 'Wage a war to end all wars.' So...rest assured that I will always bear in mind that this is the cornerstone of any arrangement between us."

The woman hesitated for a moment, then nodded.

"Now," the man said, "I believe we were discussing price—?"

The woman had enough grace and good taste not to speak the number. Instead she looked down and tapped some keys. A price appeared in a discreet corner of the screen. There were a lot of zeroes. Some might say an absurd amount.

The man in the chair considered the price.

"I'll let you know," he said, and before she could say anything he disconnected the call.

He sat in silence for a thoughtful few moments and then turned his head ever so slightly to the other small pop-up screen.

"You may comment," he said.

"That bonnie lass and her auld—and, I might add, quite daft—Frankenstein boyfriend are trying to rob ye blind, and ye damn well know it," snapped a slender man wearing an ermine-trimmed robe. He wore a mask of polished silver through which intelligent, calculating eyes stared out.

"Is that your professional assessment of the demonstration?"

"Oh, aye, I like it well enough. Lots of lovely pyrotechnics. Hooray for the Red, White and Blue...but ah dinnieken why ye want another vendor. Which of my bloody systems have underperformed for ye?"

"What's the matter, Lord Destro? Don't you *believe* in capitalism?"

"I believe in loyalty. From vendor to customer as well as from customer to vendor."

"Mmm, that's one view, but it's self-corrupting. Competition, on the other hand, encourages innovation, shortens time to market, and allows for more rational discussions of price."

"Don't be daft. I'm fair scunnered with these games. There's a trust issue here as well."

"Trust is earned."

"And haven't I earned your trust?"

"Allow me to modify that statement. Trust needs to be continually earned."

The man with the silver face said nothing.

"Dr. Prospero is offering some exciting new technologies. His hybrid Skyjack/Tempest intrusion software is probably worth the price he's asking for the whole package. I don't really need the exosuit, though admittedly there are some members of the Crimson Guard who would enjoy field testing it." He paused. "Really, Destro, if you had a mobile tactical command unit like Caliban we might not be having this conversation."

"I can make one, as ye damn well know."

"'Can make one' is far less appealing to me than 'have one now.' I can have the schematics for Dr. Prospero's technology ten minutes after a wire transfer to the Caymans. Can you do that for me?"

Lord Destro's face was inert steel, and yet it seemed to convey both anger and menace.

The man in the comfortable chair chuckled. "I thought not."

"You know you can't trust him," said Destro. "Unless you're so soft that you *believe* that he's doing this all for morality and greater good."

"Mmm, and all this time I thought *you* were an idealist, and yet you are always willing to take my money. What are you saying? That idealism is merely a candy coating over a poisoned apple?"

"Are you comparing me to that maniac?" demanded Destro.

"If you're uncomfortable with the question, then forget I said anything. Contact me when you have something for me to consider."

"'Consider'? In the name of the wee man! What about our agreements?"

"Free market," said the man with an airy wave of the hand. "Sadly, it's become a free market."

He disconnected the call and reached for his wine, sipped it. And smiled.

-6-

Destro Castle
Scotland
Lord Destro reached out and tapped a key to disconnect his end
of the call. The white static vanished on the screen. He slowly stood
and walked slowly across the room, his steps measured and his
posture thoughtful. His two dogs—great brutes of black hounds
named Cu Sith and Boky—lifted their heads and watched him. They
knew their master and his moods, and they were not at all fooled by
the calm façade; just as they were not surprised when their master
suddenly snatched up a silver and crystal goblet and threw it the
length of the room.

Boky *whuffed* softly.

Cu Sith bared a fang and growled low in his throat.

Destro sighed and bowed his head.

Honor was a ten ton weight at times. He'd known about
Prospero for years and had worked with him off and on. A
gentleman's agreement was supposed to be in place. Prospero would
bring his drones and software systems to him and Destro would in
turn broker them to Cobra. Now it was clear to a blind man that
Prospero had no intention of including Destro in any part of this
exchange. Not even so much as a finder's fee for having introduced
the old tosspot to the Commander. And Destro had lent Prospero
some of his own systems and even one of his top men, Han Kong, to
speed the development along. Kong, of course, had finessed a few
things according to Destro's requirements, none of which were
shared with Prospero. That wasn't dishonorable, that was common
sense self-defense.

This presentation…now that was so sharp a slap in the face that
Destro swore he could actually feel it on his skin.

"Damn ye for a Sassenach!" he said in a fierce whisper,
conjuring images in his mind of that old bastard being torn to red
rags by the dogs.

He felt insulted, betrayed. Hurt.

He had even tried to give Prospero a chance to make it right.
He'd gone through that with Miranda to suggest very quietly and

discreetly that the old man stop hunting on another man's preserve. When that hadn't worked he'd appealed directly to the egotistical old swine. Nothing. Not even a returned phone call.

Instead, the Commander called him and offered him the opportunity to covertly observe Prospero's impromptu test.

There were times he wished he was a mackerel fisherman. This life could be so bloody frustrating.

"Honor among thieves," he said aloud. "Aye, and pigs may fly."

The dogs got up and came over to him, leaning their huge shoulders against him, whimpering softly. Destro bent and stroked their flanks, doing it slowly, letting the action soothe him. Dogs were always the best of companions, and no joke. Loyal by nature's design and incapable of guile.

"Ye shaggy monsters," he said with rough affection. They licked his hands and chuffed.

Destro took a long breath and let it out. Then he cocked his head to one side as if listening to an inner voice.

"Ah...you are a glaikit moron," he told himself. Beneath his mask, he smiled. Then he turned back toward the computer and looked at the screen as if he could still see Prospero in his metal suit. And still hear the Commander's velvet mockery of a voice.

"Free market be damned."

He stalked back to his computer terminal and began hammering keys. He used a signal re-router to spin-worm his way into the Department of Defense database, blank-trailing his entry by a code-rewriter that wiped out all traces of the intrusion. Then he accessed the inactive employee data files and brought up the login for Dr. Han Kong.

Still smiling, he tapped in the password.

"Welcome, Dr. Kong," said a soft computer voice.

Destro laughed softly to himself. "Free market is it, ya bas? I've got your number and no mistake. Let's all make free, and devil take the hindmost."

-7-

The Island
Tactical Observation Room #1

Flint stared through the reinforced glass at the flaming wreckage and gave a low whistle. "That's…beautiful."

"I don't think that would be the adjective I'd choose," muttered Doc Greer.

Flint grunted. "The pacifist doesn't like things blowing up. Enormous surprise, Doc."

"It's not just that. One man did all that. Granted the attack vehicles were all automated, but from what I can see it wouldn't have played out any differently had there been real men and women on the field. One man."

Scarlett added, "One man in a half-billion dollar combat suit cross-linked to targeting satellites and using counter-encryption intrusion software."

"My point exactly," agreed Doc.

Flint turned away from the fires still burning out in the desert. "What adjective would you prefer?"

"Offhand?" said Doc. "Terrifying."

"Then you're going to live in fear, Doc, because this is the new face of warfare. Congress and NATO are going to line up to shovel money into this project."

Something caught their eyes and they both turned toward the window as the man in the combat rig walked by. Light from the observation deck spilled out through the window and traced the outline of the stalking figure. Prospero was totally encased in armor painted with the alternating pixilated slate gray, desert sand, and foliage green of the universal camouflage pattern used by the U.S. Military. The exoskeleton was neither sleek nor handsome. Instead it looked like an ugly and improbable collection of pipes and plates fuse-welded in a way to be deliberately unpleasant to the eye. However its massive height gave it grandeur and its performance in the field inspired a sense of dread.

It stopped and turned toward them. From outside this viewport blended into the landscape, invisible even to infrared and NVG, but the blank steel face of the titan swiveled around so that it was facing the Joes inside.

"God almighty," breathed Doc.

Then the massive metal arm came up into a formal salute, snapping it off with a touch of swagger instead of the crisp military precision that would have been more in keeping with the thing's

~ 82 ~

robotic appearance. But the Joes knew full well that this was no robot, nor was it a drone. A man hung suspended within the metal body, his slightest move instantly activating a reciprocal move by the exoskeleton.

And though they could not see the face of Dr. Allyn Prospero, they knew that the old scientist was smiling.

"Okay," said Scarlett as the thing turned and stalked away. "I'll go with 'terrifying,' too."

"I might have understated it," murmured Doc.

The hatch door behind them hissed open and they turned to see Prospero in the exoskeleton. Desert winds whipped tendrils of residual smoke around him and he looked like a statue of one of the Greek titans standing there. Immense, impossibly powerful.

With a hiss of hydraulics, the iron giant stalked into the room and stopped a dozen feet away. A robotic voice spoke from external speakers.

"*Powering down. Caliban combat systems off line.*"

A golf cart came whirring out of a side corridor and as it rolled to a stop the tech crew jumped out, each of them holding tools. Professor Miranda was with them, her expression neutral. Two men with impact wrenches went to work on the chest plate. Another unlimbered a heavy cable and plugged it into a socket on the back of the suit. Professor Miranda unfolded a short metal step ladder and mounted it to reach the face plate. The team worked with practiced efficiency as Flint and Doc watched, and with the speed of a race team pit crew, they had the major components removed and set aside to reveal Dr. Prospero suspended in the sling harness.

"How did Caliban perform?" Miranda asked.

The old man was bathed in sweat but grinning like a happy child.

"He was magnificent!" said Prospero. "Absolutely magnificent."

Professor Miranda smiled with obvious relief and pleasure.

Scarlet nudged Flint with an elbow and mouthed the word '*he.*'

Flint had caught it. He, not *it.* He turned to Doc, but Doc was already up to speed on that. He had his lips pursed in thought. Flint knew that they weren't happy thoughts.

Miranda disconnected the last of the straps and then descended the ladder to allow Prospero to disengage the harness straps and step down. She offered her hand to steady him, and when he was off the ladder she fetched a cane from the golf cart and handed it to him.

Prospero leaned on the cane. "Thank you, my dear."

"And how do *you* feel?"

It took a moment for Prospero to answer that. He turned and stared at the dissembled mechanical monster. While it was clear that he was physically exhausted, his face came alight with a complex series of emotions. He cut a quick look at the Joes standing nearby and then touched the woman's cheek.

"I feel *wonderful!*" he said. "Young and alive."

Doc cleared his throat and entered the little bubble of their private conversation. "I'd like to give you a brief post-action exam, Doctor."

Prospero stiffened. "Nonsense. I'm perfectly fine as you can see."

"You're flushed and perspiring heavily and—"

"The suit was hot and I just ran four miles," interrupted Prospero.

"—and you're seventy-four years old."

Prospero laughed aloud and nodded toward the machinery. "Not when I'm in there! It's very much like sky-diving, or driving a formula one. After a while you can't tell where you end and the machine begins. It's so exhilarating. I was a *god* out there!"

Doc nodded. "Sure, but you're not in there all the time. And right now it looks like your blood pressure could pop rivets out of plate steel."

"I'm fine."

"I'll be the judge of that."

Prospero met Doc's eyes and the moment stretched around them. Professor Miranda shifted to stand next to the old man, using body language rather than words to show her support.

Flint watched all of this and very nearly stepped over to stand beside Doc, but that would turn the moment into bad drama. Instead he said, "The test was pretty amazing, Dr. Prospero; and you have a right to be proud of the Caliban exosuit. Consider me a fan. However our friends in Congress aren't paying us just to watch. Our team is here to evaluate everything, and that does mean *everything*. If Doc Greer wants to examine you, then let's all put it down to dotting the I's and crossing the T's."

Prospero opened his mouth to say something, and from the taut pull of his lips it was likely to be something biting. They had been warned that the old scientist was a cantankerous SOB, but Flint wasn't interested in enabling cranky behavior.

It was Professor Miranda who broke the tension of the moment.

"We understand completely, Chief," she said with a smile, touching Prospero on the arm and then turning the full wattage of her smile on Flint. She stepped closer to him, pitching her voice as if they shared a private conversation. "Chief Warrant Officer Flint, as a soldier with significant field experience you must be familiar with the exuberance that comes with combat exertion."

"Somewhat," Flint said neutrally.

Professor Miranda stepped a bit closer, looking up into Flint's eyes; and Flint was suddenly very aware of how truly beautiful the professor was. He made his face turn to stone.

"All those juices flowing," Miranda continued, "the awareness of your own power. The understanding of your potential for great things."

Flint cut a look at Doc, who was trying so hard to hide a smile that the effort looked painful.

"Um, yes, ma'am," mumbled Flint. "I suppose I do."

"Call me Elsbeth, Chief *Flint*." She loaded his name with enough hidden meanings to sink a battleship.

A few feet away Scarlett softly cleared her throat. She had been watching with amusement and professional interest as Miranda attempted to dazzle Flint. She shifted her posture as a way of breaking the trance through distraction, and in a very businesslike tone said, "If everything plays out the way it looks like it will, once we crunch the numbers...I think we can safely say that you just changed the face of warfare for the next generation."

Professor Miranda began to say something else, but Flint stepped sideways—out of the potent energy of her personal space—and angled himself to address both she and Prospero.

"When Doc is done with his exam I would love to sit down over coffee and hear everything about what went on out there." He looked at Prospero. "I've never seen *anything* like that."

Prospero studied him for a few moments, clearly trying to determine whether he was being 'handled' or if the praise was genuine. Then a smile seeped slowly onto Prospero's mouth as he considered those words. He took a deep breath and let it out slowly, deflating the ball of tension he'd been holding in his chest.

"It's encouraging to know that you are a person of vision," he said.

"Are you kidding?" said Flint. "We're all certified soldier geeks. We love gadgets."

"You have no idea how much," Scarlett said under her breath.

"So," Flint concluded, "this stuff is straight from heaven."

Prospero's smile became genuine. He nodded and offered his hand to Doc.

"Forgive my terseness."

Doc's hand was only a microsecond slow in responding, but they exchanged a firm grip.

"Perfectly understandable. Just watching you had my own blood pressure nearly off the scale." He gestured toward the side corridor. "Shall we?"

Doc and Prospero walked away together. Professor Miranda lingered for a moment, giving Flint an enigmatic look and a very appealing pink-lipped smile. Then she turned and followed. The tech crew finished their work and piled back into the golf cart and vanished, leaving Flint and Scarlett alone in the observation chamber. Silence filled the room, and they turned and walked slowly over to the window. The fires had burned down to embers out there on the sand.

"How's *your* blood pressure, cowboy?" asked Scarlett.

He laughed. "Don't start."

"Me? *I* wasn't starting anything, but you looked like you were ready to drop down on one knee and propose."

Flint snorted. "She's cute, but her only interest in me is in how much she can run interference for Prospero."

"So, you're not smitten by the geeky brunette with glasses?"

"I think we all know what a slippery slope *that* is."

Scarlett gave him a knowing wink and sat down on the edge of the desk. "I think Miranda is every bit as formidable as her boss."

"Agreed. Which means everybody needs to keep their eyes open at all times." Flint tapped the topmost button on his uniform shirt. "You get all that, guys?"

"Every word," said a man's voice.

The receiver bug looked like a freckle on the inside of Flint's left ear. Scarlett had an identical one on her right ear. The voice belonged to Christopher M. Lavigne. 'Law' to the rest of the Joes. In the background his dog, Order, gave a single sharp bark as if he, too, was acknowledging.

"I heard it, too," said a second voice. Laser Rifleman Anthony 'Flash' Gambello.

General Hawk had sent a full team. Law and his canine partner were reviewing the facility security systems, with two computer experts—a Brooklyn tech-geek called Jukebox and a Japanese woman codenamed Schoolgirl—as backup. Flash had been running the drone systems from a truck parked way out in the desert, and his team included the beefy and always-grinning Australian Bruiser and Shock Jock, a sniper from San Antonio. The last two Joes here at the Nevada base were a diminutive man who was, despite the unfortunate call sign of Teacher's Pet, a first class shooter; and Monster, a hulk of a kid straight out of Force Recon and three tours in the Middle East. They were all listening in on the call, though only team leaders chimed in on the conversation.

"Opinion?" Flint asked.

Flash said, "I think you and Professor Miranda will have lovely children."

"Secure that crap, soldier," barked Flint, though he was smiling. "Give me your *professional* opinion."

"Of what?" asked Flash. "The Caliban unit? Totally kicked my ass, and that's somewhere between very cool and very, very scary."

"Agreed," said Law. "I was watching the whole thing from the security office. I had the action on fifteen screens and it was scary as hell on every screen."

Scarlett said, "On the other hand, considering that this is a military system, 'scary' is what we want."

No one responded to that for a moment, then Law said, "Y'know guys, this is a pretty strange back road for anyone who's ever been a pair of boots on the ground. On one hand we all dig the idea of replacing vulnerable flesh and blood soldiers with metal and motherboard drones. On the other hand...have these guys even *watched* science fiction? Automated systems? Artificial intelligence combat machines? That never ends well."

"It's not AI," corrected Scarlett. "They're drones. Remote operated and—"

"Yeah, yeah, I know. Short step from remote to automated, though. I mean...it's the next natural step in development. Congress ups the budget for Prospero and next thing you know it's '*Ahll be bahhk...*'"

"Geek-centric paranoia noted, Law," said Flint. "That'll look good in the report."

"So," said Flash, "what's *your* take on the good Dr. Prospero, boss?"

"On or off the record?" asked Flint.

"Off."

"He's halfway to being nuts."

"Only halfway?" asked Flash.

Flint chuckled. "Hey, I just met the man a few hours ago, guys. Jury's still deliberating."

"Well, from where I'm sitting," said Flash, "which is out here trying to figure out how one old dude in a friggin' tin suit handed me my ass...I'm going to put my vote in right now. Guy's scary *and* nuts. And I'll bet a shiny nickel that he was grooving on it, too. Sitting there in the middle of all those fireworks like he was conducting the 1812 Overture."

Scarlett raised an eyebrow to Flint. "He's got a point. Prospero took a bizarre risk just now. He could have used a less valuable subordinate for that test. Instead he put his own life on the line to prove how effective his system is."

"Personal pride?" suggested Law. "The Caliban unit is a major career high."

"Maybe. We'll go into that later."

"Couple other things to go over later, too," said Law. "The security systems are a little weird."

"Weird as in vulnerable?

"Weird as in totally *in*vulnerable. I've never seen any system with this many safeguards and redundancies."

"Better safe than sorry," quipped Flash.

"I suppose," Law said, but he sounded uncertain.

"Okay...team meeting in thirty minutes. My quarters."

"We all going to compare our homework?"

"Yeah, and then we'll braid each other's hair and have a pillow fight."

They were all laughing as the call was disconnected.

Outside, the last of the fires was out now and the desert was in total darkness.

Scarlett turned to Flint. "At the risk of sounding like a cliché," she began, "but something about this place gives me the creeps."

"Yeah," said Flint, "I know what you—"

Anything else he was going to say was suddenly cut short as screams tore through the night. They whirled toward the access corridor.

"What the hell—?"

Those words were likewise drowned out. This time by the harsh rattle of automatic gunfire.

And then all of the lights went out.

-8-

The room seemed to explode around them.

"Down!" Flint and Scarlett yelled it at the same moment, and then they were diving for cover as someone with an automatic weapon opened up from the side corridor. Bullets chopped into the desks and chairs, tore jagged chunks from the poured linoleum floor, hammered into a Coke machine and blew sparks out of it, and burned through the air above their heads like a swarm of angry bees.

Flint hit the floor in a chest-first dive that sent him sliding toward the wall with the Coke machine. Soda hissed and sprayed from a dozen holes in the casing, but Flint couldn't see it. Except for the nearly continuous muzzle flashes at the far end of the room, there was no light.

"Who the hell's firing?" yelled Scarlett as she rolled behind a heavy desk. She had her pistol out but the barrage of rounds was too heavy to risk leaning out to return fire.

"What's happening?" everyone on the com-link was yelling at once.

"We're taking fire," barked Flint. "We need back-up!"

"Go Joe!" bellowed several Joes at once.

Backup was on its way, but Flint didn't feel comforted. The automatic gunfire was continuous. He kept waiting for the pause as the shooter or shooters swapped magazines, but there was no break at all. He pressed his head to the floor and risked a quick look. Almost instantly the gun barrel fanned around to chop the exact spot. He jerked his head back amid a swarm of splinters and ricocheting lead.

"That's belt-fed," he shouted, and Scarlett nodded. "Mini-gun on a cart I think. I can see some of it in the flashes."

"Cover me!" she snapped, and without waiting for his nod, Scarlett got into a crouch, racked the slide on her weapon, and threw herself sideways toward another desk eight feet away. It was a powerful dive but not a pretty one, lacking her usual athletic grace. She twisted in midair as she jumped, firing toward the mini-gun, each recoil warping her flight path. In the darkness and thunder it was impossible to tell if she hit any of the hostiles.

The gun instantly pivoted to track her, but as it did Flint rose up fast and opened up on it, aiming for the shadows just above the muzzle, knowing it was where the gunner had to be. Every shot hit home, every shot was true and straight.

The mini-gun kept firing.

"The hell...?"

Scarlet landed hard and slewed around while continuing to fire. When the slide locked back, she rolled behind the desk and fished out another mag.

There was no break at all in the gunfire.

The desks behind which they were hiding were disintegrating and pretty soon it would be like trying to hide behind Swiss cheese.

Flint would have given his left hand for a couple of fragmentation grenades.

And, as if wishing could make it so, there was a tremendous explosion that rocked the entire room and a red fireball that punched into the ceiling and then flattened out. The sprinklers and the security lights both came on at the same time and it looked like red tears falling from a black sky.

The minigun was finally silent.

"Clear!" bellowed a deep bass voice.

Flint and Scarlett rose up together from their hiding places and their laser swept over the hulking form of Monster—who held a combat shotgun with over and under grenade launchers. Water from the sprinklers danced along the gnarled lumps of his massive arms and shoulders. He was not a handsome man, but at that moment both Scarlett and Flint could have kissed him.

"Clear!" called another voice as Teacher's Pet skidded into the room from the far side. He had his M5 in his hands and whipped it back and forth as he checked the corners and behind obstacles. "Clear!" he yelled again.

Suddenly then the lights came on, flooding the room.

The sprinklers shut off with a hiss.

The red emergency lights dimmed.

Silence settled around them.

As if everything was normal.

-9-

Teacher's Pet lowered his shotgun. "Flint, Scarlett...what the bloody hell happened here?"

Flint got carefully to his feet and scanned the room. His ears still rang with the thunder of the gunfire. Amid the phantom echoes he heard Law and Flint yell at him.

"Dial it down," he growled. "No casualties here. Anyone else taking fire?"

"No, but it sounded like you were in a war zone," said Law. "What the hell—"

"Unknown," cut in Flint. "We have zero intel and that's got to change. I want everyone to hold tight until I give the word. Stay on line."

"Look," said Scarlett as she carefully crossed the room. Flint joined her, and Pet gave a long whistle.

The minigun was a tangled mess of twisted metal that sagged from its pedestal. The vehicle on which it had been mounted looked like a golf cart except that there was no seat for a driver.

Monster hurried over to it, his shotgun ready to finish what his grenades had started...but there was no need.

There were also no bodies.

He looked up in puzzlement.

"Zero hostiles," grunted Monster. He was six feet ten and built like a Bradley. His bulk filled the corridor and he looked around irritably as if annoyed there was no one with a pulse he could shoot. "Where the hell'd they go?"

"I don't think they went anywhere," Scarlett said as she poked at the rubble with the toe of her boot. The floor was carpeted with spent shell casings. Thousands of them. Huge drum magazines anchored each side of the cart.

"Huh?"

She didn't answer right away. "Never saw a minigun like this. Dual belts leading to a central firing chamber that feeds into the same set of rotating barrels."

"Worse than that," said Flint. He tapped a scorched metal box that hung from the pedestal on a tangle of wires. "Look at this."

Teacher's Pet bent forward and peered at it. "Is that a CPU?"

"Ah," Scarlett said as if she was expecting that.

Pet looked at the others, his eyes filling with anger as he realized what it all meant. "Ah…c'mon, man, you frigging kidding me here?"

Scarlett studied the wiring. "There's an antenna array, too." She straightened. "This is—"

"What in God's name is happening here?" interrupted a fierce voice and they turned to see Dr. Prospero come sweeping into the room. He wore trousers and an undershirt. Doc was right on his heels and it was clear they had just run there from the medical suite. Professor Miranda was a half step behind them. She had a small .25 automatic in her hands, but she held it with professional competence. As soon as they saw the ruined desks and the mangled remains of the mini-gun they stopped in their tracks.

Prospero's face went purple with rage and he wheeled on Flint. "You maniac! You destroyed a four hundred thousand dollar prototype and—"

"Hold it right there, Doctor," interrupted Flint with steel in his voice. Prospero paused. Flint kicked at the shell casings and sent a score of them skittering toward the scientist. "In case you've suddenly gone blind, that prototype of yours just tried to kill us."

"Nonsense. The Kobold 118 is incapable of—"

"If Monster hadn't taken it out Scarlett and I would be dog food."

"Impossible."

Flint felt his control slipping. "I'm sorry...did you say 'impossible'?"

Prospero was not one for backing down. He stepped close so that he and Flint were almost nose to nose. "Yes, *Chief*," he said in a way that suggested that Flint's rank was of less consequence than a used Kleenex. "Kobold is a drone system. It can't 'try' to do anything. *Trying* is an act of deliberate will."

"No kidding," said Flint icily. "So what does *that* tell us about what just happened?"

Prospero's eyes cut back and forth between Flint and the drone. Doubt clouded his features. "I..." he began, but did not finish the sentence.

"Let me check the system," said Professor Miranda quietly as she stepped forward at an angle that forced Flint and Prospero to step away from each other. It was a deliberate move calculated to dial down the tension, and everyone allowed it. A shouting match was not going to increase operational efficiency. She unclipped a small toolkit from her belt and selected a screwdriver. She quickly undid the four tiny screws that fastened the faceplate to the CPU casing. There was a small *pop* as she pulled it off.

"The security tapes were intact," she announced. "I had to break them to take the faceplate off." She showed the cover to the Joes. The security tapes were slowly turning color from beige to red. "Breaking the tapes releases chemicals that change the color. They were normal color when I opened it."

"Always the same color?" asked Scarlett.

Miranda shook her head. "No. Beige was Monday's color, which is when I last worked on this unit. I select a new color for every day."

"How many people have authority to install the security tape?" asked Teacher's Pet.

"Only Dr. Prospero and myself," she answered. "And when either of us does that we're under constant video surveillance. The digital files are stored in the security office."

Flint tapped his ear mike. "Law, you get that?"

"Copy that. On it."

Prospero scowled as he realized that others beside the Joes in the room were eavesdropping on the conversation. He said nothing, but his expression conveyed his displeasure.

Flint managed not to fall down and die.

He tapped his earbud again. "Yo, Joe! Headcount and location. Did anyone take any fire?"

Immediately the other Joes scattered in and around the Island sounded off.

"Bruiser on deck—I'm outside with Flash. We're checking the perimeter. Zero hostile contact."

"Shock Jock here, Chief. Quiet as church out here. I'm running scans on the drones Dr. Prospero tore up. No one out here but us Joes."

"Schoolgirl in the house. I'm down in Operations," Schoolgirl replied. *"No one home, everything shut down and locked."*

"Good," said Flint. "Jukebox...where are you?"

"I'm in the generator shed, Flint," Jukebox said. *"Got a lot of boards fried down here. Halo never kicked in, so I've been putting out fires."*

"Deliberate?"

"Could be...but it's hard to say. Looks like a mother of a power surge."

"Okay, everyone stay on station and stay on the line." He gave them a brief rundown of what happened. A lot of theories got thrown around but nobody came up with a reason to think that they were experiencing an actual attack.

"Hope the Doc's toys are still under warranty," quipped Flash.

Flint grunted and turned to Prospero. "I want a complete rundown of every single malfunction you've had that resulted in a weapons discharge."

But the scientist was already shaking his head. "Malfunctions? No, no, no...there haven't been any."

"Not one?"

"No," insisted Prospero, "and there *can't* be because as I said, this system is a drone, it has no autonomous capabilities."

"I know." Flint smiled thinly at Prospero. "As you've heard, my team is on the line with us right now and a full-scale search is underway."

"Affirmative," said Flash in his ear.

"This is sabotage, Chief," said Prospero. "Odd that it only happened after your team arrived."

Flint took a challenging step forward. "You want to explain that comment—?"

"Wait..." said Professor Miranda in such an urgent tone that everyone turned toward her. She held a penlight and was using it to examine the inside of the CPU. "Oh my God! Doctor...look at this."

Prospero and Flint gave each other two seconds of the Alpha Dog glare and then they turned to see what the professor had found.

"What is it?" demanded Prospero.

Miranda handed the unit to the senior scientist, who immediately frowned as he laid eyes on the inner workings. "This isn't right," he said softly.

"What isn't?" asked Flint.

Prospero ignored him and instead directed his comments to Professor Miranda. "This is one of Kong's devices. The AI256?"

"I think it's the 257," said Miranda. "Look, it has a smaller microprocessor unit and—"

"Whoa—stop right there," ordered Flint. "What is an AI256, and why do you two look like you just swallowed scorpions?"

Prospero plucked a plastic-coated unit the size of a button from the CPU and held it up between his thumb and forefinger. He waved it in Flint's face. "This is your villain, Chief."

"What is it?"

"It's an artificial intelligence module designed for the next generation of unmanned tactical combat vehicles."

"Artificial intelligence?" Flint's heart sank. In his earjack he heard Flash curse.

"Yes, Chief," said Prospero.

"One of your toys?"

"I don't *do* AI," he said as if that field of science was akin to selling crack in middle school playgrounds.

"Who does? AI was on last year's budget report. You signed off on it."

"Dr. Kong's team did all of...that." Prospero still looked like he was sucking a lemon. "Kong was working on full automation systems. It was a small department and I had no plans to include it in this year's budget request."

"And yet it just *happens* to be in the CPU of one of *your* combat drones?" asked Scarlett, one eyebrow arched.

"I obviously had nothing to do with that," said the scientist, dismissing even the possibility of such a thing. "I said Dr. Kong's team *was* working on this. Kong had a stroke five months ago. He's in a coma in Las Vegas and is not expected to recover. I believe that is in the same report from last year."

In his ear, Law said, "*Yep, it's there. Blink and you miss it, though.*"

Flint said, "Who's continuing Kong's project?"

"There were only three people on his team," explained Prospero. "None of them is advanced enough to lead the project. They're all a half-step up from lab monkeys. Kong never used top people. He didn't like to share the byline on any potential patent, so most of his team are graduate assistants with low level clearance. They only worked on peripheral aspects of the hardware. None of them wrote code for the operational systems. Besides...I shut the whole project down until a suitable replacement could be found."

"And—?"

"I haven't spent a lot of time looking. As I said, AI is not the primary goal of this project. The Island is a drone shop."

Flint digested this. "Who has access to their research and materials?"

"I do."

Flint gave Miranda a hard look. "Who else?"

She shook her head. "Only Dr. Prospero. We certainly didn't plant the AI unit."

That served up a moment of silence as the Joes and the scientists processed the implications.

"Swell," said Doc with a sigh.

Flint touched his earbud. "Law...it's confirmed that we have zips in the wire. Lock this place down. Bruiser, you stay outside with Flash. Seal the perimeter. Nothing gets in or out. Shock Jock, I want you inside with Schoolgirl. I want all staff locked into their rooms. Personally check all doors. Law—initiate J-94 security redirects. Blank all keycards and replace them with our team code."

"You can't do that—" began Miranda furious.

"Shut up," barked Flint. "Jukebox...lock yourself into the power shed. I don't want another lights out."

"On it."

Immediately red lights mounted high on the walls flashed with crimson urgency. A recorded female voice spoke from speakers mounted below the lights:

"THE ISLAND IS GOING INTO LOCKDOWN. ALL STAFF WILL OBSERVE SECURITY PROTOCOL ALPHA 1. REPEAT..."

To Monster and Teacher's Pet Flint said, "Coordinate with Law. Everyone is on two-man patrol. You find anyone—*anyone*—from senior staff to pot-washer third class that's not locked in their assigned quarters and obeying all of the Alpha Security protocols, you bag 'em and drag 'em. I will want to have a talk with them."

They saluted and headed out.

"You copy all that, Law?"

"*On it. I'm downloading the fingerprint and retina scans of the whole staff to team PDAs. Everyone should verify the identities of every single staff member. Anyone can wear a nametag.*"

"Good call."

Flint eyed Prospero and Miranda. He debated locking them in their rooms, too, until his team had a chance to sweep the entire facility. The Island was a big place. He also wanted to get out of there and think it through alone. He was still jumpy from all the adrenaline that had been dumped into his bloodstream during the brief but harrowing firefight. It made it hard to maintain the air of detachment that he preferred to show, especially in front a of touchy high-maintenance jackass like Prospero.

He took the device and held it up.

"So what does it mean, doctor? If this thing had an AI predecessor then there isn't a need for an operator, correct?"

"Correct," said Prospero. "Under normal circumstances the drone would have an operator uplinked to a satellite or a plane, or perhaps a ground spotter. As the operator received intel he would direct the flight-plan or drive-plan of the drone. Our latest generation has better optical systems, including the Ariel series of airborne cameras. They're too agile to be hit by most conventional weaponry and too small to appear on radar." He paused. "I released twenty of them when I went out into the desert for our test."

Flash, who was still an invisible audience to all this, murmured, "*News to me, boss. I never spotted them.*"

Flint did not acknowledge the voice in his ear, but he knew that the rest of the Joes heard it. None of them would like the idea of tiny spycams flitting around.

"There was nothing in your quarterly reports about these Ariel units, Dr. Prospero."

Prospero shrugged. "The Ariels are biomimetic units—small drones designed to look and behave like insects, birds, or animals. In the case of the Ariels, they look like fireflies. They're new."

"So new that you have working prototypes in the field since your last report, which was—what?—six weeks ago?"

Prospero dismissed it with a wave of his hand. "I'm sure they are in the report, Chief. They'll have had a number-letter code. The nickname 'Ariel' was picked recently."

Although that was probably a legitimate answer, Flint was not leaping to accept it. His skepticism must have shown on his face, because Prospero bristled. "You don't believe me?"

Flint looked at him, then down at the still smoking machine and the carpet of spent shells. Then his cold eyes refocused on Prospero.

"Right now, Doctor...I don't trust anyone who didn't come on the chopper with me. That means if you're not a Joe you're a suspect." Prospero turned livid and opened his mouth, but Flint beat him to it. "If you don't like it, Dr. Prospero, then that's just too damn bad. Before you explode all over me take a second to remember whose name is going to be on the report that goes to NATO and the President. If you want me to sign off on a positive report, then dial down the pompous attitude and try working with us. That means full disclosure. No more of this 'oh, I forgot to mention it' crap. You'll tell me everything and you'll God damn tell me up front and when I ask for it. Is that understood?"

"That's outrageous. This is blackmail, it's—"

"The word you're fishing for is 'extortion.'"

Silence crashed around them and Scarlett thought she could feel the temperature of the room drop about forty degrees.

"Very well," Prospero said eventually, but it looked like speaking those two words was more painful that having teeth pulled without Novocain.

Flint studied him, and then gave a curt nod.

"Then tell me about this thing." He held up the AI processor. "Does this require any real-time human assistance?"

"No. That replaces the need for spotters of any kind. Kong's field within artificial intelligence was learning computers and their tactical uses."

"How advanced is this thing?"

"It has generational memory and has an extrapolative assessment hunter-killer subroutine based on established predator-prey behavior models."

"Oh boy," murmured Doc. "I'm not a computer expert, but even I can tell how bad that could be."

Prospero sniffed. "Well, it *is* designed to replace individual soldiers in the field. The whole purpose of such weaponry is to reduce human assets and—"

"We know," said Flint. "So are drones. But what you're describing here is an autonomous killing machine."

"*Ahll be bahhk,*" Law repeated in his ear.

Flint winced.

"Don't be naïve," said Prospero. "Computers and robots are only as autonomous as we allow them to be. Humans program them, and every AI system that exists or ever will exist will have override commands and failsafe systems."

"You're sure about that? Are there limits to the autonomy in self-learning systems?"

"No. Autonomy is a word we deliberately misuse. The autonomy goes only as far as the parameters written into the operational software."

"They can't evolve beyond that?"

"Absolutely not."

Flint looked at Scarlett. She gave the tiniest shake of her head. She wasn't buying Prospero's rant either.

"Then that leaves us with only one option," Flint said. "And I think you already know what that is."

"Impossible," Miranda said under her breath.

"A saboteur within the Island," Prospero said flatly.

"Yep. Either an infiltrator, in which case your security isn't as good as it should be—"

"Impossible," snapped Prospero.

"—or one of your people is working for the bad guys," concluded Flint.

Prospero was already shaking his head. "No, no, no, no..."

"*Got to agree with him, Flint,*" said Law in Flint's ear. "*Like I said, there are safeguards on the safeguards on this stuff.*"

"No." Prospero said it a final time and without the possibility of contradiction. He folded his arms and stared at Flint, defying him to argue.

"We need to keep an open mind," began Scarlett, "because any—"

That was as far as she got.

Something small flitted past her face—a tiny fluttering thing that glimmered like polished steel. She waved at it in annoyance. There was almost no sound. Just a tiny *pop!*, like a bubble bursting—and then Scarlett uttered a soft cry and fell forward. Tiny bits of metal debris fell like glittering dust.

Flint reflexively stepped forward and caught her.

"Hey, what's—?"

Scarlett's eyes were wide as saucers and filled with terror and pain. She opened her mouth to say something but instead coughed bright red blood onto Flint's shirtfront.

"I..."

Her eyes lost focus and she went totally limp in his arms.

Then the lights went out again.

And the gunfire started once more.

-10-

The Ice House

The Commander poured himself another glass of wine. The big central screen displayed a shaky green and black image from a hovering night vision camera. He watched Scarlett fall, saw her blood seed the air like drops of black oil.

Other monitors showed different views of the Island compound. Inside and out.

Small devices flew or rolled or scuttled through the darkness toward the Joes.

It did not matter to him if the Joes lived or died. There were some tactical advantages either way.

It did not matter to him if Prospero or Destro won this round, because there was no way for a completely clean win. However it played out, it would shave millions off of the asking price of anything they brought to him.

He smiled.

This was real entertainment. This was an entirely new spin on the concept of a 'price war,' and he was delighted.

-11-

Observation Room

Once more the darkness was absolute except for flashes from gunfire.

Except this time the flashes were not the rapid-fire growl of a minigun firing from a fixed position. Instead they were smaller, almost delicate *pops* that seemed to appear randomly from different parts of the room.

"What the hell is this?" bellowed Doc as he fumbled to find Flint and Scarlett in the dark.

"Sprites," yelled Professor Miranda. "Oh my God...someone launched Sprites at us. Get down...get down!"

At the same time Prospero hissed: "Don't move...freeze! They're motion trackers."

But something did move in the dark.

"Flint...I saw Scarlett, is she—?"

There was another *pop!*

"Ah...*God!*" and in the tiny muzzle flash Flint saw Doc stagger as something hit him between the shoulders. He collapsed against Flint and drove him and Scarlett to the ground in a tangle of too many arms and legs.

Pop! Pop!

Doc's body trembled as he was hit twice more and then he lay totally still.

Flint was buried under Doc's solid weight and the muscular heft of the unconscious Scarlett. He was also afraid to move.

He was wearing BDU's but he wasn't in battle dress. No Kevlar, no spider-silk weave in any of his clothes. He had a sidearm, but from what he had seen in the flash the machines were tiny, about the size of a chicken's egg.

"Keep perfectly still," said Prospero slowly in the uninflected way a person does when he speaks without moving his lips. "They can only track movement."

"Heat...infrared...?" demanded Flint.

"No. They're prototypes."

"Drones?"

"Drop and Pops," whispered Miranda.

Flint's heart sank. Drop and Pops were a covert anti-personnel device that had been in development years. Small, self-contained units with tiny filament wings, a motor, and a barrel loaded with a single shot. The bullets were low caliber hollow-points. Deadly if they hit the head or chest cavity, potentially crippling everywhere else. They were intended to be dropped by a fixed-wing drone over a mass of troops. Each device—*Sprites,* as they were called—would seek out the first moving target, close to within a meter and discharge its round. As it fired it would use gunpowder boosted by a single discharge of all juice left in the battery. They were single use and disposable. And they were supposed to be at least eighteen months away from practical field testing.

He listened to the darkness and heard a swarm of them overhead.

Christ.

Warmth was spreading over his throat and chest and with horror he realized that Doc and Scarlett were both bleeding, their blood seeping into his clothes. Just the thought of it burned him like acid.

Lying there, immobile and helpless, was maddening; but he knew that even with the lights on the tiny hunter-killers were too small to bring down with small arms fire.

"What's the battery life on these things?" he whispered, keeping his own lips from moving. He didn't know if the Sprites were really sensitive enough to pick up on the movement of lips, but if Prospero was being careful than so damn-well was he.

"Less than five minutes," answered Prospero.

Five minutes could be four minutes too long if the Sprites had clipped an artery in Scarlett or Doc. Worse if one of them had a head wound.

At the same time the thought of lying still for five minutes felt like a life sentence.

How long had it been already?

Twenty seconds?

Thirty?

Certainly not much more than that.

"Law—?" he whispered.

The voice was right there. *"What the hell's going on, Flint?"*

Speaking very slowly and softly, Flint told him.

"God! Monster and Pet are inbound to your twenty. One minute."

Flint almost yelled for him to stop them. Then he had an idea.

"Frag the doorway."

A pause, then Law said, *"Copy that."*

Time dragged and Flint's nostrils were filled with the sharp coppery smell of fresh blood.

Come on, come on, he said to himself, willing the two Joes to get here, and willing Doc and Scarlett to hold on. *No Joe dies on my watch, damn it.*

A booming bass voice yelled from across the room: "Frag out!"

And a second later the double doors leading to the main corridor blew inward as a fireball shattered wood and twisted metal and threw pieces fifty feet into the room.

A split second later the air was filled with dozens of *Pop-Pop-Pops!* The Sprites blasted the flying debris, each round creating more flying debris.

Pop-Pop-Pop!

There was a second big explosion as another fragmentation grenade struck the wall by the Coke machine. The soda dispenser seemed to leap into the air and pirouette and before it landed there were more small shots.

Pop-Pop-Pop!

Then silence.

-12-

The Island—Security Office

Christopher M. Lavigne—'Law' to the Joes—was trapped in a black box.

When the main lights all through the Island went out, so did every electrical system in the security room. Order, a muscular shepherd, stood somewhere in the inky nothingness to his left and barked steadily. Deep-chested warning barks.

Law fumbled at the gadgets on his vest until he found his flashlight and he turned it on, dialing the lens from beam to full blaze so that the security room was suddenly filled with pale blue-white light.

"Hush," he snapped to the dog and Order instantly obeyed. The shepherd's eyes were as black as a desert demon's in the gloom, their pupils reflecting pinpoints of light.

Law tapped his earbud.

"Law to Flint, over?"

There was a burst of static, then a sound like a fragment of an explosion and part of a yell, then more static. He dialed through a dozen command and team channels and got nothing but white noise.

"Screw this," he said and grabbed for the door handle.

It turned an inch and stopped.

Locked.

He knew from his analysis that the security ops room was essentially a modular vault built into one corner of the Island facility. It had a GSA Class 5 vault door capable of withstanding up to sixty minutes of penetration delay against battering attacks, and intense and concentrated hand tool attacks, and being able to withstand both 7.62mm and 5.56mm multiple shot ballistic attacks without penetration. In short, Law wasn't going to force it open or shoot off the lock. There was supposed to be a failsafe system for emergencies of this kind, allowing trapped security officers to open the door using a special day code.

Law had the day code, but the touchpad on the inside of the door was dark. Even with the backup generators out, that shouldn't be possible. The touchpad was operated by batteries.

"Uh oh," he said. "We are in deep doo-doo."

Order barked again. The sound was loud and the echoes banged around inside the vault with nowhere to go and no way to escape.

-13-

Observation Room

Flint turned at the sound of running feet and the jiggling beams from two gun-mounted flashlights. Hands reached out of the dark and suddenly the oppressive weight on Flint's chest eased as Monster pulled Doc off of him and then Scarlett. Teacher's Pet kept watch, moving his weapon in perfect time with the alert back and forth turn of his head.

"I think we're clear," he said under his breath. "Gimme some good news, Monster."

"Oh…man. Doc's bad. Count two…no three wounds. Two are through and throughs, upper back and love handle. Those aren't the problem. He's got a third hole off center of his spine, right between the shoulder blades and no exit wound. Let me work."

He had his first aid kit open and his big hands were busy. All of the Joes were qualified as medics. In their line of work it was crucial.

Flint crawled over to Scarlett. Pet kept looking over his shoulder at her, his expression a mixture of anger and alarm.

"Boss?" called Pet. "How's—"

"I'll live," growled a female voice.

"Scarlett?" Flint grinned as he put the light on her face.

She was awake and her eyes, though glazed with pain, were clear.

"Where are you hit?"

She grunted and then hissed. "Left thigh."

"You went out..."

"Something hit the back of my head. Crap...I think I bit my tongue."

Flint examined her scalp. There was a bloody groove across the middle of the occipital bone. "Good thing you are the stubbornest woman I ever met."

"What?"

"Hard head. Bullet creased your skull. You were out for almost five minutes."

Five long damn minutes, he thought.

Scarlett cursed, then a wave of nausea hit her like a punch and she turned aside and threw up.

"That's attractive," Flint said, and Scarlett replied with a particularly obscene gesture.

Monster was still busy with Doc Greer, so while Scarlett was still wiping her mouth, Flint flicked out his lock-knife and slit her pants leg, cutting it from boot to upper thigh and tearing the flaps back.

"Don't fall in love down there," Scarlett said, giving him an evil glare.

"I'll restrain myself." He set down his knife and tentatively probed the wound. "Missed the artery."

"Halle-freaking-lujah," she said then snarled and bared her teeth. "Damn, Flint, why not just hit it with a God damn hammer?"

"Stop being such a girl."

Scarlett picked up his knife and tapped him on the upper thigh with the tip of the blade. "You're one flick of the wrist away from being a girl yourself, mister."

"Noted."

"Chief," said Teacher's Pet in an urgent whisper.

"Busy."

"Chief...you better look."

Flint turned and shone his light. Professor Miranda was sprawled in a heap a dozen feet away. She seemed to float in a lake of blood. Nearby Prospero was staring at her, his eyes wide, mouth hanging open in an almost comical expression of complete shock. Then he turned to Flint and there was such a deep sense of helplessness and need in his eyes that it struck Flint to the heart.

"Please..." Prospero whispered. "I don't...I...I don't..."

"Go!" said Scarlett, pushing his shoulder.

Flint scrambled over to her, knee-walking through the blood. Miranda's brunette hair lay spread around her, her glasses on the floor by her cheek. Flint pressed his fingers into her throat, found a pulse, but it was weak and thready.

"She's alive..."

"Thank God," gasped Prospero.

Flint bent close to see if he could hear her respiration. Then he heard it. A wet hissing sound, very faint. He tore open her jacket and listened. It was there, louder. Wetter.

"Christ, I've got a sucking chest wound here." He tore open the woman's shirt and there was the wound. The bullet had gone in low on her torso, right at the bottom of the lung.

"Monster...is Doc stable?"

"Yeah, but—"

"Then leave him. I need hands over here. Right now."

But Monster was already there, opening a field trauma kit. They moved fast.

"Can you help her?" begged Prospero, his voice trembling at the edge of breaking.

"Shut up and let us work."

The bullet had punched a hole in Miranda's chest cavity effectively unsealing the normally airtight lung sack. With every breath Miranda's lung took in blood and collapsed a bit more. Flint wasted no time cleaning the wound. That was far less important and could be done later. If there was a later.

"Patch," Flint said, and instantly Monster tore the cover off of a pre-packaged chest seal. Flint took it and pressed it gently into place, making sure the seal was tight. The seal had a one-way flutter valve so that with each exhale, air in her chest would be pushed out from underneath the patch, while each inhalation would pull the patch firmly against the wound to seal it and keep air from coming in through the bullet hole. Once it was in place Flint could hear Miranda's breathing begin to settle in a relatively normal rhythm. As normal as it could be until a real medic could be found.

"I think she's stabilized," Monster said.

Flint tapped his earbud. "Law...we need a medic down here."

The only reply was silence.

"Law!"

Nothing.

"Jukebox...Schoolgirl. Report, damn it."

Nothing but static.

"I got nothing either," said Pet. "White noise."

Flint rolled Miranda onto her wounded side so that gravity would help keep the seal in place. He checked her airway and leaned back.

"Damn," Monster whispered. "What the hell are we into here?"

Flint got to his feet and walked over to Prospero. "She's lost a lot of blood and we need to get her to medical."

The old man shook his head slowly, his voice a faint mumble. "This wasn't supposed to happen. No more blood...no more death...damn it...this wasn't supposed to..."

Without knowing that he was going to do it, Flint grabbed a handful of Prospero's undershirt and held him there. "Listen to me...I don't know what the hell is going on here, but whatever it is it's happening with your toys."

"This wasn't supposed to happen..."

Flint drew his pistol and shoved the barrel hard up under Prospero's chin. "What wasn't supposed to happen? Start talking and I swear to God, if you lie to me I will kill you. Look into my eyes. Tell me if you believe me."

"Y-Yes."

"Then you tell me what the hell is going on."

Prospero licked his lips. Flint pushed the barrel harder.

"Tick tock."

Prospero spoke a single word. It answered everything and at the same time asked a thousand more questions.

He said, "Cobra."

-14-

Dead Lake

The machine rolled through the night in near silence. The low-pressure tires barely chuffed the sand and the battery-driven motor was in a sound muffler. Bruiser never heard it coming.

His first warning was when the drone rolled past a perimeter sensor and a small red dot flashed to life on the computer screen on Bruiser's forearm.

He whirled, bringing his M5 up, calling it in.

But there was only static on the team channel.

Through the green clarity of his night-vision, Bruiser saw the machine. Recognized it for what it was.

He opened fire immediately.

But he was a tenth of a second too late.

The silence and darkness was torn apart by the continuous roar of the minigun.

Bruiser—or the thing that had been Bruiser—was flung against the corner of the wall and the barrage of bullets was so intense and heavy that his body stood erect and at attention as thousands of rounds tore him to rags.

-15-

Observation Room

Flint bent close and snarled.

"Talk fast."

"I needed the money and—"

"Really? You want to play that card with me. Do I look like a sympathetic man?"

Something changed in Prospero's eyes. They lost some of their fear and it was replaced by a jaded coldness. "Very well. It doesn't matter why I did it. I did it."

"Did what?"

Prospero told him. He had been approached by a man he originally thought worked for the security division of the Department of Defense. That was both true and a lie—the man did work for the DOD, but he also worked for a black market weapons broker who had been hired to reach out to Prospero. Him, and men like him. At first Prospero turned it down. He turned it down a dozen times over a two year period, not so much out of patriotism but out of fear that it was a government sting of some kind.

Then he started believing in the man. Money was involved in that process. Money was always involved. But over time Prospero felt his heart change. The money became less important than the nature of the work, and its potential. His drones could effectively remove man from the combat field. No lives would ever have to be lost. Wars would become a contest of technology, and ultimately mankind might step away from the need for war.

The other man seemed to share this impassioned view, this Big Picture perspective that justified any covert or clandestine steps taken to achieve such a noble end.

Once they had struck a bargain, the man said that his boss wanted to acquire the Caliban combat system. Not the hardware. Just copies of all schematics and the complete Skyjack/Tempest software system. They haggled over the price for another seven months. During that time the broker himself emerged and introduced himself. He was a foreign national who had himself sold weapons systems and other technologies to the same client.

"Who was he?"

"I never knew his name," said Prospero. "I never met him. He was a voice on the phone."

"What *do* you know about him?"

Prospero hesitated. "He's a Scotsman."

Flint cursed.

"You know him?" asked Prospero, surprised.

"Unfortunately, and I plan to hang his head on my wall. Unless you want your head to be hung next to it, keep talking. If you're working *for* this client, for Cobra...why are your systems going off the rails."

"I don't *know!* It has to be sabotage."

Flint studied him, looking for the lie, but seeing only outrage and fury.

Prospero *didn't* know.

"Tell me something I can use, damn it."

"First...you have to understand two things."

"I'm listening."

"You saved Miranda's life. You may think I'm a cold-hearted bastard, but I...I love her. *We* are in love. I know the age difference is—"

"Save it for Oprah."

"My point, Chief Flint, is that you *had* to save her, which means *they* betrayed me. Betrayed us. They tried to kill the woman I love."

"You looking for revenge?"

"Of course," Prospero said coldly. "I'm a man, just like you."

Flint almost slapped him with a sarcastic comeback, but he held his tongue.

Prospero nodded. "The other thing I need you to understand is that...while I admit that at first this was about the money, it became about the work. About the goals. The Caliban unit, the other technologies...they really will save lives. American lives at first, and then as combat becomes mechanized to the point that these systems cancel each other out it will save lives on all sides."

"Bull. If the machines stop working, then people will go back in the field."

"No...the machines would deadlock each other, but they would make the actual field of combat too dangerous for men. It would end the game in a stalemate."

"That's it? Your newfound higher motives are about creating a new Cold War?"

"A Cold War is better than endless slaughter." Prospero's eyes glittered. "We are a warlike and savage race, and you know that every bit as well as I do. Just because our intellect has evolved to the point where we can appreciate and even defend ideals it doesn't change the aggression built into our DNA. We're a predator species. We *take* what we want. Look at America's history. Eminent domain?

That is a polite label for centuries of landgrabs, slaughter and ethnic genocide."

Flint said nothing.

"Once I realized that the Caliban systems could bring us to a bloodless stand-off, I saw that, however dubious my initial motivations may have been, I had *found* my purpose."

"Tell it to Congress and the U.S. Attorney. I'm not your lawyer, your confessor or your friend. I'm going to ask you one more time and then I'm going to show you just how savage a human being can be." He bent close. "How can I stop these things?"

The old man stared at him for two long seconds, then he licked his lips. "Nothing I did could possibly be responsible for this. It has to be the AI chips. Kong only made a few of the chips. They were very difficult to make, and they're too big to fit into the Sprites. Those are still drones and someone had to have launched them. There has to be somebody *here*, there has to be a handler."

"On site? What's the operational range?"

"A few miles, but the fences have jammers. Otherwise the prototypes might pick up all kinds of confusing signals. Nothing from outside the fence can get inside. And there's one more thing, Chief."

"What?"

"None of the drones have the articulation needed to enter the generator shack and blow out the fuses. And it can't have been an EMP or the drones themselves would—"

"Yeah, I got it." He stepped back and eyed Prospero in the dim glow of the flashlight's beam. "I'm going to bury you for this," he said.

The old scientist said nothing.

Suddenly gunfire erupted from the doorway.

Flint spun in time to see Teacher's Pet go flying backward as another of the minigun Kobolds rolled into the room.

There was movement to Flint's right and he cut a quick look just as Prospero vanished into the darkness.

Doc was helpless on the floor.

Scarlett pulled her sidearm and returned fire. Monster knelt in front of her and was firing his big shotgun. He was screaming Pet's name like a war cry.

"Monster!" Flint bellowed over the din. "Frag it!"

Monster yanked a fragmentation grenade and rose up to throw it. He was strong and he had a good pitching arm. The grenade flew into the flash-lit shadows. But Monster never lived to see it hit the target. Bullets tore into the big man's chest and he fell backward, landing at the same moment the minigun drone blew up.

Flint ran to where Monster had fallen, but the Joe was past all help.

Grief and rage were like a furnace in Flint's chest. Even so, he couldn't pause to mourn his friend's death. Instead he took the remaining grenades—frags and flashbangs—and all remaining ammunition.

He turned to Scarlett and gave her half of the grenades.

"Look," he began, but she gave a fierce shake of her head.

"Go!" she snarled. "Find them...*stop* this thing."

-16-

Inside the Island

Flint ran through the darkness. He had looted Teacher's Pet as well and wore the dead Joe's helmet, and his pockets were heavy with grenades and magazines. The NVD allowed him to move fast.

Once he was out of the observation wing, he had to cut down a long access tunnel to get to the security vault. The comlink was still dead, but between bursts of gunfire he could hear voices. Screams.

It had to be the staff.

"Yo, Joe!"

The cry came from his left and Flint skidded to a stop and wheeled around. Two figures emerged from behind a stack of crates. Law and Order.

The security tech was covered with blood and his left arm hung limp at his side. Order limped beside him and the dog's eyes were wild with a predatory gleam that looked more like a wolf than a German shepherd.

"How bad are you hurt?"

"Shrapnel in the shoulder," Law answered. "What the hell is happening?"

In a few terse sentences Flint gave him the basics.

"That doesn't make sense. It was Doctor Prospero who just got me out of the vault. Him and that weird iron suit of his."

"*What?*"

"Yeah, just now. He ripped the door right off the hinges. Wouldn't have thought it was possible. He told me to get to the observation deck and help Professor Miranda. She said was hurt..."

There was another burst of gunfire, down the corridor and around the bend.

Law nodded. "Prospero went that way. One of those minigun drones attacked us. Prospero charged after it and tore it apart. Literally. By hand. It exploded, which is how I got nailed. He left me here and said he was going to Ops."

"Okay. Get to the observation deck. Doc's out, Miranda's down, and Scarlett took one in the leg. Keep 'em safe."

"Count on it. But...where are you going?"

"That way," Flint said and ran off in the same direction Prospero had taken.

Order's fierce barks seemed to chase him through the darkness.

An explosion shook the whole place and the shock wave nearly knocked Flint off his feet. When he rounded the corner he saw four more of the minigun drones. Two were smoking, their parts twisted from the blast. The others looked like they had been torn apart by an angry giant.

Along one wall was a row of doors and Flint realized that he was in the first chamber of the staff wing. Most of the doors were still locked shut, but a few had been torn open and there were bodies slumped inside and out. Two or three white-coated figures staggered dazedly through the smoke, their faces smudged with dirt, their clothes singed and streaked with blood.

Flint ran.

He was following a trail of destruction. Prospero had somehow managed to get into his Caliban exosuit and was hunting the drones in his own facility. The power of the Caliban unit was incredible. Steel doors had been ripped from their hinges, doorways smashed to allow the monstrosity to pass through. And everywhere there were dead bodies and drones.

With a sinking heart Flint realized that his team had not been able to get everyone into their chambers before the drones attacked. Men and women lay sprawled like broken dolls.

And in the mess hall, Flint saw a heartbreaking sight. Jukebox and Schoolgirl, two of the newest members of his team, had apparently tried to mount a defense in order to protect a dozen staff members. They had tossed heavy tables onto their sides and set up a firing position. The floor was littered with countless spent shell casings. Jukebox's M4 and Schoolgirl's M5 were still in their hands, the barrels still smoking. But both of the Joes were down. They had taken round after round and gone down fighting.

Behind them, nine of the staff still huddled—weeping and trembling—in a corner between the kitchen entrance and the juice bar. Flint read the scene as he rushed through it. His Joes had destroyed five of the miniguns. Five.

But there had been six.

The last one was smashed flat as if a gigantic fist had pounded it into debris.

Prospero.

Had he gotten here too late? Had he tried to save the Joes as well as the staff? It looked that way, but it didn't make sense to Flint. Prospero had to know that if the drones were stopped then he was going to jail for the rest of his life.

Yet he was trying to save people.

Why?

Flint ran on. Eating his grief, clamping down on his pain.

Something hit him hard in the side and Flint felt himself tumbling, spinning. He struck the wall and slid to the floor, his whole left side ablaze.

I've been shot, he realized.

Darkness and nausea washed over him, but he fought it down, shoved it back.

The shock of the impact erased the immediate awareness of the shot. He had no idea where it had come from.

Then there was a second shot. It pinged off the wall near his head, missing him by inches.

Flint could use his right arm well enough and he sent six shots downrange with his Sig Sauer. There was a scream and then the sound of running. His NVD was askew and by the time he straightened it all he saw was a flash of white.

Not a soldier. Had to be one of the staff. The traitor.

He was sure of it.

The only one? Or part of a sleeper team?

He was inclined to think that there were more. Too much was happening too fast.

He got to his feet and probed his side. The bullet hadn't penetrated, but had instead hit at an angle on his ribcage and slashed him as surely as if he'd been hacked with a sword. When he took a breath he almost screamed. At least two ribs were broken. He could feel the jagged end of one of them tenting the skin. He took a deep breath and pushed it back into place.

He did scream then.

The world danced a sickening jig around him, but he ground his teeth. If he fell, he knew he'd never get up.

He began limping forward, forcing his mind to think through the problem. That was how to defeat the pain. That was how he'd survive.

"Kong's team," he said between gritted teeth.

What about them?

Kong had built the AI chip. Was Prospero correct when he said that Kong's team was all third rate? Or was arrogance clouding the man's judgment. At that moment Flint would have bet a month's pay that it was one of Kong's team who had installed that chip. And that some or all of that team were finessing this situation.

Why?

He staggered on, following a trail of bloody footprints. He'd scored a hit. Nice. As he ran, Flint thought about Prospero's mention of a 'Scotsman.'

Destro. Had to be.

Destro *was* known for AI systems, as well as other weapons that smudged the boundaries between 'in development' and 'science fiction.'

That fast Flint understood it. The competing weapons designers. The 'client.' Backstabbing and sabotage were not exactly unknown to that crew of maniacs.

If Destro was afraid that another top-of-the-line weapons manufacturer would come and crowd him out of the market, what better way to handle it? Let the man finish his masterpiece—the Caliban exosuit and the Skyjack intrusion software—then discredit him during an inspection and take the system for himself. He could then sell it to Cobra without losing the broker's fee; and Destro was genius enough to retro-engineer it.

It made sense, though Flint wondered at how twisted *he* was becoming if this made sense to him.

He rounded a bend and saw the open sky and the vast, black desert.

He saw Flash running at him, the smoking ruin of a laser rifle in his hands, his face flash-burned and bloody. There was an explosion and Flash was flung twenty feet through the air. Flint tried to dodge, but Flash was a screaming missile that struck him full in the chest.

-17-

Outside of the Island

Flint could barely breathe.

He crawled out from under Flash's body, reached down to touch his friend's throat, felt the pulse. Weak, but still there.

Pain was everywhere. Flash's damaged laser rifle had struck Flint in the face, and blood dripped from a deep gash on his cheek. One eye was puffed shut and the whole world had a distant, tinny sound.

And the pain.

It was hard to find somewhere to put his thoughts that was not already flooded with agony.

It was all coming apart. Gunfire rattled on and on. There were screams from inside the complex and then a huge series of explosions. One, two, five...too many to count. Fires burst through the roofs of a dozen buildings sending showers of sparks into the sky so that it looked like the stars themselves were dying and falling.

Flint ran out into the compound, moving fast despite the pain, using hard cover instead of shadows, moving from tree to rock to wall, his pattern random and unsymmetrical. He was hurt, he knew that much. The warmth running down the inside of his clothes wasn't all sweat. He could smell the sharp copper tang of his own blood.

His blood, and the blood of others.

Doc. Law. Scarlett, too. In his mind all he could see was blood.

Blood…and those *things*. The minigun drones. The Sprites. Were they real or was his damaged brain replaying the horrors of the last hour?

He ran and ran, his breath burning in his lungs.

He stumbled and went down, hitting chest-first and sliding, tasting sand in his mouth. He came to rest in the middle of the east parade ground. Exposed, vulnerable.

The screams began to die away. They did not fade like volume turned down on an iPod. They were cut off. Sharply, abruptly, in time with new bursts of gunfire.

Flint felt his consciousness begin to fade as fatigue or damage took hold of him.

"No," he mumbled, spitting sand out of his mouth. "No!"

If he passed out now, he knew that he would never wake up. Not in this world. *They* would find him. Find him and tear him apart.

He tried to get to his hands and knees, but he felt too weak, too used up.

"No!" he growled, louder this time, and the harshness in his own voice put steel into his muscles. He rose, inch by agonizing inch until he was upright on his knees.

In the distance he could hear one of *them* coming.

A metallic clang, the squeak of treads.

How far? A hundred yards? Less?

Flint set his teeth and tried to get to his feet. No way he was going to die like this. If this was his last firefight, then by God he was not going out on his knees.

Pain flared in his side. He couldn't remember what had hit him. Bullets? Shrapnel?

It didn't matter, he forced one leg up, thumped his right foot on the ground, jammed the stock of his M5 on the ground, and pushed.

It was like jacking up a tank.

He rose slowly, slowly.

The squeak of the treads was closer. All of the screams had stopped.

Even the gunfire seemed to have died away.

"No!" he snarled and heaved.

He got to his feet and the whole world spun around him. He almost fell. It nearly ended right there, but Flint took an awkward sideways step and caught his balance.

The world steadied.

The squeak of treads was close. So close. Too close.

Flint turned.

It was there. Massive, indomitable against the firelit columns of smoke. It rolled to a stop ten feet away. It was like the minigun drones that had slaughtered most of his team...but this one was bigger, and with a hiss of hydraulics the black mouths of two electric cannons swung toward him. He raised his own gun.

The miniguns could fire more than four thousand rounds per minute, per gun.

He wasn't sure he could even pull the trigger.

Flint bared his bloody teeth in a grin that defied the machine, defied logic, and defied the certainty of death that towered over him.

"Go Joe!" he yelled.

And fired.

Then something came out of the darkness to his left and slammed into the drone with the sound of a train wreck. There was a scream of twisted steel and one of the guns fired, but the rounds chopped a line through the sand a yard to Flint's right.

From the tangle of wreckage a monster rose, gleaming and ugly and huge. It punched down at the drone, shattering the gearbox; it grabbed the active gun and tore it from the pedestal and flung the smoking weapon a hundred yards into the dark.

Then silence collapsed around Flint, and he sprawled onto the sand, his gun falling from his nerveless fingers.

The giant moved toward him, clanking with each step, its metal skin smoking. There was a hydraulic hiss and the faceplate rose to reveal the madman inside the monster.

"It's over," he said. "I set an EMP bomb. It will detonate in two minutes. The drones are done. Everything is done."

Flint tried to speak, tried to form a word.

"W-why?"

Prospero smiled. A strange, enigmatic smile.

"You didn't believe me when I told you earlier, Chief," he said, "but I really have come to believe in the work. There will be blood— there *has* been blood, and I regret that more than I can express...but eventually this technology will make open warfare impossible. My drones were meant to fight other drones. That's the point. Let the machines battle over politics and oil and religion. Let men be safe."

He shook his head. "There will be a new cold war. It's inevitable. Cold as steel, Chief. The drones and iron giants will become walls between men, and ultimately men will have to stop killing each other."

"Sounds nice," gritted Flint, "but I have dead friends here who wouldn't think much of that plan."

Prospero waved his gigantic arm. "None of this was supposed to happen. This was sabotage. This is a perversion of everything I stand for."

"You got into bed with Cobra," Flint said with a cold sneer. "What did you *expect* would happen?"

Prospero's eyes shifted away. "I had his word. The Commander. He gave his word that my systems would never be used against human assets. Only against other machines of war."

Flint turned his mouth and spat blood onto the sand. "You're a God damn liar," he said. "Or you are the greatest fool who ever walked the earth."

Prospero shook his head again. "You love war, Chief. You're incapable of understanding the higher purpose in all of this."

"Maybe. I know people, though, and you can tell yourself whatever fiction will get you through the night, but anyone who does this does it for one purpose only. Money."

Prospero's eyes were unreadable in the glow from the burning buildings.

"Believe what you will," he said. "But then why did I save you?"

Before Flint could answer, the faceplate slid back into place and the *Caliban* unit stalked off. Flint could hear its clanging footsteps as it headed away—not into the desert, but back into the burning building.

Then the darkness and shock and blood loss reached for Flint and took him down into the world of shadows.

-18-

The Island

A Joe rescue team landed thirty-one minutes later.

By then the EMP had done its work and all of the drones lay still and silent. Merely machines now.

Medical teams were flown in from Area 51. Doc Greer was in the worst shape and he was airlifted to a Las Vegas hospital for emergency surgery. Scarlett, Law, Flash, and Flint were all battered, but none of them were in any immediate danger. Order would need a vet's attention.

The only member of the team unaccounted for was Shock Jock. His body was never found and the search was ongoing. Had he been with Kong's team? A mole inside the Joes? It was a horrible thought.

Or would his body be found buried under the tons of rubble of what was once the Island?

Flint thought about that as the chopper lifted him and the other survivors into the air.

Monster, Schoolgirl, Teacher's Pet, and Jukebox were still down there. Bodies in black rubber bags. Heroes whose real names would never appear in any headline. Heroes who had died fighting a battle the public would never know about. What had happened at the Island was classified. The death toll would be attributed to an industrial generator explosion. There would be no medals awarded.

There would be four more photos on the wall of the Pit. And the world would move on.

Flint sipped water to wash the taste of blood from his mouth.

Prospero had gotten away. He had gone into the burning building and taken Professor Miranda in his steel arms and then…vanished. Walked out through the smoke, leaving a hole big enough for Law and Scarlett to pull Doc Greer's body out to safety as the building collapsed in flames around them.

From the air, Flint watched the last of the buildings go crashing down. There wasn't enough water in the desert to fight that kind of conflagration. It would all be ash and charred metal.

It was a defeat. The Joes had lost before, but this felt somehow worse. Dirtier.

Prospero was out there. The Caliban unit was out there. So was Skyjack.

Destro, too.

And Cobra.

Flint stared down at the destruction and ate his pain and endured.

This was a defeat, but the war would go on.

-19-

Ice House

The Commander sat in his chair and sipped a lovely red wine. The *Goldberg Variations* played softly, filling the room with beauty. On the screens in front of him Destro and Prospero were screaming at each other from two separate secure locations. Each of them had called him within twenty-four hours after the Island incident; each of them boiling with righteous rage. They screamed about betrayal, about the sabotage of efforts. They each vowed revenge and retribution. And seeded through their diatribes, each threw covert pitches at the Commander about how their particular technologies were the only sane course worth pursuing, and they fired off coded emails with revised prices. Over and over again, even as the war of screams and threats raged.

The Commander conferenced their calls together and sat back to watch the fireworks.

"Ah," he said to himself, "I do love the free market."

Author's Note on "The Death Song of Dwar Guntha"

Celebrated anthologist John Joseph Adams is a frequent co-conspirator of mine. I've done stories for a number of his anthologies, ranging from apocalyptic to zombies to the Land of Oz. He's always fun to work with, and he's demanding enough to encourage writers to do some of their best work.

This next story is one I did for his book *Under the Moons of Mars: New Adventures on Barsoom*, which contains all-original stories set in the world of John Carter of Mars, the creation of Edgar Rice Burroughs. The anthology included stories by some amazing writers including Joe R. Lansdale, Peter S. Beagle, Garth Nix, Chris Claremont, S.M. Stirling, Catherynne Valente, and others.

My story, though set in that world, uses John Carter only as a minor supporting character. I wanted to view Barsoom through different eyes than the former Confederate soldier transporter from Earth. I wanted to tell the story of another kind of fighting man of Mars.

The Death Song of Dwar Guntha: A Story of John Carter of Mars

-1-

My name is Jeks Toron, last padwar of the Free Riders, and personal aide to Dwar Guntha. When he dies, however he dies, I pray I will go with him into the realm of legends and that our song will be sung in Helium for a thousand thousand years.

That is not a heroic boast—I won't fall upon my sword at the death of my captain; but I have been in a hundred battles with him, and we have grown old together...and war is not an old man's game. For odwars and jedwars, perhaps, but not for fighting men.

Dwar Guntha? Ah, now there is a fighting man. Was he not with John Carter when the Warlord raided the fortress of Issus? Aye, he was there, leading the mutiny of loyal Heliumites against the madness of Zat Arras. He was a man at arms in the palace when Carter was named Jeddak of Jeddaks—Warlord of all Barsoom. And in the years that followed, how many times did Guntha ride out at the head of the Warlord's Riders? Look closely at Dwar Guntha's face and chest, and in the countless overlapping scars you'll see a map of history, a full account of the wars and battles, rescues, and skirmishes.

Now, though...?

John Carter himself is old. His children and grandchildren, and grandchildren of his grandchildren are old. We red men of Helium are long-lived, but that old witch time, as they say, catches up to everyone. Guntha's right arm is not what it was, and I admit that I am slower on the draw, less sure on the cut, and less dexterous in the riposte than once I was. Even the heroes' songs for which I and my family have been famous these many generations have become echoes of old tales retold. In these days of peace there are few opportunities for songmakers to tell of great and heroic deeds; just as there are few opportunities for warriors to pass into song in a moment of glorious battle.

It seems to me, and to Guntha, that we live in an age of city men. City men, or perhaps "civilized" men, seek deaths in bed, just as our great grandfathers once sought that long, last journey down the River Iss.

We spoke of such things, did Dwar Guntha and I, as we sat before a fire, warming our hands on the blaze and our stomachs with red wine. The moons chased each other through the heavens, leaving in their wakes a billion swirling stars. Tomorrow might be our last day, and so many days lay behind us. It sat heavily upon Dwar Guntha that our last great song may already have been sung.

I caught him looking into the flames with a distance at odds with the hawk sharpness he usually displayed.

"What is it?" I asked, and he was a long time answering.

Instead of speaking, he straightened, set aside his cup, and drew his sword from its sheath of cured banth hide. Guntha regarded the blade for a moment, turning it this way and that, studying the play of reflected firelight on the oiled steel. Then with a sigh he handed it to me.

"Look at it, Jeks," he said heavily. "This is my third sword. When I was a lad and wearing a fighting man's rig for the first time I carried my father's sword. A clunky chopper of Panarian make. My father was a palace guard, you know. Served fifty years and never drew his weapon in anger. First time I used the sword in a real battle I notched the blade on a Tharkian collar. Second time I used it the blade snapped. When Zat Arras fitted out the fleet to pursue John Carter after he'd returned from Valley Dor, Kantos Kan himself gave him a better sword. Good man, that. He was everything Zat Arras was not, and the sword he gave was a Helium blade. Light and strong and already blooded. It had belonged to a padwar friend of his who died nobly but had no heirs. I used that blade for over twenty years, Jeks. It tasted the blood of green men and black men, of plant men and white apes. And, aye, it drank the blood of red men, too."

He sighed and reached for his cup.

"But I lost it when my scouting party was taken prisoner in that skirmish down south. Now, why do I tell you, Jeks? That's where we met, wasn't it? In the slave pits of An-Kar-Dool. Remember how we broke out? Clawing stones from the floor of our cell and tunneling inch by inch under the wall? Running naked into the forests, wasted by starvation, filthy and unarmed."

I smiled and nodded. "We were armed when we returned."

Guntha smiled, too, and nodded at the blade. "That was the first time I used that sword. I took it from the ice pirate who sold us into slavery. I snuck into his tent and strangled him with a lute string, and for a time I thought I would throw this sword away as soon as its immediate work was done."

"That would have been a shame," I said as I hefted the sword, letting the weight of the blade guide the turn and fall and recovery of my fist on my wrist. The balance was superb, and the blade flashed fire as it cut circles in the air.

"And so it would," he agreed, and his smile faded away by slow degrees. "Yet look at it, Jeks. See the nicks and notches that have cut so deep that no smith can sharpen them out? And along the bloodgutter, see the pits? Shake it, you can feel the softness of the tang and if you listen close you can hear it cry out in weary protest. I heard it crack yesterday when we fell upon the garrison that was fleeing this fort. Hearing it crack was like hearing my own heart break."

I lowered the sword and looked at him. Firelight danced in his eyes, but otherwise his face might have been the death mask of some ancient hero.

"I know of fifty songs in which your sword is named, Guntha," said I. "And twice a dozen names it has been given. Horok the Breaker. Lightning Sword of the East. Pirate's Bane and Thark's Friend. Those songs will still be sung when the moons are dust."

"Perhaps. They are old songs, written when each morning brought the clash of steel upon steel. What do we hear each morning now? Birdsong." He grunted in disgust. "Call me superstitious, Jeks, or call me an old fool, but I believe that my sword has sung its last songs."

"There is still tomorrow. The pirates will come and try to take this fort back from us."

"No," he said, "they *will* take it back, and they will slaughter us to a man and bury our bodies in some forgotten valley. No one will see us die and no one will write our last song."

"A death in battle is a death in battle," I observed, but he shook his head.

"You quote your own songs, Jeks," he said, "and when you wrote it you were quoting me."

"Ah," I said, remembering.

"Tomorrow is death," said Guntha, "but not a warrior's death. We will try and hold the walls and they will wear us down and root us out like lice. Extermination is not a way for a warrior to end his own song. There are too few of us to make a stand, and all of us are old. Where once we were the elite, the right hand of John Carter, now we are a company of dotards. An inconvenience to a dishonorable enemy."

"No—" I began but he cut me off with a shake of the head.

"We've known each other too long and too well for us to tell lies in the dark. The sun has set on more than this fortress, Jeks, and I am content with that." He paused. "Well…almost content. I am not a hero. I'm a simple fighting man and perhaps I should show more humility. I have been given a thousand battles. It is gluttony to crave one more."

Again I made to speak and again he shook his head. "Let me ramble, Jeks. Let me draw this poison out of my spirit." He sipped wine and I refilled both of our cups. "I have always been a fighting man. Always. I could never have done temple duty like my father. Standing in all that finery during endless ceremonies while my sword rusted in its sheath for want of a good blooding? No…that was never for me. Perhaps I am less…civilized than my father. Perhaps I belong to an older age of the world when warriors lived life to its fullest and died before they got old."

"You've fought in more battles than anyone I've ever heard of," I said. "Perhaps more than the great Tars Tarkas or the Warlord himself. You've *been* in most of their battles, and a hundred beside."

"And what is the result, Jeks? The world has grown quiet, there are no new songs. The Warlord has tamed Barsoom. He's broken the Assassins Guild and exposed the corruption of the nobles in the courts of Helium, made allies of the Tharks and Okarians; overthrew the Kaldanes, driven out most of the pirates except these last desert scum, and brought peace to the warring kingdoms."

"And *you* were there for much of that, Guntha. This very sword sang its song in the greatest battles of all time."

"Ah, friend Jeks, you miss my point," he said. He sipped his wine and shook his head. "It is *because* of all those battles, it is *because* of all the good that has been done with sword and gun and airship that I sit here, old and disgruntled and…yes…drunk. It is because of the quiet of peace that I feel so cheated."

"Cheated?"

"By myself. By our success. I never wanted to die the way my father did—an old man drooling down my chest while his great-

great-grandchild swaddled him in diapers. Nor would I want to live on in 'retirement,'" he said, wincing at the word, "while my sword hangs above a hearth, a relic whose use is forgotten and whose voice is stilled."

We sat there, both of us staring into the fire.

I took a breath and held out his sword. He looked at it the way a man might regard a friend who has betrayed him.

"Better I should break it over a rock than let it fail in a pointless battle."

"Take it, Guntha," I said softly. "I believe it still has one song left to sing."

His hand was reluctant, but finally he did take it back and slid it with a soft rasp into its sheath.

"What song is left to old men, Jeks?"

"Tomorrow."

He shook his head. "You weren't listening. Tomorrow is a slaughter and nothing more. We will rise and put on our weapons and gear, and then we will die. No one will write that song. No victory will be won. It will be a minor defeat in a war that will pass us by. We are small and peripheral to it, as old men are often peripheral things. No, Jeks, though we may wet our blades in the dawn's red glow, there is nothing..." His voice trailed off and stopped. Guntha drew a breath and straightened his back, staring down in his cup for long moments as logs crackled and hissed in the fire. "Gods," he said softly, "listen to me. I am an old woman. The wine has had the better of me. Forget I spoke."

"Do you say so?" I asked, cocking my head at him.

He forced a smile onto his seamed face. "Surely you can't take my ramblings seriously, old friend. Nor hold them against me after we've drained our cups how many times? Who am I, after all? Not an odwar or a jeddak. A dwar I am and a dwar shall I die—though..." he paused and looked around at the men who slept under rough blankets on the wooden walkway behind the parapets of the small stone fort. "Truly, for a warrior what greater honor is there than to have been the captain of men such as these? Surely none of *my* songs would have ever been sung had it not been for the company of such as they."

"One might say so of all heroes, Guntha," I pointed out. I took the wineskin and filled our cups.

"Not so. John Carter needs no company of men to help him. Even old, he is stronger than the strongest."

"He is not of this world," I reminded him. "Besides...how many times has he been captured during his adventures? How many times has his salvation relied on others? On warriors? Even on women and men from other races? The great Tars Tarkas has saved his life a dozen times."

"Just as John Carter saved his," Guntha fired back.

"Which only makes my point. What man is a hero without another warrior or ally at his back?"

"Like you and me," conceded Guntha, then gave another nod to the sleeping soldiers. "And these creaky old rogues."

"Just so. And it is because men need other men in order to live long enough to *become* heroes that I am able to write songs. Otherwise...no one would be alive to tell me the tales that *become* my songs."

"And I thought your lot made it all up," Guntha said, though I knew he was joking.

"We...*embellish* to be sure," I said unabashedly. "All heroes are handsome, all princesses beautiful, all dangers fell, all escapes narrow, and all victories legendary. You, for example, are taller, slimmer, and better looking in my songs."

We laughed and toasted that.

"But see here," Guntha said, warming to the discourse, "surely there is another kind of hero in songs. The hero whose tale is sung over his grave."

"Ah, you speak of the tragic hero who dies at the moment of his fame. Is it a death song you crave now, Guntha? Since when do like sad songs?"

"Not all death songs are sad. Some are glorious, and many are rallying cries."

"They are all sad," I said.

Guntha shook his head. "Not to the fallen. Such songs are not melancholy, Jeks. Such songs are perhaps the truest hero's tale for they capture the warrior at the peak of his glory, with no postscript to tell of the dreary and ordinary days that followed. There are many who would agree that a hero should never outlive his own song. I know I would have no regrets."

"I would have one," I said.

"Eh?"

"If you were to die in such a glorious battle, you know that I would be by your side. Our men, too. We would all go down together, our blood filling the inkwells of the songmakers."

"So what is your regret?"

I smiled. "I am just arrogant enough to want to outlive our deaths so that *I* would be the one to write that song."

Guntha laughed long and loud. Some of the sleeping men muttered and pulled their blankets over their heads.

"By Iss, Jeks, you'll have to teach your ghost the art of crafting songs."

We laughed, but less so this time, and then we lapsed into a long silence. Guntha and I looked out beyond the battlements of our stolen outpost, past the glow of torches, into the velvety blackness of the night. The moons were down now and starlight was painted on the silks of ten thousand banners and a hundred thousand tents. Cookfires glowed like a mirror of the constellations above. Guntha went and leaned on the wall and I with him, and we stared at the last army of the Pirates of Barsoom. Three hundred thousand foot soldiers and a cavalry of five thousand mounted knights.

Resting now, waiting for dawn.

It was a nice joke to call them pirate scum and a rabble army, but the truth was there before us. It was one of the greatest armies ever assembled, and it marched on Helium and the lands of the Warlord. Would our lands go down in flames? We told ourselves "no." We had learned long ago to believe that John Carter, Jeddak of Jeddaks, would find a way to rally and respond and soak the dead soil of Barsoom in the blood of even so vast an army.

I knew that this was the core of Guntha's despair. He wanted to be there, he wanted to be with the Warlord when the true battle came. Even though he believed that his next battle would be his last, he wanted that battle to matter, to mean something. To be legendary.

We were a nuisance who took this fortress by luck and audacity, but as Guntha said, we would be swatted before the sun was above the horizon. We would not see the Warlord's fleet of airships fill the skies from horizon to horizon. We would not be there when the last— truly the last—great battle of our age was fought. We would already be dead. Forgotten, buried in the rubble of a fort that still stood only because it was inconvenient to take it from us in the dark. There would be no moment to shine, no glory, no notice. There would only be death and then a slide into nothingness as memories of us were overlaid by the songs that would be written about the real battle.

"Perhaps the Warlord will come with the dawn," I said. "The messengers we sent were well-mounted."

He gave another weary shake. "No. They would need to fly on wings to have reached even the most distant outposts. Had we an airship...but, no. John Carter will come, and he will come in all his might and wrath, but our song, my friend, will have ended long before."

"You would never have made a songmaker," I said. "You don't know how to write an ending to your own tale."

"Ha," he laughed, "and that is what I've been trying to tell you all evening."

-2-

Guntha woke me at the blackest hour of night. Only cold starlight washed down upon him as he crouched over me. For my part I came awake from a dream of battle.

"What is it?" I cried. "Are we beset?

My sword was half-drawn from its sheath when he caught my wrist. "No, sheath your sword, my friend," said he. "Just listen to me for a moment and then I'll let you rest."

"Speak then," I said quietly, mindful of the men who slept around us.

"What I said earlier...they were weak words from an old tongue, and I ask that you forgive them."

"There is nothing to forgive."

"Forget them, then. I spoke from old age and regret, but as I lay upon my blanket I thought better of my words, and of my life. To blazes with death songs and glory, and to Iss with the ego of someone to whom the Gods have granted a thousand graces. I said that I was a Dwar and by heaven I will die as one. Not as a hero in some grand song, but a simple man doing a simple job for which he is well-suited. A loyal soldier for whom his daily service to his lord is both his purpose and his reward." He took a breath. "I have had my day, and there need be no more songs for me. None to write and none to sing. Not for me, Jeks, and not for us. The song is over. All that remains is to do one last day's honest work and then I shall lay me down with a will, content that I have not betrayed the trust placed upon me."

I was tempted in my weariness to make light of so bold a speech at such an unlikely hour, but the starlight glittered in his eyes like splinters of sword steel. And all the shadows re-sculpted his face so that as he turned this way and that he was two different men. Or perhaps two different versions of Dwar Guntha. As he turned to the right it seemed to me that I looked upon a much younger man—the young dwar I met in the dungeons so many years ago; and when he turned to the other side, the blue-white starlight transformed his face into a mask as of some ancient king. Neither aspect betrayed even a whisper of the doubt or weakness that had been in his voice scant hours before.

I sat up and put my hand on his shoulder. "Dwar Guntha," I said, "you would have made quite a singer of songs."

He chuckled. "Don't mock me. It's just that I had second thoughts after I lay down."

"Tell me."

"If we are to die tomorrow—or, today, as I perceive that dawn is not many hours away—then at least let us satisfy ourselves to usefulness."

"I don't follow."

"What would you rather do, Jeks? Be an insect to be smoked out of the cracks in these ancient walls and ground under foot...or die as a fighting man?"

"You ask a question to which we both know the answer. The latter, always."

"Then when the sun ignites the morning, let us not wait for death behind these walls. Let us ride out instead."

I smiled. "Ride out?"

"Aye! A charge. We might make the upland cleft, where the slopes narrow before they spill out onto the great plains. It's a bottleneck and we could fill it. With our thoats, we could make a wall of spears." Guntha slapped his thigh. "By the gods I would bear death's ungentle touch, but I will not—*can not*—bear it without blood upon my steel. Even if my blade breaks on iron circlet or skull beneath, then let it break thus, red to the hilt."

"Ride out?" I asked again. "Sixteen against one hundred thousand?"

"Better than sixteen quivering behind battlements they don't have the numbers to defend."

"We wouldn't last a minute."

"And, *ah!*—what a minute it would be."

"No songs," I said.

"No songs," he agreed. "The only song that need be written today is that of John Carter, Jeddak of Jeddaks, as he fills the sky with ships and rains fury down upon this pirate scum. This is it, you know. This is the last battle. Even if we survived tomorrow—and there is scant chance of that—war is over for our generation. Once this army is crushed, then there will be peace on Barsoom. Peace! And it was our swords, Jeks, that helped to bring about such a glorious and blessed and thoroughly depressing turn of events. No...let us ride out to our doom and the dooms of those who first oppose us. The Free Riders of Helium, sailing to paradise on a river of pirate blood."

I laughed. "A singer of songs, indeed!"

We smiled at each other then. Dawn was coming and we both knew that only one last sleep awaited us now.

"I'll go wake the others," said I. "I think they will be pleased!"

And so they were.

-3-

Dawn did indeed come early, and with it the silver voices of a thousand trumpets. My head ached with the hot hammers of the wine-devils, but I was in my battle harness before the pale sunlight clawed its way over the horizon. Before the first echo of the trumpets had yet had time to reach the distant mountains and come back to us, we swung open the gates to the outpost and the Free Riders rode out into the dawn.

Such a sight it must have been, could I have but seen it from a lofty perch. Sixteen men in heavy armor from another age. Spears and lances, warhammers and swords, polished and glittering

The pirates scrambled to meet us, the pike men and foot soldiers grabbing up pieces of armor even as they counted our numbers and laughed. Had I any thoughts of surviving the day I, too, might have laughed; but I knew a great secret that they did not. We were sufficient to our purpose: plenty enough men to die.

We raced to the upland cleft, which was a natural fissure in the red rock through which only half a dozen horses could pass at once. The footing was bad and you needed a trailwise thoat to navigate it at the best of times. All other passes were much stepped or littered with boulders, which forced the army to funnel into the pass. Hence the reason they had stopped for the night. We did not flatter ourselves that that great monster of an army had paused for us.

Dwar Guntha rode before the company, his ancient sword held high.

A dwar from the pirates cupped hands around his mouth and bade Dwar Guntha to surrender.

"Surrender, old man! Beg for your life and my jeddak may spare it!" he taunted.

Guntha never stopped smiling, even as he hefted his spear and threw it with great power and accuracy into the throat of the pirate dwar.

"There is our surrender," Dwar Guntha cried aloud. "We will write our names in the book of death with pirate blood. Have at you bastards, and may the desert demons feast upon your cowardly bones!"

The pirates stared at the body of their fallen captain for a long moment, and then with a great roar like a storming sea, they swept toward us.

We formed ranks and drew into the cleft and only when the first wave of them rushed up the hill at us we charged out to meet them. Spears flashed like summer thunder and the air was filled with a treasure house of bright red rubies.

Ah, the killing.

Guntha and I fought side by side, our thoats rearing and slashing with steel-shod feet. The enemy was so determined to run us down that they sent lancers and foot soldiers in rather than archers. After all, who were we but a few old men on old horses?

It was an arrogance that cost them dearly. And yes, it would have made a glorious song. A battle song. A death song that would be remembered long after our bones were dust. Alas.

Each of the Riders was a veteran of countless battles. Old maybe, but deft and clever and ruthless. They laughed as they fought, delighting in the expressions of shock on the faces of much younger men who learned too little and too late that wisdom and experience often trumps youth and vigor. They came at us in that narrow defile and we took them, shouting our ancient songs of war as the blood ran like a brook around our ankles.

But there were one hundred thousand of them. Though they sent not a single man who could stand before the least of us, they had men to spare and no sword arm can fight without fatigue forever.

I saw Kinto Kan fall, his body feathered with arrows but his own quiver empty and the dead heaped around him—two score and six to be his slaves in death. Ben Bendark, known as Thark-Killer before the Warlord forged the alliance, swung his war axe, that great cleaver of a hundred tavern songs, and the head of a pirate jed flew from his shoulders. I never saw where it landed. Bendark gave a wild cry of red triumph even as spears pierced his chest and stilled his mighty heart. He fell next to his brother, Gan, who smiled even in death, his mighty hands clenched forever around the shattered throats of the men who killed him.

Hadro Henkin, the sword dancer from Gathol, leaped and turned and cut men from the saddle and slipped between spears and left a path of ruin behind him. He made it nearly to the chariot of the jeddak himself before a dozen spearmen converged and brought him down. His best friend, Zeth Hondat, screamed like a banth and threw himself at the spearmen, cutting them down one-two-three-four. Seven fell before the jeddak raised a huge curved sword and cut Zeth nearly in twain.

These things I saw and more. The waves of pirates were as limitless as the dunes of a desert. An ocean of spears and swords, but Dwar Guntha had chosen our spot well and we held the high ground while they were forced into a narrow killing chute. We slaughtered five times our number. Ten times. *More.* And still they came. As I parried and thrust, cut and slashed, I could not help but compose our song in my head. Despite the melancholy musings of last night, this was a glorious end. This was such an end that perhaps the pirates themselves would write the song. Not a hero's lament or stirring death song, but a tale of desert demons who it took an army to overthrow. We would be the monsters to frighten children on dark nights, and that would please Dwar Guntha. It was a way to strike once more into the heart of our enemy.

In a moment's brief reprieve I called to him. Guntha bled from a dozen cuts and leaned heavily on his saddle horn.

"What a song!" I cried.

"Sing it with your blade," he laughed, and they were on us again.

Then I saw three things occur in close succession, and what a wonder they were to behold.

First, I saw the fresh wave of pirates swarm toward us. These were burly men, not the foot soldiers or light skirmishers; these were the cream of their cavalry on fresh thoats, led by the fierce jeddak in his war chariot. Dwar Guntha reared up on his thoat, the reins flying free, a spear in one hand and his ancient sword in the other. With a cry so fierce and powerful that it momentarily stilled the war shouts of the pirates, Guntha thrust the spear deep into the roaring mouth of the chariot's lead thoat, and as the beast fell the chariot tilted forward to offer the jeddak up to Guntha's sword. The blade caught red sunlight and then flashed down, cleaving gold circlet and black skull even as the jeddak thrust his own great blade forward into Dwar Guntha's chest. Guntha's blade snapped as he predicted it would, but only on a killing stroke. His last, and a masterful one it was. The pirates could never reckon this day's victory without counting a terrible cost.

Dwar Guntha fell, and that was the second thing I saw. He fell and as he did so the entire battle seemed to freeze into a shocked moment. The pirates recoiled back as if the sight of a hero's fall and their own champion's death stole the heart from them.

And then I turned to see the third thing, and I knew then why the entire army of pirates has stalled in this moment.

The sky was full of ships.

Hundreds of them. Thousands. The great combined host of Helium and the Tharks, together in a fleet such as no man has seen in the skies of Barsoom in fifty thousand years. I do not know how our scout reached the capital in time. Perhaps he found a patrol in their airship and flew like a demon wind to spread the news and sound the alert. I will never know, and do not care. John Carter had come, and that was all that mattered. He had come...and with the greatest force of arms this world could yet muster. Here, to this barren place by a forgotten outpost. Here to fight the last battle. Whoever won this war would rule Barsoom forever.

John Carter, warlord of warlords, grown wise in his years, knew this and he brought such a force that the pirates howled in fear.

But...ah, they did not throw down their weapons.

I will honor them enough to say that, and to say that they made a fight of it that *will* make songs worth singing.

Yet, my heart was lifted as I looked up and saw a fleet so vast that it darkened the skies.

Or...was it my eyes that grew dark?

I felt a burning pain and looked down to see the glittering length of a sword moving through me below my heart.

I laughed my warrior's laugh and I slew my slayer even as the air erupted with the barrage of ten thousand airships firing all at once.

And the voice of the singer faded, even to his own ears.

-4-

It was a cold night in Helium. The moons were like chips of ice in the black forever that stretched above the royal palace.

John Carter drew his cloak more tightly around him. He was still a tall man, still strong, though great age had slimmed him. Slender and hard as a sword blade.

He leaned a shoulder against a pillar and looked out over the city. Even this late there was the sound of music and laughter. The sounds of peace. How long had it been thus, he mused. So many nights of so many years without the clang of steel on steel? He sighed, content that his people lived without fear, and yet secretly craving those old days when he and Tars Tarkas rode out to face monsters and madmen and hordes of bloodthirsty enemies.

Those were memories of a different world than this.

He heard a sound behind him and saw Kestos, the singer, gathering up his scrolls after a night of composing songs for a pending festival. When the young man noticed Carter watching, he bowed.

"My prince," he said nervously, "I did not mean to disturb you...I'm just leaving—"

Carter waved it off. "No. Tarry a moment, Kestos. Tarry and entertain an old man. Sing me a song."

"Of what would you have me sing, my prince? Of the spring harvest? Of the dance of the moons above—"

"No. Gods, no. Kestos, sing me one of the old songs. Sing me a song of heroes and battle."

"I...know but a few, my prince. I can sing of your victory over the—"

"No. I know my own songs. Sing to me the death song of Dwar Guntha. That's a good tale for a night like this."

The young man looked embarrassed. "My prince, I am sorry...but I don't know that song."

Carter turned and studied him. "Ah...you are so young. To not know the great songs is so sad."

"I...I'm sorry..."

Carter smiled. "No. Sit, young Kestos and I will sing you the song. Learn it. Remember it, and sing it often. Some songs should never be forgotten."

And as the moons sailed through the black ocean of the sky, John Carter, Warlord of all Barsoom, sang of the last charge of the great Free Riders.

And such a tale it was. All of the heroes were tall and handsome, all of the enemies were vile and dangerous, and each of the heroes slew a hundred and then died gloriously upon a mountain of their foes.

Or, so it goes in the song.

Author's Note on "Chokepoint"

If you're at all familiar with my work you'll know that I have a special fondness for my life-impaired fellow citizens (aka zombies). This is one of my favorites of the zombie stories I've written. It was written as the lead story for issue #2 of *The Univited*, a webzine of horror stories.

This story is technically a sequel to two of my novels, *Dead of Night* and *Fall of Night*, which are—in their way—prequels to George A. Romero's *Night of the Living Dead*. You don't need to have read either of those novels in order to read this; nor do you need to be familiar with that landmark movie. Though, come on...you *should* watch Romero's flick. It's a piece of history and it started the entire zombie genre.

Chokepoint

-1-

The lieutenant said to hold it.

So we're holding it.

Chokepoint Baker: five miles up a crooked road, fifty miles from the command post, a hundred miles from the war.

They dropped us here three days after what the radio has been calling First Night.

Couple days later, I heard a DJ out of Philly call it Last Night. But the news guys always do that hysterical shit. If it's going to snow, they start talking about blizzards; two guys shove each other outside a Wal-Mart, and it's rioting in the streets. Their amps are always dialed up to eleven.

Guess that sort of thing's infectious, because we got rousted and rolled before dawn's early light.

As we climbed down off the truck, Lieutenant Bell took me aside. We'd known each other for a while and he usually called me Sally or Sal, but not that day. He was all Joe-Army. "Listen up, Corporal," he told me. "The infection is contained to the west side of this river. There are two other bridges; closest is eight klicks downstream. We're spread pretty thin, so I can spare one fireteam per bridge. This one's yours."

The bridge was rusted steel that had once been painted blue, a lane of blacktop going in each direction. No tollbooth, no nothing. Pennsylvania on one side, New Jersey on the other.

"You think you can do that, Corporal?"

I grinned. "C'mon, Loot, a couple of Cub Scouts could hold that bridge with a slingshot and a wet fart."

I always cracked him up, drunk or sober, but now he just gave me the *look.* The officer look.

I straightened. "Yes, sir. We'll hold it."

"You are authorized to barricade this bridge. Make sure nothing gets across. Nothing and no one, do you understand?"

For what? Some dickheads rioting on the other side of the state? I wanted to laugh.

But there was something in his eyes. He lowered his voice so it was just heard by the two of us. Everyone else was handing empty sandbags and equipment boxes down from the truck. "This is serious shit, Sally. I need you to do this."

I gave a quick right-left look to make sure no one could hear us. "The fuck's going down, man? You got the bug-eyes going on. This is a bunch of civilians going apeshit, right?"

Bell licked his lips. Real nervous, the way a scared dog does.

"You really don't know, do you?" he asked. "Haven't you been watching the news?"

"Yeah, I've seen the news."

"They aren't civilians," he said. "Not anymore."

"What does that—?"

A sergeant came hurrying over to tell us that everything was off-loaded. Bell stepped abruptly away from me and back into his officer role. "Are we clear on everything, Corporal Tucci?"

I played my part. "Yes, *sir.*"

Bell and the sergeant climbed back into the truck and we watched its taillights through a faint smudge of dust. My guys—all three of them—stood with me. We turned and looked at the bridge. It was rush hour on a Friday, but the road was empty. Both sides of the bridge.

"What the hell's going on?" asked Joe Bob—and, yeah, his actual name on his dog tags is Joe Bob Stanton. He's a redneck mouth-breather who joined the Reserves because nobody in the civilian world was stupid enough to let him play with guns. So the geniuses here decided he should be an automatic rifleman. When they handed him an M249 Squad Automatic Weapon, he almost came in his pants.

I shook my head.

"Join the Navy," said Talia. "See the world."

"That's the Navy," said Farris. "We're the National damn Guard."

"That's my point," she said.

"C'mon," I said, "let's get this shit done."

It took us four hours to fill enough sandbags to block the western approach to the bridge. Four hours. Didn't see a single car the whole time.

At first that was okay, made it easier to work.

Later, though, none of us liked how that felt.

-2-

I was the Team Leader for this gig. Corporal Salvatore Tucci. I'm in charge because everyone else on the team was even greener than me. Army Reserves, man. I'm in technical college working on a degree in fixing air conditioners, and I'm the most educated guy on the team. Cutting-edge, 21st century Army my ass.

A lot of the guys who enlist are dickheads like Joe Bob.

The other two? Farris is a slacker with no G.E.D. who mops up at a Taco Bell. They made him a rifleman. And our grenadier, Talia? Her arms and her thighs are a roadmap of healed-over needle scars, but she doesn't talk about it. I think she maybe got clean and signed up to help her stay clean.

That's Fireteam Delta. Four fuck-ups who didn't have the sense to stay out of uniform or enough useful skills to be put somewhere that mattered.

So here we are, holding Checkpoint Baker and waiting for orders.

We opened some M.R.E.s and ate bad spaghetti and some watery stuff that was supposed to be cream of broccoli soup.

"Dude," said Farris, "there's a Quiznos like three miles from here. I saw it on the way in."

"So?"

"One of us could go and get something…"

"Deserting a post in a time of crisis?" murmured Talia dryly. "I think they have a rule about that."

"It's not deserting," said Farris, but he didn't push it. I think he knew what we all thought. As soon as he was around the bend in the road he'd fire up a blunt, and that's all we'd need is to have the lieutenant roll up on Farris stoned and A.W.O.L. On my watch.

I gave him my version of the *look.*

He grinned like a kid who was caught reaching in the cookie jar.

"Hey," said Talia, "somebody's coming."

And shit if we didn't all look the wrong way first. We looked up the road, the way the truck went. Then we realized Talia was looking over the sandbags.

We turned.

There was someone on the road. Not in a car. On foot, walking along the side of the road, maybe four hundred yards away.

"Civvie," said Talia. "Looks like a kid."

I took out my binoculars. They're a cheap, low-intensity pair that I bought myself. Still better than the 'no pair' they issued me. The civvie kid was maybe seventeen, wearing a Philadelphia Eagles sweatshirt, jeans, and bare feet. He walked with his head down, stumbling a little. There were dark smears on his shirt, and I've been in enough bar fights to know what blood looks like when it dries on a football jersey. There was some blood on what I could see of his face and on both hands.

"Whoever he is," I said, "someone kicked his ass."

They took turns looking.

While Talia was looking, the guy raised his head, and she screamed. Like a horror movie scream; just a kind of yelp.

"Holy shit!"

"What?" Everyone asked it at the same time.

"His face…"

I took the binoculars back. The guy's head was down again. He was about a hundred yards away now, coming on but not in a hurry. If he was that jacked up then maybe he was really out of it. Maybe he got drunk and picked the wrong fight and now his head was busted and he didn't know where he was.

"What's wrong with his face?" asked Farris.

When Talia didn't answer, I lowered the glasses and looked at her. "Tal…what was wrong with his face?"

She still didn't answer, and there was a weird light in her eyes.

"What?" I asked.

But she didn't need to answer.

Farris said, "Holy fuck!"

I whirled around. The civvie was thirty yards away. Close enough to see him.

Close enough to see.

The kid was walking right toward the bridge, head up now. Eyes on us.

His face…

I thought it was smeared with blood.

But that wasn't it.

He didn't have a face.

Beside me, Joe Bob said, "Wha—wha—wha—?" He couldn't even finish the word.

Farris made a gagging sound. Or maybe that was me.

The civvie kid kept walking straight toward us. Twenty yards. His mouth was open, and for a stupid minute, I thought he was speaking. But you need lips to speak. And a tongue. All he had was teeth. The rest of the flesh on his face was—gone.

Just gone.

Torn away. Or…

Eaten away.

"Jesus Christ, Sal," gasped Talia. "What the fuck? I mean—what the *fuck?*"

Joe Bob swung his big M249 up and dropped the bipod legs on the top sandbag. "I can drop that freak right—"

"Hold your goddamn fire," I growled, and the command in my own voice steadied my feet on the ground. "Farris, Talia—hit the line, but nobody fires a shot unless I say so."

They all looked at me.

"Right fucking now," I bellowed.

They jumped. Farris and Talia brought up their M4 carbines. So did I. The kid was ten yards away now, and he didn't look like he wanted to stop.

"How's he even walking with all that?" asked Talia in a small voice.

I yelled at the civvie. "Hey! Sir? Sir...? I need you to stop right there."

His head jerked up a little more. He had no nose at all. And both eyes were bloodshot and wild. He kept walking, though.

"Sir! Stop. Do not approach the barricade."

He didn't stop.

Then everyone was yelling at him. Ordering him to stop. Telling him to stand down, or lie down, or kneel. Confusing, loud, conflicting. We yelled at the top of our voices as the kid walked right at us.

"I can take him," said Joe Bob in a trembling voice. Was it fear or was he getting ready to bust a nut at the thought of squeezing that trigger?

The civvie was right there. Right in our faces.

He hit the chest-high stack of sandbags and made a grab for me with his bloody fingers. I jumped back.

There was a sudden, three-shot *rat-a-tat-tat.*

The civvie flew back from the sandbags, and the world seemed to freeze as the echoes of those three shots bounced off the bridge and the trees on either side of the river and off the flower water beneath us. Three drum-hits of sound.

I stared at the shooter.

Not Joe Bob. He was as dumbfounded as me.

Talia's face was white with shock at what she had just done.

"Oh...god..." she said, in a voice that was almost no voice at all. Tiny, lost.

Farris and I were in motion in the next second, both of us scrambling over the barricade. Talia stood with her smoking rifle pointed at the sky. Joe Bob gaped at her.

I hit the blacktop and rushed over to where the kid lay sprawled on the ground.

The three-shot burst had caught him in the center of the chest, and the impact had picked him up and dropped him five feet back. His shirt was torn open over a ragged hole.

"Ah...Christ," I said under my breath, and I probably said it forty times as we knelt down.

"We're up the creek on this," said Farris, low enough so Talia couldn't hear.

Behind us, though, she called out, "Is he okay? Please tell me he's okay."

You could have put a beer can in the hole in his chest. Meat and bone were ripped apart; he'd been right up against the barrel when she'd fired.

The kid's eyes were still open.

Wide open.

Almost like they were looking right at...

The dead civvie came up off the ground and grabbed Farris by the hair.

Farris screamed and tried to pull back. I think I just blanked out for a second. I mean...this was impossible. Guy had a fucking hole in his chest and no face and...

Talia and Joe Bob screamed, too.

Then the civvie clamped his teeth on Farris's wrist.

I don't know what happened next. I lost it. We all lost it. One second I was kneeling there, watching Farris hammer at the teenager's face with one fist while blood shot up from between the bastard's teeth. I blinked, and then suddenly the kid was on the ground and the four of us—all of us—were in a circle around him, stomping the shit out of him. Kicking and stamping down and grinding on his bones.

The kid didn't scream.

And he kept twisting and trying to grab at us. With broken fingers, and shattered bones in his arms, he kept reaching. With his teeth kicked out, he kept trying to bite. He would not stop.

We would not stop.

None of us could.

And then Farris grabbed his M4 with bloody hands and fired down at the body as the rest of us leapt back. Farris had it on three-round burst mode. His finger jerked over and over on the trigger and he burned through an entire magazine in a couple of seconds. Thirty rounds. The rounds chopped into the kid. They ruined him. They tore his chest and stomach apart. They blew off his left arm. They tore away what was left of his face.

Farris was screaming.

He dropped the magazine and went to swap in a new one and then I was in his face. I shoved him back.

"*Stop it!*" I yelled as loud as I could.

Farris staggered and fell against the sandbags, and I was there with him, my palms on his chest, both of us staring holes into each other, chests heaving, ears ringing from the gunfire. His rifle dropped to the blacktop and fell over with a clatter.

The whole world was suddenly quiet. We could hear the run of water in the river, but all of the birds in the trees had shut up.

Joe Bob made a small mewling sound.

I looked at him.

He was looking at the kid.

So I looked at the kid, too.

He was a ragdoll, torn and empty.

The son of a bitch was still moving.

"No," I said.

But the day said: *yes.*

-3-

We stood around it.

Not him. *It.*

What else would you call something like this?

"He…can't still be alive," murmured Talia. "That's impossible."

It was like the fifth or sixth time she'd said that.

No one argued with her.

Except the kid was still moving. He had no lower jaw and half of his neck tendons were shot away, but he kept trying to raise his head. Like he was still trying to bite.

Farris clapped a hand to his mouth and tried not to throw up...but why should he be any different? He spun off and vomited onto the road. Joe Bob and Talia puked in the weeds.

Talia turned away and stood behind Farris, her hand on his back. She bent low to say something to him, but he kept shaking his head.

"What the hell we going to do 'bout this?" asked Joe Bob.

When I didn't answer, the other two looked at me.

"He's right, Sally," said Talia. "We have to do something. We can't leave him like that."

"I don't think a Band-Aid's going to do much frigging good," I said.

"No," she said, "we have to—you know—put him out of his misery."

I gaped at her. "What, you think I'm packing Kryptonite bullets? You shot him and he didn't die, and Farris...Christ, look at this son of a bitch. What the hell do you think I'd be able to—"

Talia got up and strode over to me and got right up in my face.

"Do something," she said coldly.

I wasn't backing down because there was nowhere to go. "Like fucking *what*?"

Her eyes held mine for a moment and then she turned, unslung her rifle, put the stock to her shoulder, and fired a short burst into the civvie's head.

If I hadn't hurled my lunch a few minutes ago, I'd have lost it now. The kid's head just flew apart.

Blood and gray junk splattered everyone.

Farris started to cry.

The thunder of the burst rolled past us, and the breeze off the river blew away the smoke.

The civvie lay dead.

Really dead.

I looked at Talia. "How—?"

There was no bravado on her face. She was white as a sheet, and half a step from losing her shit. "What else was there to shoot?" she demanded.

-4-

I called it in.

We were back on our side of the sandbags. The others hunkered down around me.

The kid lay where he was.

Lieutenant Bell said, "You're sure he stopped moving after taking a headshot?"

I'm not sure what I expected the loot to say, but that wasn't it. That was a mile down the wrong road from the right kind of answer. I think I'd have felt better if he reamed me out or threatened some kind of punishment. That, at least, would make sense.

"Yes, sir," I said. "He, um, did not seem to respond to body shots or other damage."

I left him a big hole so he could come back at me on this. I wanted him to.

Instead, he said, "We're hearing this from other posts. Headshots seem to be the only thing that takes these things down."

"Wait, wait," I said. "What do you mean 'these things'? This was just a kid."

"No," he said. There was a rustling sound and I could tell that he was moving, and when he spoke again, his voice was hushed. "Sal, listen to me here. The shit is hitting the fan. Not just here, but everywhere."

"What shit? What the hell's going on?"

"They...don't really know. All they're saying is that it's spreading like crazy. Western Pennsylvania, Maryland, parts of Virginia and Ohio. It's all over, and people are acting nuts. We've been getting some crazy-ass reports."

"Come on, Loot," I said—and I didn't like the pleading sound in my own voice. "Is this some kind of disease or something?"

"Yes," he said, then, "maybe. We don't know. *They* don't know, or if they do, then they're sure as shit not telling us."

"But—"

"The thing is, Sally, you got to keep your shit tight. You hear me? You blockade that bridge and I don't care who shows up—nobody gets across. I don't care if it's a nun with an orphan or a little girl with her puppy, you put them down."

"Whoa, wait a frigging minute," I barked, and everyone around me jumped. "What the hell are you saying?"

"You heard me. That kid you put down was infected."

The others were listening to this and their faces looked sick and scared. Mine must have, too.

"Okay," I said, "so maybe he was infected, but I'm not going to open up on everyone who comes down the road. That's crazy."

"It's an order."

"Bullshit. No one's going to give an order like that. No disrespect here, *Lieutenant,* but are you fucking high?"

"That's the order, now follow it..."

"No way. I don't believe it. You can put me up on charges, Loot, but I am not going to—"

"Hey!" snapped Bell. "This isn't a goddamn debate. I gave you an order and—"

"And I don't believe it. Put the captain on the line, or come here with a signed order from him or someone higher, but I'm not going to death row because you're suddenly losing your shit."

The line went dead.

We sat there and stared at each other.

Ferris rubbed his fingers over the bandage Talia had used to dress his bite. His eyes were jumpy.

"What's going on?" he asked. It sounded like a simple question, but we all knew that it wasn't. That question was a tangle of all sorts of barbed wire and broken junk.

I got up and walked over to the wall of sandbags.

We'd stacked them two deep and chest high, but suddenly it felt as weak as a little picket fence. We still had a whole stack of empty bags we hadn't filled yet. We didn't think we'd need to, and they were heavy as shit. I nudged them with the toe of my boot.

I didn't even have to ask. Suddenly we were all filling the bags and building the wall higher and deeper. In the end, we used every single bag.

-5-

"Sal," called Talia, holding up the walkie-talkie, "the Loot's calling."

I took it from her, but it wasn't Lieutenant Bell, and it wasn't the captain, either.

"Corporal Tucci?" said a gruff voice that I didn't recognize.

"Yes, sir, this is Tucci."

"This is Major Bradley."

Farris mouthed, *Oh shit.*

"Sir!" I said, and actually straightened like I was snapping to attention.

"Lieutenant Bell expressed your concerns over the orders he gave you."

Here it comes, I thought. *I'm dead or I'm in Leavenworth.*

"Sir, I—"

"I understand your concerns, Corporal," he said. "Those concerns are natural; they show compassion and an honorable adherence to the spirit of who we are as soldiers of this great nation."

Talia rolled her eyes and mimed shoveling shit, but the Major's opening salvo was scaring me. It felt like a series of jabs before an overhand right.

"But we are currently faced with extraordinary circumstances that are unique in my military experience," continued Major Bradley. "We are confronted by a situation in which our fellow citizens are the enemy."

"Sir, I don't—"

He cut me off. "Let me finish, Corporal. You need to hear this."

"Yes, sir. Sorry, sir."

He cleared his throat. "We are facing a biological threat of an unknown nature. It is very likely a terrorist weapon of some kind, but quite frankly, we don't know. What we do know is that the infected are a serious threat. They are violent, they are mentally deranged, and they will attack anyone with whom they come into contact, regardless of age, sex, or any other consideration. We have reports of small children attacking grown men. Anyone who is infected becomes violent. Old people, pregnant women...it, um...doesn't seem to matter." Bradley faltered for a moment, and I wondered if the first part of what he'd said was repeated from orders *he* got and now he was on his own. We all waited.

And waited.

Finally, I said, "Sir?"

But there was no answer.

I checked the walkie-talkie. It was functioning, but Major Bradley had stopped transmitting.

"What the hell?" I said.

"Maybe there's interference," suggested Joe Bob.

I looked around. "Who's got a cell?"

We all had cell phones.

We all called.

I called my brother Vinnie in Newark.

"Sal—Christ on a stick, have you seen the news?" he growled. "Everyone's going ape-shit."

"SAL!"

I spun around and saw Talia pointing past the sandbags.

"They're coming!"

They.

God. They.

-6-

The road was thick with them.

Maybe forty. Maybe fifty.

All kinds of them.

Guys in suits. Women in skirts and blouses. Kids. A diner waitress in a pink uniform. A man dressed in surgical scrubs. People.

Just people.

Them.

They didn't rush us.

They *walked* down the road toward the bridge. I think that was one of the worst parts of it. I might have been able to deal with a bunch of psychos running at me. That would have felt like an attack. You see a mob running batshit at you and you switch your M4s to rock'n'roll and hope that all of them are right with Jesus.

But they walked.

Walked.

Badly. Some of them limped. I saw one guy walking on an ankle that you could see was broken from fifty yards out. It was buckled over to the side, but he didn't give a shit. There was no wince, no flicker on his face.

The whole bunch of them were like that. None of them looked right. They were bloody. They were ragged.

They were mauled.

"God almighty," whispered Farris.

Talia began saying a Hail Mary.

I heard Joe Bob saying, "Fuck yeah, fuck yeah, fuck yeah." But something in his tone didn't sell it for me. His face was greasy with sweat and his eyes were jumpier than a speed freak's.

The crowd kept coming to us. I'd had to hang up on Vinnie.

"They're going to crawl right over these damn sandbags," complained Farris. The bandage around his wrist was soaked through with blood.

"What do we do?" asked Farris.

He already knew.

When they were fifteen yards away, we opened up.

We burned through at least a mag each before we remembered about shooting them in the head.

Talia screamed it first, and then we were all screaming it. "The head! Shoot for the head!"

"Switch to semi-auto," I hollered. "Check your targets, conserve your ammo."

We stood in a line, our barrels flashing and smoking, spitting fire at the people as they crowded close.

They went down.

Only if we took them in the head. Only then.

At that range, though, we couldn't miss. They walked right up to the barrels. They looked at us as we shot them.

"Jesus, Sal," said Talia as we swapped our mags. "Their eyes. Did you see their eyes?"

I didn't say anything. I didn't have to. When someone is walking up to you and not even ducking away from the shot, you see everything.

We burned through three-quarters of our ammunition.

The air stank of smoke and blood.

Farris was the last one to stop shooting. He was laughing as he clicked on empty, but when he looked back at the rest of us, we could see that there were tears pouring down his cheeks.

The smoke clung to the moment, and for a while, that's all I could see. My mouth was a thick paste of cordite and dry spit. When the breeze came up off the river, we stared into the reality of what we had just done.

"They were all sick, right?" asked Talia. "I mean…they were all infected, right? All of them?"

"Yeah," I said, but what the hell did I know?

We stood there for a long time. None of us knew what the hell to do.

Later, when I tried to call the Major again, I got nothing.

The same thing with the cells. I couldn't even get a signal.

None of us could.

"Come on," I said after a while, "check your ammo."

We did. We had two magazines each, except for Farris, who had one.

Two mags each.

It didn't feel like it was going to be enough.

Talia grabbed my sleeve. "What the hell do we do?"

They all looked at me. Like I knew what the fuck was what.

"We hold this fucking bridge," I said.

-7-

No more of them came down the road.

Not then.

Not all afternoon.

Couple of times we heard—or thought we heard—gunfire from way upriver. Never lasted long.

The sun started to fall behind the trees, and it smeared red light over everything. Looked like the world was on fire. I saw Talia staring at the sky for almost fifteen minutes.

"What?" I asked.

"Planes," she said.

I looked up. Way high in the sky there were some contrails, but the sky was getting too dark to see what they were. Something flying in formation, though.

Joe Bob was on watch, and he was talking to himself. Some Bible stuff. I didn't want to hear what it was.

Instead, I went to the Jersey side of the bridge and looked up and down the road. Talia and Farris came with me, but there was nothing to see.

"Maybe they made a public service announcement," said Talia. "Like the Emergency Broadcast Network thing. Maybe they told everyone to stay home, stay off the roads."

"Sure," I said in pretty much the same way you'd say 'bullshit.'

We watched the empty road as the sky grew darker.

"We could just leave," said Farris. "Head up the road. There's that Quiznos. Maybe we can find a ride."

"We can't leave the bridge," I said.

"Fuck the bridge."

I got up in his face. "Really? You want to let *them* just stroll across the bridge? Is that your plan? Is that what you think will get the job done?"

"What job? We're all alone out here. Might as well have been on the far side of the goddamn moon."

"They'll come back for us," I said. "You watch; in the morning there'll be a truck with supplies, maybe some hot coffee."

"Sure," he said, in exactly the same way I had a minute ago.

-8-

That night, there were a million stars and a bright three-quarter moon. Plenty of light to see the road. Only one of them came down the road. Talia was on watch and she took it down with a single shot to the head. She let the thing—it used to be a mailman—walk right up to the sandbags. It opened its mouth, even though it was too far away to bite, and Talia shot it in the eye.

Then she sat down and cried like a little girl for ten whole minutes. I stood her watch and let her cry. I wished I could do that. For me, it was all stuck inside and it was killing me that I couldn't let it go.

-9-

Farris got sick in the night.

I heard him throwing up, and I came over and shined my flashlight on him. His face was slick with sweat. Joe Bob went back to the wall and Talia knelt next to me. She knew more First Aid than I did, and she took Farris's vitals as best she could.

"Wow, he's burning up," she said, looking at his fever-bright eyes and sweaty face, but then she put her palm on his forehead and frowned. "That's weird. He's cold."

"Shock?" I asked, but she didn't answer.

Then she examined the bite and I heard her gasp. When I shined my light on Farris's arm, I had to bite my lip. The wound on Farris's wrist was bad enough, but there were weird black lines running all the way up his arm. It was like someone had used a Sharpie to outline every vein and capillary.

"It's infection," said Talia, but I knew that it was worse than that.

"God," gasped Farris, "it's blood poisoning."

I said nothing, because I thought it was worse than that, too. Even in the harsh glare of the flashlight, his color looked weird.

Talia met my eyes over the beam of the light. She didn't say anything, but we had a whole conversation with that one look.

I patted Farris on the shoulder. "You get some sleep, man. In the morning we'll get a medic down here to give you a shot, set you right."

Fear was jumping up in his eyes. "You sure? They can give me something for this?"

"Yeah. Antibiotics and shit."

Talia fished in her first-aid kit. There was a morphine syrrette. She showed it to me and I nodded.

"Sweet dreams, honey," she said as she jabbed Farris with the little needle. His eyes held hers for a moment, and then he was out.

We made sure he was comfortable and then we got up and began walking up and down the length of the bridge. Talia kept looking up at the moon.

"Pretty night," I said.

She made a face.

"*Should* be a pretty night," I amended.

We stopped for a moment and looked down at the rushing water. It was running fast and high after that big storm a couple of days ago, and each little wave-tip gleamed with silver moonlight. Maybe fifteen, twenty minutes passed while we stood there, our shoulders a few inches apart, hands on the cold metal rail, watching the river do what rivers do.

"Sally?" she asked softly.

"Yeah?"

"This is all happening, right?"

I glanced at her. "What do you mean?"

She used her fingers to lightly trace circles on the inside of her forearm. "You know I used to ride the spike, right? I mean, that's not news."

"I figured."

"I've been getting high most of my life. Since...like seventh grade. Used to swipe pills from my mom's purse. She did a lot of speed, so that's what I started on. Rode a lot of fast waves, y'know?"

"Yeah." I was never much of a hophead, but I lived in Newark and I'd seen a lot of my friends go down in flames.

"Until I got clean the last time, I was probably high more than I was on the ground."

I said nothing.

"So," she continued, "I seen a lot of weird shit. While I was jonesing for a hit, while I was high, on the way down. You lose touch, y'know?"

"Yeah."

"People talk about pink elephants and polka-dotted lobsters and shit, but that's not what comes out of the woodwork." She shivered and gripped the rail with more force. Like it was holding her there. "And not a day goes by—not a fucking day—when I don't want a fix. Even now, twenty-three months clean, I can feel it. It's like worms crawling under my skin. That morphine? You think I haven't dreamed about that every night?"

I nodded. "My Uncle Tony's been in and out of twelve steps for booze. I've seen how he looks at Thanksgiving when the rest of us are drinking beers and watching the ball game. Like he'd take a knife to any one of us for a cold bottle of Coors."

"Right. Did your uncle ever talk to you about having a dry drunk? About feeling stoned and even seeing the spiders come crawling out of the sofa when he hasn't even had a drop?"

"Couple times."

"I get that," she said. "I get that a lot."

I waited.

"That's why I need you to tell me that this is all really happening; or am I lost inside my own head?"

I turned to her and touched her arm. "I wish to Christ and the baby Jesus that I could say that you're just tripping. Having a dry drunk, or whatever you'd call it. A flashback—whatever. But…I ain't a drunk and I never shot up, and here I am, right with you. Right here in the middle of this shit."

Talia closed her eyes and leaned her forehead on the backs of the hands that clung so desperately to the rail. "Ah…fuck," she said quietly.

I felt like a total asshole for telling her the truth.

Then Talia stiffened, and I saw that she was looking past her hands. "What's that?"

"What?"

She pointed over the rail. "In the water. Is that a log, or…?"

Something bobbed up and down as the current swept it toward the bridge. It looked black in the moonlight, but as it came closer we could see that part of it was white.

The face.

White.

We stared at it…and it stared back up at us.

Its mouth was open, working, like it was trying to bite us even as the river pulled it under the bridge and then out the other side. We hurried to the other side and stared over, watching the thing reach toward us, its white fingers clawing the air.

Then it was gone. A shape, then a dot, then nothing.

Neither of us could say a word.

Until the next one floated by. And the next.

"God, no…" whispered Talia.

We went back to the other side of the bridge.

"There's another," I said. "No…two…no…"

I stopped counting.

Counting didn't matter.

Who cares how many of them floated down? Two, three hundred? A thousand?

After the first one, really, who cared how many?

Talia and I stood there all night, watching. There were ordinary civilians and people in all kinds of uniforms. Cops, firemen, paramedics. Soldiers. I wished to God that I had a needle of heroin for her. And for me.

We didn't tell the others.

-10-

I'm not sure what time the bodies stopped floating past. The morning was humid and there was a thick mist. It covered the river, and maybe there were still bodies down there, or maybe the fog hid them.

We stood there as the fog curled gray fingers around the bridge and pulled itself up to cover everything. The wall of sandbags, Joe Bob, the sleeping figure of Farris, our gear. All of it.

Talia and I never moved from the rail, even when it got hard to see each other.

"They'll come for us, right?" she asked. "The Lieutenant? The supply truck? They'll come to get us, right?"

"Absolutely," I said. She was a ghost beside me.

"You're sure?"

"They'll come."

And they did.

It wasn't long, either, but the sun was already up and the fog was starting to thin out. Talia saw them first and she stiffened.

"Sally..."

I turned to look.

At first it was only a shape. A single figure, and my heart sank. It came down the road from the direction our truck had come, walking wearily toward us from the Jersey side. In the fog it was shapeless, shambling.

Talia whimpered, just a sound of denial that didn't have actual words.

"Fuck me," I whispered, but before I could even bring my gun up, the fog swirled and I could see the mishmash stripes of camouflage, the curve of a helmet, the sharp angles of a rifle on its sling.

Talia grabbed my arm. "Sally? Look!"

There was movement behind the soldier, and, one by one, shapes emerged. More camos, more tin pots.

More soldiers.

They came walking down the road. Five of them. Then more.

"It's the whole platoon," Talia said, and laughter bubbled in her voice.

But it was more than that. As the mist thinned, I could see a lot of soldiers. A hundred at least. More.

"Damn," I said, "they look bone-ass tired. They must have been fighting all night."

"Is it over?" she asked. "Have we beaten this goddamn thing?"

I smiled. "I think so."

I waved, but no one waved back. Some of them could barely walk. I could understand, I felt like I could drop where I stood. We'd been up all night watching the river.

"Talia, go wake up Farris and tell Joe Bob to look sharp."

She grinned and spun away and vanished into the veil of fog that still covered the bridge.

I took a second to straighten my uniform and sling my rifle the right way. I straightened my posture and stepped off the bridge onto the road, looking tough, looking like someone who maybe should get some sergeant's stripes for holding this frigging bridge. Army strong, booyah.

I saw Lieutenant Bell, and he was as wrung out as the rest of them. He lumbered through the fog, shoulders slumped, and behind him were gray soldiers. Even from this distance I could tell that no one was smiling. And for a moment I wondered if maybe this was a retreat rather than a surge. Shit. Had they gotten their asses kicked and these were the survivors? If so...Bell would have his ass handed to him and I wouldn't be going up a pay grade.

"Well, whatever," I said to myself. "Fireteam Delta held the bridge, so fuck it and fuck you and hooray for the red, white, and blue."

A breeze wandered out of the south and it blew past me, swirling the mist, blowing it off the bridge and pushing it away from the soldiers. The mass of gray figures changed into khaki and brown and green.

And red.

All of them.

Splashed with...

I turned and screamed at the top of my lungs. "*TALIA! Joe Bob, Farris!* Lock and load. Hostiles on the road..."

The breeze had blown all the mist off of the bridge.

Talia stood forty feet from the wall of sandbags. Her rifle hung from its sling, the sling in her hand, the stock of the weapon on the blacktop. She stood, her back to me, staring at Joe Bob.

At what was left of Joe Bob.

Farris must have heard something. Maybe a sound I made, or Talia's first scream. He froze in the midst of lifting something from Joe Bob's stomach. Some piece of something. I couldn't tell what, didn't care what.

Farris bared his teeth at us.

Then he stuffed the thing into his mouth and chewed.

Where he wasn't covered with blood, Farris's skin was gray-green and veined with black lines.

Behind me I heard the shuffling steps of the soldiers as the first of them left the road and stepped onto the bridge.

Talia turned toward me, and in her eyes I saw everything that had to be in my own eyes.

Her fingers twitched and the rifle dropped to the asphalt.

"Please," she said. Her mouth trembled into a smile. "Please."

Please.

I raised my rifle, racked the bolt, and shot her. She was never a pretty girl. Too thin, too worn by life. She had nice eyes, though, and a nice smile. The bullets took that away, and she fell back.

I heard—*felt*—someone come up behind me.

Some*thing.*

Probably Bell.

I turned. I still only had two mags. Less three bullets.

There were hundreds of them.

I raised my rifle.

Author's Note on "Clean Sweeps"

My first-ever short story was *Pegleg and Paddy Save the World*, which will be included in *The Wind Through the Fence and Other Tales*, a companion to this volume. My second story was the Sherlock Holmes tale contained herein. But *Clean Sweeps* was my third story, and it was my third genre. With short fiction you get to jump around a lot, trying new things, having fun, growing as a writer, reaching new readers, driving headlong into new territory.

The genre for this story is 'military science fiction.' Spaceships and combat. I had some wicked fun with this one.

Clean Sweeps

-1-

Cloaking devices are science fiction. Relics of old *Star Trek* shows from the last century. We don't have cloaks, we never had cloaks. And we don't have any chameleon circuits or shit retroengineered from alien craft.

What we got is stealth technology. We got LOT—Low Observability Technology. It doesn't make our birds invisible, but it pretty much makes the radar and motion scanners look in the wrong place, or misunderstand what they're seeing. We can look like a big black hole in the middle of the sky. We can look like space junk. Or, we can look like feedback and sensor static. I always liked LOT that makes us look like static because most of the stations have been out here so long that their systems are older than dinosaur shit. Most of what they see nine to five is static.

That works for me. It keeps us from getting shot out of the black before we can put boots on the deck.

We tune our LOT systems to read the static backwash from the sensor arrays of any ship or base we approach, and then the computers work out some kind of math wizard fluctuating algorithm that matches the normal radio wave crap the universe has been kicking out since the big balloon popped.

Surprise always helps, but we didn't know how much of that was on our side. We were hoping to surprise the shit out of *them*. I'm a big fan of catching the bad guys with their dicks in their hands. Makes for a better raid.

Yeah, I know what the press says. WorldNews and SolarAP both have this thing for firefights—which they insist on called 'shoot-outs'—like we're the O.K. fucking Corral. Army PR sends them maybe six to eight mission video files a month, but do the clean sweeps ever make the Net? Nope. Not a one unless it's a god damn slow news day in the middle of August, where they'll report on crop growth or dig up some old celeb for a 'where are they now?' space filler.

But somebody pulls a trigger and it's a breaking story. And these news fucks don't give a red hot flying shit if it's a bad guy, a Federal Ranger, or one of our boys in Free-Ops that either fires the shot or takes the hit. Bullets and blood, man, that's all they care about; and the bigger the body count the bigger the ratings.

We Free-Ops guys only ever get press if something goes wrong, so we've been on the news…what, maybe five times in four years? And of those, the first three were during the mine riots following the cluster-fuck with the unions. That whole thing took less than a week. Since then the only time Free-Ops made the news was back in '93 when Captain Lisa Stanley got killed while her team was running down some pirates running the alley between Phobos and Deimos. I mean, come on, Stanley was killed when a stray shot hit an O2 tank in the airlock. I saw the official reports, and the conclusion I drew from it was that she probably tripped on one of the landing sleds the pirates used when they breeched the cargo ship. She tripped and popped off a round that bounced all over the airlock until it punched into the O2 tank. It was her bad luck that it was after they'd re-pressurized. Twenty seconds earlier there'd have been no spark, and no death, and no story.

The news jackasses made her a hero across half the Network. My guess? If Stanley hadn't been a California blonde with yabos out to there the news people wouldn't have run with it as long as they did. That and they're always starved for action stories. There's only so much mileage you can get from politicians making assholes of themselves or celebrities getting caught fucking the wrong wife.

The other time was a real firefight—excuse me, 'shoot-out'— between my team and the Chinese hit team that tried to declare sovereignty over the New Tibet colony on Io. That one was a real ball-burner. My boys—Jigsaw Team—were on point, with Delta, Baker, and Zulu Teams on fast-follow and a squadron of Jackhammers giving close air support. The Chinese team was sharp, even I have to give them that. There were a lot of them, they were well armed, well-trained, and they weren't afraid of us. No sir, not one little bit.

It wasn't until we were on the ground that our forward spotters sent back the news that we were outnumbered and outgunned. Outnumbered like four to one, which can give serious pause even to a bunch of heartbreakers and life-takers like I got in Jigsaw. But by then we were in the pipe, riding the adrenaline high, breathing the helmet gas that triggered all those useful dopamine receptors. We were juiced and jazzed, and when the smoke cleared we had a whole lot of dead Chinese. And some dead Tibetans, too, but what the fuck could we do? The Chinese hid among the colonists, and they even put Tibetans in their own uniforms. We shot anyone with a red star.

Here's how the bullshit plays out, though. First the press are up our ass all the way through the raid. They're doing advance stories on the men and women of Free-Ops. You know, those schmaltzy human interest things where they show vidcaps of the soldiers as kids, riding horses on the farm or taking their first EVA at Disney Lunar. Then during the battle they're getting video-only live feeds from helmet cams. The brass didn't let them hear our team chatter during the raid.

When the battle was over they spent two days canonizing everyone from the first wave of shooters down to the cooks in the galley of the drop ship. Heroes all.

Then they find out that three colonists took fire during the raid. Suddenly we're reckless killers who can't tell a friendly face from an enemy's—and remember, we're talking Chinese and Tibetans here, and everyone dressed the same. We're fried by the press. It's a great story, it kept the news feeds buzzing for weeks.

Then, when that cooled down they have the big clanking balls to ask if they can go on every other raid. And the fucking brass—*our* fucking brass—says yes.

Tells you everything you need to know about why I think the whole Solar System is populated with nutcases.

And, yeah…they're on this run with us now. At least we don't have it as bad as the Federals who have that weekly show. FEDS. You've seen it, where they do the fly-alongs with the Federals, following the busts with handhelds and helmet cams. Mostly busting mouth-breathing bozo drug runners or low-level pirates who are too stupid to know how to dodge a full-lit Federal wagon broadcasting siren calls on all frequencies. I ask you.

We came at the Tower with the sun behind us, alternating speed and using LOT to look like feedback from old wiring to anyone who was looking. And they were looking, don't get me wrong, but this is a clever stunt and we were pretty good at it. So good that on Jigsaw's last six hard infils we'd had zero shots fired on either side. Before anyone knows we're even a reality we're breeching fore and aft airlocks and our Jackhammers are suddenly broadcasting sweetlock signals. The bad guys go from thinking they're all alone in the big black to having twenty ugly-ass special operators coming into their ship from ass and mouth and every rocket and missile in the catalog cocked and locked from point blank. That's not a time to make a stand. It's a time to trigger an isolated EMP to fry your computer records, drop your guns on the deck and stand around looking extremely cooperative.

That's what we were expecting on this run, too.

The mission was routine. The Tower was a forty year old barrel-style deep space manufacturing plant that used to make ball bearings and alloy pipes before the company went bust. After that it was empty for ten years and then got bought by some investors who filed papers saying they were going to retool it for drilling equipment to supply mines on Jupiter's moons.

Then, get this, our intel people get a hot tip from some news guy from SolarAP that the Tower is really making weapons. Nothing exotic, but enclosed gas shell rifles that you can use in any atmosphere including zero atmosphere. Only two kinds of people need guns like that. Guys like me and pirates.

It was a no brainer to order a raid. You don't let assholes mass produce guns that you know for damn sure are not going to be used for hunting or home defense. Since the news guys brought us the tip they got to ride along during the raid. It was a dream come true for them.

I didn't like it, but I'm a Sergeant. There isn't one person above my pay grade who gives a hemorrhoidic rat's ass what I like or don't like.

We planned it right, though, and even did some dry runs on the infil using a similar plant orbiting Luna. My team had the fastest in-time, so we drew the lead on the breech.

Our tactical bird is a SV-117 Bullet, one of the new frictionless electric motor boats fired torpedo fashion from the bow of the transport. We go in fast and our battery power is used mostly for steering and braking. The Bullets are all short-range, and we were launched from two thousand miles out. The entire nose-package of the Bullet has jamming gear tuned to the transport so we don't ring any bells unless they have towed metal detectors. Which this tub didn't.

What the Tower did have, though, was gravity. It was in a nice spin that suggested a 360 surface pull. Probably not earth gravity, but enough so that we could run rather than float. I hate floating in a fight.

"Twenty seconds to soft dock," our pilot called. We were all ready. Ten tough apes in EVA flexsuits, armed to the teeth and ready to kick a little gunrunner ass. We all had SolarAP cameras exterior-mounted on our helmets. We also had a ridealong in the person of Alex Tennet, a reporter for SolarAP. He used to be a big shot, but his career had been tanking for years. One of those guys who was never in the right part of the Solar System when anything interesting was happening. Bringing the tip about the gunrunners was the first big thing to happen to him in fifteen years, and he confided to me back on the transport, "You know, Sarge, if I hadn't lucked into this...I'd be burning off the rest of my career doing weather reports on Ganymede."

"Lucky you," I said. He was a news guy, so I hated him on principle, but he was okay when the cameras were off. I didn't like having to take him along on a raid, but the brass thought it would look good. A nice PR hit for us.

Like we needed good PR. Or *any* PR. We're soldiers. It's not like we're in the Navy. Nothing glamorous. Grunts with guns is what we were. But, like I said, nobody above my pay grade gives a shit what I think, and just about everyone's above my pay grade.

So Tennet got to come along. Luckily I could switch his audio feed off so I didn't have to listen to him give a blow-by-blow account of all this.

We docked without a sound, and the vibration was so soft through our ship that I knew it couldn't be felt in the Tower.

"Jigsaw in place," I reported.

"Zulu in place," came the reply. Our brother team was soft-docked at the other airlock.

"Deploy blowback skirt."

"Roger that, skirt deployed."

"On my mark," I said. "Everybody watch your fire and check your targets. Nobody dies who doesn't have to. Everybody lives, everybody comes home."

"Hooah," I heard from everyone. The old Ranger cry was always a comfort right before a battle. It came with a hell of a lot of history, and most of that history was of success.

By now the pilots of both bullets would have spinners on the airlock wheels.

I counted it down.

On zero the pilots initiated the hard-rips that spun the airlock wheels faster than any man could manage it, and the airlocks were literally torn open. The blowback skirts caught any flying debris and shot-injected oxygen into the airlocks. Then our hatches swung open and we used the elastic slings to launch ourselves from the Bullets into the airlocks. The skirts kept the docking collars pressurized, so we went straight for the inner hatches.

"It's locked," my corporal said.

"Blow it," I growled.

He already had the burst patch attached with magnets and we wrapped our frag caps around us and did the ol' duck and crouch as the patch blew apart the internal computers on the hatch. Tennet—the dumbass—tried to get a good shot of the blast, so I had to drag his ass down and under cover.

The second the locks were toast the corporal—Hastings—yanked open the door.

"Go! Go! Go!" I bellowed and then we were all running into the Tower. I led the way with Hastings on my three o'clock and Tennet on my six. He could get some nice footage of my ass if he wanted. Maybe that would help his sorry ratings.

The corridor was dark so I threw Starbursts ahead of us. The little marble-sized LEDs ignited and flooded the corridor with blue light.

In my helmet mic I could hear the same process happening for Zulu team. Man, there's nothing like military precision.

We raced through one hatch after another. Most were filled with huge machines whose nature or purpose was beyond me. Then we reached the galley, startling the cook who was in the process of sliding a big tray of pot pies into the oven.

He had time to say, "What the fuck—?" before I kicked him in the nuts and pistol whipped him to the deck. Yeah, I know, he's just a cook. But if you're working for the bad guys then you're a bad guy. At least in my view, and it kept things nice and simple.

The adjoining corridor spilled out into a huge manufacturing plant that smelled of oil and sweat. There had to be fifty guys in there. Big sonsabitches, with the arms and shoulders you only get from hauling around pigs of iron or steel in a gravity environment. No space muscles. No flab.

Then something really weird happened, and from that point on everything went to shit.

One of the guys, a Turkish-looking guy wearing a Kufi pointed a big wrench at us and shouted: "Pirates!"

It all went crazy. The Turk swung the wrench at me with incredible force. The gravity was maybe half-earth, which means a big son of a bitch like him could swing a thirty pound wrench real damn fast. I tried to duck, but the edge of the wrench caught me on the shoulder pad and knocked me ten feet into a stack of pipes.

My gun discharged as I was hit and I stitched a line of rounds across the floor. I didn't see the bullets hit, but I heard the screams.

And then the force of my body knocked the stack of pipes over and hundreds of pounds of half-inch pipes were hammering down on me. I dropped my gun and buried my head in my arms and curled my body into a ball. But even so I took a hell of a beating. Pipes whacked me in the shoulders and ribs and hips and thighs. The clang was like insanely loud. My visor cracked and I ducked inside my helmet to keep plastic splinters from blinding me.

Through it all I could hear the chatter of gunfire, yells, screams, and the unmistakable thud of heavy metal on flesh.

"Shit!" I cursed and tried to worm my way out from under. I had to get back into this fight. Suddenly two of the bars right over me were pulled back and I saw Hastings there, crouching down, pushing the bars aside. Tennet, the reporter, stood gawping behind him, his handheld camera shifting back and forth from the battle to me. He hadn't lifted a frigging hand to help Hastings dig me out.

"Sarge!" Hasting yelled. "You all right?"

"Help me up," I said. He grabbed my arm and pulled me out from under the pile, and I staggered as more of the pipes clanged and rolled down around me. There was a flash and a bang and suddenly Hastings was down, his faceplate smashed by a hard-shell flare and as I watched in total horror the flare exploded inside his suit. Our flexsuits are designed to be fireproof. It's saved our lives a hundred times...but the fire is supposed to be on the outside. The flare burst inside his suit and within a second the suit ballooned out as the fire ignited the oxygen inside and roasted Hastings alive. He screamed like I'd never heard a person scream before, and the expanding gasses ballooned his suit for a moment before he fell out of sight. There wasn't a god damn thing I could do about it.

A separate fire ignited inside of me. Pure white-hot rage!

Tennet caught the whole thing on camera and for a moment our eyes met. His face was white with shock but his eyes were alight. Adrenaline can do that. Even at the worst of times it can make you feel totally alive.

My rifle was gone, lost under all the debris, so I pulled my sidearm.

The room was a melee. The gunrunners badly outnumbered us and two of my guys were down. Dead or hurt I couldn't tell. The rest had taken up shooting positions behind pieces of machinery, and they'd littered the deck with bodies. But the numbers were bad. The gunrunners had a variety of weapons—flares, hatchets, wrenches, hand-welders. No guns, which was kind of weird. They worked in teams, two men holding up a big piece of plate steel and moving it forward like a shield while others crowded behind it, throwing stuff, popping flares over the barricades behind which my guys hid. We had the better weapons, but they sure as hell had the numbers. And I could see more men pouring into the room from the far end.

I tapped my com-link and called for Zulu Team, but the unit was dead. It was smashed along with most of my helmet.

I pushed Tennet behind me and took up a shooting posture, legs wide and braced, weapon in a two-hand grip with my arms locked in a reinforced triangle. I fired careful shots and dropped seven men with six shots, and for a moment it stalled the rush of the gunrunners. I was at a right angle to their advance, which created a nice cross-fire situation. If I conserved my ammo we might pull this out of the crapper.

Then something occurred to me and it jolted me so hard that I took my finger off the trigger.

"Christ! These aren't gunrunners," I said aloud. I turned to Tennet. "Does your comlink work?"

He lowered his camera and tapped his throat mic. "No...it's malfunctioning."

"Fuck. We have to get word to the fleet. This is a cluster-fuck. These aren't gunrunners. Look at 'em. They're machinists, factory workers. That's why they called me a pirate. They think we're the bad guys. Shit."

Tennet picked up a length of steel pipe and held it defensively, then abruptly pointed past me. "Sergeant! Behind you!"

I whirled around. There was nothing. I heard a voice behind me say, "I'm sorry."

It was Tennet, and it was an odd thing to say.

It was even odder when he slammed the pipe into my head.

-2-

I heard bones crack and felt myself fall. The taste of blood in my mouth was salty sweet. Sparks burst from the wiring in the machines and fireworks ignited in my vision. I fell in a pirouette, spinning with surreal slowness away from the point of impact. As I turned I could see the gunrunners renewing their advance on my remaining men. I could hear the chatter of gunfire from the other end of the room. Was it Zulu Team? Had they broken through? Or was it the gunrunners with Zulu's guns?

As I hit the deck I wondered why the gunrunners didn't have their own guys. It seemed strange. Almost funny. Gunrunners without guns.

And why had they called us 'pirates'?

I sprawled on the ground, trying to sort it out. Trying to think. I felt blood in the back of my nose. I tasted it in my mouth.

I wanted to cough, but I couldn't.

A shadow passed above me. Raising my eyes took incredible effort. I couldn't manage it. But the shadow moved and came around to bend over me.

Tennet.

His eyes were still wide and excited...but he was smiling. Not an adrenaline grin. I've seen those. This was different. Almost sad. A little mean. A little something else, but I couldn't put a word to it. My head hurt so much. Thinking was hard. He dropped the pipe.

He bent close. The noise around us was huge but it also seemed distant, muffled. My left eye suddenly went blind.

Tennet was speaking. But not to me. His camera was pointed past me.

"...as the shootout rages on, the brave men of Jigsaw team are clearly over-matched by the determined resistance of the gunrunners."

Firefight. That's the right word, but though my mouth moved I couldn't get the word off my tongue.

He clicked off the camera and looked down at me.

"Thanks," he said.

I shaped the words 'for what?'

"Ratings, Sergeant. This is sweeps week. This story will get me back in the big chair. I'll be an anchor again before your bodies are cold."

"The...tip-off..." I managed.

He nodded. "Good PR for everyone. Your bosses will leverage this for increased funding. The militia will get more money for security. And I get an anchor's chair. Everyone's a winner."

I was sinking into the big black. I could feel myself moving away from the moment, sliding out of who I was. "You mother...fucker..." I gasped with what little voice I had.

"Hey," he said, "you told me at least twenty times that you never get to pull a trigger, that good soldiering doesn't require heroes. That's a sad epitaph for a career Free-Ops agent." He bent even closer. "I just made you a hero, Sergeant. I just made you a *star!*"

I wanted to grab him by the neck and tear his head off. I wanted to stuff his camera down his throat. I wanted to destroy the hard drive and all its images of my men fighting and dying.

But I didn't have anything left.

So, with the gunfire like thunder around me, and the screams of good men dying on both sides, I closed my eyes. I knew that he'd turn his camera back on, that he'd film my last breaths. That he'd use my death—and the deaths of my men—to get exactly what he wanted.

But what the fuck. That's show business.

Shit.

Author's Note on "Long Way Home"

Many writers break into the fiction business by writing short stories and then make the jump to novels. I did it the opposite way. I wrote a trilogy of supernatural thrillers first and that resulted in getting invitations to write short stories. However once I got the short fiction bug I found out that it was a great way to enhance my novels by telling new stories that take place before or after the events in the books.

My first three novels were *Ghost Road Blues, Dead Man's Song,* and *Bad Moon Rising*—collectively known as the Pine Deep Trilogy. This story takes place several years after the events described in the Trilogy. You do not need to have read those books in order to read— and hopefully enjoy—this little tale set in a troubled town in rural Pennsylvania.

Long Way Home

-1-

Donny stood in the shadow of the bridge and watched the brown water. The river was swollen with muddy runoff. Broken branches and dead birds bobbed up and down—now you see 'em, now you don't—as the swift current pulled them past.

The river.

Jeez, he thought. *The river.*

He remembered it differently than this. Sure, he'd lived here in Pine Deep long enough to have seen the river in all her costumes. Wearing gray under an overcast sky, running smoothly like liquid metal. Dressed in white and pale blue when the winter ice lured skaters to try and cross before the frozen surface turned to black lace. Camouflaged in red and gold and orange when early November winds blew the October leaves into the water.

Today, though, the river was swollen like a tumor and wore a kind of brown that looked like no color at all. It was like this when Halloween was about to hit. You'd think a town that used to be built around the holiday, a town that made its nut off of candy corn and jack-o-lantern pumpkins and all that trick or treat stuff would dress up for the occasion. But no. This time of year the colors all seemed to bleed away.

The last time he had seen the river was on one of those summer days that made you think summer would last forever and the world was built for swimming, kissing pretty girls, drinking beer, and floating on rubber inner tubes. It was the day before he had to report for basic training. He'd been with Jim Dooley, he remembered that so clearly.

Jim was going into the navy 'cause it was safe. A red-haired Mick with a smile that could charm the panties off a nun, and a laugh that came up from the soles of his feet. You couldn't be around Jim and not have fun. It was impossible, probably illegal.

They'd driven twenty miles up Route 32 and parked Donny's piece-of-shit old Ford-150 by Bleeker's Dock. The two of them and those college girls. Cindy something and Judy something.

Cindy had the face, but Judy had the body.

Not that either of them looked like bridge trolls, even without makeup, even waking up in Jim's brother's Boy Scout tent in the woods at the top of Dark Hollow. They were both so healthy. You could stand next to them and your complexion would clear up. That kind of healthy.

And with Jim around they laughed all the time.

Nothing like pretty girls laughing on a sunny day, as the four of them pushed off from the dock and into the Delaware. Way up here, above the factories down south, way above the smutch of Philadelphia, the water was clean. It was nice.

On that day, the water had been slower and bluer. It hadn't been a dry summer, but dry enough so that in shallow spots you could see the river stones under the rippling water. Judy swore she saw a starfish down there, but that was stupid. No such thing as freshwater starfish. Or, at least Donny didn't think so.

Didn't matter anyway. That was the last time Donny saw Judy. Or Cindy or even Jim for that matter. The girls went back to college. Jim went into the navy.

Donny went into the army.

It all seemed like a long time ago.

Way too fucking long.

It was no longer summer. October was burning off its last hours. Even if the river looked like sewer water at least the trees were wearing their Halloween colors.

Donny stood by the bridge and watched the brown river sweep the broken, dead things away. There was some message there, he thought. There was at least a Springsteen song there. Something about how nothing lasts.

But Donny was no more a songwriter than he was a philosopher.

He was a man who had spent too long coming home.

Donny climbed up from the bank and stepped onto the creosote-soaked planks of the bridge. It was a new bridge. The old one had been destroyed in the Trouble.

He'd missed that, too.

He'd read about it, though. Probably everybody read about it. That shit was how most people first heard of Pine Deep. Biggest news story in the world for a while. Bunch of militia nutjobs dumped all sorts of drugs into the town's water supply. LSD, psychotropics, all sorts of stuff. Nearly everybody in town went totally ape shit. Lots of violence, a body count that dwarfed the combined death tolls of Afghanistan and Iraq. Eleven thousand six hundred and forty-one people dead.

So many of the people that Donny knew.

His folks.

His cousin Sherry and her kids.

And Jim.

Jim had come home on leave from the navy. He hadn't taken a scratch in boot camp, had been posted to an aircraft carrier, was halfway through his tour and filling his letters with jokes about how the worst thing that happens to him is the clap from getting laid in every port in the Pacific.

Jim had been stabbed through the chest by a drugged-out corn farmer who claimed—swore under oath—that he was killing vampires.

How fucked up was that?

The massacre in Pine Deep changed the world. Like 9/11 did. Made the great big American paranoia machine shift its stare from everyone else in the world to its own backyard. Domestic terrorism. No one was safe, not even at home. Pine Deep proved that.

Eleven thousand people dead.

It had happened ten years ago. To the day. The militia goons had used the big Pine Deep Halloween Festival as its ground zero. Thousands of tourists in town. Celebrities. Everyone for miles around.

If the militia assholes ever had a point, it died with them. The press called them "white supremacists," but that didn't make sense. Most of the people in Pine Deep were white. WASPs, with some Catholics and a handful of Jews. Except for a few families and some of the tourists, there wasn't enough of a black or Latino or Jewish or Muslim presence to make a hate war point. It never made sense to Donny. The people in town were just caught up in the slaughter. Either they wound up taking the same drugs, or the red wave of insanity just washed over them.

Donny had been in Iraq, midway through his second tour.

He'd been over there, killing people, trying not to die from insurgent bullets or IEDs, fighting to protect the people at home. But the people at home died anyway.

Donny never did figure out how to react to it, and standing here now on this new bridge didn't make it any clearer. The death of so many at home, neighbor killing neighbor, felt like a sin. It felt like suicide. Even though he knew that with all those drugs in the water no one could ever be held responsible for what they did. Except those militia dickheads, and Donny wished there was at least one of them alive that he could hunt down and fuck up.

"Damn it, Jim," he said to the air.

He stared across the bridge to the thick stands of oaks and maples and birch trees. From here, in the sun's fading light, it was hard to tell if the trees were on fire or if it was just the red blaze of dying leaves.

Donny adjusted the straps of his backpack and stretched out one foot. Somehow taking this step would be like crossing a line.

But between what and what, Donny had no idea.

He was no philosopher.

He was a soldier coming home.

-2-

It seemed to take forever to walk across the bridge. Donny felt as if his feet were okay with the task but his heart was throwing out an anchor.

He paused halfway across and looked back.

Behind him was a million miles of bad road that led from here all the way back to Afghanistan and Iraq. He was amazed he'd made it this far home. Donny always figured he'd die on a cot in some dinky aide station in the ass-end of nowhere, way the hell out on the Big Sand. God knows the world had tried to kill him enough times. He touched the row of healed-over scars that were stitched diagonally from left hip to right shoulder. Five rounds.

Should have died in the battle.

Should have died in the evac helicopter.

Should have died in the field hospital.

Lost enough blood to swim home.

The dead flesh of the scars was numb, but the muscle and bone beneath it remembered the pain.

And beneath that suffering flesh?

A heart that had ached to come back home, when there was a home to come back to. Now that heart beat a warning tattoo as if to say, *this is not your home anymore, soldier.*

This isn't home.

All the way here, with every mile, every step, he wondered why, after all these years away, he was coming back here at all.

He closed his eyes and felt the river wind blow damp across his cheeks.

The house he grew up in wasn't even his anymore. Attorneys and real estate agents had sold it for him. His parents' stuff, his sister's stuff, and everything he'd left behind when he joined the army had either gone to the Salvation Army or into storage.

Donny realized he didn't know where the key was for that. A lawyer had sent it to him, but...

He gave himself a rough pat-down, but he didn't have any keys at all.

No keys, no change in his pockets, not even a penknife to pry open the storage bin lock.

Shit.

He turned and looked back as if he could see where he'd left all of that stuff. Did someone clip him on the bus? Was it on the nightstand of that fleabag motel he'd slept in?

How much was gone?

He patted his left rear pocket and felt the familiar lump of his wallet, tugged on the chain to pull it out. He opened it, and stared at the contents.

Stared for a long time.

Donny felt something on his cheeks and his fingers came away wet.

"Why the fuck are you crying, asshole?" he demanded.

He didn't know how to answer his own question.

Slow seconds fell like leaves around him.

A car came rumbling across the bridge, driving fast, rattling the timbers. Crappy old Jeep Grand Cherokee that looked so much like the one Jim used to drive that it tore a sob from his chest. Sunlight blazed off the windshield so he couldn't see the driver. Just as well. Maybe it meant the driver couldn't see a grown man standing on the fucking bridge crying his eyes out.

"You pussy," he told himself.

The car faded into the sun glare on the other side but Donny could hear the tires crunching on gravel for a long time.

Donny sniffed back the tears, shoved his wallet back into his pocket, took a steadying breath, and then raised his head, resolved to get this shit done.

He crossed the bridge, paused only a moment at the end of the span, and stepped onto the road.

In Pine Deep.

Home.

-3-

Donny walked along Route A32.

Unless he could thumb a ride it was going to take hours to get into town. There were miles and miles of farm country between here and a cold beer. So far, though, no cars. Not a one.

As he passed each farm he thought about the families who lived there. Or...used to live there. Donny had no idea who was still here, who'd moved out after the Trouble, or who hadn't made it through the war zone the militant assholes had created. He'd gotten some news, of course. The Tyler family was gone. All of them. And the Bradys.

The farm to his right, though, was the old Guthrie place. One of the biggest farms in town, one of the oldest families. Old man Guthrie had died before the Trouble. Or, maybe at the start of it, depending on which account he'd read. Guthrie had been gunned down by some gun thugs up from Philly. Donny couldn't remember if the thugs were hiding out in Pine Deep, or they broke down there, or whether they were part of the white supremacist nut-bags. Either way, one of them popped a cap in Mr. Guthrie, and that was a shame 'cause the old guy was pretty cool. Always ready to hire some town kids to pick apples and pumpkins, and pay them pretty good wages. Always smiling, he was. Deserved better than what he got.

Beyond the rail fence the late season corn was high and green, the thick stalks heavy with unpicked ears. Two crows sat on the top bar, cawing for their buddies to join them, but the rest of the birds were way up in the air, circling, circling.

What was it they called a bunch of crows, he wondered? He had to think back to Mrs. Gillespie in the third grade. A pod of whales, a parliament of owls, and a...

A murder of crows.

Yeah, that was it. So, what was it when there were only two crows? Attempted murder?

Donny laughed aloud at his own joke and wished Jim was here. Jim usually came up with clever shit like that. Jim would have liked that joke, would have appreciated it. Would have patted him on the back, fist-bumped him, and then stolen the joke for his own repertoire. Which was okay. Jokes are free and everyone should take as many as they could, that's how Donny saw it.

Smiling, Donny walked along the rail fence. Up ahead he saw an old guy on a ladder wiring a scarecrow to a post. The scarecrow was dressed in jeans and a fatigue jacket, work gloves for hands, and a pillowcase for a head. Straw and shredded rag dripped from the sleeves and pants cuffs. Shoes were mismatched, a Converse high-top sneaker and a dress shoe with no laces. Donny slowed to watch the man work. The man and the scarecrow were almost silhouetted by the sun. The image would have looked great on a Halloween calendar. A perfect snapshot of harvest time in the American farm country.

He liked it, and smiled.

"Looks great," he said when he was close enough.

The old guy only half-turned. All Donny could see was grizzled white hair and wind-burned skin above pale eyes. He nodded at Donny's fatigue jacket.

"Afghanistan?"

"Yes, sir," answered Donny.

"You left the war," said the old man.

"No, sir...I reckon the war left me. It's over. They're cycling most of us home."

The old man studied him for a few long seconds. "You really think the war's over?"

Donny didn't want to get into a political debate with some old fool.

"I guess that's not for me to decide. They sent me home."

"Did they?" The man shook his head in clear disapproval and said, "The war's not over. No sirree-bob, it's not over by a long stretch."

Donny didn't know how to respond to that, so he began edging further up the road.

"Son," said the old man, "some folks join the army to fight and some join to serve. What did you join for?"

"To protect my home and my family, sir." It sounded like a bullshit platitude, even as he said it, but in truth it really was why Donny enlisted. Ever since 9/11, he was afraid of what might happen here at home, on American soil. Donny knew that he wasn't particularly smart and he was far from being politically astute, but he knew that he wanted to do whatever he could to protect those who couldn't protect themselves. In school, it had been Jim at his back, who kicked the asses of bigger kids picking on the geeks and dweebs. Donny hated a bully. As far as he saw it, terrorists were just bullies of a different wattage.

"Gonna be dark soon," said the old guy, apropos of nothing.

Donny glanced at the angle of the sun.

"Yeah. In a while, I s'pose."

"We all got to do what we can."

With those words, the old man nodded to himself then turned back to his work. After half a minute Donny realized that there was nowhere to go with that conversation.

Gonna be dark soon.

Yeah, well, sure. Happens a lot around nighttime.

Crazy old fuck.

Donny walked on.

When he was just at the end of the Guthrie fence he heard a sound and turned to see a man riding a small tractor. Far, far away, though. Way on the other side of a harvested field. The tractor looked like one of those really old kind, the ones that looked a little like a 1950s hotrod. It chugged along, puffing smoke but not really making much noise. At least not much of it reached Donny. Only an echo of an echo.

He cupped his hands around his eyes to try and see who was riding it. But all he could see was a man in coveralls with hair that could have been white or blond.

Even so, Donny lifted his hand and waved.

The man on the tractor waved back.

Maybe another old guy, but not an old fuck.

It was a simple conversation between strangers a mile apart. Donny wondered if it was a stranger, though. Might have been another of the Guthries. Or it might have been someone working for them. Or, hell, maybe it was whoever bought the farm if the surviving Guthries sold it after the Trouble. Didn't much matter. It was just nice to see someone.

Anyone.

The Guthrie farm ended at Dark Hollow Road, and Donny lingered at the crossroads for a moment, staring down the twisted side road. Not that he could see much, certainly not all the way to the Passion Pit where everyone went to get high or get laid, but it was down there. That's where he and Donny went with those two girls. Last place he went in town before he climbed onto a bus to go learn how to be a soldier.

That last good night and day. All those laughs, the snuggling, cuddling sex in the tent with Judy, while Jim and Cindy screwed each other's brains out in a sleeping bag by their campfire. A great night.

But then he thought about Judy. She hadn't written to him, not once in all the time he was away. He never heard from her after that night.

That was strange. It felt bad. For a long time it made him wonder if he was lousy in the sack, but over time he realized that probably wasn't it. Judy had gone to college and that was a different world than a war half a world away. Maybe the sex and the pot they'd smoked was some kind of close-one-door-open-another thing. Like he and Jim were doing with their last blast weekend before going to war.

Maybe.

He'd written to her, though.

Four letters with no replies before he got the idea that she wasn't ever going to write back.

In some way he supposed she was as dead to him as his folks and town. And Jim.

"Jesus, you're a gloomy fuck, too," he told himself. He turned away from Dark Hollow Road and the dead memories, disgusted with himself for thoughts like that.

On the road, the traffic was still a no-show, so he drifted into the center of the two-lane, liking the sound his heels made on the blacktop. A soft but solid *tok-tok-tok*. The echo of it bounced off the walls of trees that divided one farm from another.

At the top of a hill he looked down a long sweep and the beauty of his town nearly pulled more tears from him. The farms were not the geometrically perfect squares of some of the agricultural areas he'd seen. Some were angled this way, others turned that, with hedgerows and fences and rows of oaks to create borders. Cornfields swayed gently like waves on a slow ocean. Pumpkins dotted green fields with dots of orange. Autumn wheat blew like marsh grass in the soft breeze.

High above, a crow cried out with a call that was so plaintive, so desperately sad that the smile bled away from Donny's features. With the distortion of distance and wind, it sounded like the scream of a baby. Or the banshee wail of a woman kneeling over the body of a dead child.

Donny had seen that image, heard that sound too many times. In Iraq, in Afghanistan.

He touched his shirt over the scars, remembering pain. Remembering all the dying that went on over there.

But it went on here, too.

While he was gone, his town died, too.

Except for the one car that crossed the bridge, there hadn't been a single vehicle on the road. A tractor in a field hardly counted. And only two old sonsabitches at the Guthrie place. All of the other fields and the whole length of Route A32 were empty. It was Halloween. The road should have been packed with cars. Jeez...had the Trouble totally killed the town's tourism economy? That would seriously blow. Just about every family in town had their income either tied to farming stuff like Indian corn and pumpkins or to attractions like the Haunted Hayride, the Haunted House, the Dead-end Drive-in, and other seasonal things. Had the Halloween Festival been revived? Could he have been wrong about the town starting to come back from the Trouble?

It was weird.

Donny felt suddenly scared. Where *was* everyone else?

Had the town died for real?

Had he come home—come all these miles—to a ghost town?

High above the far row of mountains he saw a white cloud float between him and the sun. Its vast purple shadow covered most of the horizon line and as it sailed across the sky toward him, it dragged its dark shadow below, sweeping the land, brushing away details with a broom of darkness.

The belly of the cloud thickened, turned bruised and was suddenly veined with red lightning.

A storm was coming.

He hadn't noticed it building, but at the rate it was growing it was going to catch him out here on the road.

He suddenly wondered if that's what the old guy on the ladder was trying to say.

Gonna be dark soon.

He looked over his shoulder at the road he'd walked. It was a black ribbon fading out of sight as the shadows covered it. Up ahead was eight miles of hills between him and a bar or a Motel 6. He chewed his lip as he debated his options. The breeze was stiffening and it was wet. It was going to rain hard and cold. And soon.

Maybe he could go back and ask one of the guys at the Guthrie place for a ride into town. Or a dry spot on a porch to wait it all out.

He could have done that.

Didn't.

Instead he let his gaze drift over to the thick wall of oaks and pines beyond the closest field. He could haul ass over there and stay dry under the thick canopy of leaves. Yeah, sure, you weren't supposed to stand under trees in a lightning storm, but you weren't supposed to stand out in a cold rain and catch pneumonia either.

Thunder snarled at him to make up his mind. The first big raindrops splatted on the blacktop.

He cut and ran for the trees.

-4-

As he ran he thought he saw the car again. The Jeep Grand Cherokee that looked like Jim's. It bumped along the rutted length of Dark Hollow Road, a dozen yards to his right, beyond the shrubs and wind-bent pines.

The car was heading the same way he was. Going away from the main road, following an unpaved lane that only went to one spot. The Passion Pit that had long ago been carved out of the woods by generations of hot-blooded teenagers so they could try and solve the mysteries that burned under their skin. Donny had lost his cherry there. So did most of the guys and girls he grew up with. Getting popped at the Pit was a thing, one of those rite of passage things. It was cool. It was part of being from this town. It was what people did.

That car, though, why was it heading here right now? Wrong time of day for anything but a quickie. Wrong weather for anything at all. No tree cover over the Pit. Rain would sound like forty monkeys with hammers on the roof of an SUV like that.

The car kept on the road, going slow like it was keeping pace with him.

Eventually it would reach the Passion Pit, and so would he.

How would that play out?

If it was a couple looking for privacy, they weren't going to be happy to see him. But, Donny thought, if it was someone who took a wrong turn in a heavy rain, then maybe he could leverage a ride in exchange for directions.

Worth a shot.

But the car pulled out ahead of him, bouncing and flouncing over the ruts, splashing mud high enough to paint its own windows brown. Donny watched it go.

"Nowhere to go, brother," he told the unseen driver.

Donny angled toward the road, thinking that if the car was going to turn around at the Pit then he wanted to be where he'd be seen.

He jogged through the woods, staying under the thickest part of the leafy canopy, sometimes having to feel his way through rain-black shadows.

When he got to the edge of the clearing he jerked to a stop.

The car was there.

Except that it wasn't.

It was the wrong car.

Same make, same model. Same color. The muddy tire tracks curved off the road and ended right there. Those ruts were only just now filling with rainwater.

But it had to be the wrong car.

Had to be.

"What the fuck...?" Donny said aloud.

The car sat there at the edge of the Pit.

Maybe not "sat." Hunched. Lay. Something like that. Donny stared at it with a face as slack as if he'd been slapped silly.

The car was old. Rusted.

Dead.

The tires were nothing but rags, the rims flecked with red rust. There were dents and deep gouges in the faded paintwork. Spider-web cracks clouded the windshield. The side windows were busted out; leaving only jagged teeth in black mouths. Creeper vines snaked along the length of the SUV and coiled around the bars of the roof rack.

The car was dead.

Dead.

Cold and rusted and motherfucking dead.

He didn't know what to do. He didn't know how to think about something like this. His mind kept lunging at shreds of plausibility and reason, but they were too thin and slippery to grab. This made no sense.

No goddamn sense.

He stood just inside the wall of the forest. It was thinner here and rain popped down on him. Hitting his shoulders and chest and forehead like a big wet finger jabbing him every time he tried to concoct an explanation for it.

He turned and looked at the curving tire tracks. No chance at all that they belonged to any other car than this. He looked at the car. No way it had driven past him. He looked at the road. There was nowhere else to go. The Pit was the only destination on that road. The Pit was the only place wide enough to turn around and go back, and besides, Donny had been close enough to the road to have definitely seen something go past him.

It made no sense.

No sense.

No sense.

Donny didn't realize that he was crying until the tears curled past his lips and he tasted salt.

"Oh, man," he said as he sagged down into a squat, buttocks on heels, palms over his face, shoulders twitching with tears that wanted to break like a tide from his chest. His voice sounded thin, like it was made out of cracked glass. "Oh shit, oh shit, oh shit."

"Yeah," said a voice behind him. "It's all total shit."

Donny almost jumped out of his skin. He whirled, rose to his feet, fists balled, heart hammering, ready to yell or fight or run.

Instead he froze right there, half up, bent over, mouth open, heart nearly jerking to a halt in his chest.

A figure stood fifteen feet away. He'd managed to come this close without making a sound. Tall, thin, dressed in a Pine Deep Scarecrows football shirt. The shirt was torn, with ragged cloth drooping down to expose pale skin beneath; the material darkened as if by oil or chocolate, or...

Donny felt his own mouth fall open.

The world seemed to fall over sideways.

The figure had a big shit-eating grin on his face.

"Hey, Donny," said Jim.

-5-

"What the fuck?"

It was all Donny said, and he said it five or six times.

Jim laughed.

"No," growled Donny, "I mean what the fuck?"

"Guess you're the fuck," said Jim. "Christ on a stick, you should see the look on your face."

"You can't," began Donny. "I mean...you just can't. You can't..."

"Yeah," agreed Jim. "But I guess I can."

"No."

"So can you."

"Can what, man?" screamed Donny. "This is crazy. This is totally fucked."

Jim spread his hands in a "what can I say" gesture.

Donny pointed an accusing finger at him. "You died, you stupid shit. You *died!*"

A shadow seemed to pass over Jim's face and his smile faded a bit. Not completely, but enough.

Enough to let Donny know that Jim didn't really find this funny.

Somehow, in a way Donny couldn't quite identify, that realization was worse.

Tears burned on Donny's face. It felt like acid on his skin.

Jim stepped closer, and with each step his smile faded a little more. He stopped a few feet away, the smile gone now. Donny saw that Jim's face was streaked with mud. His skin gleamed as white as milk through the grime.

"You died," Donny said again, his voice less strident but no less hurt.

"Yeah," said Jim, "I did. Kind of blew, too."

Donny said, "What...?"

"The whole death thing? Blows elephant dick."

"What are you...?"

"For one thing, it hurt like a bitch." Tommy touched his throat. "Nothing ever hurt that much before. Not even when I busted my leg when I fell off the ropes in gym class and the bone was sticking out. Jeez, remember that? You almost hurled chunks."

Donny said nothing. He wasn't sure he could.

"They had to carry me out of school. I was crying and shit 'cause it hurt so bad."

"That was when we were kids," said Donny weakly. "Fourth grade."

"Yeah," agreed Donny. "Long time ago. Lot of ships have sailed since then, huh?"

Donny just looked at him.

"But the day I died? Man...that was something else. The pain was red hot. I mean red fucking hot. And all the time it was happening I kept trying to scream." His voice was thin, almost hollow, and Jim's eyes drifted away to look at something only he could see. Memories flashing on the inside walls of his mind. It was something Donny understood, even if he could understand nothing else that was happening.

"Help me out here, Jim," said Donny slowly. "You remember...dying?"

"Sure."

"How?"

Jim gave him a half-smile. "I was there, dude. I was paying attention to that shit."

"No, assface, how do you remember dying? How can you remember dying? I mean, how's that even possible?"

Jim shrugged. "I just remember. The pain in my throat. How hard it was to try and breathe. The air in my lungs feeling like it was catching fire. Shit, there's no part of that I'll ever forget." He glanced at Donny and then away again. More furtive this time. "I remember how scared I was. I pissed my pants. Imagine that, man. Me dying and pissing my pants and even with all that pain I think I felt worse 'cause I gave myself a golden shower. Isn't that fucked up? I mean, how pathetic is that? I'm dying, some motherhumper is tearing my throat out with his teeth, and I'm worried about what people will think when they find out I juiced my shorts."

Donny looked at Jim. At his neck.

"That's not how you died," he said.

"What?" asked Jim.

"That's not how you died. That's not what happened."

"Yeah," said Jim, "it is."

"The hell it is. I read about it in the papers, saw it on the Net. Heard about it from people in town who lived through that shit, the Trouble. Some drugged-out farmer stabbed you in the chest."

Donny jabbed Jim in the chest with a finger, right over the place where his friend's shirt was torn. He jabbed hard. Twice.

"Right there, man. They said you got stabbed with a big piece of wood right there."

Jim stepped back out of poking distance. There was a look on his face that Donny couldn't quite read. Annoyance? Anger? And what else? Shame?

"Oh," said Jim. "Yeah, well, there was that."

"That's how you—"

"No," Donny said, cutting him off. "It's not how I died."

"But..."

"When that happened," continued Donny, "I was already dead."

-6-

Donny said, "What?"

Jim touched the spot on his chest where he'd been poked. He tried to push the torn material back into place to cover it, but the shirt was too ragged.

"Um," he said, and strung that word out for as long as he could.

"What the hell are you trying to say?" demanded Donny. "You got to start making sense out of this shit."

"Sense? Damn, man, you don't ask for much." Jim shook his head. "I was killed, man, but not by that ass pirate with the stake."

"'Stake,'" said Donny, tasting the word and not liking it one bit.

"It's all part of the way they look at us. They think that stakes and all that shit really works."

"W-what?"

"Stakes. It's just bullshit man."

"What are you talking about? C'mon man, don't do this to me," pleaded Donny.

"Dude," said Jim sadly, "it's already done. I died when I got bit. I was already dead when I got staked."

"Already dead...?"

Jim nodded.

Donny stared at him, his mouth forming words, trying to shape sounds out of broken echoes of what Jim had just said.

"You got...*bit*?"

"Bit, yeah."

"By...what?"

"The fuck do you think bit me? The tooth fairy?"

"But are you trying to say that you were killed by a...a...?"

"Go on, man, nut-up and say it. Put it the hell out there."

Donny licked his lips and tried it, forced the word out of his gut, up through his lungs, and out into the world. As he struggled to say it, Jim said it with him.

"A vampire."

"Yeah," said Jim, "I got bit by a goddamn vampire. How totally fucked up is that?"

They stood there staring at each other as the heavens wept and the trees shivered.

"Before you totally lose it," said Jim, "just think about it. All those stories about the Trouble? All that wild shit everyone was saying about how when everyone got stoned from the drugs the militiamen put in the water they started seeing werewolves and ghosts and vampires. You read about that, right?"

Donny said nothing.

"Well, there really wasn't any white militia...not like the papers said. There was a jackass who was a racist prick, but he was working for someone."

"Who?" asked Donny in a ragged voice.

Jim shrugged. "Doesn't matter. A big bad mothergrabber from Europe somewhere."

"A vampire?"

"Oh yeah. He started killing people, turning 'em into vampires and shit. Then there was a big-ass fight and people started killing each other, killing the vampires, vampires killing civilians. It was totally fucked up."

"And...you?"

"Oh, they got me like ten days before the shit hit the fan. I was home on leave and I was on the way over to Jessie Clover's place. You remember her from school? Brunette with the ass? I started banging her the day I got home and I was tapping that every night. I was on my way to her place for some pussy when someone grabbed me and dragged me over a hedge."

"A vampire?" asked Donny.

"Shit yeah it was a vampire, but here's the nut-twister...the vampire was that kid, Brandon Strauss. You know him, fourteen or fifteen, something like that. Hung out with Mike Sweeney all the time."

Donny nodded numbly.

"Kid's half my size, but he's got all these vampire super powers and shit," said Jim. "I tried to beat the shit out of him, and I got some good shots in, too, but...like I said, he's got that strength and speed. That part of the vampire legend is true. Speed, strength. Hard to hurt. Hard to kill. And...always hungry."

Donny took an immediate step backward.

"Hey," said Jim, "no, man...don't be like that. You're my road dog. I'm not going to hurt you."

"You're a fucking vampire, man," said Donny.

"Yeah, well, that part sucks."

They stood there, cold and awkward as the rain fell. Donny pointed to his friend's chest.

"You did get stabbed though, right?"

"Yeah, and that hurt, too. Hurt like a bastard. That's the thing...even being, um, like dead and all? We still feel pain. And that hurt. Not as much as Brandon killing me, but it was bad."

"What happened?"

Jim's eyes darted away again. "He was alive," he said. "Even though he was looped on drugs from the water, he was alive. I was hurt...and I was hungry."

"Oh, shit..."

"Yeah," said Jim. "It kind of blows. I mean...it's evil and all that, but for some reason I don't really seem to give much of a shit about that. It's nasty. It's messy, and even though I have to kill, I really can't stand the fucking screaming. Oh, man, you think it's bad when you're like at a concert and everyone's yelling? For me, it's like that but like ten times worse. All that heightened sense of hearing crap...it sounds good, it sounds like superhero shit, but then when you actually hear a full-throat, balls-to-the-wall death scream, you go about half deaf. Your head wants to explode and the pain drives you bat shit."

He stopped as if considering the kind of picture his words were painting.

He sighed.

"Long story short, man," he half-mumbled, "I only died that one time. And if I'm careful and smart and follow the rules, I won't ever die again."

Donny echoed those last four words. "Won't ever die again."

"Yeah."

"But you're killing other people?"

Donny looked momentarily surprised. "Oh, the vampire thing. No, man, that's yesterday's news. I don't hunt like that."

"What do you mean?"

"What I said. I haven't made that kind of kill in years, man. Not since right after the Trouble."

Donny narrowed his eyes. "You expect me to believe that?"

"Shit, man, you can believe what you want. But it's true. I can live off of animals. There's a whole state forest right here. As long as I feed every couple of weeks, I'm good to go. The taste blows, but I figure it's kind of like being a vegan. It may not taste good but it's better for my health."

"Why? What made you stop?"

"The Big Bad got killed. That night when the town burned, somebody must have killed the vampire that started all this."

"Who?"

"Shit if I know. I wasn't there when it happened. I was, um...doing other stuff."

"Killing people?"

Jim looked away once more. "You don't understand how hard it is. The hunger? It screams in your head. Especially back then, especially when the Big Bad was alive. It was like he juiced us all, amped us up. You couldn't fight it. And when he died? Christ, it was like a part of me died, too. I wanted to die. Really, man, I wanted to kill myself."

"But you can't die."

Jim snorted. "Everything can die."

"But you said that you couldn't die."

"No, I said that if I was careful I wouldn't die. Not the same thing."

Donny frowned. "You can die?"

"Sure. That night, when we had the Trouble? Couple of hundred of us died."

"There were that many?"

"Yeah. Would have been thousands if the Big Bad had his way. But we almost all died that night."

"Almost all? There's more like you?"

Jim didn't answer that, but that was answer enough.

"This is bullshit," grumbled Donny. Then he corrected himself. "This is nuts."

"It's the world, man. Bigger, weirder, badder than we ever thought. And lately it's started to get worse. There's more...of them, of people like me."

"Vampires," Donny supplied.

Jim flinched. "Yeah. More vampires and maybe something coming—something like the Big Bad we had—coming back. People...or something...are starting to hunt. Not animals, like we been doing...but humans."

"What do you mean something's coming? What's coming?"

Jim said, "Bad times are coming, Donny. Bad times are here. It's getting dark and there's something coming. I...can feel it. I can feel the pull. It's Halloween, man. Stuff...happens on Halloween. Halloween kicks open a door. You're from here, you know that. Something's going to take a bite out of town."

"No," said Donny, dismissing all of this as if it was unreal.

His gaze drifted over to the rusted out car. Jim followed his line of gaze.

"Is that yours?" asked Donny.

"Yeah. I miss that old heap. We had some fun with that."

"It's a wreck."

"Well, yeah. Been like that for years."

"But I saw you driving it."

Jim frowned.

"No, man."

"I did. On the bridge and then ten minutes ago."

"Really," said Jim, "that car's deader than me. It's *dead* dead, you know?"

"No, I don't know," snapped Donny. "None of this makes sense. I finally manage to get home, and you want me to just accept all this shit?"

Jim shrugged.

"It's bullshit," snarled Donny suddenly. "This? All of this? It's bullshit."

"It is what it is."

Donny stepped forward and suddenly shoved Jim. "Don't give me that crap, Jim. We went to fucking war, man. We enlisted to fight for this, to protect all of this." He waved his arms as if to indicate the whole of Pine Deep and everyone in it. "And while we're out there fighting real bad guys—terrorists, the Taliban, Al-Qaeda and shit—you're trying to tell me that vampires came in and killed everyone I know? You want me to believe that?"

Jim spread his hands again.

Donny shoved him again. "No! I fought every day to get back home. I bled to get back home. Do you have any idea how many firefights I've been in? How many times I was nearly killed? How many times I got hurt? Do you have any idea what kind of hell I went through?"

"I know, man."

"No you don't. You went into the navy, Jim. You played it safe. But I went to fucking war. Real war. I fought to protect....to protect..."

Fresh tears ran down his face. They felt as cold as the rain.

Colder.

"And it's all for shit. There are more like you out there. They're going to keep feeding on my town. They're going to make a punk out of me because they'll just take away everything I fought for."

Jim looked at him, and there was a deep sadness in his eyes. "Donny...believe me, man, I do know what you went through. I know all about it. Everything."

"Oh yeah? And how the hell are you supposed to know that shit? You get psychic powers, too?"

"No, man...I read it."

Donny blinked. "Read it?"

"Yeah."

"Read it where?"

A single tear broke from Jim's right eye. It carved a path through the grime on his face. "I may sleep under the dirt, dude, but I do read the papers. I read all about you."

"What are you...?"

"They did a whole big story on you. Donny Castleberry, Pine Deep's war hero." Jim shook his head. "Donny...I read your obituary, man."

Donny said nothing.

"They had the whole story. You saving a couple of guys. Getting shot. They played it up big, too. Said that you killed four Taliban including the one who shot you. You went down swinging, boy. You never gave up the fight."

Donny said nothing. What could he say? How could he possibly respond to statements as ridiculous as these? As absurd?

The ground seemed to tilt under him. The hammering of the rain took on a surreal cadence. None of the colors of the forest made sense to him.

He touched his chest, and slowly trailed his fingers slantwise across his body, pausing at each dead place where a bullet had hit him.

He wanted to laugh at Jim. To spit in his face and throw his stupid words back at him. He wanted to kick Jim, to knock him down and stomp him for being such a liar. He wanted to scream at him. To make him take back those words.

He wanted to.

He wanted.

He...

He fought to remember the process of recovering in the hospital in Afghanistan, but he couldn't remember a single thing about it. Not the hospital, not a single face of a nurse or doctor, not the post-surgical therapy. Nothing. He remembered the bullets. But it seemed so long ago. He felt as if there should be weeks of memories. Months, maybe years of memories. His discharge, his flight back to the States. But as hard as he tried, all he could grab was shadows.

After all, he couldn't remember how he came to the bridge that crossed the river to Pine Deep. None of it was in his head.

None of it was....

Even there?

"God..." he breathed. If, in fact, he breathed at all.

"I'm sorry," said Jim. "I'm so sorry."

Off away in the woods there was a long, protracted shriek. It was female. Cold and high and completely inhuman.

It's getting dark.

"What is that?" he asked.

Jim shook his head. "I don't know. Not really. Whatever it is, it's not right, you know?"

Donny said nothing.

"When it screams like that, it means that it's starting to hunt."

"It's a vampire, though," said Donny hoarsely.

"Yeah," said Jim. "I think so. Some...kind of vampire. Something I haven't seen before. Something bad."

Donny turned and looked toward the road. "And it wants to kill Pine Deep."

"It doesn't care about the town. It just wants the people."

"No," said Donny. He wiped at the tears in his face. The wetness was cold on the back of his hand. As cold as ice. "I didn't fight and..."

He couldn't bring himself to say the rest.

Fight and die.

"I didn't come home...come *back*... just to see terrorists destroy my town."

"Terrorists?" Jim almost laughed. "They're not terrorists, man, they're..."

But his words trailed off, and it was clear from his expression that he was reevaluating the word "terrorists."

"Donny?" he asked.

"Yeah?"

"I don't have any inside track on this shit," Jim began, "but I wonder if that's *why* you're back."

Donny said nothing.

"What if the town needed you and you were...I don't know....*available?*"

Donny said nothing, but inside his head something went *click*.

"You said that you can die," he murmured.

"Yeah."

"Can you tell me...how?"

Jim only paused for a single second. "Yeah," he said.

The scream tore the air again. Deep in the woods, hidden by the rain. But coming closer, angling through the darkened forest and the pounding storm, toward Pine Deep.

"Maybe you're right," said Donny. And as he said those words he felt a smile force its way onto his mouth. He couldn't see it, but he knew that it wouldn't be a nice smile. Not pleasant, not comforting.

He turned to Jim.

"All bullshit aside, Jim, we both signed up to serve. To protect our homes and our folks and our town, right?"

Jim nodded.

"So...let's serve. Let's be soldiers," said Donny. "You tell me how to kill them, and I'll bring the fight right to them. Right fucking to them."

"Are you serious?" asked Jim.

A third scream slashed at the air.

Donny touched the dead places on his chest.

"Yeah," he said, and he could feel a small, cold smile form on his mouth. "Dead serious."

Jim looked at him and his eyes filled with fresh tears. Not of pain, nor of fear. There was love there. And joy. And something else, some indefinable quality that Donny could not label.

"Okay," said Jim. "Dead serious."

The scream came again, louder and closer than before.

Donny stared in the direction of the approaching monster.

And he smiled.

A soldier's smile.

Author's Note on "Mister Pockets"

This is the second of four Pine Deep stories in this collection, and like *Long Way Home*, takes place after the events in the Trilogy.

It's also a dual homage to two great writers I've had the good fortune to meet and get to know. The first is Ray Bradbury, who—along with Richard Matheson—was a mentor of mine when I was a young teen. The other is Stephen King, who I met at the Edgar Awards the year he was named Grand Master. Ray and Steve have not only become household names, their stories—long form and short—have added significantly to the body of fine American literature. Their impact and influence on countless writers cannot be understated. Ray was a kind and decent man; Steve is a kind and decent man. They each also put their mark on creepy stories about kids in small towns. So, this one is for them.

Mister Pockets

-1-

There were towns like Pine Deep.
A few.
But not many.
Luckily, not many.

-2-

The kid's name was Lefty Horrigan.

Real name.

His father was a baseball fanatic and something of an asshole. Big Dave Horrigan thought that naming his only son Lefty would somehow turn the boy into a ballplayer, ideally a pitcher with a smoking fastball and a whole collection of curves and breakers. Big Dave played in high school and might have made it to the minors if he hadn't screwed up his right shoulder in Afghanistan during the first year of the war. It wasn't a shrapnel hit from an IED or enemy gunfire. Big Dave had tripped over a rock and fell shoulder-first onto a low stone wall, breaking a lot of important stuff. When he got home and got his wife pregnant, he transferred his burning love of the game to Lefty. Papered the kid's room in baseball images. Bought him a new cap and glove just about every year. Took him all the way to Philly to watch the Phils. Subscribed to every sports channel on the Net and had Lefty snugged up beside him from first pitch to last out.

Yeah, Lefty was going to go places. Lefty was going to be the ball playing star of the Horrigan clan, by god so he was.

Lefty Horrigan hated baseball.

He wasn't entirely sure he'd have loathed baseball as much if his name had been Louis or Larry. Lefty was pretty damn sure, however, that being hung with a jackass name like that was not going to make him enjoy the sport. No way.

He was a small kid for his age. A little chubby, not the best looking kid who ever pulled on a pair of too white, too tight gym shorts in the seventh grade. He had an ass and he had a bit of a gut and he had knocked knees. When he ran the hundred yard dash the gym teacher threw away the stopwatch and pulled out a calendar. Or so he said. Often.

When the other kids lined up to climb the rope, Lefty just went over and sat down. His doctor's note got a lot more workout than he did, and it had more calluses than his hands did. Nobody thought much of it. Fat kids didn't climb the rope. Fat kids sucked at gym class and none of them went out for sports unless it was on a dare.

And it didn't much matter.

Nobody bullied Lefty about it. This was farm country, out beyond the suburban sprawl and infil of Bucks County, out where Pennsylvania looked like it did on holiday calendars. Not the gray stone towers of Philadelphia or the steel bridges of Pittsburgh, but the endless fields of wheat and corn. Out here, a fat kid could ride a tractor all day, or work the barns in a milking shed. Weight didn't mean much of anything out there.

So it didn't mean much in gym class.

Most that happened was people made certain assumptions if you were the fat kid. They knew you wouldn't volunteer for anything physical. They knew you were always a good person to tap for a candy bar. They knew you'd be funny, because if you weren't good looking you had to be funny to fit in. Lefty was kind of funny. Not hilarious enough to hang with the coolest kids, but funnier than the spotty lumps that orbited the lowest cliques in the social order. Lefty could tell a joke, and sometimes he watched Comedy Central just to cram for the school days ahead. Stuff Jon Stewart or Stephen Colbert said was usually good for a pat on the back or a smile from one of the smarter pretty girls. If he made them laugh once in a while he was part of the group, and all judgment pretty much ended there.

But his dad was still on him about baseball.

Fucking baseball, Lefty thought. What was the big freaking deal with baseball? A bunch of millionaires standing around in a field, spitting tobacco and adjusting their cups as if their dicks were crowded for room. Once in a while one of them would have to run to catch a ball.

Shit.

Lefty worked harder than that pedaling his bike up Corn Hill. That was more of a workout than most of those guys saw in a whole game. And biking all the way across town or, worse, out to one of the farms, probably took more effort than playing a whole series. Lefty was sure of it. Just as he was sure that one of these days puberty would kick in so that he grew tall enough to stretch his ass and gut into a leaner hide. Just like Mom said would happen.

So far, though, he had hair on his balls, hair under his arms, pit-sweat stink that could drop an elk at forty paces, and painful erections every time he saw either of the Mueller twins walk past. But he hadn't grown an inch.

At the same time, his dad was hoping that the growth spurt would somehow unlock the baseball gene that must be sitting dormant in him. Big Dave usually hovered between hopeful expectation and active denial about his son's views on the American pastime.

-3-

He saw someone cut in front of him and head across the street. Old Mr. Pockets, the town's only homeless person. What grandpa called a 'hobo.'

Mr. Pockets looked like he was older than the big oaks that lined the street. Older than anything. Even through the thick gray dirt caked on his skin, the hobo's face was covered in thousands of lines and creases. His brown eyes were so dark they looked black, deep-set as they were and half hidden under bushy brows that looked like sickly caterpillars. Mr. Pockets wore so many layers of clothing that it was impossible to tell what was what. The only theme was that everything he seemed to wear—shirts, jackets, topcoats, aprons—had pockets. Dozens and dozens of pockets into which he stuffed whatever it was he found in the gutters and alleys of town.

Lefty smiled at Mr. Pockets and the old man paused halfway across the street and stared at him in the blank way he does, then he smiled and waved. Mr. Pockets, for all of his personal filth, had the whitest teeth. Big and white and wet.

Then he turned away and went trotting down a side street. Lefty rolled forward to watch him and saw that there was something going on half a block away. So, he pushed down on the pedals and followed the hobo, curious about what the cops were doing.

There was an ambulance parked halfway onto the curb outside of Colleen's Knit-Witz yarn shop. And two patrol cars parked crookedly, half blocking the street and slowing traffic to a gawking crawl. Lefty pulled his bike as close as he could get, but all he saw was the chief and a deputy talking in the open doorway of the shop.

The chief of police was a weird little guy who walked with a limp. A long time ago, before the Trouble—and everything in Pine Deep was measured as being *before* the Trouble or after it—Chief Crow had owned a store right here in town. A craft store, where

Lefty's cousin Jimmy used to buy comics. Jimmy was dead now. He'd been badly burned in the Trouble and hung himself six years ago.

Lefty only barely remembered the Trouble. He'd been five at the time. For him it was a blurred overlap of images. People running, people screaming. The state forest on fire. Then all those helicopters the next day.

In school they all had to read about it. It was local history. A bunch of militia guys dumped some drugs into the town water supply. Drove everyone batshit. People thought that there were monsters. Vampires and werewolves and things like that.

A lot of people went crazy. A lot of people died.

Every Halloween the local TV ran the movie they made about it, *Hellnight*, in continuous rotation for twenty-four hours. Even though in the movie there really *were* monsters, and the militia thing was a cover up.

Lefty'd seen the movie fifty times. Everyone in town had. It was stupid, but there were two scenes where you could see tits. And there was a lot of shooting and stuff. It was pretty cool.

Chief Crow wasn't in the movie—the sheriff back then had been a fat guy name Bernhardt who was played by John Goodman, who only ever played fat guys. But the guys in school said that the chief had gotten hurt in the Trouble and that was why he walked with a limp.

Now the chief stood with his deputy, a moose name Sweeney who nobody in town liked. Sweeney always wore sunglasses, even at night. Weird.

A friend of Lefty's broke out of the crowd and came drifting over. Kyle Fowler, though everyone called him Forks. Even his parents. The origin of the nickname wasn't interesting, but the name stuck.

"Hey, Left," said Forks. He had a Phillies cap on and a sweatshirt with Pine Deep Scarecrows on it.

"S'up?"

They stood together, watching the cops do nothing but talk.

"This is pretty f'd up," said Forks. He was one of the last of their peer group to make the jump from almost cursing to actually cursing. Saying 'f'd up' was a big thing for him, though, and he lowered his voice when he said it.

"Yeah?" asked Lefty, interested. "I just got here. What's happening?"

"She's dead."

"Who's dead?"

"Colleen," said Forks. "I mean Mrs. Grady. Lady who owns the store."

"She's *dead*?"

"Dead as a doornail."

"How? She was old, she have a heart attack or something?"

Forks shook his head. "They don't call the cops out for a heart attack."

That was true, at least as far as Lefty knew.

"So how'd she die?"

"Don't know, but it must be bad. They have some guy in there taking pictures and I heard Sheriff Crow say something about waiting for a forensics team from Doylestown."

Lefty cut a look at him. "Forensics? For real?"

"Yeah."

"Wow."

"Yeah."

Forks started to say something, then stopped.

"What—?" asked Lefty.

His friend chewed his lip for a minute, then he looked right and left as if checking that no one was close enough to hear him. Actually there were plenty of people around, but no one was paying attention to a couple of kids. Finally, Forks leaned close and said, "Want to hear something really weird?"

"Sure."

Forks thought about it for another second and then leaned closer. "Before they pushed the crowd back, I heard them talking about it."

"About what?"

"About the way she died."

The way Forks said it made Lefty turn and study him. His friend's face was alight with some ghastly knowledge that he couldn't wait to share. That was how things were. This was Pine Deep and stuff happened. Telling your friends about it was what made everything okay. Saying it aloud gave you a little bit of power over it. So did hearing about it. It was only *knowing* about it but not talking about it that made the nights too dark and made things move in the shadows. Everyone knew that.

Forks licked his lips as if what he had to say was really delicious. "I heard Sheriff Crow and that big deputy, Mike Sweeney, talking about what happened."

"Yeah?" asked Lefty, interested.

"Then that doctor guy, the dead guy doctor..." Forks snapped his fingers a couple of times to try and conjure the word.

"The coroner."

"Right, then he showed up and started to go inside, but the sheriff stopped him and said that it was dark in there."

Lefty waited for more, then he frowned.

"Dark? So what?"

"No, look, all the lights are on, see?"

It was true, the Knit-Witz shop blazed with fluorescent lights. And, in anticipation of Halloween, the windows were trimmed with strings of dark brown and orange lights. All of the shadows seemed to be out here on the street. Underfoot, under cars, in sewer grates.

"Yeah, but the sheriff told the coroner guy that it was dark in there. And you know what the doctor did?"

"I don't know, get a flashlight?" suggested Lefty.

"No, dummy, he *crossed* himself," said Forks, eyes blazing.

"Crossed...?"

Forks quickly crossed himself to show what he meant. Lefty made a face. He knew what it was, it was just that it didn't seem to fit what was happening.

Then Forks grabbed Lefty's sleeve and pulled him closer. "And Deputy Sweeney said, 'I think it's *them*.' He leaned on the word 'them,' like it really meant something."

They stared at each other for a long time. It was Lefty who said it, "You think it's happening again?"

Forks licked his lips again. "I don't know, man, but..."

He didn't say it, but it was there, hanging in the air between them, around them, all over the town.

Like an echo of last summer.

Nine people died in the space between June second and August tenth. A lot of bad car crashes and farm accidents. In every case the bodies were mangled, torn up.

It wasn't until the seventh death that the newspapers began speculating as to whether these were really accidents or not. That thought grew out of testimony and an inquest by the county coroner who said he was troubled by what he called a 'paucity of blood at the scene.' The papers provided an interpretation. For all of the physical damage, given every bit of torn flesh, there simply was not enough blood at the crime scenes to add up to what should be inside a human body.

In August, though, the deaths stopped. No explanation, and apparently no further speculation by the coroner. It just ended.

They turned and looked at the open door of Knit-Witz.

I think it's them.

Lefty swallowed dryness.

It's dark in there.

"You know what I think?" asked Forks in a hushed voice.

Lefty didn't want to know, because he was probably thinking the same thing.

"I think it's the Trouble again."

The Trouble.

Lefty looked away from the store, looked away from Forks. He studied the sky that was pulled like a blue tarp over the town. It was wrinkled with lines of white clouds and the long contrails of jets that had better places to be than here. A single crow stood on the roof of the hardware store across from Knit-Witz. It opened its mouth as if to let out a cry, but there was no sound.

Lefty felt very small and strange.

Movement to his left caught his eye and he turned to see Mr. Pockets five feet away, bending to pick through a trash can.

Lefty touched his jacket pocket. He had a Snickers bar and he pulled it out.

"Here," he said, holding it out to the old hobo.

Mr. Pockets paused, one grimy hand thrust deep into the rubbish, then he slowly turned his face toward Lefty. Dark eyes looked at the candy bar and then at Lefty's face.

The smile Mr. Pockets smiled was very slow in forming. But it grew and grew and for a wild moment it seemed to grow too big. Too wide. Impossibly wide, and there appeared to be far too many of those big, white, wet teeth.

But then Lefty blinked, and in the same instant he blinked Mr. Pocket's closed his mouth. His smile was now nothing more than a curve of lips.

"May I?" he asked with the strange formality he had, and when Lefty nodded, the old hobo took the candy bar with a delicate pinch of thumb and forefinger. Mr. Pocket's fingernails were very long and they plucked the bar away with only the faintest brush of nail on flattened palm.

The hobo held the candy up and slowly sniffed the wrapper from one end to the other with a single continuous inhalation of curiosity and pleasure.

"Peanuts," he said. "Mmm. And milk chocolate—sugar, cocoa butter, chocolate, skim milk, lactose, milkfat, soy lecithin, artificial flavor—peanuts, corn syrup, sugar, milkfat, skim milk, partially hydrogenated soybean oil, lactose, salt, egg whites, chocolate, artificial flavor. May contain almonds."

He rattled off the ingredients without ever looking at the wording printed on the label.

Forks was watching the cops and didn't seem to notice any of this happening. Which was kind of weird, thought Lefty.

Mr. Pockets began patting his clothing, a thing he did when he found something he wanted to keep. His hands were thin, with long spidery fingers, and he went pat-a-pat-pat-patty-pat-pat, making a rhythm of it until finally stopping with one hand touching a certain pocket. "Yes," said Mr. Pockets, "this one has an empty belly. This one could use a bite."

And into that pocket he thrust the Snickers bar. It vanished without a trace, and Lefty was so mesmerized that he expected the pocket to belch like a satisfied diner.

Mr. Pockets smiled and asked, "Do you have another?"

"Um...no, sorry. That was all I had."

The smile on Mr. Pockets' mouth didn't match the humor in his eyes. They were on a totally different frequency. One was friendly and even a little sad, but there was something really off about the smile in the old man's eyes. It seemed to speak to Lefty, but not in words. In images. They flitted through his head in a flash. Too many to capture, too strange to understand. Not shared thoughts. No more than looking at a crime scene was a shared experience.

"No," Lefty gasped, and he wasn't sure if he was repeating his answer or saying something else. "I don't have anything else."

Mr. Pockets nodded slowly. "I know. You gave me what you had. That was so nice, son. Soooo nice. That was generous. How rare a thing that is. I thank you, my little friend. I thank you most kindly."

It was the most Lefty had ever heard Mr. Pockets say at one time and he realized that the old man had an accent. Or...a mix of accents. It was a little southern, like people on TV who come from Mississippi or Louisiana. And it was a little...something else. Foreign, maybe? European or maybe just...Yeah, he thought, *foreign*.

"You..." began Lefty but his voice broke. He cleared his throat and tried again. "You're welcome."

That earned him another wide, wide grin, and then Mr. Pockets did something that Lefty had only ever seen people do in old movies. He winked at him. A big, comical wink.

The hobo turned and walked away, lightly touching his pockets.

Pat-a-pat-pat.

After a moment Lefty realized that he was holding his breath and he let it out with a gasp. "Jeez..."

Forks finally looked away from the crime scene. "What?"

"Man that was freaking *weird*."

"What was?"

"That thing with Mr. Pockets."

"What thing?"

Lefty elbowed him. "You blind or something? That whole thing with me giving him my Snickers bar and all."

Forks frowned at him. "What are you babbling about?"

"Mr. Pockets..."

"Dude," said Forks pointing, "Mr. Pockets is over there."

Lefty looked where his friend was pointing. On the far side of the street, well behind the parked ambulance, Mr. Pockets was standing behind a knot of rubberneckers.

"But...how...?"

Forks said, "Look man, it's getting late. I need to get a new calculator at McIlveen's and get home. I got a ton of homework and besides..."

Forks left it unfinished. Nobody in Pine Deep ever needed to finish that sentence.

It was already getting dark.

"See ya," said Lefty.

"Yeah," agreed Forks, and he was gone.

Lefty pulled his bike back, turned it under him, and placed his right foot on the pedal, but he paused as he saw something across the street. Mr. Pockets was standing by the open alley way, but he wasn't looking into it; instead he was looking up. It was hard for Lefty to see anything over there because that side of the street was in deep shade now. But there was a flicker of movement on the second floor. A curtain fell back into place as someone up there dropped it. Lefty had the briefest after image of a pale face watching from the deep shadows of the unlighted window. Someone standing in darkness on the dark side of the street. Pale, with dark eyes.

A woman? A girl?

He couldn't be sure.

Mr. Pockets turned away and glanced across the street at Lefty. He smiled again and touched the pocket into which he'd placed the Snickers. He gave the pocket a little pat-a-pat, then he walked into the alley and disappeared entirely.

Lefty Horrigan see-sawed his foot indecisively on the pedal.

It was nothing, he decided. All nothing.

But he didn't like that pale face.

It's dark in there.

"Yeah," Lefty said to no one, and he pushed down on the pedal and drove away.

-4-

Lefty chewed on all of this as he huffed up the slope at the foot of Corn Hill, standing on the pedals to force them to turn against the pull of gravity. Aside from Lefty's own weight, his bike's basket was laden with bags of stuff he needed to deliver before dark. His afterschool job was delivering stuff for Association members and now he was behind schedule.

The sun was already sliding down behind the tops of the mountains. A tide of shadows was washing across the farmers' fields toward the shores of the town.

He rode on, fast as he could.

Pine Deep had a Merchants Association comprised of fifty-three stores. Most of the stores sold crafts and local goods to townsfolk and tourists. Lefty and two other kids earned a few bucks making deliveries for people who couldn't spare the calories to carry their own shit to their cars, their homes, or in some cases to their motel units. On October afternoons like this Lefty enjoyed the job, except for that fucking Corn Hill. In the winter he called in sick a lot, and he never lost his job because people always assumed a fat kid got sick a lot.

Lefty pumped his way up Corn Hill until he reached Farmers Lane, turned and coasted a bit while he caught his breath. He had four deliveries to make today. The first was here in the center of town, and he made the stop to drop a bag of jewelry supplies—spools of wire and glue sticks—to Mrs. Howard at the Silver Mine. She tipped him a dollar.

A dollar.

Which bought exactly what? Comics were two-ninety-nine or a buck more. Even a Coke was a buck and a half. But he pasted on one of the many smiles he kept in reserve and made sure—upon her reminder—not to bang the door. She told him that every day. Every single day.

Then Mrs. Howard went back to gossiping with two locals about what was happening down at Knit-Witz. It seemed that the town already knew.

The town, he supposed, always knew everything. It was that kind of town.

As he climbed onto his bike, Lefty heard someone mention The Trouble, and the others cluck about it as if they were sure bad times were coming back. People threw out The Trouble for everything from a weak harvest to too many blowflies around a car-struck deer on Route A32. Everything was The Trouble coming back.

It's dark in there.

Lefty wondered if there really was something, some connection. The town might know—or guess—but he didn't. And he didn't like the half-guesses that shambled around inside his head.

He turned around and found Corn Hill again and went three steep blocks up to the Scarecrow Inn to deliver some poster paint. They were gearing up for Oktoberfest and had two of the waitresses making signs. The bartender told one of the waitresses to give Lefty something. The girl, Katelyn, a seventeen year old who lived a few houses down from the Horrigans, gave the bartender's back a lethal stare and gave Lefty fifty cents.

Lefty stood there, legs wide to straddle his bike, holding the handlebar with one tight fist and staring past the quarters on his open palm to the girl's face. He didn't say anything. Anyone with half a brain could understand. She did, too. She understood and she didn't give a wet fart. She waited out his stare with a flat one of her own. No, not entirely flat. A little curl of smirk. Daring him to say something.

Katelyn was pretty. She had a lot of red curls and big boobs and she wore a look that told him that no matter what he said or did, this was going to end her way.

Hers. Never his.

Not now. Not ever.

Not just because he was a thirteen year old fat kid.

Not just because she had the power in the moment.

She gave him the kind of look that said that this was small town America, he was fat and only moderately bright, living in a town that fed on fat and moderately bright people. They fueled the machinery and they greased the wheels. Her look told him, in no uncertain terms, that when she was eighteen, she'd blow this town like a bullet leaving a gun.

She would. He wouldn't.

It was *always* going to be like this. She'd always be pretty. No matter what else he became. Even if he grew a foot and learned to throw a slider that could break the heart of a major league batter. She would always be pretty.

Here in Pine Deep, she had him by the nuts. And she fucking well knew it.

Lefty slowly closed his hand, feeling the coins against his skin. Strangely warm, oddly moist. He shoved his hand into his pocket but didn't immediately let go of the quarters.

Katelyn still stared at him.

They both knew that he would break eye contact first. It was the way it was supposed to work. The universe turned on such immutable realities.

Lefty wanted to tough it out, but...

He lowered his eyes and turned away.

Katelyn didn't laugh, didn't even give a victorious snort. It wasn't compassion or manners. He simply wasn't worth the effort, and they both knew it. In two minutes she would have forgotten the encounter entirely.

He knew he'd wear that moment when they put him in his coffin.

And that was the way these things worked, too.

He got onto his bike, holding it steady with one hand as he began to coast down Corn Hill. When he was far enough away he put his sneakers down and let the tread skid him to a slow stop. Then he took the coins out of his pocket, unfolded his hand, and looked at two silver disks. Two quarters. A 1998—and didn't there always seem to be a 1998 coin in every handful of change?—and a 2013. Still new looking though it was a few years old now.

The coins were still warm. Warmer now for having been in his pocket.

He raised them to his face and peered at them.

Sniffed them.

And licked them.

He had no idea at all he was going to do that.

He immediately pulled his head back, disgusted, wincing, wanting to spit.

Except…

Except all of those were fake emotions, fake reactions, and he knew it. He played out the drama, though. He even went so far as to raise his left hand to throw the coins away.

And yet after he sat there on his bike for another two or three minutes he could still feel the coins in his fist, and his fist was in his pocket.

The taste of the warm, damp silver was on his tongue.

He had an erection that he didn't know what to do with.

Not out here, right here on Corn Hill, right here in front of the world.

Lefty felt sick. On some level, he felt sick.

He knew he should feel sick.

He wasn't *like* that. He wasn't no fucking pervert.

Lefty threw the coins away.

Except that isn't what he did.

In his mind that's what he did, but the coins jingled in his pocket as he headed out of town to make his next delivery. With each pump of his legs he pretended that he couldn't hear them.

-5-

Lefty's last delivery was all the way out of town, way out on Route A32. The Conner farm. The sun was fully behind the mountains now and although the trees on the top looked like they were burning, the flat farmlands were painted with purple shadows.

"Shit, shit, shit," Lefty said aloud as he rode along.

The Conner's weren't home but there was a note on the door to leave the parcel on the porch swing-chair. He saw that they'd left him a tip.

An apple and a little Post-it that said, "Thanks!"

The note had a smiley face.

He picked up the apple and stared at it.

"Jesus Christ," he said and threw the apple as far as he could. It sailed all the way across the yard and hit the garden fence.

Dad would have approved. A fastball with a nice break down and to the left. A batter would break his heart swinging at that.

"Fuck," he said, annoyed even that he'd thrown a good ball. Somehow it felt like an extra kick in the nuts.

He stomped down the steps and along the red brick walkway, then stopped when he realized he *was* stomping. He couldn't see himself, but the image of a disappointed fat kid stomping was disgusting. It disappointed him in his own eyes.

Lefty straightened, squared his shoulders, and walked with great dignity to where his bike leaned against the garden gate. A pair of Japanese maples grew on either side of the entrance, their pruned branches forming a leafy arch over the walkway. Lefty made himself stop and look at the trees for a moment because he was still pissed off.

His eyes burned as if he was going to cry, but Lefty cursed aloud at the thought of tears.

"You're so fucking stupid," he told himself.

And he sniffed as he reached for his bike. He glanced up at the sky and then along the road. There was no way he was going to get home before full dark.

His heart beat the wrong way in his chest as the truth of that hit home. It was like being punched in the sternum.

It's dark in there.

It's dark.

"Yes," said a voice behind him, "it's dark."

-6-

Lefty jumped and whirled. He lost his grip on the bike and it fell over with a clatter.

A woman stood behind him.

Tall.

Pretty.

Short red-gold hair snapping in the freshening breeze. Floral print house-dress flapping around her thighs.

Mrs. Conner.

She smiled at him with ruby red lips.

"I..." he began but didn't know where to go with that.

"You didn't eat your apple," she said. "And it was so ripe."

He looked down at the apple. It had hit the fence hard and burst apart, the impact tearing the red skin to reveal the vulnerable white flesh.

But the apple was all wrong. The meat of the apple wasn't white, it was gray and pale maggots writhed in it. Lefty recoiled from it, taking an involuntary step backward.

He bumped into the post and spun around.

It wasn't the fence post.

It was Mrs. Conner.

He yelped and spun around to where she should have been, to where she just was. But she wasn't there. She was here.

Right here.

So close.

Too close.

Much too close.

The top buttons of her housecoat were open. He could see the curves of her breasts, the pale yellow lace of her bra. The blue veins beneath her skin.

"It looks delicious," she said. "Doesn't it?"

He didn't know if she was talking about the apple or about...

No.

He did know.

Of course he knew.

It's just that it wasn't right. Not in any moral sense. It wasn't right because it didn't make sense. This didn't happen. Not even in his wet dreams. This never happened. Probably not even to the hunky guys on the football team in high school. Not to thirteen year olds. Not to fat kids.

Not really.

Not ever.

Mrs. Conner moved a step closer and he simply could not take his eyes off of her cleavage. The half melon shapes of her breasts defined by shadows that curved down and out of sight behind the cups of her bra and the buttons that were still buttoned.

He stared at those breasts, looking at them, watching the rise and fall of her chest.

Except...

Except.

The breasts did not rise and fall.

Because the chest did not rise and fall.

Not until Mrs. Conner took a breath in order to speak.

"Ripe," she said. "Ripe for the picking."

Lefty slowly raised his eyes from those shadow-carved breasts, past that ruby-lipped mouth, all the way to the eyes of the woman who stood so close.

To eyes with pupils as large as a cat's.

Eyes that, he knew at once and for certain, could see in the dark.

In any darkness.

He felt himself growing hard. Harder than before with Katelyn. Harder than ever in any of his dreams. Hard enough to hurt. To ache like a tumor, like a punch. There was no pleasure in it, no anticipation of release. It hurt, and he knew, on every level of his young mind, that hurt—that *pain*—was the point of this. Of all of this. Of everything in his life and in this odd day. Hurt was the destination at the end of this day. He knew that now even if he'd never even suspected it before.

It's dark in there.

And it was dark out here, too. And darkness called to him from the shadow beneath her breasts.

"So ripe," she said.

And he said, "Please..."

He was not asking for anything she had, not for anything she was. Not for those lips, or for those breasts. Or for any fulfillment of a fantasy that was too absurd even for his fevered midnight dreams.

"So, so ripe," said Mrs. Conner as she reached out and caressed his cheek with the backs of her pale fingers.

He shivered.

Her fingers were as white and as cold as marble.

"And juicy," she said as she bent to kiss him.

With those red, red lips.

Lefty wanted to shove her away. Wanted—*needed*—to run as fast as his stubby legs would go. Wanted to get onto his bike and ride faster than the wind, ride faster than the sunset. Ride fast enough to leave the darkness behind.

That's what he wanted.

But all he could do was stand there.

Her lips, when she kissed his cheek, were colder even than her fingers. Her breath, colder still.

"Please," he whispered.

"Yes," she said.

Those were not parts of the same conversation, and they both knew it.

She kissed his cheeks, his slack lips. When he closed his eyes she kissed his eyelids and delicately licked the tears that slid from beneath his lashes. Then she kissed his jaw.

And his throat.

Her tongue traced a line along his flesh and whenever his heart beat, she gasped.

"Please," he said again and his breath was so faint, the word so thin that he knew that it was his last breath. Or, maybe he could take one more. A deep one, so he could scream.

He felt her lips part. Felt the hard sharpness of something touch his skin.

Two points, like needles.

"No," said a voice.

Mrs. Conner was still so close when she turned her face that for a moment she and Lefty were cheek-to-cheek. Like lovers. Like people squeezing into a booth to take a photo. The coldness of her flesh was numbing.

But more numbing still was the figure that stood behind them. Not in the road, but on the red brick garden path, as if somehow he'd snuck over the fence so he could surprise everyone from behind.

A figure in tatters of greasy gray and the faded colors of countless garments.

A figure that smelled of earth and sewers and open landfills.

A figure whose lined and seamed face beamed a great smile.

Mr. Pockets.

-7-

Mrs. Conner said, "Go away."

Her voice was cold, sharp, without the sensual softness of a moment ago.

Mr. Pockets just stood there.

"This meat is mine," snarled Mrs. Conner. And with that she jerked Lefty nearly off his feet, pulling him in front of her. Not as a shield but to put him on display. Her property.

Her...

What?

She'd called him *meat*.

Tears burned channels down Lefty's face.

The old hobo kept smiling.

"Get away," said Mrs. Conner.

He stood his ground.

Mrs. Conner pointed at him with one of her slender, icy fingers. "Go on now," she said in a voice much more like her own, without sex in it but still with passion. "Go on, *git*."

The wind gusted and Mr. Pockets closed his eyes and leaned into the wind like he enjoyed the cold and all of the smells the breeze carried with it. Lefty thought the wind smelled like dead grass and something else. A rotten egg smell. Lefty wasn't sure if the wind already had that rotten egg smell, or if it came from the hobo.

Mrs. Conner tensed and took a single threatening step toward Mr. Pockets.

"Get your disgusting ass out of my yard, you filthy tramp," she growled. "Or I'll make you sorry."

"You'll make me sorry?" said the hobo, phrasing it as if it was a matter of great complexity to him. His speech was still southern mixed with some foreign accent Lefty couldn't recognize. "What in the wide world could that mean?"

Mrs. Conner laughed. Such a strange laugh to come from so pretty a throat. It was how Lefty imagined a wolf might laugh. Sharp, harsh and ugly. "You don't know what kind of shit you stepped in, you old son of a bitch."

"Old?" echoed Mr. Pockets, and his smile faded. He sighed. "Old. Ah."

Lefty tried to pull away but the single hand that held him was like a shackle of pure ice. Cold, unbreakable. The fingers seemed to burn his skin the way metal will in the deep of winter.

"Let me go," he said, wanting to growl it, to howl it, but it came out as a whimper.

"Let him go," said Mr. Pockets.

"He's *mine*."

"No," said the hobo, "he's mine."

Mrs. Conner laughed her terrible bark of a laugh again. She shook Lefty like a doll. "You really don't get it, do you shit for brains?"

"What don't I get?" asked the old man.

"You don't know what's going on here, do you? Even now, you don't get it? You're either too stupid or you've pickled what little brains you ever had with whatever the fuck you drink, but you just don't get it. I'm telling you to leave. I'm giving you that chance. I don't want to dirty my mouth on you, so I'm letting you walk away. You should get down on your knees and kiss the ground where I'm standing. You should pray to God and thank Him for little mercies, 'cause I—"

"No," said Mr. Pockets, interrupting.

"What?"

"No, my dear," he said and there was less of the southern and more of the foreign accent in his tone, "it's you—and anyone like you—who doesn't understand. You're too young, I expect. Too young."

She tried to laugh at that, but there was something in Mr. Pocket's voice that stalled the laugh. Lefty heard it, too, but he didn't know what was going on.

Or, rather he did know and could not imagine how any thought he had, any insight he possessed, or any action he took could change this from being the end of him. The hardness in his pants had faded and now he had to tighten up to keep from pissing down his legs.

The woman flung Lefty down and he hit the gatepost, spun badly and fell far too hard. Pain exploded in his elbow and knee as he struck the red bricks, and as he toppled over he hit the back of his head. Red fireworks burst in his eyes.

Through the falling embers of sudden pain, he saw Mrs. Conner bend forward and sneer at Mr. Pockets. Her face contorted into a mask of pure hatred. The sensual mouth became a leer of disgust, the eyes blazed with threat.

"You're a fucking idiot for pushing this," she said, the words hissing out between gritted teeth.

Between very, very sharp teeth.

Teeth that were impossible.

Teeth that were so damned impossible.

"I will drink the life from you," said Mrs. Conner, and then she flung herself at Mr. Pockets, tearing at him with nails and with those dreadful teeth.

Lefty screamed.

In stark terror.

In fear for himself and for his soul.

But his fear became words as he screamed. A warning.

"*Mr. Pockets!*"

However Mr. Pockets did not need his warning. As the woman pounced on him, he stepped forward and caught her around the throat with one gray and dirty hand.

And with that hand he held her.

She thrashed and spat and kicked at him. Her fingernails tore at his face, his clothes. Her feet struck him in the groin and stomach and chest.

He stood there and held her.

And held her.

Every blow that landed knocked dust from him. Lefty could feel the vibrating thuds as if they were striking him, the echoes bounced off the front wall of the Conner farmhouse.

And Mr. Pockets held her.

Inches above the ground.

Then, with infinite slowness, he pulled her toward him. Toward his smiling mouth.

He said to her, "Oh, you are so young. You and those like you. Even the ones you think are old. What are they anyway? Fifty years old? The oldest living in these mountains, the one who came from far away and settled here, the one who made you, he isn't even three centuries old. Such a child. A puppy. A maggot that will never become a fly." As he spoke, spit flecked her face.

Mrs. Conner squirmed and fought; no longer trying to fight. She tried to get away.

Mr. Pockets pulled her close and licked the side of her face, then made a face of mild disappointment.

"You taste like nothing," he said. "You don't even taste of the corruption you think defines you. You haven't been what you are long enough to lose the bland flavor of life. And you haven't acquired the savory taste of immortality. Not even the pungent piquancy of evil."

"You don't...know...what you're...doing..."

Mrs. Conner had to fight to gasp in little bits of air so she could talk. She didn't need to breathe, Lefty understood that now, but you had to breathe in order to speak, and the hand that held her was clamped so tight. He could hear the bones in her neck beginning to grind.

Mr. Pockets shook her. Once, almost gently. "You and yours hunt these hills. You are the boogeymen in the dark, and I suspect that you feed as much off of their fear of you as from the blood that runs through their veins. How feeble is that? How pathetic." He pulled her close, forcing her to look into his eyes. "You think you understand what it is to be old? You call yourselves immortal because some of you—a scant few—can count their lives in centuries. You think that's what immortality is?"

Mr. Pockets laughed now, and it was entirely different from the lupine laughter of Mrs. Conner. His was a laughter like distant thunder. A deep rumble that promised awful things.

Lefty curled into a ball and wrapped his arms around his head.

"If you could count millennia as the fleeting moments of your life, even then you would not be immortal. Then, all you would be is old. And there are things far older than that. Older than trees. Older than mountains."

His hand tightened even more and the soft grinding of bone became sharper. A splintery sound.

"You delight in thinking that you're evil," whispered Mr. Pockets. "But evil itself is a newborn concept. It was born when a brother killed a brother with a rock. And that was minutes ago in the way real time is counted. Evil? It's a game that children play."

He pulled her closer still so that his lips brushed hers as he spoke.

"You think you're powerful because monsters are supposed to be powerful. But, oh, my little child, only now, I think, do you grasp what *power* really is."

"…please…" croaked Mrs. Conner.

Lefty's bladder went then. Heat spread beneath his clothes, but he didn't care.

"You think you understand hunger," murmured Mr. Pockets as gently as if he spoke to a lover. "No. Not with all of your aching red need do you understand hunger."

Then Mr. Pockets opened his mouth.

Lefty watched him do it.

He lay there and watched that mouth open.

And open.

And open.

So wide.

So many white, white teeth.

Row upon row of them, standing in curved lines that stretched back and back into a throat that did not end. A throat of teeth that was as long as forever. Mrs. Conner screamed a great, terrible, silent scream. Absolute terror galvanized her; her legs and arms flailed wildly as Mr. Pockets pulled her closer and closer toward those teeth.

As Lefty Horrigan lay there, weeping, choking on tears, pissing in his pants, he watched Mr. Pockets eat Mrs. Conner. He ate her whole. He ate her all up.

He swallowed her, housecoat and shoes and all.

The old man's throat bulged once and then she was gone.

The world collapsed down into silence. Even the crickets of night were too shocked to move.

Lefty squeezed his eyes shut and waited for everything he was to die. To vanish, skin and bone, clothes and all, like Mrs. Conner.

He waited.

Waited.

The cold breeze ran past and across him.

And he waited to die.

-8-

When Lefty Horrigan opened his eyes, the yard was empty.

Just him and his bike.

The rotten, shattered apple lay where it had fallen, visible only as a pale lump in the thickening darkness.

Mr. Pockets was gone.

Even so, Lefty lay there for a long time. He didn't know how long, but the moon was peering at him from above the mountains when he finally unwrapped his arms from around his head.

He got slowly to his feet. His knee and elbow hurt almost as much as the back of his head. The pee in his pants had turned cold.

He didn't care about any of that.

The wind blew and blew and Lefty let it scrub the tears off his cheeks.

He limped toward the gate and opened it and bent to pick up his bike.

Something white and brown fluttered down by his feet, caught under the edge of one pedal. It snapped like plastic.

Lefty bent and picked it up. Straightened it out. Turned it over in his hands.

Read the word printed in blue letters on a white background on a brown wrapper.

Snickers.

There was only the smallest smudge of milk chocolate left on the inside of the wrapper.

Lefty looked at it, then he looked sharply left and right. He turned in a full circle. Waiting for the worst, waiting for the trick.

But it was just him and the night wind and the bike.

He looked at the wrapper and almost—almost—opened his fingers to let it go.

He didn't though.

Instead he bent and licked off the chocolate smudge. Then he folded the wrapper very neatly and put it into his pocket.

He wasn't sure why he'd taken that taste. It was a weird, stupid thing to do.

Or maybe it was something else.

A way of saying something in a language he couldn't speak in words. And a way of expressing a feeling that he knew he would never be able to really understand.

He patted the pocket where he'd stored the wrapper. A little pat-a-pat.

Then Lefty Horrigan stood his bike up, got onto it, and wet, cold, sore and dazed, he pedaled away.

Through the darkness.

All the way home.

Author's Note on "Property Condemned"

Although this is the third Pine Deep story included in this collection, it is unique in three important ways. Firstly because it is a prequel, of sorts, to the Pine Deep Trilogy. Second, because it was the first Pine Deep story I ever wrote. And third, because it was the lead story in the first issue of a wonderful horror webzine, *Nightmare Magazine*, edited by my friend John Joseph Adams.

Nightmare Magazine is a horror companion to John's award-winning *Lightspeed* science fiction e-zine. I encourage you to try both of them. And in the meantime, welcome once more to Pine Deep.

Property Condemned

-1-

The house was occupied, but no one lived there.

That's how Malcolm Crow thought about it. Houses like the Croft place were never really empty.

Like most of the kids in Pine Deep, Crow knew that there were ghosts. Even the tourists knew about the ghosts. It was that kind of town.

All of the tourist brochures of the town had pictures of ghosts on them. Happy, smiling, Casper the Friendly Ghost sorts of ghosts.

Every store in town had a rack of books about the ghosts of Pine Deep. Crow had every one of those books. He couldn't braille his way through a basic geometry test or recite the U.S. Presidents in any reliable order, but he knew about shades and crisis apparitions, church grims and banshees, crossroads ghosts and poltergeists. He read every story and historical account; saw every movie he could afford to see. Every once in a while Crow would even risk one of his father's frequent beatings to sneak out of bed and tiptoe down to the basement to watch Double Chiller Theater on the flickering old Emerson. If his dad caught him and took a belt to him, it was okay as long as Crow managed to see at least *one* good spook flick.

Besides, beatings were nothing to Crow. At nine years old he'd had so many that they'd lost a lot of their novelty.

It was the ghosts that mattered. Crow would give a lot—maybe everything he had in this world—to actually *meet* a ghost. That would be...well, Crow didn't know what it would be. Not exactly. *Fun* didn't seem to be the right word. Maybe what he really wanted was *proof.* He worried about that. About wanting proof that something existed beyond the world he knew.

He believed that he believed, but he wasn't sure that he was right about it. That he was aware of this inconsistency only tightened the knots. And fueled his need.

His *hunger.*

Ghosts mattered to Malcolm Crow because whatever they were, they clearly outlasted whatever had killed them. Disease, murder, suicide, war, brutality...abuse. The cause of their deaths was over, but they had survived. That's why Crow wasn't scared of ghosts. What frightened him—deep down on a level where feelings had no specific structure—was the possibility that they might *not* exist. That this world was all that there was.

And the Croft house? That place was different. Crow had never worked up the nerve to go there. Almost nobody ever went out there. Nobody really talked about it, though everyone knew about it.

Crow made a point of visiting the other well-known haunted spots—the tourist spots—hoping to see a ghost. All he wanted was a glimpse. In one of his favorite books on hauntings, the writer said that a glimpse was what most people usually got. "Ghosts are elusive," the author had written. "You don't form a relationship with one, you're lucky if you catch a glimpse out of the corner of your eye;

but if you do, you'll know it for what it is. One glimpse can last you a lifetime."

So far, Crow had not seen or even heard a single ghost. Not one cold spot, not a single whisper of old breath, not a hint of something darting away out of the corner of his eye. Nothing, zilch. Nada.

However, he had never gone into the Croft place.

Until today.

Crow touched the front pocket of his jeans to feel the outline of his lucky stone. Still there. It made him smile.

Maybe now he'd finally get to see a ghost.

-2-

They pedaled through dappled sunlight, sometimes four abreast, sometimes in single file when the trail dwindled down to a crooked deerpath. Crow knew the way to the Croft place and he was always out front, though he liked it best when Val Guthrie rode beside him. As they bumped over hard-packed dirt and whispered through uncut summer grass, Crow cut frequent covert looks at Val.

Val was amazing. Beautiful. She rode straight and alert on her pink Huffy, pumping the pedals with purple sneakers. Hair as glossy black as crow feathers, tied in a bouncing ponytail. Dark blue eyes, and a serious mouth. Crow made it his life work to coax a smile out of her at least once a day. It was hard work, but worth it.

The deerpath spilled out onto an old forestry service road that allowed them once more to fan out into a line. Val caught up and fell in beside him on the left, and almost at once Terry and Stick raced each other to be first on the right. Terry and Stick were always racing, always daring each other, always trying to prove who was best, fastest, smartest, strongest. Terry always won the strongest part.

"The Four Horsemen ride!" bellowed Stick, his voice breaking so loudly that they all cracked up. Stick didn't mind his voice cracking. There was a fifty cent bet that he'd have his grown up voice before Terry. Crow privately agreed. Despite his size, Terry had a high voice that always sounded like his nose was full of snot.

Up ahead the road forked, splitting off toward the ranger station on the right and a weedy path on the left. On the left-hand side, a sign leaned drunkenly toward them.

PRIVATE PROPERTY
NO ADMITTANCE
TRESPASSERS WILL BE

That was all of it. The rest of the sign had been pinged off by bullet holes over the years. It was a thing to do. You shot the sign to the Croft place to show that you weren't afraid. Crow tried to make sense of that, but there wasn't any end to the string of logic.

He turned to Val with a grin. "Almost there."

"Oooo, spooky!" said Stick, lowering the bill of his Phillies ball-cap to cast his face in shadows.

Val nodded. No smile. No flash of panic. Only a nod. Crow wondered if Val was bored, interested, skeptical, or scared. With her you couldn't tell. She had enough Lenape blood to give her that stone face. Her mom was like that, too. Not her dad, though. Mr. Guthrie was always laughing, and Crow suspected that he, too, had a lifelong mission that involved putting smiles on the faces of the Guthrie women.

Crow said, "It won't be too bad."

Val shrugged. "It's *just* a house." She leaned a little heavier on the word "just" every time she said that, and she'd been doing that ever since Crow suggested they come out here. *Just* a house.

Crow fumbled for a comeback that would chip some of the ice off of those words, but as he so often did, he failed.

It was Terry Wolfe who came to his aide. "Yeah, yeah, yeah, Val, you keep saying that but I'll bet you'll chicken out before we even get onto the porch."

Terry liked Val, too, but he spent a lot of time putting her down and making fun of whatever she said. Though, if any of that actually hurt Val, Crow couldn't see it. Val was like that. She didn't show a thing. Even when that jerk Vic Wingate pushed her and knocked her down in the schoolyard last April, Val hadn't yelled, hadn't cried. All she did was get up, walk over to Vic and wipe the blood from her scraped palms on his shirt. Then, as Vic started calling her words that Crow had only heard his dad ever use when he was really hammered, Val turned and walked away like it was a normal spring day.

So Terry's sarcasm didn't make a dent.

Terry and Stick immediately launched into the Addams Family theme-song loud enough to scare the birds from the trees.

A startled doe dashed in blind panic across their path and Stick tracked it with his index finger and dropped his thumb like a hammer.

"Pow!"

Val gave him a withering look, but she didn't say anything.

"*...So get a witch's shawl on, a broomstick you can crawl on...*"

They rounded the corner and skidded to a stop, one, two, three, four. Dust plumes rose behind them like ghosts and drifted away on a breeze as if fleeing from this place. The rest of the song dwindled to dust on their tongues.

It stood there.

The Croft house.

-3-

The place even *looked* haunted.

Three stories tall, with all sorts of angles jutting out for no particular reason. Gray shingles hung crookedly from their nails. The windows were dark and grimed, some were broken out. Most of the storm shutters were closed, but a few hung open and one lay half-buried in a dead rosebush. Missing slats in the porch railing gave it a gap-toothed grin. Like a jack o'lantern. Like a skull.

On any other house, Crow would have loved that. He would have appreciated the attention to detail.

But his dry lips did not want to smile.

Four massive willows, old and twisted by rot and disease, towered over the place, their long fingers bare of leaves even in the flush of summer. The rest of the forest stood back from the house as if unwilling to draw any nearer. Like people standing around a coffin, Crow thought.

His fingers traced the outline of the lucky stone in his jeans pocket.

"Jeeeez," said Stick softly.

"Holy moley," agreed Terry.

Val said, "It's *just* a house."

Without turning to her, Terry said, "You keep saying that, Val, but I don't see you running up onto the porch."

Val's head swiveled around like a praying mantis's and she skewered Terry with her blue eyes. "And when *exactly* was the last time you had the guts to even come here, Terrance Henry Wolfe? Oh, what was that? Never? What about you, George Stickler?"

"Crow hasn't been here either," said Stick defensively.

"I know. Apparently three of the four Horsemen of the Apocalypse are sissies."

"Whoa, now!" growled Terry, swinging his leg off his bike. "There's a lot of places we haven't been. *You* haven't been here, either, does that make you a sissy, too?"

"I don't need to come to a crappy old house to try and prove anything," she fired back. "I thought we were out riding bikes."

"Yeah, but we're here now," persisted Terry, "so why don't you show everyone how tough you are and go up on the porch?"

Val sat astride her pink Huffy, feet on the ground, hands on the rubber grips. "You're the one trying to prove something. Let's see you go first."

Terry's ice-blue eyes slid away from hers. "I never said I wanted to go in."

"Then what *are* you saying?"

"I'm just saying that you're the one who's always saying there's no such thing as haunted houses, but you're still scared to go up there."

"Who said I was scared?" Val snapped.

"You're saying you're not?" asked Terry.

Crow and Stick watched this exchange like spectators at a tennis match. They both kept all expression off their faces, well aware of how far Val could be pushed. Terry was getting really close to that line.

"*Everyone*'s too scared to go in there," Terry said, "and—"

"And *what*?" she demanded.

"And...I guess nobody should."

"Oh, chicken poop. It's just a stupid old house."

Terry folded his arms. "Yeah, but I still don't see you on that porch."

Val made a face, but didn't reply. They all looked at the house. The old willows looked like withered trolls, bent with age and liable to do something nasty. The Croft house stood, half in shadows and half in sunlight.

Waiting.

It wants us to come in, thought Crow, and he shivered.

"How do you know the place is really haunted?" asked Stick.

Terry punched him on the arm. "*Everybody* knows it's haunted."

"Yeah, okay, but...how?"

"Ask Mr. Halloween," said Val. "He knows everything about this crap."

They all looked at Crow. "It's not crap," he insisted. "C'mon, guys, this is Pine Deep. Everybody knows there are ghosts everywhere here."

"You ever see one?" asked Stick, and for once there was no mockery in his voice. If anything, he looked a little spooked.

"No," admitted Crow, "but a lot of people have. Jim Polk's mom sees one all the time."

They nodded. Mrs. Polk swore that she saw a partially formed figure of a woman in Colonial dress walking through the backyard. A few of the neighbors said they saw it, too.

"And Val's dad said that Gus Bernhardt's uncle Kurt was so scared by a poltergeist in his basement that he took to drinking."

Kurt Bernhardt was a notorious drunk—worse than Crow's father—and he used to be a town deputy until one day he got so drunk that he threw up on a town selectman while trying to write him a parking ticket.

"Dad used to go over to the Bernhardt place a lot," said Val, "but he never saw any ghosts."

"I heard that not everybody sees ghosts," said Terry. He took a plastic comb out of his pocket and ran it through his hair, trying to look cool and casual, like there was no haunted house forty feet away.

"Yeah," agreed Stick, "and I heard that people sometimes see *different* ghosts."

"What do you mean 'different ghosts'?" asked Val.

Stick shrugged. "Something my gran told me. She said that a hundred people can walk through the same haunted place, and most people won't see a ghost because they can't, and those who do will see their own ghost."

"Wait," said Terry, "what?"

Crow nodded. "I heard that, too. It's an old Scottish legend. The people who don't see ghosts are the ones who are afraid to believe in them."

"And the people who *do* see a ghost," Stick continued, "see the ghost of their own future."

"That's stupid," said Val. "How can you see your own ghost if you're alive?"

"Yeah," laughed Terry. "That's stupid, even for you."

"No, really," said Crow. "I read that in my books. Settlers used to believe that."

Stick nodded. "My gran's mom came over from Scotland. She said that there are a lot of ghosts over there, and that sometimes people saw their own. Not themselves as dead people, not like that. Gran said that people saw their own *spirits*. She said that there were places where the walls between the worlds were so thin that past, present, and future were like different rooms in a house with no doors. That's how she put it. Sometimes you could stand in one room and see different parts of your life in another."

"That would scare the crap out of me," said Terry.

A sudden breeze caused the shutters on one of the windows to bang as loud as a gunshot. They all jumped.

"Jeeeeee-zus!" gasped Stick. "Nearly gave me a heart attack!"

They laughed at their own nerves, but the laughs died away as one by one they turned back to look at the Croft house.

"You really want me to go in there?" asked Val, her words cracking the fragile silence.

Terry said, sliding his comb back into his pocket, "Sure."

"No!" yelped Crow.

Everyone suddenly looked at him: Val in surprise, Stick with a grin forming on his lips, Terry with a frown.

The moment held for three or four awkward seconds, and then Val pushed her kickstand down and got off of her bike.

"Fine then."

She took three decisive steps toward the house. Crow and the others stayed exactly where they were. When Val realized she was alone, she turned and gave them her best ninja death stare. Crow knew this stare all too well; his buttocks clenched and his balls tried to climb up into his chest cavity. Not even that creep Vic Wingate gave her crap when Val had that look in her eyes.

"What I ought to do," she said coldly, "is make you three sissies go in with me."

"No way," laughed Terry, as if it was the most absurd idea anyone had ever said aloud.

"Okay!" blurted Crow.

Terry and Stick looked at him with a *Nice going, Judas* look in their eyes.

Val smiled. Crow wasn't sure if she was smiling at him or smiling in triumph. Either way, he put it in the win category. He was one smile up on the day's average.

Crow's bike had no kickstand so he got off and leaned it against a maple, considered, then picked it up and turned it around so that it pointed the way they'd come. Just in case.

"You coming?" he asked Stick and Terry.

"If I'm going in," said Val acidly, "then we're *all* going in. It's only fair and I don't want to hear any different or so help me God, Terry…"

She left the rest to hang. When she was mad, Val not only spoke like an adult, she sounded like her mother.

Stick winced and punched Terry on the arm. "Come on, numb-nuts."

-4-

The four of them clustered together on the lawn, knee deep in weeds. Bees and blowflies swarmed in the air around them. No one moved for over a minute. Crow could feel the spit in his mouth drying to paste.

I want to do this, he thought, but that lie sounded exactly like what it was.

The house glowered down at him.

The windows, even the shuttered ones, were like eyes. The ones with broken panes were like the empty eye-sockets of old skulls, like the ones in the science class in school. Crow spent hours staring into those dark eye-holes, wondering if there was anything of the original owner's personality in there. Not once did he feel anything. Now, just looking at those black and empty windows, made Crow shudder, because he was getting the itchy feeling that there *was* something looking back.

The shuttered windows somehow bothered him more than the open ones. They seemed...he fished for the word.

Sneaky?

No, that wasn't right. That was too cliché, and Crow had read every ghost story he could find. Sneaky wasn't right. He dug through his vocabulary and came up short. The closest thing that seemed to fit—and Crow had no idea *how* it fit—was *hungry*.

He almost laughed. How could shuttered windows look hungry?

"That's stupid."

It wasn't until Stick turned to him and asked what he was talking about that Crow realized he'd spoken the words aloud.

He looked at the others and all of them, even Val, were stiff with apprehension. The Croft house scared them. Really scared them.

Because they believed there was something in there.

They all paused there in the yard, closer to their bikes and the road than they were to that porch.

They believed.

Crow wanted to shout and he wanted to laugh.

"Well," said Val, "let's go."

The Four Horseman, unhorsed, approached the porch.

-5-

The steps creaked.

Of course they did. Crow would have been disappointed if they hadn't. He suppressed a smile. The front door was going to creak, too; those old hinges were going to screech like a cat. It was how it was all supposed to be.

It's real, he told himself. *There's a ghost in there. There's something in there.*

It was the second of those two thoughts that felt correct. Not *right* exactly—but *correct*. There was some*thing* in that house. If they went inside, they'd find it.

No, whispered a voice from deeper inside his mind, *if we go inside it will find us.*

"Good," murmured Crow. This time he said it so softly that none of the others heard him.

He wanted it to find them.

Please let it find them.

They crossed the yard in silence. The weeds were high and brown as if they could draw no moisture at all from the hard ground. Crow saw bits of debris there, half-hidden by the weeds. A baseball whose hide had turned a sickly yellow and whose seams had split like torn surgical sutures. Beyond that was a woman's dress shoe; just the one. There was a Triple-A road map of Pennsylvania, but the wind and rain had faded the details so that the whole state appeared to be under a heavy fog. Beyond that was an orange plastic pill-bottle with its label peeled halfway back. Crow picked it up and read the label and was surprised to see that the pharmacy where this prescription had been filled was in Poland. The drug was called *Klozapol*, but Crow had no idea what that was or what it was used for. The bottle was empty but it looked pretty new. Crow let it drop and he touched the lucky stone in his pocket to reassure himself that it was still safe.

Still his.

The yard was filled with junk. An empty wallet, a ring of rusted keys, a soiled diaper, the buckle from a seat belt, a full box of graham crackers that was completely covered with ants. Stuff like that. Disconnected things. Like junk washed up on a beach.

Val knelt and picked up something that flashed silver in the sunlight.

"What's that?" asked Terry.

She held it up. It was an old Morgan silver dollar. Val spit on her thumb and rubbed the dirt away to reveal the profile of Lady Liberty. She squinted to read the date.

"Eighteen-ninety-five," she said.

"Are you kidding me?" demanded Terry, bending close to study it. He was the only one of them who collected coins. "Dang, Val...that's worth a lot of money."

"Really?" asked Val, Crow, and Stick at the same time.

"Yeah. A *lot* of money. I got some books at home we can look it up in. I'll bet it's worth a couple of thousand bucks."

Crow goggled at him. Unlike the other three, Crow's family was dirt poor. Even Stick, whose parents owned a tiny TV repair shop in town, had more money. Crow's mom was dead and his father worked part-time at Shanahan's Garage then drank most of what he earned. Crow was wearing the same jeans this year that he wore all last season. Same sneakers, too. He and his brother Billy had learned how to sew well enough to keep their clothes from falling apart.

So he stared at the coin that might be worth a few thousand dollars.

Val turned the coin over. The other side had a carving of an eagle with its wings outstretched. The words UNITED STATES OF AMERICA arched over it and ONE DOLLAR looped below it. But above the eagle where IN GOD WE TRUST should have been, someone had gouged deep into the metal, totally obscuring the phrase.

Terry gasped as if he was in actual physical pain.

"Bet it ain't worth as much like that," said Stick with a nasty grin.

Val shrugged and shoved the coin into her jeans pocket. "Whatever. Come on."

It was a high porch and they climbed four steep steps to the deck, and each step was littered with dried leaves and withered locust husks. Crow wondered where the leaves had come from; it was the height of summer. Except for the willows, everything everywhere was alive, and those willows looked like they'd been dead for years. Besides, these were dogwood leaves. He looked around for the source of the leaves, but there were no dogwoods in the yard. None anywhere he could see.

He grunted.

"What?" asked Val, but Crow didn't reply. It wasn't the sort of observation that was going to encourage anyone.

"The door's probably locked," said Terry. "This is a waste of time."

"Don't even," warned Val.

The floorboards creaked, each with a different note of agonized wood.

As they passed one of the big shuttered windows, Stick paused and frowned at it. Terry and Val kept walking, but Crow slowed and lingered a few paces away. As he watched, the frown on Stick's mouth melted away and his friend stood there with no expression at all on his face.

"Stick...?"

Stick didn't answer. He didn't even twitch.

"Yo...Stick."

This time Stick jumped as if Crow had pinched him. He whirled and looked at Crow with eyes that were wide but unfocused.

"What did you say?" he asked, his voice a little slurred. Like Dad's when he was starting to tie one on.

"I didn't say anything. I just called your name."

"No," said Stick, shaking his head. "You called me 'daddy.' What's that supposed to mean?"

Crow laughed. "You're hearing things, man."

Stick whipped his ball-cap off his head and slapped Crow's shoulder. "Hey...I *heard* you."

Terry heard this and he gave Stick a quizzical smile, waiting for the punch-line. "What's up?"

Stick wiped his mouth on the back of his hand and stared down as if expecting there to be something other than a faint sheen of spit. He touched the corner of his mouth and looked at his fingers. His hands were shaking as he pulled his ball-cap on and snugged it down low.

"What are you doing?" asked Terry, his smile flickering.

Stick froze. "Why? Do I have something on my face?"

"Yeah," said Terry.

Stick's face blanched white and he jabbed at his skin. The look in his eyes was so wild and desperate that it made Crow's heart hurt. He'd seen a look like that once when a rabbit was tangled up in some barbed wire by the Carby place. The little animal was covered in blood and its eyes were huge, filled with so much terror that it couldn't even blink. Even as Crow and Val tried to free it, the rabbit shuddered and died.

Scared to death.

For just a moment, Stick looked like that, and the sight of that expression drove a cold sliver of ice into Crow's stomach. He could feel his scrotum contract into a wrinkled little walnut.

Stick pawed at his face. "What is it?"

"Don't worry," said Terry, "it's just a dose of the uglies, but you had that when you woke up this morning."

Terry laughed like a donkey.

No one else did.

Stick glared at him and his nervous fingers tightened into fists. Crow was sure that he was going to smash Terry in the mouth. But then Val joined them.

"What's going on?" she demanded.

Her stern tone broke the spell of the moment.

"Nothing," said Stick as he abruptly pushed past Terry and stalked across the porch, his balled fists at his sides. The others gaped at him.

"What—?" began Terry, but he had nowhere to go with it. After a moment he followed Stick.

Val and Crow lingered for a moment.

"Did they have a fight or something?" Val asked quietly.

"I don't know what that was," admitted Crow. He told her exactly what happened. Val snorted.

"Boys," she said, leaving it there. She walked across the porch and stood in front of the door.

Crow lingered for a moment, trying to understand what just happened. Part of him wanted to believe that Stick just saw a ghost. He wanted that very badly. The rest of him—*most* of him—suddenly wanted to turn around, jump on the bike that was nicely positioned for a quick escape, and never come back here. The look in Stick's eyes had torn all the fun out of this.

"Let's get this over with," said Val, and that trapped all of them in the moment. The three boys looked at her, but none of them looked at each other. Not for a whole handful of brittle seconds. Val, however, studied each of them. "Boys," she said again.

Under the lash of her scorn, they followed her.

The doors were shut, but even before Val touched the handle, Crow knew that these doors wouldn't be locked.

It wants us to come in.

Terry licked his lips and said, "What do you suppose is in there?"

Val shook her head, and Crow noted that she was no longer saying that this was *just* a house.

Terry nudged Crow with his elbow. "You ever talk to anybody's been in here?"

"No."

"You ever know anyone who knows anyone who's been in here?"

Crow thought about it. "Not really."

"Then how do you know it's even haunted?" asked Val.

"I don't."

It was a lie and Crow knew that everyone read it that way. No one called him on it, though. Maybe they would have when they were still in the yard, but not now. There was a line somewhere and Crow knew—they all knew—they'd crossed it.

Maybe it was when Stick looked at the shuttered windows and freaked out.

Maybe it was when they came up on the porch.

Maybe, maybe...

Val took a breath, set her jaw, gripped the rusted and pitted brass knob, and turned it.

The lock clicked open.

A soft sound. Not at all threatening.

It wants us to come in, Crow thought again, knowing it to be true.

Then there was another sound, and Crow was sure only he heard it. Not the lock, not the hinges; it was like the small intake of breath you hear around the dinner table when the knife is poised to make the first cut into a Thanksgiving turkey. The blade gleams, the turkey steams, mouths water, and each of the ravenous diners takes in a small hiss of breath as the naked reality of hunger is undisguised.

Val gave the door a little push and let go of the knob.

The hinges creaked like they were supposed to. It was a real creak, too. Not another hungry hiss. If the other sound had been one of expectation then the creak was the plunge of the knife.

Crow knew this even if he wasn't old enough yet to form the thoughts as cogently as he would in later years. Right now those impressions floated in his brain, more like colors or smells than structured thoughts. Even so, he understood them on a visceral level.

As the door swung open, Crow understood something else, too; two things, really.

The first was that after today he would never again need proof of anything in the unseen world.

And the second was that going into the Croft house was a mistake.

-6-

They went in anyway.

-7-

The door opened into a vestibule that was paneled in rotting oak. The broken globe light fixture on the ceiling above them was filled with dead bugs. There were no cobwebs, though, and no rat droppings on the floor.

In the back of Crow's mind he knew that he should have been worried about that. By the time the thought came to the front of his mind, it was too late.

The air inside was curiously moist, and it stank. It wasn't the smell of dust, or the stench of rotting meat. That's what Crow had expected; this was different. It was a stale, acidic smell that reminded him more of his father's breath after he came home from the bar. Crow knew that smell from all of the times his father bent over him, shouting at him while he whipped his belt up and down, up and down. The words his father shouted seldom made any sense. The stink of his breath was what Crow remembered. It was what he forced his mind to concentrate on so that he didn't feel the burning slap of the belt. Crow had gotten good at that over the years. He still felt the pain—in the moment and in the days following each beating—but he was able to pull his mind out of his body with greater ease each time as long as he focused on something else. How or why that distraction had become his father's pickled breath was something Crow never understood.

And now, as they moved from the vestibule into the living room, Crow felt as if the house itself was breathing at him with that same stink.

Crow never told his friends about the beatings. They all knew— Crow was almost always bruised somewhere—but this was small town Pennsylvania in 1974 and nobody ever talked about stuff like that. Not even his teachers. Just as Stick never talked about the fact that both of his sisters had haunted looks in their eyes and never— *ever*—let themselves be alone with their father. Not if they could avoid it. Janie and Kim had run away a couple of times each, but they never said why. You just didn't talk about some things. Nobody did.

Nobody.

Certainly not Crow.

So he had no point of reference for discussing the stink of this house. To mention it to his friends would require that he explain what else it smelled like. That was impossible. He'd rather die.

The house wanted us to come in, he thought, *and now we're in.*

Crow looked at the others. Stick hung back, almost crouching inside the vestibule and the wild look was back on his face. Terry stood with his hands in his pockets, but from the knuckly lumps under the denim Crow knew that he had his fists balled tight. Val had her arms wrapped around her chest as if she stood in a cold wind. No one was looking at him.

No one was looking at each other. Except for Crow.

Now we're inside.

Crow knew what would happen. He'd seen every movie about haunted houses, read every book. He had all the Warren *Eerie* and *Creepy* comics. He even had some of the old E.C. comics. He knew.

The house is going to fool us. It'll separate us. It'll kill us, one by one.

That's the way it always was. The ghost—or ghosts—would pull them apart, lead them into darkened cellars or hidden passages. They'd be left alone, and alone each one of them would die. Knives in the dark, missing stairs in a lightless hall, trapdoors, hands reaching out of shadows. They'd all die in here. Apart and alone. That was the way it always happened.

Except...

Except that it did not happen that way.

Crow saw something out of the corner of his eye. He turned to see a big mirror mounted on the wall. Dusty, cracked, the glass fogged.

He saw himself in the mirror.

Himself and not himself.

Crow stepped closer.

The reflection stepped closer, too.

Crow and Crow stared at each other. The boy with bruises, and a man who looked like his father. But it wasn't his father. It was Crow's own face, grown up, grown older. Pale, haggard, the jaws shadowy with a week's worth of unshaved whiskers, vomit stains drying on the shirt. A uniform shirt. A police uniform. Wrinkled and stained, like Kurt Bernhardt's. Even though it was a reflection, Crow could smell the vomit. The piss. The rank stink of exhaled booze and unbrushed teeth.

"Fuck you, you little shit," he said. At first Crow thought the cop was growling at him, but then Crow turned and saw Val and Terry. Only they were different. Everything was different, and even though the mirror was still there, nothing else was the same. This was outside, at night, in town. And the Val and Terry the cop was cursing at quietly were all grown up. They weren't reflections; they were real, they were here. Wherever and *whenever* here was.

Val was tall and beautiful, with long black hair and eyes that were filled with laughter. And she *was* laughing—laughing at something Terry said. There were even laugh lines around her mouth. They walked arm-in-arm past the shop windows on Corn Hill. She wore a dress and Terry was in a suit. Terry was huge, massive and muscular, but the suit he wore was expensive and perfectly tailored. He whispered to Val, and she laughed again. Then at the corner of Corn Hill and Baker Lane, they stopped to kiss. Val had to fight her laughs in order to kiss, and even then the kiss disintegrated into more laughs. Terry cracked up, too, and then they turned and continued walking along the street. They strolled comfortably. Like people who were walking home.

Home. Not home as kids on bikes, but to some place where they lived together as adults. Maybe as husband and wife.

Val and Terry.

Crow turned back to the mirror, which stood beside the cop—the only part of the Croft house that still existed in this world. The cop—the older Crow—stood in the shadows under an elm tree and watched Val and Terry. Tears ran like lines of mercury down his cheeks. Snot glistened on his upper lip. He sank down against the trunk of the tree, toppling the last few inches as his balance collapsed. He didn't even try to stop his fall, but instead lay with his cheek against the dirt. Some loose coins and a small stone fell out of the man's pocket.

Crow patted his own pocket. The lucky stone was there.

Still there.

Still his.

The moment stretched into a minute and then longer as Crow watched the drunken man weep in wretched silence. He wanted to turn away, but he couldn't. Not because the image was so compelling, but because when Crow actually tried to turn...he simply could not make his body move. He was frozen into that scene.

Locked.

Trapped.

The cop kept crying.

"Stop it," said Crow. He meant to say it kindly, but the words banged out of him, as harsh as a pair of slaps.

The cop froze, lifting his head as if he'd heard the words.

His expression was alert but filled with panic, like a deer who had just heard the crunch of a heavy footfall in the woods. It didn't last, though. The drunken glaze stole over it and the tense lips grew rubbery and slack. The cop hauled himself to a sitting position with his back to the tree, and the effort winded him so that he sat panting like a dog, his face greasy with sweat. Behind the alcohol haze, something dark and ugly and lost moved in his eyes.

Crow recognized it. The same shapeless thing moved behind his own eyes every time he looked in the mirror. Especially after a beating. But the shape in his own eyes was smaller than this, less sharply defined. His usually held more panic, and there was none at all here. Panic, he would later understand, was a quality of hope, even of wounded hope. In the cop's eyes, there was only fear. Not fear of death—Crow was experienced enough with fear to understand that much. No, this was the fear that, as terrible as this was, life was as good as it would ever be again. All that was left was the slide downhill.

"No..." murmured Crow, because he knew what was going to happen.

The cop's fingers twitched like worms waiting for the hook. They crawled along his thigh, over his hip bone. They found the leather holster and the gnarled handle of the Smith and Wesson.

Crow could not bear to watch. He needed to not see this. A scream tried to break from him, and he *wanted* it to break. A scream could break chains. A scream could push the boogeyman away. A scream could shatter this mirror.

But Crow could not scream.

Instead he watched as those white, trembling fingers curled around the handle of the gun and pulled it slowly from the holster.

He still could not turn...but now his hands could move. A little and with a terrible sluggishness, but they moved. His own fingers crawled along his thigh, felt for his pocket, wormed their way inside.

The click of the hammer being pulled back was impossibly loud.

Crow's fingers curled around the stone. It was cold and hard and so...*real.*

He watched the cylinder of the pistol rotate as the cop's thumb pulled the hammer all the way back.

Tears burned like acid in Crow's eyes and he summoned every ounce of will to pull the stone from his pocket. It came so slowly. It took a thousand years.

But it came out.

The cop lifted the barrel of the pistol and put it under his chin. His eyes were squeezed shut.

Crow raised his fist, and the harder he squeezed the stone the more power he had in his arm.

"I'm sorry..." Crow said, mumbling the two words through lips bubbling with spit.

The cop's finger slipped inside the curled trigger guard.

"I'm so sorry..."

Crow threw the stone at the same moment the cop pulled the trigger.

The stone struck the mirror a microsecond before the firing pin punched a hole in the world.

There was a sound. It wasn't the smash of mirror glass and it wasn't the bang of a pistol. It was something vast and black and impossible and it was the loudest sound Crow would ever hear. It was so monstrously loud that it broke the world.

Shards of mirror glass razored through the air around Crow, slashing him, digging deep into his flesh, gouging burning wounds in his mind. As each one cut him, the world shifted around Crow, buffeting him into different places, into different lives.

He saw Terry. The adult Terry, but now he was even older than the one who had been laughing with Val. It was crazy weird, but somehow Crow knew that this was as real as anything in his world.

Terry's face was lined with pain, his body crisscrossed with tiny cuts. Pieces of a broken mirror lay scattered around him. Each separate piece reflected Terry, but none of them were the Terry who stood in the midst of the debris. Each reflection was a distortion, a funhouse twist of Terry's face. Some were laughing—harsh and loud and fractured. Some were weeping. Some were glazed and catatonic. And one, a single large piece, showed a face that was more monster than man. Lupine and snarling and so completely *wrong*. The Terry who stood above the broken pieces screamed and if there was any sanity left in his mind it did not shine out through his blue eyes. Crow saw a version of his best friend who was completely and irretrievably *lost*.

Terry screamed and screamed, and then he spun around, ran straight across the room and threw himself headfirst out of the window. Crow fell with him. Together they screamed all the way down to the garden flagstones.

The impact shoved Crow into another place.

He was there with Val. They were in the cornfields behind Val's house. A black rain hammered down, the sky veined with red lightning. Val was older...maybe forty years old. She ran through the corn, skidding, slipping in the mud. Running toward a figure that lay sprawled on the ground.

"Dad!" screamed Val.

Mr. Guthrie lay on his stomach, his face pressed into the muck. In the brightness of the lightning, Crow could see a neat round bullet hole between his shoulder blades, the cloth washed clean of blood by the downpour.

"No!" shrieked Val. She dropped to her knees and clawed her father into her arms. His big old body resisted her, fighting her with limpness and weight and sopping clothes, but eventually Val found the strength to turn him onto his back.

"Daddy...Daddy...?"

His face was totally slack, streaked with mud that clumped on his mustache and caught in his bushy eyebrows.

Val wiped the mud off his face and shook him very gently.

"Daddy...*please*..."

The lightning never stopped, and the thunder bellowed insanely. A freak eddy of wind brought sounds from the highway. The high, lonely wail of a police siren, but Crow knew that the cops would be too late. They were already too late.

Crow spun out of that moment and into another. There were police sirens here, too, and the flashing red and blue lights, but no rain. This was a different place, a different moment. A different horror.

He was there.

He was a cop.

He was sober. Was he younger or older? He prayed that this was him as an older man, just as Val and Terry had been older.

Older. Sober.

Alive.

However the moment was not offering any mercies.

Stick was there. He was on his knees and Crow was bent over him, forcing handcuffs onto his friend's wrists. They were both speaking, saying the same things over and over again.

"What did you do? Christ, Stick, what did you *do*?"

"I'm sorry," Stick said. "I'm sorry."

On the porch of the house a female cop and an EMT were supporting a ten year old girl toward a waiting ambulance. The girl looked a lot like Janie and Kim, Stick's sisters, but Crow knew that she wasn't. He knew that this girl was Stick's daughter. Her face was bruised. Her clothes were torn. There was blood on her thighs.

"What did you do, Stick, what did you *do*?"

"I'm sorry," wept Stick. His mouth bled from where Crow had punched him. "I'm sorry."

Crow saw other images.

People he did not know. Some dressed in clothes from long ago, some dressed like everyone else. He stepped into sick rooms and cells, he crawled through the shattered windows of wrecked cars and staggered coughing through the smoke of burning houses.

Crow squeezed his eyes shut and clapped his hands over his ears. He screamed and screamed.

The house exhaled its liquor stink of breath at him.

-8-

Crow heard Val yell. Not the woman, but the girl.

He opened his eyes and saw the Morgan silver dollar leave her outstretched hand. It flew past him and he turned to see it strike the mirror. The same mirror he'd shattered with his lucky stone.

For just a moment he caught that same image of her kneeling in the rain, but then the glass detonated.

Then he was running.

He wasn't conscious of when he was able to run. When he was *allowed* to run.

But he was running.

They were all running.

As Crow scrambled for the door he cast a single desperate look back to see that the mirror was undamaged by either stone or coin. All of the restraints that had earlier held his limbs were gone, as if the house, glutted on his pain, ejected the table scraps.

And so they ran.

Terry shoved Stick so hard that it knocked his ball-cap off of his head. No one stooped to pick it up. They crowded into the vestibule and burst out onto the porch and ran for their bikes. They were all screaming.

They screamed as they ran and they screamed as they got on their bikes.

Their screams dwindled as the house faded behind its screen of withered trees.

The four of them tore down the dirt road and burst onto the access road, and turned toward town, pumping as hard as they could. They raced as hard and as fast as they could.

Only when they reached the edge of the pumpkin patch on the far side of the Guthrie farm did they slow and finally stop.

Panting, bathed in sweat, trembling, they huddled over their bikes, looking down at the frames, at their sneakered feet, at the dirt.

Not at each other.

Crow did not know if the others had seen the same things he'd seen. Or perhaps their own horrors.

Beside him, Terry seemed to be the first to recover. He reached into his pocket for his comb, but it wasn't there. He took a deep breath and let it out, then dragged trembling fingers through his hair.

"It must be dinner time," he said, and he turned his bike toward town and pedaled off. Terry did not look back.

Stick dragged his forearm across his face and looked at the smear, just as he had done before. Was he looking for tears? Or for the blood that had leaked from the corners of his mouth when the older Crow had punched him? A single sob broke in his chest, and he shook his head. Crow thought he saw Stick mouth those same two terrible words. *I'm sorry.*

Stick rode away.

That was the last time he went anywhere with Crow, Val, or Terry. During the rest of that summer and well into the fall, Stick went deep inside of himself. Eight years later, Crow read in the papers that George Stickler had swallowed an entire bottle of sleeping pills, though he was not yet as old as he had been in the vision. Crow was heartbroken but he was not surprised, and he wondered what the line was between the cowardice of suicide and an act of bravery.

For five long minutes Crow and Val sat on their bikes, one foot each braced on the ground. Val looked at the cornfields in the distance and Crow looked at her. Then, without saying a word, Val got off her bike and walked it down the lane toward her house. Crow sat there for almost half an hour before he could work up the courage to go home.

None of them ever spoke about that day. They never mentioned the Croft house. They never asked what the others had seen.

Not once.

The only thing that ever came up was the Morgan silver dollar. One evening Crow and Terry looked it up in a coin collector's book. In mint condition it was valued at forty-eight thousand dollars. In poor condition it was still worth twenty thousand.

That coin probably still lay on the Croft house living room floor.

Crow and Terry looked at each other for a long time. Crow knew that they were both thinking about that coin. Twenty thousand dollars, just lying there. Right there.

It might as well have been on the dark side of the moon.

Terry closed his coin book and set it aside. As far as Crow knew, Terry never collected coins after that summer. He also knew that neither of them would ever go back for that silver dollar. Not for ten thousand dollars. Not for ten million. Like everything else they'd seen there—the wallet, the pill bottle, the diaper, all of it—the coin belonged to the house. Like Terry's pocket comb. Like Stick's ball-cap. And Crow's lucky stone.

And what belonged to the house would stay there.

The house kept its trophies.

Crow went to the library and looked through the back issues of newspapers, through obituaries, but try as he might he found no records at all of anyone ever having died there.

Somehow it didn't surprise him.

There weren't ghosts in the Croft house. It wasn't that kind of thing.

He remembered what he'd thought when he first saw the old place.

The house is hungry.

-9-

Later, after Crow came home from Terry's house, he sat in his room long into the night, watching the moon and stars rise from behind the trees and carve their scars across the sky. He sat with his window open, arms wrapped around his shins, shivering despite a hot breeze.

It was ten days since they'd gone running from the house.

Ten days and ten nights. Crow was exhausted. He'd barely slept, and when he did there were nightmares. Never—not once in any of those dreams—was there a monster or a ghoul chasing him. They weren't those kinds of dreams. Instead he saw the image that he'd seen in the mirror. The older him.

The drunk.

The fool.

Crow wept for that man.

For the man he knew that he was going to become.

He wept and he did not sleep. He tried, but even though his eyes burned with fatigue, sleep simply would not come. Crow knew that it wouldn't come. Not tonight, and maybe not any night. Not as long as he could remember that house.

And he knew he could never forget it.

Around three in the morning, when his father's snores banged off the walls and rattled his bedroom door, Crow got up and, silent as a ghost, went into the hall and downstairs. Down to the kitchen, to the cupboard. The bottles stood in a row. Canadian Club. Mogen-David 20-20. Thunderbird. And a bottle of vodka without a label. Cheap stuff, but a lot of it.

Crow stood staring at the bottles for a long time. Maybe half an hour.

"No," he told himself.

No, agreed his inner voice.

No, screamed the drunken man in his memory.

No.

Crow reached up and took down the vodka bottle. He poured some into a Dixie cup.

"No," he said.

And drank it.

Author's Note on "Whistlin' Past the Graveyard"

This is the last of the four Pine Deep short stories in this collection, and the one that lends this book its name. It's also a personal favorite because it introduces a pair of supporting characters—Near Danny and Far Danny—who have been lurking around in my head for quite a while waiting to come onstage. They will be returning in other stories (not yet written).

Like the first two Pine Deep stories, this one takes place after the events of the Trilogy.

Whistlin' Past the Graveyard

This story takes place several years after the events described in the Pine Deep Trilogy, of which *Ghost Road Blues* is the first volume. You do not need to have read those books in order to read—and hopefully enjoy—this little tale set in rural Pennsylvania.

-1-

He had six different names.

It was Francisco Sponelli on his birth certificate, but even his parents never called him that. They called him Little Frankie most of his life. A kid's name that, once hung on him, made sure he'd never quite grow up. His father wasn't even Big Frankie. Dad was Vinnie. Big Frankie was an uncle back in Sicily but who wasn't called Big Frankie *in* Sicily; just when people talked about him. Big Frankie never set a goddamn foot on American soil.

In school—from about four minutes after he stepped onto the kindergarten playground—he was Spoons. It was better than Little Frankie in about the same way that a kick in the balls was better than catching the clap. Not a holiday either way.

In the old neighborhood in South Philly—he was Frankie Spoons for all of the six months he lived there. And that's a cool name. Made him sound like a Made Man, which he would never and could never be, but it sounded great when he walked into the taproom and someone called out, "Hey, Frankie Spoons, come on and have a beer with the grown-ups."

Actually, no one ever said exactly that, but it was in his head. It's what he heard every time he walked into the bar. Especially when he saw one of the Donatellas there, who were third or fourth cousins. It was the kind of thing they said to each other because they *were* made men. The Donatella cousins worked a protection racket their family had owned since the sixties. They all had great nicknames and they all said cool things to each other. Francisco just liked hanging out at that bar because it made him feel like a man, like a tough guy.

Then he knocked up a girl from the burbs and next thing he was living in a crappy little town called Pine Deep in the inbred Deliverance backwoods of Bucks County. Near *her* folks and family, way too far from Philly, and although it was right over the bridge from New Jersey it wasn't over the right bridge. Cross over the Delaware up there and you're in fucking Stockton or Lambertville or some other artsy-fartsy damn place where they put boursin cheese on a son of a bitching cheese-steak, which is like putting nipple rings on the Virgin Mary.

Out there in Pine Deep he was Spoonsie to the guys at the Scarecrow Tavern. Another stupid name that clung to him like cow shit on good shoes.

He longed to go back to Philly, but Debbie kept popping out kids like she had a t-shirt cannon in her hoo-hah. And any conversation involving 'sex' and 'condoms' became a long argument about a bunch of Bible shit that he was sure didn't really matter to God, Jesus, the Virgin, or anyone else. Four kids and counting. In this economy? On his pay? Seriously? God wants kids to grow up poor and stupid in a town like this?

As his Uncle Tony was so fond of saying, "Shee-eee-eee-ee-it."

But...

The nickname was only part of it. It was a splinter under the skin.

The kids? Well, fuck it. He did love them. Loved the process of making them, too, though he'd like to explore the option of stopping before he and Debbie turned their lives into one of those we-have-no-self-control-over-our-procreative-common-sense reality shows.

He suspected that she had some kind of mental damage. She seemed to enjoy being pregnant. Bloated ankles, hemorrhoids, mucus plugs, the whole deal. He was pretty sure that on some level Debbie was—to use the precise medical term—batshit crazy.

But she was also the most beautiful woman he'd ever talked to. Even now, four kids in and a bigger ass than she used to have, Debbie could look at him from out of the corners of her eyes and stop his heart.

Even now.

So...he stayed in Pine Deep.

And he worked in Pine Deep.

That was something by itself. A lot of people in town didn't have jobs. The town was still recovering from the Trouble, and the economy blew. Sure, a few of the stores had rebuilt and there was some out of town money to rebuild the infrastructure. Federal bucks. And after the town burned down, there was that big rock concert fundraiser bullshit. Willie Nelson, the Eagles, Coldplay, bunch of others including some rappers Francisco never even heard of. It was on TV with that stupid nickname: ANTI-terror. With terror crossed out. All those middle-aged rock stars, none of whom had ever even heard of Pine Deep before those militiamen torched everything, singing about unity and brotherhood. Blah, blah, blah. If any of the money they raised ever actually reached the town then it never made it into Francisco Sponelli's bank account.

All he got was an offer of free counseling for PTSD, which he didn't have, and a stack of literature about surviving domestic terrorism, which he didn't read, and a pissant break on his taxes for two years, which wasn't enough.

On the upside—which Francisco didn't think was really 'up' in any way—the Trouble had kind of passed him by. He and Debbie and the kid—only one back then—were down in Warrington watching a movie at the multiplex when it all went down. They heard it on the news driving back. The news guys said that a bunch of shit-for-brains white supremacists put drugs like LSD and other stuff into the town's drinking water and every single person went apeshit. What made it worse was that it was Halloween and the town was totally packed with tourists. All those thousands of people went out of their minds and started killing each other. Worst day of domestic terrorism in U.S. history. That much was a fact. Francisco took Debbie and the kid to her sister's in Doylestown for a week. By the time they came back Pine Deep looked like a war zone. Lot of people they knew were dead. Lot of the town was gone. Just freaking gone.

Lot of people out of work, too, because Pine Deep was built with tourist dollars.

One of the few businesses that didn't go under was the one he worked for. The one owned by Tom Gaines, Debbie's third cousin. Francisco's workload tripled, but he didn't get overtime. Gaines said he couldn't afford it because a lot of the customers couldn't afford to pay. Not right away. Some not at all.

But the job still had to be done.

And that was his life. Working for one of Debbie's family at shit for pay. Not exactly starvation wages, but it was a job with no future. Not really. Sure, he could have the job for as long as he wanted, but there was nowhere to go. There was no promotion possible. The whole company was the owner, Mr. Gaines, and him. And a couple of guys they hired by the hour to help with some heavy stuff. All of the rest of it was Francisco's to do.

Trimming all the hedges.

Pruning the trees.

Mowing the grass.

Digging the graves.

And...the other stuff.

The stuff he did at night.

So the graves wouldn't be messed with.

Mr. Gaines sometimes slipped him a couple extra bucks when things got bad. And he let Francisco drink as much as he wanted on the job.

He encouraged Francisco.

It was that kind of a job.

-2-

Before the Trouble the job wasn't really that bad. Dead people don't complain, they don't give you shit. They don't dime you out when you go into one of the crypts to smoke a joint. He could get to a level, get mellow, and that would carry him through even the longest shift.

The job was quiet except for occasionally chasing teenagers out of the crypts who'd gone there to drink or light up. Once in a while some prick vandal would use spray paint to tag a mausoleum or knock over a few headstones. But that happened in every cemetery, and everyone knew that, so Francisco adjusted to it as part of the job. The job was okay.

Even for a while after the Trouble it was tolerable. He worked mostly days, and Gaines didn't go out of his way to be a prick. The boss was cheap, but not a cheap fuck. The difference mattered.

Then things started changing.

It started with people talking. The Scarecrow was one of the few bars that wasn't burned down, and it was a good place for a plate of wings and a schooner of Yuengling at the end of a day. But the flavor of the conversation there changed as the weeks and months went on. It really started after the cops and fire inspectors sorted out the last of the bones. It had taken a lot of sweat and elbow grease to put together a list of all the dead. The official tally was eleven thousand six-hundred and forty-one. Two thirds of the whole town. Only the thing was that there weren't that many bodies. The count was short. Eighty-four short, and that's a lot of bodies to misplace.

They brought in teams of dogs to search the woods and the fields and under frigging haystacks. Still eighty-four missing.

The count stayed the same.

That's when the vandals started hitting the cemetery. Knocked-over headstones, grave dirt churned up, his tool shed broken into, beer bottles everywhere. Couple of times he discovered that someone had pissed on a grave he'd just filled in. He mentioned all this to his cousins over a poker game. Near Danny was nodding before he finished describing the disturbances.

"Sure, sure, that makes sense," said Near Danny.

"It does?" asked Francisco, confused.

"Yeah," agreed Far Danny. "People are blowin' off steam. With all that shit happening—"

"All those people dying," added Near Danny.

"All that death and shit..."

"...they're like obsessed with that death shit."

"Morbid."

"Morbid."

Francisco looked back and forth between them. "Okay, but why trash the cemetery?"

Near Danny and Far Danny said it at the same time. "Power."

Francisco said, "Huh?"

"Death came to that little fucking town and made everybody its bitch," said Far Danny.

Near Danny nodded. "And that boneyard—hell, that...what word am I looking for?"

"'Symbolizes,'" supplied Far Danny.

"Yeah, that boneyard symbolizes death. So...of course someone who lost everything's going to go take a piss on it."

"Show death that *he's* alive, that he's nobody's bitch."

The two Dannys nodded.

"Wow," said Francisco.

Then Far Danny leaned across the card table and stabbed a finger at him. "But if any of these mamluke bastards fucks with *you*, then that's different."

"It is?"

Near Danny grunted and gave him a hard sneer. "You're family."

"Nobody fucks with the family," said Far Danny. "No fucking body, you hear me, Frankie Spoons?"

"Any shit comes down you can't handle, you pick up the phone."

They sat there grinning at him like extras from a bad gangster film. Chest hair and gold chains, big gold rings, perpetual five o'clock shadow on lantern jaws. But they were the real deal. South Philly muscle who were tough on a level that Francisco could understand only from a distance. It was the kind of feeling you get looking at the big cats in the zoo.

Then the conversation turned to sports, as it always does. Could the Eagles do anything about their passing game, 'cause right now it was like watching the Special Olympics.

More weeks passed and that's when people in town started talking.

Whispering, really. Real quiet, nothing out loud. Nothing in front of anyone. The whispers started over beers. At first it was late at night, before closing, guys talking the way guys do. Talking shit. Throwing theories out there because that was the time of night for that kind of thing.

Even then people talked *around* it. They didn't so much say it as ask questions. Putting it out there.

Like Scotty Sharp who asked, "Do you think they really put drugs in the water?"

People said sure, of course they did. The Fed tested the water, they did blood tests on the people.

That's when Mike DeMarco said, "Yeah, well my sister Gertie's oldest daughter goes out with that kid, you know the one. He's an EMT up to Crestville. And he said that only about one in four people tested positive for drugs."

Then some guy would say that was bullshit and there'd be an argument. It would quiet things down. Until the next time it came back up.

Lucky Harris—and Francisco thought Lucky was a kickass nickname—asked, "Did you guys see that thing on the History Channel?"

They all did. A special about Pine Deep. Two thirds of it was the same bullshit you could get out of any tourist brochure, but then there was section near the end when they interviewed a few survivors—and Francisco wondered if they deliberately picked the ones who looked like they were either half in the bag or half out of their minds. These 'witnesses' insisted that the Trouble wasn't what the news was saying it was, that the white supremacist thing was a cover up for what was really happening. And this is where the host of the show changed his voice to sound mysterious right as he asked what the *real* truth was about the Pine Deep Massacre.

"It was monsters," said the witness. An old duffer with white around his eyes.

"What kind of monsters?" asked the host.

"*All* kinds. Vampires and werewolves and demons and such. That's always been the problem with Pine Deep...we got monsters and that night? Yeah, the monsters came to get us."

The host then condensed the eyewitness reports into a speculation that the white supremacists were really servants of a vampire king—like Renfield was to Dracula—and that the drugs in the water and all of the explosions were distractions, subterfuge.

Then there was a montage of jump shots that lasted only long enough for a dozen other witnesses to say the word 'vampire.' The segment ended with the kind of dumbass tell-nothing questions those shows always have, accompanied by stock footage of old Dracula flicks and shots of Pine Deep taken with cameras tilted to weird angles. "Was Pine Deep the site of an attack by vampires? Do the dead really walk the earth? Have creatures out of legend begun a war against the world of the living? And what about the missing eighty-four? Authorities continue to search for their bodies, but there are some who believe that these people aren't missing at all and are instead hiding...and perhaps *hunting* during the long nights in this troubled little town. Government sources deny these claims. Local law enforcement refuse to comment. But there are some...who believe."

The guys at the Scarecrow had all seen that special. Just as they had all seen the headlines of the National Enquirer which had supposed photos of vampires on the front page at least once a month.

Everybody knew about the stories. The conspiracy theories. As soon as the main shock of the tragedy died down, Jon Stewart and Stephen Colbert went ass-wild on the subject. They did bits about small town vampires. Conan started a running segment with a vampire dressed in farmer's coveralls; at the end of each segment the vampire would get killed in some funny way. He'd go out to harvest, forgetting he'd planted his fields with garlic. He'd trip over a chicken and fall on a convenient sharp piece of wood. The vanes of a windmill would cast a shadow of a cross on him. Shit like that. Making a joke out of it because it was stupid.

Vampires.

It was all bullshit.

Except that as the first year crumbled into the dirt and the next year grew up dark and strange, it got harder and harder to call it bullshit.

Especially after people started dying.

There was a rash of car accidents in town. Accidents weren't all that rare with all the twists and turns on A32, but before the Trouble it was mostly tourists who wrapped their SUVs or Toyotas around an oak tree they didn't see, or college kids driving too drunk and too fast with too much faith in underdeveloped decision-making capabilities.

But there was no tourism in Pine Deep right now. Maybe in another couple of years. Maybe if some outside group rebuilt the Haunted Hayride and the other attractions. Right now, State Alternate Route A32 was mostly empty except for farm workers coming and going to day jobs or farmer's wives heading into town to work shifts at the hospital or at one of the craft shops.

So, it was locals who started dying.

Linda Carmichael went first. Her six-year-old Hyundai went off the road, rolled and hit a parked hay bailer that was sitting at the edge of a field. The papers said that she was so badly mangled that her husband had to confirm her I.D. by looking at a mole on what was left of her torso. Francisco didn't know if he believed that part, but when he drove past the accident spot on the way to work the next day, the car looked like a piece of aluminum foil somebody'd crinkled up.

It was a matter of discussion at the Scarecrow, but the Carmichael's weren't part of their circle, so the conversation moved on to sports.

The second accident was a bus full of Puerto Rican day workers. Nine dead because the bus skidded off the road and hit a panel truck. Both drivers were dead, too. There were no witnesses, but it must have been a hell of an impact to mangle everyone that badly.

"Yeah, maybe," said Lou Tremons, "but here's the thing, Spoonsie, there were no skid marks and my cousin Davy heard Sheriff Crow say that it didn't look like a high speed crash."

"Well hell, son," said Scotty, "you can't kill that many people in a low speed crash."

They all agreed that the sheriff, who used to be a drunk a long time ago, was probably drinking again and didn't know his ass from his elbow.

The conversation turned to sports.

But the deaths kept happening.

A mailman ran his truck into a drainage ditch and went halfway through the windshield in the process. Aaron Schmidt's son flipped his motorcycle.

Like that.

All violent accidents. Every single body torn up.

Lots of blood on the blacktop.

Except...

Lou's cousin Davy heard Sheriff Crow tell his deputy that there didn't seem to be enough blood. In each case there was less than you'd expect.

When Francisco dropped that little tidbit the conversation at the bar stalled. Nobody talked sports that night. Nobody said much of anything that night. Even Francisco kept his thoughts to himself and watched the foam on his beer disappear, one bubble at a time.

The following summer was when the fires started. Everyone blamed it on the constant high temperatures, on global warming. But this was Pennsylvania not Wyoming. There was a lot of water in the state, and even with the heat there was plenty of rain. Francisco found it hard to buy that a drought killed all those people.

And a lot of people burned up, too.

Three of the Carter family went up while they slept. Only Jolene survived because she was in the Navy.

The guys all talked about that, throwing out different theories. Bud Tuckerman suggested that it was most likely bad wiring because Holly Carter always had the air conditioners going full blast, and it had been a lot of summers since her husband had bought a new unit. The other guys mumbled agreement, but nothing sounded like enthusiastic support for that theory to Francisco.

The other fires? Five dead at the Hendrickson farm when the barn went up and cooked some kids from the horse camp.

The wiring at the camp was inspected twice a year. Scotty said so because that's what he did for a living and he'd swear on a stack of fucking bibles that everything was up to code. Better than code, he said.

A lot of beers got drunk in thoughtful silence that night.

The weeks of summer burned away, and by fall there were four more fires. Two business, one hotel, one house.

That last one was a ball-buster. That's where it hit home to the guys at the Scarecrow. It was Lou Tremons who got fried.

After the funeral the guys met at the tavern in a missing man formation, with Lou's seat left empty and a glass of lager poured for him. The conversation was lively for most of the night as they all told lies about Lou. Tall tales, funny stories, some tearful memories. Francisco talked about the time he and Lou drove down to Philly to play cards with the Donatella cousins. Francisco described how Lou nearly busted a nut trying not to laugh at what everyone called the cousins. They were both named Danny, and as cousins they looked a lot alike, almost like twins, except that one of the Dannys—the one from Two Street—was really short, maybe five-seven, and the other Danny, the one who lived near Gino's Steaks, was a moose, six-seven. They looked like the same guy seen up close and far away, and long ago the Don had nicknamed the big one Near Danny and the little one Far Danny.

Francisco warned Lou ahead of time not to laugh about it to their faces. Near Danny would break his arm off and beat Lou to death with it; and Far Danny carried a Glock nine and a straight razor and he was a bad mamba-jamba. They worked the protection racket and they were a pair of guys with whom you absolutely did not want to fuck. No sir, no way.

Francisco had a private motive for inviting Lou to the game. The Donatellas always called him Frankie Spoons, and he hoped Lou would pick it up and spread it to Pine Deep. But it didn't happen.

They had fun though. Francisco caught the laughter in Lou's eyes all through the night, but Lou kept a plug in it until they were back in the car on I-95 heading north toward home.

"Then he totally lost his shit," said Francisco, and everybody had a good long laugh. Then they toasted Lou and tapped their glasses to his and drank. More than a couple of them had tears in their eyes.

Mike said, "Hey, Spoonsie, I saw a big bunch of flowers from the Donatella family. Was that the Dannys?"

"Yeah," said Francisco.

"Nice of 'em."

"Yeah. They're standup. They liked Lou."

The guys nodded. Everyone liked Lou. What wasn't to like?

"Far Danny called me," added Francisco. "After Lou...you know."

Everyone nodded.

"He said that he heard a lot of people been dying here in town."

More nods. Nobody said anything.

"Then he asks me if I thought there was anything hinky with Lou's death."

"Hinky," said Mike. Not a question, just keeping the word out there.

"Hinky," agreed Francisco.

"Why'd he want to know that, Spoonsie?" asked the bartender, Joey, who was leaning on the bar, listening like he usually did.

"Like I said, he and Near Danny both thought Lou was okay. They told me they thought he was standup."

Nods.

"I thought you said those boys were wiseguys," said Joey.

Francisco shrugged. "Yeah, well...they're not bad guys."

Which was bullshit and they all knew it, but they were Francisco's cousins and when you're related to criminals—unless they were pedophiles or like that—then whatever they did wasn't so bad. Or as bad. Or something. None of them really looked too close at it.

"If it *was* something hinky, then maybe they'd have come up here, looked into it. They're like that. Lou was my friend and he didn't shark them at cards, and they laughed at his jokes. So, I guess...you know."

They nodded. They knew.

"But I told them it was just an accident," said Francisco. "Just a string of bad luck."

They nodded at that, too, but no one met his eyes.

The only one there who was nearly silent all evening was Scotty and eventually Francisco noticed.

"What's wrong, man?" he asked. Scotty was friends with Lou, but only here at the bar. They weren't really tight.

"I don't know, Spoonsie," Scotty began, fiddling with a book of matches. He'd pulled each match off and distractedly chipped off the sulfur with his thumbnail and peeled the paper apart layer by layer.

He stopped and stared down at the pile of debris on the bar as if surprised that it was there.

"What is it?" asked Lucky Harris.

"It's just that..." Scotty began, faltered and tried it again. "It's just that I'm beginning to wonder if your cousin Far Danny is right."

"About what?" asked Francisco.

"About there being something hinky."

"About Lou's death?"

"That...and everything else that's going on in town. You know...since the Trouble."

Everyone was looking at him now, and the intensity of their attention formed a little cone of silence around that end of the bar. Francisco was dimly aware of other people, other conversations, music, the Flyers on the flatscreen, but suddenly it all belonged to another world.

"What are you saying?" asked Mike.

"I don't know what I'm saying," Scotty said in a way that said he *did* know what he was saying. Everyone waited. He took a breath and let it out. "I was watching that show again. You know the one." They nodded. "And sometimes—not all the time, but sometimes—I wonder if it's all bullshit or if maybe, y'know, there's something there."

He suddenly looked around, trying to catch everyone's eyes, looking for someone laughing at him. Francisco followed his gaze, looking for the same thing. But nobody was laughing. Nobody was smiling. Most of the guys did nothing for a few moments, then one by one they nodded.

That killed the conversation.

And it nearly stopped Francisco's heart from beating.

He saw Scotty say something completely under his breath. Francisco read his lips, though.

Scotty said, "*Jesus Christ.*"

-3-

Over the next few months things in Pine Deep seemed to swing back and forth between a rash of new deaths and periods of calm. In a weird way Francisco was more freaked out by the long spaces between the deaths. It was too much like calms before bad storms. And each one was a little longer than the last, so each time it became way too easy to start thinking that it was over. This time it was over.

Except that it wasn't over.

The guys still met at the Scarecrow. They still talked about things, and all the time what Scotty said stayed with them like they'd been tattooed with it. But they didn't actually *talk* about it. Not out loud, not in words. But through eye contact? Sure. And with silences and with things that weren't said aloud. They all knew each other well enough to have those kinds of conversations. Francisco wondered who would pick up Scotty's conversational ball and run with it.

For his part, Francisco had to deal with another effect of the increased mortality in Pine Deep. He managed a cemetery. He dug the graves.

And he didn't like what was going on at Pinelands Grove, which is what the place was called.

His discomfort with things at work started a few weeks after Lou's funeral. It was an overcast day late in October. The colors of the autumn leaves were muted to muddy browns and purples as the slate gray sky thickened into an early darkness. A wet wind was blowing out of the southwest, and the breeze was filled with the smells of horseshit and rotting leaves. Francisco was working in the west corner of the Grove, which was almost a mile from the front gate. The Grove was huge, with sections of old plots that dated back to the Civil War and even a few to Colonial times. But the west corner was new. Before the Trouble it had been a cabbage field that belonged to the Reynolds farm, but the Reynolds family died that night and the farm went to a relative who sold it cheap just to unload it. Now the only thing that was planted there were dead bodies. Nineteen in the last month. Not all of them from accidents or fires, but enough so that it was a sad place to be.

That afternoon the O'Learys, a nice young couple, buried their thirteen year old daughter. She'd been run over by a UPS truck. The truck driver tried to swerve, at least according to the skid marks on the road, but he'd clipped her and then plowed right into a tree. Two dead. Francisco didn't know where the driver was buried. Doylestown or New Hope, maybe. But little Kaitlin O'Leary went into the ground after a noon graveside service. Pretty pink coffin that probably cost too much for her family to afford. One of those sentimental decisions funeral directors count on. And, Francisco thought, Kaitlin was the only kid. She wouldn't need a car, college tuition or anything else. If buying a pink casket gave her mother even a little bit of comfort, then fuck it.

The family stayed while the coffin was lowered down by the electric winch, and they and all their friends tossed handfuls of dirt and pink roses into the hole, but Mrs. O'Leary lost it around then and her husband took her away before she had to watch Francisco dump a couple of yards of wormy dirt down on their little girl.

Francisco waited a good long time to make sure nobody came late. Then he used a front-end loader to shift the dirt. He tramped it all down with his shoes and pats from a shovel, put his equipment away, and came back to arrange the bouquets and grave blankets according to the parents' wishes. The garage was by the gate, but he didn't mind the walk. He walked four or five miles a day here at the Grove, and he was okay with that. Kept his weight down, good for the heart.

Except when he came walking across the damp grass toward the grave he could see that something was wrong.

The flowers were no longer standing in a neat row waiting for him to arrange them. They were torn apart and scattered everywhere. The grave blanket was in pieces, too. And the little teddy bear Mrs. O'Leary had left for her little girl had been mutilated, gutted, its stuffing yanked out and trampled in the dirt.

Francisco registered all of this, but what made him jerk to a stop and stand there was the condition of the grave.

It was open.

Open.

"Jesus Christ," he breathed.

In the time it had taken Francisco to drive the front-end loader back and put his gear away, someone—some fucking maniac—had come up, dug up all the dirt, and left a gaping hole.

Francisco snapped out of his shock and ran to the grave, skidded to a stop and teetered on the edge, staring down.

The coffin was exposed.

Pale pink metal, streaked with dirt.

But it was worse than that.

Much worse.

The coffin had been pried open, the seals broken.

Inside there was tufted white silk. There was a photo of the whole family at Disney World. There was a letter from Mrs. O'Leary. All of that was there.

But Kaitlin was not there.

She was gone.

Gone.

God.

-4-

That was one of the longest nights in Francisco's life. Calling Gaines. Calling the cops.

Answering a thousand questions.

The cops—Sheriff Crow—grilling him, almost accusing him.

Gaines looking furious and scared, and giving him looks.

Everybody watching as the sheriff made Francisco take a breathalyzer. Their confusion when he passed. No trace of alcohol.

All the rubberneckers showing up in crowds like someone sent out invitations.

The reporters. First the local guys, then stringers for the regional news. Then the network TV vans. Shoving cameras and microphones in his face.

Hour after hour.

Then the O'Learys showing up.

Yelling at him.

Screaming.

Mrs. O'Leary totally losing her shit. Nobody thinking that was strange, because it wasn't strange. Francisco thought about how he'd feel if this was the grave of one of his kids. He'd fucking kill someone. Himself, probably.

Francisco saw Mike and Scotty and Lucky from the Scarecrow. Some of the other guys, too. Hanging back, standing in a knot, bending now and then to whisper something to each other. Scotty nodded to him once, and that made him feel a little better. Solidarity. He was still one of them, and that wasn't a sure bet at first. Sometimes things cut you out and make you one of 'them,' one of the people the guys talk about rather than talk to.

Debbie texted him a dozen times, asking if he was okay, telling him everything was on the news, telling him things would be okay, asking when he was coming home.

It was nearly dawn before the cops cut him loose and let him drive home. By then most of the crowd was gone. His friends were gone, and the Scarecrow was closed.

Even Gaines was gone. Probably on the phone with his lawyer, worrying about how much of his money he was going to lose to the O'Learys when they sued. And, of course, they would sue. This was America, everybody sued everybody. Might even mean that Gaines would fire him, cut his losses, try to blame it all on him.

The last person left at the cemetery was Sheriff Crow.

"You can go," he said.

Francisco stood for a while, though, staring at the grave.

"Why?" he asked. For maybe the fiftieth time.

The sheriff didn't answer. Instead he asked a question he'd already asked. "And you saw no one here?"

"Like I told you. I was alone here."

"No kids?"

That was a new question and it startled him.

"What—you think some jackasses from the college—?"

"No, I mean younger kids. Did you see any young teenagers?"

"No."

"No teenage girls?"

Francisco shot him a look. "What? Like girls from Kaitlin's class?"

The sheriff just stood there, looking at him with an expression that didn't give anything away. "You can go," he said again.

Francisco trudged back to his car, confused and hurt and scared. Sad, too. He wanted to go home and hug his kids, kiss his wife, and check the locks on all the doors.

When he got into his car he checked his cell phone and saw that he'd missed a bunch of text messages. From Scotty and a couple of the guys. Shows of support. More from Debbie asking when he was coming home.

And one from Far Danny. He grunted in surprise. The Dannys sometimes texted him, mostly about sports or card games, and always on the birthdays of his kids, but he didn't expect to hear from them tonight.

The message read: *Saw u on the news, cuz. Somebody fucking with you?*

For some reason it made Francisco smile. He texted back, *Don't know what's happening. Thanks for asking.*

As he was starting his car a reply message bing-bonged. *Anybody gets in your shit, call.*

Francisco smiled again, started the car and drove home.

-5-

Francisco headed down the long, winding black ribbon of A32 with music turned up loud so he didn't have to listen to his thoughts. An oldies station. Billy Joel insisting he didn't start a fire. Francisco not hearing any of the words because you really *couldn't* not listen to your thoughts about something like this. His car was bucketing along at eighty when he topped the rise that began the long drop down to the development where he lived.

Immediately he slammed on the brakes.

Two people were walking along the side of the road, so close to the blacktop that Francisco had to swerve to keep from clipping them.

Two people.

A tall man with thinning blond hair.

A teenage girl.

Walking hand-in-hand.

They heard his car, heard the screech of his tires on the road, turned into the splash of high beams. They stared at him through the windshield.

They smiled at him.

Francisco screamed.

He screamed so long and so loud that it tore his throat raw.

The car began to turn, the ass-end swinging around, smoke rising from the rubber seared onto the asphalt, the world around the car spinning. The world in general losing all tethers to anything that made sense.

Francisco had no memory of how he kept out of the ditch or kept from rolling. His hands were doing things and his feet were doing things but his mind was absolutely fucking numb as the car spun in a complete circle and then spun another half-turn so that when it rocked to a bone-rattling stop he was facing the way he'd come, his headlights painting the top of the rise and washing the two figures to paleness.

Man and girl.

They stood there, still looking at him.

Still smiling.

Francisco kept screaming.

Screaming and screaming and screaming.

Long after the car stopped rocking.

The man and the girl hesitated, then they took a single step toward him.

Which is when the light on their faces changed from white to rose pink. Behind the car, off behind the humped silhouette of the development, the sun clawed its way over the horizon.

The man winced.

So did the girl.

Wincing did something to their mouths.

It showed their teeth.

Their teeth.

Their teeth.

The man spoke a single word, and even though Francisco couldn't hear it, he saw the shape those pale lips made.

Spoonsie.

Francisco screamed even louder.

And then the man turned and pulled the girl's hand. She, more reluctant, finally turned and the two of them ran across the road and vanished into the black shadows under the trees.

Francisco screamed once more and then his voice ran down into a painful wet rasp.

The man and the teenage girl were gone.

Lou Tremons was gone.

Kaitlin O'Leary was gone.

-6-

Francisco didn't tell anyone about what he'd seen.

By the time the sun was up and he was home and in Debbie's arms on the couch, he was more than half sure he hadn't seen what he'd seen.

Because he couldn't have.

No fucking way.

Right?

That was a long, bad day. After he got a few hours of troubled sleep, Francisco got up, stood under a shower hot enough to melt paint off a truck, dressed, and drove back to the Grove. There was yellow crime scene tape around the open grave, but no cops. The reporters and news trucks were gone, too.

Francisco called Gaines to see what was what, mostly worried about whether he still had a job. Gaines sounded bad.

"Look," he said, "can you work tonight?"

"Tonight?" Francisco hoped his voice didn't sound as bad to his boss as it did to his own ears.

"We...we can't let this happen again."

"I—"

"I'm not blaming you," said Gaines in a way that left some doubt about that. "But we need someone there."

Francisco didn't want to mention that he was actually there when this shit happened. He said he'd stay late.

The image of Lou and little Kaitlin O'Leary went walking across the fragile ice in the front of his mind.

"Bullshit," he said out loud.

That usually worked.

It didn't do shit today.

He got back in his car, drove home, went into his bedroom and got his gun. Debbie was out, the older kids were in daycare or school, and the house was empty. He sat on the edge of the bed and loaded cartridges into the magazine of a Glock nine that Far Danny had given him once.

"Hey, Frankie Spoons, this here's a good piece," said Far Danny. "Totally legal and shit. Not on any watch list."

"Good for keeping your kids safe," added Near Danny. "Long as you're living out in the fucking boonies you got to be careful."

At the time Francisco hadn't wanted a gun, but even though they were family you simply didn't argue with the Dannys.

Now he was glad they'd given him a gift like this.

Then a pang of mingled pain and fear stabbed through him.

Lou Tremons had taught him how to load and shoot the gun.

Feeling strange in more ways than he could describe, Francisco got back in his car and drove to work. There was a storm coming and the day was so overcast that it looked like twilight and it was only nine-thirty in the morning.

Francisco parked by the shed and began the slow, sad walk back to the grave. But halfway there he veered to his left into a different section. To where Lou was buried.

After a grave was filled in and the dirt had a chance to settle, Francisco brought in some rolls of sod and filled in the open dirt with green grass. It took a while for the sod to set, for the roots to anchor it to the ground beneath. It had been weeks since Lou was buried and the grass roots had long since taken.

But as Francisco slowed to a stop by the grave he could see that there was something wrong.

The sod was wrinkled. There was a distinct bump in the middle.

He squatted down and stared at it, studied it.

He licked his lips, afraid to do what he was about to do.

Then he reached out a hand and pulled at the sod.

It came away like a heavy comforter. The roots were all torn, and below the layer of sod the grave dirt was wrong. It was loose, churned.

"No," said Francisco.

He fell backward and clawed the gun out of his jacket pocket, dropped it, picked it up again, and *bang!*

His finger had slipped inside the trigger guard and the gun went off by accident. The bang was so loud that he recoiled from it, the gun bucked so hard that it fell from his hand, the bullet hit the granite headstone and whipped backward past Francisco's ear. The sound scared a hundred crows from the trees.

Francisco sat there, his ass on the wet grass, feet wide, eyes wider, heart hammering, mouth opening and closing like a fish.

Above and around him the world ticked on into the next minute, and the next.

Then something happened.

Something awful.

The sod moved.

It rippled. Twitched.

Francisco absolutely could not move. All he could do was sit and stare.

The grass cover bulged and trembled.

The Glock lay on the edge of the grave, but Francisco could only stare as it rose up and thumped down as something *moved* beneath the sod.

Then a pale worm wriggled out from under the edge of the grass cover. Thick, gray, deformed.

And another.

And another.

Five worms in all, moving through the damp earth.

Only they weren't worms and Francisco knew it. His mind screamed inside his head that this wasn't happening, that it wasn't true. But he knew.

Not worms.

Worms don't have knuckles.

Worms don't have fingernails.

Worms aren't attached to a hand.

A word boiled up inside Francisco's throat and burned his mouth. He spat it out.

"L—Lou...?"

The fingers stopped for a moment as if *they'd* heard him.

There was a sound from under the sod, under the dirt, muffled and indistinct. Like a voice heard through a closed door.

Like a voice.

Like a name.

Spoonsie.

Then Francisco was up and running as fast as he could.

He didn't remember picking up the gun, but he became aware of it pressed to his chest with both hands. Hiding it because of his mistake? Or clutching it like a talisman? There was no time, no thought, no breath to answer those questions.

His car tires kicked showers of mud and gravel and torn grass as he drove the hell out of there.

-7-

Francisco spent the whole day at the Scarecrow.

The whole day.

Joey the bartender tried to get him to talk about it, probably thinking it had to do with the big thing last night. And it did, Francisco was sure of it, but he couldn't talk about it. Not now. Maybe not ever.

The pistol was a cold weight between belt and belly flesh.

Joey must have made some calls because Lucky Harris showed up. Then Mike and Scotty. They clustered around him. Nobody said a word. For hours.

Joey put the TV on and they watched the news. Watched Family Feud. Watched The View. Watched the day get older. Outside it started to rain. There was a low snicker of thunder.

It was late afternoon inside the bar; outside it looked like the middle of the night.

Scotty was the first one to talk, to try and pry him open.

"Hey, Spoonsie, you okay...?"

Francisco felt his nose tingle and then his eyes and then before he could get away from the guys and go hide in a toilet stall, he was crying. Really crying. Sobs, shoulders twitching, tears and snot running down his face.

Any other time the guys might have fucked with him. Made fun, handled it like dicks because that's what guys do when emotions get real for anything except the Super Bowl. But not after last night.

Scotty—the closest their group had to a hard-ass--reached out and took Francisco's hand, gave it a squeeze, but didn't let it go.

"We're here, brother," he said softly.

Without wiping his face, without looking up, Francisco said, "I saw that little girl."

And he told them what he'd seen on the road.

Lou Tremons.

Kaitlin O'Leary.

Walking hand-in-hand.

Smiling at him.

With all those long, white teeth.

Saying his name.

And then...the five white worms under the dirt. And that voice down there in the dirt. Saying his name again.

Mike pressed a wad of paper napkins into his hand. Francisco stared at them for a moment unable to comprehend what they were or what they were for. Then he wiped his face and his nose. Mike patted him on the back.

Joey poured some shots and they all had one.

No one told him he was crazy. No one asked him if he was sure. Maybe if this was another town. Maybe if the Trouble had never happened. Now, though…no one tried to tell him that he was wrong or suggest that he'd imagined it.

It was Lucky who asked, "What are you going to do?"

It was unfortunately phrased. What are *you* going to do.

Not *we*.

There's a line. If you stand on one side of it and let a statement like that go uncorrected, then the line becomes a wall. The moment stretched and everyone at the bar knew that Francisco was suddenly on one side of the wall, and they were on the other.

Lucky tried to fix it without fixing it. "Spoonsie…you should just say fuck it. You should call Gaines and tell him to shove his job up his ass."

Francisco shook his head. "I can't."

No one had to ask why. This was Pine Deep, and this was America, and if the economy blew in the rest of the country then it was going deep throat in Pine Deep. There were no other jobs.

"I got Debbie and the kids," Francisco said.

It was a stupid thing to say. Crazy. Impossible because the town had become impossible. The job was impossible.

But there were no other doors marked 'exit.'

For better or worse, this was his town.

His *family* lived here.

And he had nowhere else to go, nowhere else he could go.

The gun in his belt weighed a thousand pounds.

His heart weighed more.

-8-

When he was drunk enough so that his legs could carry him and his terror, he staggered into the bathroom, locked himself into a stall, turned and leaned heavily against the door. It took nearly four full minutes to convince himself not to put the barrel of the gun into his mouth and blow his troubles all over the walls.

Inside his head, some maniac had started a slide show, flashing high-res images onto the walls of his brain.

A pink coffin resting on the canvas straps, ready to go into the ground.

The same pink coffin open. Tufted silk. An eviscerated teddy bear.

Cold dirt on white teeth.

White fingers grubbing through the soil.

Lou Tremons calling his name. On the road, under the ground.

Monsters.

In his town.

"God…help me."

And as if in answer to his prayers he heard the bing-bong alert of a new incoming text message.

How's it going?

It was from Far Danny.

Francisco almost laughed.

How's it going?

Well, fuck me, cuz, I think I'm growing a crop of vampires, that's how it's going. How the hell are things with you? How's the leg-breaking business? Any goddamn vampires in the protection racket?

Those thoughts tumbled through his head and a laugh bubbled at the edge of his control. He had to fight it back because it was the wrong kind of laugh. The kind you don't ever want to let get started because there's no way you can stop it. That kind of laugh can break something you know can't be fixed.

He stared at the stupid message.

How's it going.

So, instead of laughing, instead of going totally apeshit out his mind, Francisco did something else equally crazy.

He called Far Danny and told him exactly how things were going.

Every goddam bit of it.

-9-

Far Danny took it pretty well.

After a bit.

At first he got a little mad and asked Francisco if he was fucking with him.

Then he asked him if he was drunk.

And he asked if he was crazy.

Francisco said no to the first question, yes to the others, but he didn't take back anything he said. He couldn't. It was out there. He wasn't even afraid of pissing off the Dannys. Things had changed and getting his ass kicked by his goombah cousins didn't seem so scary anymore.

Far Danny said, "Debbie and the kids? They okay?"

Francisco stiffened. It was already dark outside. He'd been here in the bar all day.

"Oh, god..."

-10-

Francisco ran out of the bathroom with the Glock in one hand and his car keys in the other. Lucky and Scotty and the others yelled and started to make a grab for him, misunderstanding what he was doing, but Francisco blundered past them and headed out into the rain.

He drove badly and way too fast.

He sideswiped a mailbox and tore some expensive stuff off the side of his car, and he didn't give a cold shit about it. The storm was pounding down on the hood and windshield and Francisco fast as he could all the way out of town, along the wet black tongue of Route A32, into his development, up to his front door, skidding to a sloppy stop and splattering mud ten feet high on the front of his house. Left the car door open, ran onto the porch, banged the door open.

Scared the hell out of Debbie, who was putting supper on the table.

The kids started yelling. The baby started screaming.

Debbie saw the gun in his hand and the look in his eyes and she started screaming, too.

It took a long time to calm everyone down.

He had to calm down a lot to manage it.

He put the gun on top of the fridge, out of any kid's reach.

He closed and locked the front door. Checked the whole house. Locked and pinned the windows. Took the cross down off the bedroom wall, the one Debbie's grandmother had given them for their wedding. Heavy, with a silver Jesus nailed to it.

Francisco had to lie to make Debbie calm down.

He told her there was an escaped criminal in town. A madman.

She looked at the cross in his hand and then at the top of the fridge, and deep lines cut into her pretty face.

"Frankie," she said very softly—too quiet for the kids to hear, "is this about...the Trouble?"

He stared at her, floored.

"What...? How do you...?"

She shrugged. "At the beauty parlor. The girls. We...talk."

Outside the rain hammered the door and the thunder beat on the walls.

An hour later Lou Tremons kicked open the front door.

-11-

Francisco and Debbie screamed.

So did the kids. Even the baby, who didn't know what was going on.

Lou smiled. He seemed to like the screams.

He was dressed in mud and rain water and his funeral clothes. He had Kaitlin O'Leary with him. And three other people. People Francisco had buried in closed coffins because they were supposed to have been too badly mangled in car wrecks or burned in fires. But they looked whole now.

They were smiling, too.

Wet lips, long white teeth. Red eyes.

Debbie screamed again and broke away from Francisco's side, throwing herself between the vampires and her children. Francisco raised the cross, holding it up like a torch against the darkness.

A couple of them flinched. The little O'Leary girl hissed and backed away.

Lou Tremons said with a wicked grin, "Yeah, well, here's the thing, Spoonsie...I'm a fucking atheist. If we don't believe in something it can't hurt us, and I don't believe in that shit."

A voice behind him said, "Do you believe in *this* shit?"

Lou turned. Everyone turned.

Far Danny stuck the barrel of a shotgun under Lou's chin and pulled the trigger.

As it turned out, Lou was able to grasp the concept of buckshot.

Francisco screamed.

Debbie and the kids screamed.

Kaitlin O'Leary screamed.

The other vampires screamed.

Near Danny yanked the pull cord on a chainsaw.

He screamed, too. But for him and his smaller cousin, the screams sounded a lot like laughter.

-12-

Francisco sat on beach chairs between Near Danny and Far Danny.

It was the last day of October.

Halloween.

That night at the house was ten days ago, but it felt like ten years ago.

Debbie and the kids were staying with Far Danny's mother in South Philly. Just for a little while. Until things calmed down. Until things got straightened out.

Scotty was gone. After that night at the bar, after what Francisco told them about Lou's grave, he'd driven to a motel of town, then came back the next morning and put his house up for sale. Mike and the other guys were still here, though. But the nights at the Scarecrow were long and mostly silent. No one wanted to talk about what was going on in town.

The Dannys went back to Philadelphia for a few hours then came back with suitcases. They moved into Francisco's house. Near Danny slept on the couch. Far Danny slept in the La-Z-Boy. They'd brought more guns and other stuff.

The bodies of Lou Tremons and the others were back in the ground. Francisco had done that quietly, when no one was looking. The cemetery was a big place and these days not even the college kids went there to hang out.

Only Kaitlin's body was above ground. It was in the morgue. It had been 'found' by a motorist on the highway. No one could explain how she managed to get a big piece of sharpened wood buried in her chest. Some kind of post-mortem mutilation by the madman who dug her up. That's what the papers said.

Sheriff Crow came and asked Francisco some questions, but not as many as he expected. And the sheriff had a strange, knowing look in his eyes. He gave Francisco a smile and a pat on the shoulder and that was the end of it.

Of that part of it.

Now it was ten days after the Dannys had come to Francisco's house.

Ten days after a slaughter that would probably keep his kids in therapy for the rest of their lives. Something to deal with. Something *else* to deal with.

The three of them sat on beach chairs. There was an open plastic cooler between Francisco and Far Danny.

"Beer me," said Far Danny, and Francisco dug into the ice, pulled out a longneck bottle of Stella, popped the top and handed it to his cousin. He opened a fresh one for himself.

They drank.

Sitting in a row. Three thirty-something guys. Cousins. Drinking beer in a graveyard as the sun tumbled over the autumn trees and down behind the mountain.

The grave in front of them was a new one.

A construction worker named Hollis who'd died when scaffolding collapsed on him. Or so the story went. Lots of injuries, not enough blood at the scene.

"Smart the way they do that," said Near Danny.

"Fucking up the body so you can't tell," agreed Far Danny.

Francisco sipped his beer.

They watched the bare patch of dirt that Francisco has filled in and patted down three hours ago.

They'd brought a wheelbarrow with them. The handles of two shotguns stuck out the back, flanking the plastic grip of the Black and Decker chainsaw. There were other things in the wheelbarrow, too. Practical things. Holy water from St. Anne's. The priest there was a fourth cousin. A Donatella. Bottles of garlic oil and Ziploc bags of garlic powder. From Aldo's Pizza on Two Street. Stuff like that.

There wasn't a lot of conversation.

Francisco had said his thanks. He'd wept his thanks, clinging to Debbie and the kids while looking up at the blood-splattered Dannys. It had all been said. And it was all understood. This was family.

You do not fuck with family.

Not even if you're an undead blood-sucking soulless fiend. No sir.

To have kept thanking the cousins would have been weak. And even though he was not a strong man, Francisco knew that.

The sun fell away and the purple shadows flowed over the cemetery.

Near Danny lit a Coleman camp lantern.

They had another beer.

Far Danny lit a joint and they passed it back and forth.

The dirt trembled.

The joint paused in mid-handoff, Far Danny to Francisco.

The dirt shivered and danced as something beneath it moved.

Near Danny sighed, bent forward, grabbed the handle of the chainsaw and sat back with it. Watching the dirt.

Francisco took the doobie and had a nice, long hit. Blew blue smoke out over the grave.

The dirt bulged as something pushed upward. Rising. Coming out.

Near Danny handed the chainsaw to Francisco.

"Yo, Frankie Spoons," he said. "You're up."

Francisco took the chainsaw.

But it was Frankie Spoons who stood up with it, jerked the ripcord, and stood wide-legged, waiting for the dead to rise.

Author's Note on "Cooked"

This is a standalone horror story that isn't part of any other world and not attached to my other novels. Just a weird, strange, sad little tale about justice, love, friendship, revenge, and voodoo.

Cooked

-1-

Billy Sparrow was high.

Almost high.

The 'almost' part was a bitch. It was a heartbreak.

He needed to get high enough to fly away, like Cooter promised they could do.

But he wasn't high enough for that.

For Billy the high used to start before he even clicked his lighter to smoke the ice. Meth was always like that, you even think about it you get a tingle in the balls and a flutter behind the eyes. High before you're high, that's what Cooter used to say.

Cooter used say a lot of stuff.

Cooter was pretty funny. He had Billy laughing the first time they smoked meth. Called it methandfriendofmine. That was funny.

He and Cooter would smoke so much they'd get pipe-drunk and then everything was funny. Peeling wallpaper was funny. A cockroach swimming in his cereal bowl was funny. Even watching Carla, that scratchity-ann crank hoe, pick at her blisters was funny.

That was a long time ago.

The anticipation wasn't the same.

The high wasn't the high anymore.

Now, when Billy popped a lighter under the quartz all he felt was bad stuff. His stomach was full of bees and there were thorns in his head. Even when he sucked in that first lungful and the world fell off its hinges. That used to be epic. That used to be the fucking *it*.

Now it was like opening a door into a haunted house.

Cooter was in that haunted house, too.

Sitting there, grinning at him with crooked teeth surrounded by charred skin, staring with eyeballs that had been boiled white in the fire.

If Billy smoked too long he could see Cooter die all over again. It was like a big DVR playing the scene over and over again in his head. Surround-sound and everything. No amount of smoke could bury that, and the deeper into the high Billy went to hide from it, the clearer the picture got.

-2-

They'd come in a couple of Escalades. Farelli and his posse of six wiseguy wannabes from Newark, rolling up to Cooter's little place on DeFrane Street. White boys dressed like they thought the *Sopranos* was on the Fashion Channel. Pointy shoes and tight pants and shirts open to show Neanderthal hair on their chests. Acting tough, hoping to be noticed by guys who *are* tough. Talking trash.

Carrying baseball bats and gas in red plastic cans.

Billy was in the attic, huddled over the last fumes in a pipe. He heard the shouts, but at first that didn't mean shit to him. You get high, you hear stuff. Some highs are good, some highs blow. People steal shit from each other. There are fights. It's no big deal.

But then the shouts turned to screams.

Screams weren't part of it. Meth doesn't take you down that avenue. Billy staggered to his feet and looked down the attic stairs. There were no doors anywhere. Billy remembered he and Cooter taking them off, but he couldn't remember what that had been about.

The screams were loud enough to poke holes in the envelope of his high.

He crept down to the second floor and leaned over the bannister. There they were.

The dickheads from Seventh Avenue. Farelli's thugs were like a pack of dogs. Billy lost count of the number of times they beat him up. Rubbed his face in dogshit. Kicked him in the balls. Always laughing about it. Always grabbing their own nuts and yelling 'Eat me!' every time they saw Cooter. Always calling Cooter faggot or nigger or other shit.

Worse than a pack of dogs, Billy thought. Dogs won't fuck with you for no reason. Billy Sparrow didn't hate very many things, but he hated Farelli and his crew.

Farelli lived in the house with all those statues of the Virgin Mary on their lawn. The virgin and a bunch of dumb-ass plastic pink flamingos.

Billy had a vague memory of him and Cooter stealing some of them the other night. Or was it last night? What the fuck did they do with them?

They stole all sorts of shit. Flamingos, those goofy little lawn gnomes, a statue of a black guy dressed like a jockey. That one really pissed Cooter off. Billy didn't know why. Sure, Cooter was black but he wasn't a jockey. But it pissed Cooter off, and when Cooter gets pissed he gets funny.

Billy remembered what they'd done with the stuff they stole. The gnomes and flamingos were all on the front lawn here, with the Virgin Mary and the lawn jockey snuggled down in the crab grass together. Cooter couldn't take their clothes off—they were statues, after all—but the way he laid them down said it all. With the gnomes and pink birds watching. It was fucking hilarious.

Afterward, when they were about to get high, Cooter said that he'd have to move that shit before his uncle saw it. Uncle Conch Boukman was a hard-headed, short-tempered old man who moved to New Jersey after his village in Haiti was destroyed in that earthquake. Cooter was his only relative, but to Billy they were so different that it was hard to tell that there was any connection.

But Uncle Conch brought a little money with him, and he paid the mortgage off on Cooter's pad.

The screams from downstairs punched Billy in the head and it shook him out of the memories of last night.

Farelli and his goon squad were all there. So were a whole mess of Cooter's friends. Couple of kids Billy knew, too. Maybe ten people, hanging out, getting high. One guy—the uptown kid who brought some quality ice with him—with the shorts down around his knees so Carla could give him a courtesy BJ. But Carla wasn't blowing him. Or anybody. Billy looked at her and saw her face burst apart as a baseball bat hit her.

She screamed and then the bat hit her and she couldn't scream anymore. Carla fell back and she fell weird, like she had no bones in her neck.

That's when it all went crazy.

That's when Farelli's thugs went apeshit. Bats and chains.

Farelli stood in the center of the living room and even from upstairs Billy could see that there was a bulge in Farelli's pants. He was rock-hard watching this shit. Billy knew about that. His old man had been like that sometimes. Getting serious wood because using a belt on Billy and his sisters felt that good. Made him feel that jazzed.

That's when Billy heard Cooter come crashing into the room, swinging a mop handle and catching Farelli's cousin, Tony, right across the forehead.

There was a moment when Billy thought it would all be over right there and then. Everyone and everything froze solid. Even the screaming stopped for just a second.

Billy wanted to scream a warning. He wanted to shout at Cooter and everyone else. Tell them to run, tell them to get the fuck out.

While there was still a chance.

-3-

But there was no chance.

Cooter knew it when he came charging out of the kitchen with the mop.

Farelli and his goons knew it before they loaded into their Escalades. They knew it when they stopped at the Lukoil to fill up their red gas cans.

Even the zoned-out stoners knew it. Carla probably knew it, too, right up until the bat knocked her head loose on her neck.

Billy knew it. Billy knew that all of them—greaser or meth-head— were born into this. Into this moment, like they were all bowling balls thrown down polished wood alleys but all the alleys were designed to converge into one spot. No pins. Just a bunch of bats and gas cans and a mop handle.

The moment became unstuck when Farelli laughed.

The right kind of laugh will do that.

Cooter looked at him and Farelli looked back.

Billy screamed then.

Nobody heard him, because everyone was screaming. The bats went up and down and around and around, and somebody kept painting all of the drowsy, doped-up, screaming faces with red.

Cooter tried to run.

They splashed him with gas.

Farelli flicked a cigarette at him.

Cooter made it all the way to the second floor. Billy tried to help him. Swatting at the flames that were wreathed around Cooter's face. Billy shoved him into the bathroom, knocked him down with burned hands into the tub. Turned on the water.

But by then there were flames coming up through the floor.

The water filled the tub, but fire reached up with long yellow fingers between the floor boards and drove Billy back. From the bathroom doorway he watched the inferno heat boil the water in the tub. Where Cooter was.

When Billy dove through the second floor window, he saw three things.

The Escalades driving away, laughter tumbling out of the open windows.

The faces of pink flamingos and lawn gnomes and the mother of Jesus staring up at him with plastic eyes.

And then the hedges reaching up at him with a thousand green fingers.

-4-

Billy got out of the hospital the day they buried Cooter.

He was the only one at the graveside. Billy and the priest, who didn't even look at him. And a brass urn full of ashes.

Billy's hands were burned. He had bandages around his face and under his clothes. Billy felt the fire still burning in his skin and the screams still burning in his head. They would have kept him in the hospital but despite everything they say about providing medical coverage if you don't have money, they will kick a meth head out after a couple of days. He didn't have any money, so he walked home. Back to Cooter's.

The house was a blackened shell. The fire department had been able to save the front steps. The rest was cinder.

Billy sat down on the top step, rested his elbows on his knees, hung his head, and cried until there was no moisture left in his body. The urn sat next to him. No one had claimed it, so they'd given it to him, and he carried it all the way back.

He stayed there all day, talking to Cooter in his head.

Cooter didn't say shit, though.

Two days later Billy bought some rock. Smoked it. Saw Cooter. They slopped on the couch and played video games. They talked about living and dying. They hung out.

When the rock was gone and the high broke apart into little pieces of reality, Cooter went back to sleeping in his urn. Billy went back to the burned-out house, sat down on the step next to the ashes. And cried.

That was life.

That was every day.

On the sixth day after the funeral, on the long downslope of a high, Billy sat on the step with his head in his hands. He heard a car pull up and stop, but he didn't look up.

"You that white boy," said a voice.

Billy looked up slowly. Moving fast hurt. It broke blisters. So, Billy moved like he was old. Uncle Conch stood on the soot-covered little bit of pavement that ran between the two halves of the front lawn. He wore a black suit and a shirt the color of snow. His hat hid most of his face so that only his chin and mouth were in the light. He had dark lips and cigarette-yellow teeth.

"You that white boy," he repeated, his thick Haitian accent making everything sound like a song. "You was friends with Cooter."

"I guess," said Billy. He realized that his nose was running and he sniffed. Tasted some tears, so he wiped his eyes.

Uncle Conch looked down at the urn. "That my Cooter?"

Billy nodded. "You weren't at the funeral, so they said I could have his ashes."

"Yeah," said the old man, "I'm too close to the grave my ownself for me to want to visit a boneyard."

That made sense to Billy, and he nodded.

After a while, Uncle Conch said, "You and Cooter always doing the drug."

He never said 'doing drugs' or 'smoking meth.' Doing the drug.

"I guess."

Uncle Conch stepped a little closer. He had bad legs and leaned heavily on a cane that was carved with snakes and skulls.

"Why you do the drug?"

"What?"

"The drug. Why you and my Cooter always do the drug? Where it take you?"

Billy thought about that. "Away, I s'pose."

"You suppose? You don't know?"

"Away."

Billy stared down at the lawn. The heat had withered the grass to brown strings, and the fire hoses had turned that to clingy seaweed. The tendrils were wrapped around the legs of half-melted flamingos and the throats of charred gnomes.

Another shuffling step closer. "Tell me," he said.

Billy squinted up. "Why do you want to know about that stuff?"

Uncle Conch lowered himself down to the step. It took a long, painful time for the old man to do it. Billy tried to help, but he was too badly burned. When he was down, Uncle Conch took a minute to catch his breath and he produced a spotless white handkerchief and mopped his brow. Billy was pretty sure he'd never seen anyone use a handkerchief before, not outside of a movie.

"Tell me, boy," wheezed Uncle Conch, "why you and my Cooter always want to go away? What you want to get away from?"

Billy looked past him to the street, but what he was seeing was the open mouth of the grave before they lowered the box. The mound of dirt was a brown heap that they didn't bother to cover with one of those green AstroTurf mats. Nobody gave enough of a shit even for that.

"I don't know."

"Tell me, boy. I got to know."

Billy looked at him. "Why? What does it matter now?"

"It matters to me. Cooter may not be a saint, but he all the family I had left. Tell me what he wanted to do. Let me carry that for what time I got left. Give me that much so I don't bury his dream, too."

Billy stared at Uncle Conch for almost a minute before he could answer. "You were in Haiti when we were growing up," he said. "Cooter and me were always getting kicked around, you know?"

"No, I don't know. Tell me."

"I don't know...I saw Haiti on the news and stuff. I know that you guys had it worse down there than we had here..."

"Poor is poor is poor," said Uncle Conch. "Kid starving in the street don't measure his hunger 'gainst some other kid he never met. Kid still hungry. Kid still cries when he hungry."

"Yeah, but it wasn't just that. Cooter's mom was pretty cool—she was your daughter?"

Uncle Conch shook his head. "My sister's daughter. Only one of us to leave Haiti in a hundred years."

"Until you."

The old man shook his head. "I live here, boy, but I ain't ever left Haiti. Haiti is home. I'm a Boukman—you know what that mean?"

Billy shook his head.

"My many-times-great granddaddy was Dutty Boukman, a *houngan* from Jamaica who settled in Haiti. Let me tell you what a *houngan* is," said Uncle Conch. "That's a sorcerer, a priest of the old religion. Dutty led the first slave revolt in Haiti. He that strong. He that fierce a man. Once Dutty shucked off his chains no man could put them back on again. Them French they had to shoot him a hundred times to bring Dutty Boukman down. Why so many times? Because Dutty was filled with the *loa* of Kalfu—and that is one powerful spirit. Kalfu is the *loa* of the crossroads and every slave who ever died had to stand before that spirit and tell Kalfu how they died and who killed them. Kalfu got so angry he looked for the right man, the right slave, to open a doorway in his soul, to let him come through. That's what Dutty Boukman did. Dutty's heart was so filled with hate for the slavers that he opened up the door in his soul and let Kalfu come walking through. Oh, now Kalfu is not Casper. You know Casper, the friendly ghost? Like on TV? No, Kalfu not like that. Kalfu controls all the evil forces of the spirit world. He bring bad luck and hard justice. Dutty was filled with that dark magic and when he told all the other slaves to rise up, they rise up. That was 1791. By 1794 slavery was abolished in Haiti. That's how strong Dutty Boukman was. That's the blood that flows right pass the crossroads. The river of dark blood that flows over the years from him to me." He paused and sadness filled his eyes. "And to Cooter. And that river of blood end with Cooter, but it don't make the little boy strong. All that river did was wash him away, and up in heaven his mama is singing a sad song."

The birds in the trees seemed to echo that music.

"I live here, but Haiti is in me." Uncle Conch touched his chest. "When I die here, my soul will be buried in Haiti."

Billy nodded. That was something he could understand. "Cooter and me always wanted to find a place that we could call home. My mom died when I was two, so I never got to know her. Cancer. Sucks, but I was over Cooter's all the time. His mom was so great, you know? She was always singing songs."

"Little Bird," said Uncle Conch, and there was a smile buried down inside the wrinkles on his face. Sad and deep and real. "That's what we called her. Little Songbird."

"She was great. She was the best. But…you know, she died, too. A bus hit her. I mean, how random and fucked up is that? How does God allow a bus to hit someone like her? Fucking bus should have hit my dad. Or Cooter's dad. Those two assholes should have had a fleet of busses hit them. Fuckers."

Uncle Conch nodded. "I didn't know that about her husband. Not until I get a letter and she tell me. I was putting money together to come here and talk to that man when I get the other letter. 'Bout the bus."

They sat and thought about it.

"You didn't come, though," said Billy. It wasn't an accusation. He was putting it out there to see what it looked like.

Uncle Conch nodded. "I didn't come. Not till after the quake."

"Yeah."

"I think the quake was a judgment on me."

Billy looked at him. "What?"

"The *loa*—they know what kind of man I am."

"Cooter said you were a priest, too," said Billy. "They said in your village back on the island people thought you could do magic and stuff. Tell the future, cure all sorts of diseases and raise dead people. He said you were a good guy."

The words were kindly meant, but Uncle Conch looked sad. "What Cooter know? All he knows is what his mama, Little Songbird, tell him, and what she know? Over here her whole life, just hearing 'bout things in letters. No…it's the *loa* who know the truth. They know that I carry Boukman blood—hero blood—and they know I studied the ways of the *houngan*, but they also know I ain't done much with it 'cept make myownself happy. Drink and pussy and some deviltry to make the long nights scream. Yeah, you can fool your family but you can't fool the *loa*." He paused and Billy did not interrupt. "Maybe I'm a bad man, white boy. Maybe I'm a bad man like Cooter's dad. Like your dad."

Billy said nothing.

But then Uncle Conch shook his head. "No, not like those cockroaches. I don't put my hand on a woman and I don't put my hand on a baby. Even so…I'm a bad man. I done bad things." He nodded to the rhythm of his own thoughts. "Haiti a bad place. Hard place to be a good man. Easy place for a bad man to be a bad man. Bad is more fun."

"I—"

Uncle Conch laughed. A deep, rumbling laugh that had no humor in it. "Don't worry, white boy, I ain't going to do bad things to you."

"You weren't bad to Cooter."

The old man sighed and ran his fingers along the outside of the brass urn. "I wasn't good to him, neither."

"You paid his bills, man. You gave him a place to live."

Uncle Conch turned and looked at the charred walls behind him. "All I gave that boy is a place to die, and I think he was dead before they cooked him in there."

But Billy shook his head. "No, man, that's just it. Cooter and me...we could always get free. We could get away anytime we liked."

The old man's brows knitted. "How? How you and my Cooter get free?"

When Billy didn't answer, the old man nodded.

"The pipe," said Uncle Conch.

"I guess."

"That got you away?"

"Yeah."

"All the way away?"

Billy thought about it. "At first, yeah."

"What happened at first?"

"At first, man, we'd light a pipe and take one hit and we were gone. Really gone. We were flying." He closed his eyes to summon the memory, and his body swayed as if he was gliding on the winds, riding the thermals, high above it all. "That's how we escaped, man."

"Escaped?"

"Cooter's dad. Mine. When Cooter's dad went to jail, we sailed so high that night. Oh, god, we were all the way up. Flying like birds."

When he opened his eyes, Uncle Conch was not looking at him. Instead he was studying the soot-blackened flamingos.

"That why you got these birds all over the lawn?"

Billy sniffed back more tears. "That was Cooter's idea. He said that maybe if we got high enough we'd fly way up in the sky, like the flamingos. You ever see them? They soar up there, not a care in the world, just floating on the wind like nothing beneath them matters. Nobody can touch them up there. They're so high. And so free." He looked at the melted wings of the pink plastic birds. "Now Cooter's gone and all the flamingos are dead. Cooked, man. It's all cooked."

A sob broke in Billy's chest and he hugged his ribs with bandaged hands as he wept for Cooter.

Uncle Conch laid a hand on Billy's trembling shoulder.

"Why'd they have to do that?" sobbed Billy. "Why'd they have to do all that? So we stole their yard stuff. So we took some stupid pink birds and stupid gnomes and that other stuff. If they were mad about it, most they should have done was mess us up a little. They done that plenty of times. All they had to do was knock us around a little and take their stuff back. And, look, man, they didn't even take their shit. All that stuff's still here. What was it all about, man? What's the point of anything if they didn't even take their stuff back?"

He kept crying and his voice crumbled beneath the weight of it. The only word he could manage was, "Cooter…"

Then Uncle Conch bent close and whispered in his ear.

"Now you listen to me, boy," he said, "I told you once that I'm a *houngan* and the blood of Dutty Boukman run through my veins. Told you that my many-times grandfather got so mad, so damn mad, that he opened up a door in his soul and let something evil come right on through."

"Kalfu," said Billy.

"The *loa* Kalfu, lord of the crossroads, bringer of hard justice." Uncle Conch picked up the urn. "I just 'bout pissed on everything good there was in the Boukman name. I left my Little Songbird to get knocked around by a weak, bad man. I let her boy die trying to fly away from this shithole. I done that. I could have changed it, but I didn't, so I done that."

Billy shook his head, but Uncle Conch was staring at the urn. He opened it and looked at the soft gray nothing that was Cooter.

"I done this," he murmured. "I got no one else alive on this earth who is blood kin to me. The Boukman name, proudest blood of my people, dies when I die. And if I die this moment, right now, then that blood turns to piss that ain't worth hosing off the street."

He drew a long breath.

"But I got me a little breath left and a little blood yet, and I got me a heart that is so full of hate that it wants to burst open and break the world. So what you think I should do?"

Billy said nothing. His eyes were huge and round.

"You 'member Cooter said I could magic, white boy. Pretend I'm a genie in a bottle and you can ask one wish. What that wish going to be?"

Billy looked at the urn and down at the melted flamingos and then up at the endless blue sky. "I guess I'd want two wishes," he said.

"What wishes, boy?"

"I'd want to see Cooter again. He's my best friend, you know? He's the greatest, Cooter's the king. I'd want to see him again. Not with burns on him, though. Like he was yesterday morning. Laughing and happy, singing to himself like the way his mom used to. That's what I'd wish for."

A tear broke from Uncle Conch's eye and wandered over the million seams and lines in the old man's face, burning like hot silver.

"And what's your second wish? You want me to burn those boys who burned Cooter? You want me to raise the devils of hell to burn them? Or how about I call the *loas* of vengeance and we turn these melted gnomes into a pack of monsters to hunt *that* pack of monsters. I could do that. That's dark magic. I call Kalfu and I could do that."

But Billy shook his head. "No...if I only had one more wish after that, I'd want Cooter and me to fly out of here. Far away. Like flamingos, but not melted ones. Not fly like we're smoking ice, but really fly. All the way into the sky. That would be the shit, man. That's what Cooter would want."

Uncle Conch stared at Billy for a long, long time.

"That's all you want? You can have all the revenge you want and instead you want to fly away with my Cooter like a couple of birds?"

Billy closed his eyes.

"Big pink flamingos, man. So high...so free..."

-5-

Billy thought he said more to Uncle Conch, but he couldn't hear his own words. Another sob hitched his shoulders.

But it wasn't a sob, of course. He knew that. When he opened his eyes, he knew that much.

Far, far below the Passaic River curved along the edge of Newark, but from up here it looked like a blue ribbon. Billy turned to say something to Uncle Conch, but it wasn't the old man. It was Cooter. Big and pink and riding free. Billy called out to him, but his voice sounded different. It didn't sound like his voice. And it didn't sound wrong. It sounded right. It sounded too right.

Billy closed his eyes and he laughed in that strange new voice as he and Cooter flew free.

Uncle Conch took his time getting to his feet. He was old but parts of him were even older, used up before their time. He braced himself on his cane and began lumbering toward his car.

In his chest, his heart hammered like old drums. Fast, insistent, powerful. Pain darted up and down his left arm.

But he hummed as he walked to his car. He knew that he wasn't going to die in the next five minutes. Not that soon. When he got to the curb he turned and looked at the debris in the yard. The flamingos were gone, and that made him smile. For just a moment. It would be the last of Uncle Conch's smiles to touch that face.

Then his eyes fell on the little singed and half-melted gnomes. Nasty looking little things. Stupid things. White man's idea of what looked good on a man's lawn.

The eyes that looked on the gnomes were Uncle Conch's for one blink longer. Then with the next blink the eyes changed from dark brown to fiery red. The smile on the old mouth changed, became broader, brighter. No longer the pained smile of a dying man but the vital smile of something far more powerful. In his chest the old heart began hammering to a rhythm that was many times older than the body around it. A rhythm many times older than the pavement beneath the scuffed shoes. Many times older than the country in which he stood. As old as hate, and that was so very old.

"Rise up, my brother spirits," said the voice that was no longer Uncle Conch's. Nor was the language English, or French, or Creole.

On the lawn, there was a small sound, a tiny groan, a rasp of plastic. One of the lawn gnomes raised its singed and sooty head. The white beard was streaked with ash, the eyes were melted holes. The mouth was stamped into the plastic. But then the plastic lips trembled and the whole body trembled with effort and finally there was a *popping* noise as the mouth opened. Broken, twisted plastic in a zigzag gash. The little creature smiled, and its wide and wicked grin was exactly the same as what was now stretched across Uncle Conch's mouth. The mouth that had belonged to Uncle Conch, when there had been an Uncle Conch.

"Rise up, brother spirits," repeated Kalfu, using Uncle Conch's borrowed mouth. Each word was exhaled on a hot breath that blew through the open door of hate in the ancient body. "They are serving dinner on Seventh Avenue. White meat, served rare. All you can eat."

One by one the melted gnomes opened empty eyes and ripped open jagged mouths. Hungry mouths. They rose unsteadily to their feet, tottering toward the open car door beside which Kalfu, their brother, waited.

Author's Note on "The Death Poem of Sensei Ōtoro"

Sometimes a story waits patiently in a writer's head until the right moment for it to be written. This is one of those. And it involves several of my favorite elements—weird history, horror, action, and martial arts—particularly the sword arts of the Samurai. I've been a lifelong practitioner of Japanese martial arts and have always wanted to write a tale set in Feudal Japan. This is it.

The Death Poem of Sensei Ōtoro

-Ichi-

Ōtoro knelt by the doorway to contemplate the cherry blossoms as the late afternoon breeze dusted them from the branches. The courtyard was a softly rippling sea of white and pink.

"Beautiful," he murmured.

The servant girl came and poured more tea and the fragrance of jasmine perfumed the air. He nodded his thanks but did not touch the cup until she was gone. Ōtoro didn't know this girl and didn't like her furtive looks. Might be curiosity—everyone was curious about a stranger until they knew the story—and it might be suspicion. Anyone who was not suspicious in these times was a fool; but suspicion could have so many meanings. He kept his sword hand on his thigh until she had closed the door and her soft footsteps had vanished down the hall.

In the courtyard of the inn blossoms fell like silent tears from the trees. Ōtoro sipped his tea. It was a little too strong; the girl had hoped to impress him with its scent so that he wouldn't notice that she'd over-brewed it. He took a second sip and set the cup aside.

Beyond the holly hedge he saw the tops of two heads bobbing their way toward him. Ōtoro considered the angle of the sun. They were right on time and he appreciated promptness. The two men emerged from behind the holly, paused to orient themselves, saw the open door and angled that way. The older man was Ito, a daimyo of considerable wealth and connections; his young companion was unknown to Ōtoro.

Ito was perhaps sixty, in fine silks, the other less than half his age in less expensive clothes. Both wore two swords—it confirmed what Ōtoro had learned about Ito, that he was a traditional Samurai, a devout Buddhist rather than a Christian. The Christians did not carry the shorter sword, the *wakazashi*, as it was against their religion to commit seppuku, even when faced with a loss of honor. Ōtoro disliked and distrusted this spreading departure from the values by which his family had lived for centuries, though he was realistic enough to accept that some changes were inevitable. Europe was closing its fist around Japan and eventually even the age of the samurai would pass.

One day, he knew; but it was a day he would never live to see. Like the samurai culture itself, his time was nearly over.

The visitors drew closer. Ito walked with casual confidence, his companion affected a gamecock strut. They came to the edge of the courtyard and the younger man strode forward, body erect as a statue, his gait that of an experienced but arrogant veteran. The young man made as if to keep walking but Ito stopped him with an arm across his chest. The older man looked out across the unbroken sea of cherry blossom petals and his face changed from a purposeful frown to a softer look, eyes scanning the color, lips parting slightly. The younger man just looked past the beauty to where Ōtoro sat.

A samurai and a fool, mused Ōtoro.

Ito looked up and made eye-contact with Ōtoro across the forty feet of color. He bowed ever so slightly. Not yet an introduction—but clearly an acknowledgment of the moment. It was that, more than any of the letters and presents Ōtoro had so far received or anything that was said or given later, that decided his mind. Because of the blossoms Ōtoro knew that he would help this man, that he would kill whomever he wanted killed.

-Ni-

Ōtoro lifted his fingers an inch and Ito took that as an invitation to enter the courtyard. He stepped into the blossoms and now it was okay that his footsteps disturbed them. Beauty is meant to behold, it is not meant to endure. The younger man followed him across the courtyard, his strut increasing as they approached.

They stopped again about ten feet away and everyone bowed. Ōtoro and Ito both lowered their eyes when they bowed; the young fool did not. He probably still lacked confidence in who and what he was supposed to be. Dogs are like that. Men shouldn't be.

"Ōtoro-san," the older man said. "It is my great pleasure to meet you."

"Ito-sama. Please be welcome."

Ito nodded toward his companion. "This is Kangyu, my nephew and heir."

At closer range Ōtoro realized that the old man's companion was not a grown man at all but was instead a tall boy of maybe sixteen years. His erect posture and aggressive manner were probably more for show—a display intended to convince others as well as himself that he was a man and a samurai. Seeing this, Ōtoro relented from his previous assumption that Kangyu was a fool. He was merely young.

Ōtoro gave Kangyu a small bow, not out of any real respect but because Ito's statement surprised him and the bow hid his reaction. Ito had three sons. This boy could not possibly be any closer than fourth in line to inherit the clan's considerable wealth. Ōtoro hid his surprise behind good manners.

"Please be comfortable. The girl will bring saké if you wish, or tea."

The guests knelt and Ito pulled his swords from his belt and set them beside him. Kangyu did not; the younger man's hands fidgeted on the scabbard.

Ōtoro tapped a small bell with a stick and the girl appeared with a fresh pot of tea, clean cups, and a tray of rice cakes. She poured and withdrew.

"The tea is very fragrant," Ito said but he didn't drink any and Ōtoro knew that this was a segue from politeness to business, but now that it came to it Ito seemed to hesitate, his face pale and damp from exertion, and Ōtoro wondered if the hesitation was sadness, sickness, or perhaps a trace of weakness.

"Ito-sama," Ōtoro prompted, "your letter indicated that this was a matter of both grave importance and some urgency."

The old man studied him for a moment, then gave a curt nod. "Importance? Yes, without a doubt. Urgent?" He smiled a weary smile. "That's relative, all things considered."

"Timely, perhaps?" Ōtoro suggested.

"Timely indeed." Ito took a breath. "I am dying, Ōtoro-san."

Ōtoro was careful not to move or show anything on his face. Less than a year ago that statement would have been one of indifference to him. People tended to die, old men more so. Now, however, death was a spirit who whispered in Ōtoro's ear. Death, he reflected, takes on so many new meanings when you are, yourself, dying.

But there was more to it than that. Death had reached out its hand across the entire nation and many thousands had died. The coastal merchants called it the 'Spanich Disease,' attaching the label based solely on a popular belief that the plague originated among the passengers on a Spanish trading vessel. That claim had never been substantiated, though the government burned three Spanish traders to the waterline and issued an inflexible warning to all others to steer clear of all Japanese ports.

Ōtoro studied Ito for the signs of the disease, but although the old man's skin was pale it was not gray. There were no visible signs of unhealed bites or sores. On the other hand, clothing hid so much and a bite could be anywhere. Even so, this man was still able to speak. If he did have the Spanich Disease, it could not be very far advanced.

It did make Ōtoro wonder more about the presence of Kangyu. Was his nephew traveling with him as a bodyguard, or as a *kaishakunin*—the person entrusted with the death cut during seppuku?

Ito must have been reading his thoughts because he smiled and shook his head. "No, Ōtoro-san, I don't have the Spanish Disease. I have a wasting sickness of the bowels. A cancer." He made a small gesture. "Not the most dignified way to die, and not the ideal end for a samurai."

The old man's eyes were penetrating as he said this, and there was an expectant quality to the fragment of a smile on his mouth.

After allowing a moment to come and go, Ōtoro said, "All things die."

"And some in better ways than others," Ito replied, and Ōtoro nodded to acknowledge the point.

"Are you looking for a kaishakunin?"

"No, Kangyu will be my second when it comes to that."

Ōtoro almost smiled. The boy looked absolutely terrified at the thought, and Ōtoro guessed that for all his posturing and strutting, this boy's sword had never yet coaxed blood from the flesh of another person. He looked positively green at the thought.

"Then how may I be of service? I'm no doctor."

"I know exactly what you are, Ōtoro-san. You come very highly recommended. My good friend daimyo Chiyojo has spoken so highly of your services for ten years now. No, don't be alarmed—he is my cousin and we have no secrets between us, though none pass through me to anyone else."

Ōtoro cut a small glance at Kangyu, but Ito shook his head.

"I say now only as much as I need in order to impress upon you the fullness of my confidence in your abilities," assured Ito.

After a pause, Ōtoro shrugged. "Many people can kill and I am not an assassin."

"If I wanted an assassin, sensei, there are many schools of ninja I could hire. And the countryside teems with ronin if all I wanted was someone competent with a sword. No," said Ito slowly. "If artless slaughter was what I wanted I could have hired a gang and it would be done. I came looking for a warrior. A true samurai."

Ōtoro sipped his tea, nodded. "What is it that you want done?"

Ito picked up his own cup and gazed into its depths as if it was a window into his own thoughts. "There is a rumor in the city…"

"A rumor?"

"About you," said Ito, raising his eyes. "About your future."

Ōtoro waited.

"I have heard idle gossip that you have been putting your affairs in order, that you have sold your estate and your holdings, that you have given much of the proceeds to the monks. They say that you are nearing your death. Some think that you have become disgusted with this world, or with the politics of our nation, or with the influence of Europe, or with some point of honor. There are many bets on when you will commit seppuku."

"Is that what the gossipers say? And does a man of your position listen to wagging tongues?"

"Occasionally. Not all gossip is mere chatter and noise."

Ōtoro said nothing.

"There are many opinions on this," continued Ito. "It seems that you are a very popular man, sensei. One might go as far as to describe you as a folk hero."

"Nonsense."

Ito raised an eyebrow. "False modesty?"

"Self-knowledge," countered Ōtoro. "I have met heroes. They lay down their lives for causes, they throw away their lives for their clans."

"You wear two swords…"

"And I would commit seppuku without hesitation for the right reason. I have found, Ito-sama, that most 'causes' are transient things. To die for a whim or to soothe the feelings of a nobleman who feels slighted—these things are not worthy of a good death."

"What is a good death?" asked Ito. "To you, I mean. To your mind."

"The aesthetic of the samurai is to find beauty in a violent death, the death of one in his prime, a death in harmony with life."

The boy, Kangyu, interrupted and blurted, "The Way of the Samurai is found in death. When it comes to death, there is only the quick choice of death."

Ōtoro and Ito looked at him.

"You quote the *Hagakure* well," said Ōtoro, "but do you understand it?"

Kangyu puffed up his chest. "It is the desire of every samurai to die gloriously in battle amid a heap of his enemies."

Ito heaved out a great sigh of disappointment. Ōtoro affected to watch the dragonflies flit among the flowers.

"What?" demanded Kangyu, perplexed by the reaction. "Uncle, you know that I can recite every passage in the—"

"You can recite the passages," said Ito, "but how many times have I told you that you do not interpret them correctly?"

"What other interpretation is there but that a samurai yearns to die in glorious battle? And I am not afraid to die, uncle," the boy insisted. "I will swim into eternity on a river of my enemy's blood."

Ito turned to Ōtoro. "Do you see? This is what the younger generation has come to. When I hear such things I do not despair of my own death, even one as ignoble as that which approaches. It will spare me from witnessing such a world through the eyes of a helpless dotard."

Kangyu began to protest but Ito held up a hand and the boy snapped his jaws shut as if biting off his words. It was clear to Ōtoro that Ito's heart was breaking at the thought of his clan's lineage being handed over to so misguided a child as Kangyu. It was a sad end for a house whose bloodlines had produced some of the nation's greatest heroes. Like the nation itself, Ōtoro thought, becoming soft and losing a true connection to the old ways. Entropy was a great evil that no sword could slay.

"We were speaking of idle gossip," said Ōtoro, steering the conversation back onto its road.

"We were speaking about heroes," Ito corrected.

Ōtoro smiled and shook his head. "And as I said, I'm not one of those. Heroes will march unflinching into a storm of arrows to defend a point of philosophy. And why? Because they believe that to die in such a way guarantees the favor of heaven and the enduring praise of those who live on to record his passing in song and story. They die well, to be sure, and those songs and plays are written, but their deaths are, in the end, without meaning, without effect, and without true beauty."

"How can they lack beauty if their deaths live on in songs?" snapped Kangyu.

"Singers exaggerate to make the mundane seem extraordinary," said Ōtoro. "However a truly beautiful death does not require a single word of embellishment. It is a sacred thing, shared between the samurai, his enemy, and with heaven. No other witnesses, no further praise is required."

"But how would anyone know if the death was beautiful?" insisted Kangyu.

"A perfect death only matters to he who passes through it."

"No," said Kangyu and he gave a fierce shake of his head. "Beauty does not exist unless it is witnessed."

"When a samurai knows he is going to die," said Ito thoughtfully, "he often writes a poem. A bit of haiku to try and convey his understanding of life and death, of honor and beauty. The simplicity and elegance of the verse is all that eloquence requires."

The boy opened his mouth to reply, but this time he lapsed into silence without a command or rebuke. His eyes became thoughtful as he considered his uncle's words.

"Ôuchi Yoshitaka wrote one two hundred years ago," said Ōtoro. He closed his eyes and recited. "Both the victor and the vanquished are but drops of dew, but bolts of lightning—thus should we view the world."

Ito nodded. "An ancestor of mine, Shiaku Nyûdo, who died hundreds of years ago, wrote this poem. 'Holding forth this sword I cut vacuity in twain; In the midst of the great fire, a stream of refreshing breeze!' Now that is the poetry of death."

Ōtoro met Ito's eyes and much was said between them that was not spoken aloud. They were both true samurai, and they both understood what Kangyu did not or, perhaps, could not.

"So," said Ōtoro at length and changing the subject, "is it only gossip that brings you all the way here?"

Ito smiled faintly. "Hardly that. I have come for two reasons, sensei."

Ōtoro inclined his head to indicate that the old man should continue.

"First I came to satisfy my curiosity, for I, too, have wondered about these rumors, just as I, too, have a theory for why you have been divesting yourself of all of your worldly possessions. I believe that you, like me, are sick, Ōtoro-san. I believe that you, like me, are dying."

Ōtoro said nothing, but the moment when he should have denied such a claim came and went. Ito nodded to himself. They watched as a breeze stirred the branches and caused more of the lovely blossoms to fall like slow, pink rain.

"And the second reason for your visit?" asked Ōtoro.

"I want you to kill my family, Ōtoro-san."

-San-

Ōtoro stared at him.

"Which family members do you want killed?" His eyes darted briefly toward Kangyu, but Ito shook his head.

"My nephew and his two sisters will inherit my estate," said Ito. "My sons are..." He let the rest hang.

"Are they dead?"

Ito's eye shifted away. "Who can define 'death' in these times?"

"Ah," said Ōtoro, grasping the implications. "The Spanich Disease?"

Ito nodded.

Ōtoro frowned. "But you say that you do not have the disease."

"No, I do not. I was not with my sons when they... *contracted*... it. It consumed them and swept through their households. My wife, too."

Tears glistened in Ito's eyes, but they did not fall.

"I am sorry to hear this," said Ōtoro gently. "Will you tell me what happened?"

Ito turned to look out at the cherry blossoms as they fell. Already the path he and Kangyu had walked had been covered.

"How much do you know of this disease?"

Ōtoro considered. "Not much. I have been in retirement here for some time." He paused. "Putting my affairs in order, as you guessed. I know what people in the countryside are saying."

"Gossip?" asked Ito with a small smile.

"Not all gossip is mere chatter and noise," said Ōtoro. "As a wise man once put it."

Ito nodded, still smiling, though his smile was filled with sadness.

"The stories say," continued Ōtoro, "that the disease came to our shores aboard a Spanish trader, and that much I believe. They say that it strikes and spreads very quickly. There are stories that whole towns have been overrun, and that government troops have razed those towns to the ground to keep the infection from spreading."

"All of that is true," agreed Ito. "But what the gossips do not know is that the government is worried. The Emperor is worried. Each time they think the disease has been contained and all carriers killed, it crops up again in another place."

"Then it is carried on the wind itself. There are diseases like that."

Ito shook his head.

"What then?" probed Ōtoro. "Is it a plague that hides among the fleas on vermin? Do you remember what those Jesuits said about the plague that slaughtered nearly a third of the people in Europe? You can burn a village and kill all infected people, but how do you build a wall that will keep out rats and mice?"

"No," said Ito. "That is not how the disease is spread."

"Then how?"

Instead of answering, Ito asked, "What have you heard about the disease itself?"

Ōtoro poured more tea and considered. "They say that the disease comes on very quickly, that it brings with it lethargy and a spiritual malaise. The inflicted become strange and solemn, seldom speaking again once the disease has overcome them. Often they are violent, perhaps hysterical in their suffering. Death follows soon after."

Ito glanced at him. "Is that all you heard?"

"No, but the other rumors are nonsensical. The villagers say that the disease does not die with the victim, nor does it let the victim lie quietly in the grave. There are wild tales that say the victims become possessed by *jikininki*, the hungry ghosts the Buddhists believe in. People believe that the *jikininki* have come to punish our people for allowing the Europeans to corrupt us. From there the gossip descended into fantasy and I stopped listening. But then…people are always ascribing spiritual interference with everything. A dog barks at night and it is ghosts. A child is born with a birthmark and it is a sure sign of demonic possession." Ōtoro waved his hand in disgust.

"Not all gossip is a lie," Ito reminded him.

"Do you say so?" asked Ōtoro. "Then tell me where the truth is in these fanciful stories? We Buddhists believe in many things, but on a hundred battlefields I have never yet seen a ghost or demon. They may exist, but what proof is there that they interfere in the ways of steel and flesh?"

"Let us be frank, Ōtoro-san," said Ito. "We are both dying."

Ōtoro raised an eyebrow. "You know, then?"

"Yes. As I said, the gossip about you is nonstop. You have no family...?"

"No. They were killed in the war with the Yuraki clan. While I was crushing their army on the field, their assassins came over the walls of my estate and murdered my wife, my children, my parents."

"I read about that!" said Kangyu excitedly. "You rode into the Yuraki camp and strangled the daimyo in front of his remaining generals, and then cut them all to pieces. It was magnificent!"

Ōtoro wanted to slap the young man, and clearly the twitch of his uncle's arm suggested that he was using a great deal of personal control to keep his hand from loosening Kangyu's teeth. The boy saw their expressions and lapsed into a confused silence.

The serving girl came with a fresh pot of fragrant tea.

"So, Ōtoro-san," said Ito, "is it true? Are you dying? I know it is rude and impertinent to ask this in such a bold way, but since I discovered I was dying I find myself taking many liberties."

Ōtoro smiled. "I am dying. Like you, I have a cancer. It gnaws at my bones."

They sat in the silence of their shared understanding. Two dead men. Two samurai who drank tea in companionable silence there on the brink of the abyss. Kangyu, young and vital and with all of his years before him, might as well have been a shadow on the moon.

"We are both old," said Ito, "but you are younger than me. You are still strong. Under...other circumstances...you might have lived to become a general of a great army, or a lord with charge over many hundreds of samurai."

Ōtoro shrugged.

"And in some distant battle you would have found that beautiful death. A moment of balance between life and unlife. You would have danced there on the edge of a sword blade and found peace." Ito paused. "But there are no wars left to fight. Peace—damn it for all eternity—is a wasteland for warriors. That is, I believe, why you sometimes accept small missions. You are not a ronin, you are a warrior in search of a meaningful war."

"Yes...you do understand. But, Ito-sama, how does this involve my killing your family?"

"Ah," said Ito, and he took a roll of silk from an inner pocket of his coat and spread it out on the floor. The silk was decorated with the faces of several people, all painted in the ultra-realistic Chinese style. "My wife, my three sons, my two daughters." The old man's voice faltered as he caressed the silk portraits.

Ōtoro allowed a moment before he said, "Which of them do you want killed?"

Ito turned back to face him and his eyes looked a thousand years old. "All of them," he said.

They had shared two bottles of saké and a dish of rice cakes and the sun had set quietly behind a wall of clouds. The servant girl had lit the lanterns, and now brown moths buzzed in the cooling air.

Ito spread a map out on the floor. It showed a small island two hundred miles due south of the port city of Osaka, out in the emptiness of the Philippine Sea. The daimyo tapped the spot with his forefinger. "Keito Island."

"I've not heard of it."

"It has no military value except that clans like mine send their families there during times of crisis. There are fifty estates there, and their presence has always necessarily been kept secret."

"This is where your family is now?"

Ito hesitated before nodding agreement. "My wife retired there to be with our eldest daughter during the birth of her first child. A boy...I've not yet seen. Six weeks ago one of my sea captains came to me to report that the regular supply ship to Keito had not returned on schedule and had instead been found adrift, almost washed ashore on Shikoku. My captain sent five of his crew aboard and as he watched with a telescope he saw the crew of the supply ship come boiling out of the hold like maggots the moment his men were aboard. They overwhelmed the five men and..."

"The Spanich Disease was aboard the supply ship?"

Ito mopped his face with a cloth. "Forty men, all of them as gray as ghosts, moaning like demons. The five crewmen were torn apart on the main-deck. Torn to pieces and...consumed."

As hard as he tried to keep a shudder of revulsion from shaking his whole body, Ōtoro felt it pass through him. His forearms pebbled with gooseflesh.

"I had heard accounts of this disease," continued Ito. "Of how the infected wasted away with a sickness no doctor could cure and then against all logic came back to a kind of half-life in which they do nothing but prey on living men and devour their flesh. It is easy to see why so many people believe that these are jikininki—the returning spirits of gluttons and impious men whose unnatural appetites brought them back to life to feast upon the living."

Ito paused again. It was clear that he was having to pull each word from his own mouth.

"Listen to me, Ōtoro-san," he said, "I am Buddhist, but I am also an agnostic. I began losing faith in ghosts and demons long ago, and even this current disaster did not at first ignite sparks of belief in me. Like most of the other samurai I believed that the plague was probably just that: a disease whose symptoms caused strange and violent behavior. I've seen victims of rabies and of other disorders. That was sickness, not possession. But then I heard the story of the Spanish ship *Infanta Christa* which had sailed into the island port of Shinjujima bringing a cargo of tapestries from Turkey and spices from the Arab states for some domestic merchant whose name was still unknown. The ship flew the yellow plague flag and was put under quarantine out in the roads, well away from the docks...but witnesses claimed to have seen people jumping off the ship—ostensibly men driven to suicide by fear of the wasting disease—but who were later seen walking out of the surf to attack fishermen. Naturally, when I'd first heard the story I doubted any of it was true because the news criers always exaggerate; but then I started hearing accounts from colleagues—men I trust. Scores of local ronin were suddenly booking passage to Shinjujima to take jobs with town security or to bolster the household protection for the merchants. Within a month the going rate for a week's employment had quadrupled. Then the stories began circulating that some of these ronin were deserting their new jobs because the enemy was not what they expected. These were neither diseased people who merely had to be contained, nor were they Europeans deliberately spreading a disease. These were the corpses of the people who had died of the Spanich Disease. Do you understand me, Ōtoro-san? The corpses."

Ōtoro pursed his lips for a moment. "I've heard some of those same stories, but not from the lips of trustworthy witnesses. Always second or third-hand."

Ito nodded. "That was the case with me for many weeks, but then I heard that large numbers of people were booking passage to Keito. Nearly every one of the important families who maintained estates there were sending their women and children to the island for protection."

"I have not heard that."

"It was kept very quiet," explained Ito. "Information was shared only by those of us who owned land there. We did not want to inspire an invasion of the island by everyone who wanted to escape the disease."

Ōtoro nodded. "Go on."

"I sent most of my household there, keeping only my brother's son and a strong detachment of samurai to guard my estates and warehouses. My grand-daughter had just given birth to my first grandson. After nine grand-daughters I finally had a grandson. I thought that my family would be safe there, but after weeks and weeks I had no word from Keito. Then rumors began circulating among my fellow land-owners. Rumors that the Spanish plague was already on the island. Can you imagine my horror, Ōtoro? I had done everything I could to protect my family and my clan, to insure that the family name would continue." He reached out and placed a trembled hand on Kangyu's arm. "My nephew may now be the last person to bear our clan name, and that is a terrible responsibility for one so young."

"Uncle, I..." began Kangyu, but Ito shook his head.

Ōtoro said, "What did you do when you heard the rumors?"

"Last week I sent my fastest war galley with twenty of my most seasoned and trusted samurai to scout the island. Their orders were to protect my family and evacuate them if necessary. Three days ago that galley returned to my dock with only a skeleton crew aboard. The captain of my galley said that when he tied up to the wharf behind my estate and the samurai debarked, a large group of people came rushing out of the compound. They fell upon the samurai. Of twenty seasoned fighters, only two made it back to the ship, and both of them were badly mauled. The captain cast off and narrowly escaped having his ship overrun. The wounded samurai succumbed to the sickness and died, but within minutes they came alive again. If 'alive' is a word that has any meaning. They opened their eyes, they rose from where they had fallen, and they attacked the crew. Many men died in the fighting that ensued. The captain ordered all of the dead to be thrown overboard, and by then he had seen the correlation between a bite and the inevitable transformation into one of the hungry dead. He ordered his remaining, uninfected crewmen to kill anyone who had so much as a scratch, and all of the bodies were cast into the sea. With only a few sailors remaining, the galley limped home. I sent them all to their deaths, just as I had sent my own family to...to..."

"Uncle, please...be easy with yourself," said Kangyu with more gentleness than Ōtoro would have expected. "You did the right thing. How could you have known what would happen?"

Ōtoro decided he liked the boy after all. He was trying very hard to be a man in a family whose men had all died...or were dying. Bravado, in the face of such circumstances, could be forgiven.

Ito nodded and took a deep, steadying breath. "Several of my friends sent boats to the island," he continued. "But not one has returned. The island must be completely overrun. It has become a place of death."

"I am sorry for your loss, Ito-sama," said Ōtoro, bowing.

"There is more," said the daimyo. "There is one thing that anchors my hope to my sanity and it is why I have come here today and disturbed your retirement."

"Tell me."

"After my ship had cast off the captain took the fastest route home, which meant that he passed behind the east end of the island. My estate is there, perched high on a sheer cliff. I chose the spot because there is no beach and it is inaccessible from sea and therefore safe from raiders or pirates. By twilight's last light, the captain saw a figure running along the cliff. A woman." Ito took a breath. "My daughter-in-law, Haru, wife of my second son. She was clearly in flight and was likely making her way to the caves below the edge of the cliff. We keep some stores there in case of an emergency. Haru was carrying a bundle with her, clutching desperately to her bosom."

"Your grandson?" asked Ōtoro.

"I do not know. It could have been my grandson or it could have been another child. Or a pet, or a bundle of food. There is no way for me to know. And, perhaps it doesn't matter. That was last week and by now my entire family is dead. My grandson...will have been consumed."

Seconds fell slowly around them, drifting down through the silence likely the blossoms outside, but lacking all beauty.

"I may be a samurai and a killer, Ōtoro-san," said Ito heavily, "but those are masks I wear. When I take off my swords and my kimono I am only a man. A husband, a father, a grandfather. I am my clan, Ōtoro-san. I love them above all else."

The tears brimming in the old man's eyes broke and fell, cutting silver lines through his seamed and weathered cheeks. Even then he sat straight and proud, a man of great character and dignity.

Ōtoro said, "Why do you come to me? You could hire an army to assail the island."

A ghost of a smile flickered across Ito's tear-streaked face. "As I said, you are a hero. Even if you do not agree with that assessment."

Ōtoro said, "I am one man, Ito-sama. If a warship and twenty samurai could not penetrate the island to rescue your family, what do you expect me to accomplish? Even setting aside for the moment that I am dying—as you are dying—and cancer in my bones does not grant me any immunity to a plague."

"I sent men in force, without secrecy," said Ito. "It is my belief—supported by the scant reports of the surviving crew—that the plague victims were alerted by the presence of the ship and the sounds of soldiers debarking and marching through the forests. Drawn by such things the infected attacked in force and my men were devoured." The old man shook his head. "One man, however, could come ashore quietly, avoid being noticed and therefore avoid being infected."

The girl brought warm saké and Ito drank a full cup.

"There are younger and healthier men who would take this mission…"

"I'll do it!" cried Kangyu, but Ito shook his head again.

"No, nephew. This is not a mission for the young. This is not a job for anyone with a pocketful of unspent years."

Ōtoro said nothing, though he agreed with the sentiment.

"What would you think this one man could accomplish? Are you looking for a spy—?"

"No," said Ito. "I am looking for death."

"Death?"

"Death's grace. A sword stroke is a great mercy," said Ito. "It is a clean death, and if delivered by a samurai of sterling reputation, a true samurai, then honor would be restored. Death would take the infected in truth, and that death would be beautiful because it would be correct. It would be just."

Ōtoro drank his saké.

Ito said, "There is another thing, my friend. I know your politics, and I believe I understand your idealism. I know that you have gone into battle so many times in defense of the innocent. Even of innocent peasants in towns that would have been overrun by gangs of bandits. I am samurai enough to know why."

Ōtoro said nothing.

"You believe power without purpose is vain, ugly, unworthy."

"It is without honor," said Ōtoro.

"Yes, without honor," agreed Ito. "My family has been so dishonored by this foreign disease that the grave will not even accept them. No one should have to live with shame they did not earn."

"Ah," said Ōtoro softly. "You want me to act as their *kaishakunin*, to provide the death cut that they are unable to take themselves."

Ito nodded. "Not only will you restore the honor of my samurai sons, but you will be rescuing the helpless from the bondage of this dreadful curse. Including my newborn grandson. All will be freed. No matter which way your sword cuts, it will do heaven's work."

"But uncle," said Kangyu, "no one could escape that island. It must be completely overrun by now. You are sending him to his death."

"Yes," said Ito. "To certain death. To a quicker death than that which an unjust fate offers him."

Ōtoro smiled. "And, as you say, Ito-sama, there are far worse deaths."

"Now I will tell you one more thing, Ōtoro-san," added Ito. "Time is very short. I have it on reliable authority that the Emperor is going to have Keito burned next week. They are rounding up infected and even suspected infected and they'll transport them to the island. Within six days there will be many thousands of them there. You would never be able to find my family. And, when all of the infected are there, the fleet will use cannon and mortars to shell the estates, and fire bombs to reduce everything to ash."

"Would that not end the misery of your family?" asked Ōtoro.

"Tell me, Ōtoro-san," said Ito, "could you sit here, safe and comfortable, while rough and rude soldiers burned your suffering family?"

The smile on Ōtoro's lips became thinner, colder. It was enough of an answer.

"Besides," said Ito, "I don't know if fire will do what needs to be done. I know—I have *seen*—that a neck cut will do it. Remove the head and the infected are released into ordinary death. Nothing else seems to work."

"Why?" asked Ōtoro.

"No one knows. This disease does not kill as we understand it," said Ito. "Death will not take them and they will have no rest. They are corpses roaming the earth like damned things. When I close my eyes I think of my wife staggering around, dead and rotting, trailing the rags of her fine silks, hungry for fresh meat. And then I think of my grandson. How small a meal he would make…"

Kangyu made a small, soft gagging sound.

Ito closed his eyes for a moment. Then he opened them and the old man's eyes were hard and steady. "My sons were samurai of the old traditions. Good men, dedicated to *bushido*; men who deserved to die on a battlefield, or in a duel, or as old men at the end of a life lived to its fullest. Now they are denied that and even denied the mercy of committing seppuku. It is not right, Ōtoro-san. This plague destroys more than flesh. It is a blasphemous thing. I do not know if ghosts or demons are at work here, but the very nature of the disease is an insult to the very nature of honor. It removes any chance of beauty in death. I am an old man and I no longer have the strength, otherwise I would go myself. I would make of it my last battle, and it would be one worth fighting. If I found all of my family infected and roaming the earth like monsters, I would cut them down and in doing so would free them from dishonor and horror. With every cut I would ease their pain while giving them the clean and honorable death that they deserve." He paused. "My nephew is a good swordsman for all that he is brash and young, but he is the last male of my house. I cannot spend his life as if it was a coin in my pocket. And I am unable to see this done myself. As for others…there are few who would undertake the mission and fewer still that I would trust to accomplish it with skill and honor and compassion. And that, my friend, is why I come to you, to the sword master Sensei Ōtoro."

Kangyu shook his head. "But Uncle...you would send him to certain death..."

"Of course," said Ito. "And what a wonderful death it would be. Filled with purpose and honor..."

"And beauty," said Ōtoro.

Ōtoro drank some saké as blossoms fell from the trees.

"Very well, Ito-sama," Ōtoro said in a voice that was very quiet and calm, "it will be my honor to serve you in this matter."

-Shi-

Ito's war galley set sail on the next outgoing tide. Ito was aboard, as was Kangyu. The plan was to sail to within twenty miles of the island and drop Ōtoro over the side in a small fishing boat. Then the ship would make a wide circle of the island, returning to the drop-off point at sunrise. If, after that time, Ōtoro had not returned, then the ship would sail back to the mainland.

Ōtoro knew that there was little chance that he would make that rendezvous, and he figured that this part of the plan was there more to soothe Kangyu's conflicted feelings than to offer him a hope of rescue.

As the ship sailed on, Ōtoro sat by himself in a posture of meditation, listening inside his body for the places where the bone cancer had weakened him. He was still strong enough to compensate for anything he was aware of. At least he had not yet reached the point where his bones would become brittle. With luck, he would never experience that level of sickness and humiliation.

For a time, Ito and Kangyu knelt on either side of him, all three of their faces turned toward the setting sun. Much was said without words during that time. Between Ōtoro and Ito, and perhaps between both older samurai and the young man who would one day become a lord of men.

The trip was without incident.

Later, when the captain told them that they were in position, Ōtoro and Ito exchanged a bow, and Kangyu helped Ōtoro into the boat.

Once Ōtoro was settled in the thwarts, Kangyu placed one foot on the ship-side ladder, but then he paused and turned.

"I...I would have done this for my uncle," he said. "I would have done this for my family."

Ōtoro smiled at him. "I know you would," he replied.

Kangyu glanced up at the rail of the ship far above and then thoughtfully back at Ōtoro. "Sensei...even if you manage to do what my uncle wants...there are so many of the infected on the island...too many for one man to fight. You know that they'll get you. They'll infect you."

Ōtoro nodded.

"And then you'll become one of them."

"There is always *seppuku*," said Ōtoro.

"How, though? In the midst of an army of infected dead, how will you have time to prepare yourself and read your death poem and cut your stomach? How?"

But Ōtoro did not reply to that.

"I could come with you and act as *your* second and—"

"And then who would be there for you?" asked Ōtoro. "No, young samurai, your strength is needed for a different fight than this one. Be strong, be alive, and be what your uncle needs you to be."

The boy studied him for a long moment, then nodded.

"I hope I see you again," said Kangyu.

Ōtoro cast off the line and used his oar to fend his boat away from the ship. He turned the boat and found the current. A few minutes later he raised his sail and bore away toward Keito Island. He did not look back to see how long Kangyu remained there on the side of the ship, watching him.

-Go-

Ōtoro made landfall in the middle of the afternoon. Keito Island was a lush crescent-shaped hump of green rising from the blue waters, the remnants of the volcano it had once been visible in the spikes of black rock that showed here and there through the foliage. The far side of the island was shadowed under a pall of smoke. Something big had burned but Ōtoro judged the fire to be at least half a day old. A fire last night.

Ito had given him a small French telescope and Ōtoro extended it and examined the coastline. The beach was littered with boats, and each one was a wreck, their hulls smashed in, broken oars scattered on the sand. He lowered the glass and frowned. It was too regular and too thorough to have been storm damage. Could the local militia have done that to prevent the infected people from fleeing? He thought it likely. A desperate act, but a smart one.

He scanned the island for an hour and saw little else of value. Just the lingering smoke and the corners of the walls of a few compounds amid the trees. He did not see a single person, alive or dead. He folded the telescope and sailed toward Keito Island, ran the boat up onto the sand, and hid it among the reeds of a small lagoon. He slung his katana across his back, which was better for running. Various knives and weapons were secured in pockets throughout his garments, cushioned with silk to prevent clanking.

A three-quarter moon rose above the island and it gave him enough light to read his map and pick his way through the woods, following clearly marked paths that had once been neatly edged and swept, but which were now being reclaimed by creeper vines and broadleaf plants. No one had tended these paths in weeks. Insects screamed at him and owls mocked him as he ran.

The Ito compound was at the east end of the island, but Ito had been right about the lack of a useful beach and the sheer height of the towering cliffs. While resting in the boat, Ōtoro had committed the map of Keito to memory. There was a main road that linked all of the estates to the only harbor; however there were dozens of small paths cut through the forest. Some were for use by servants, others for the patrolling guards—a cadre made up of four samurai from each of the households on the island—and a few private walking paths that wandered through the beautiful woods. Ōtoro took one of these, partly because it was unlikely anyone would be out for a casual stroll during a plague outbreak, and partly because it took him to within a hundred yards of the eastern-most edge of the Ito estate, and less than two hundred yards from a small goat path that lead up along the rocky face of the cliffs.

He made excellent progress across Keito, though, but when he was nearly halfway there he saw another samurai standing in the woods directly ahead.

Ōtoro froze.

The man wore the light turtle-shell armor of a sea-going trade guard, and he stood with his back to the path. Ōtoro could see that the man wore a single sword—a low-ranking guard, and that there was a symbol painted on the back-plate of his armor which Ōtoro recognized as the crossed feathers of the Asano family, one of the Tokugawa retainer clans. The Asano compound was next to Ito's, so this was either a household guard or one they had lent to the island's security force.

Ōtoro crept closer to the man, making no sound on the path as he closed to ten yards, then to five. The Asano guard turned. Ōtoro was sure he had made no noise, but still the guard swung around as if something had drawn his attention, his head tilted like a dog's as he sniffed the air.

In the off chance that the guard was uninfected and was actually patrolling these woods, Ōtoro whispered the island's current call-sign, provided for him by Ito. "Tiger."

The response was supposed to be: 'Eagle.'

The guard opened his mouth, but not to speak. Instead he let out a low and inarticulate moan that somehow spoke eloquently of an inhuman and aching hunger. A wordless, nearly toneless groan that chilled Ōtoro to the marrow. The clouds passed from in front of the moon and the white light showed the Asano guard's face in all its horrific clarity.

The man had no nose. There was just a ragged hole in which maggots writhed. One eye hung from its tendril of nerve, rolling against the bloodless cheek. The man's mouth was open, the lips torn and pasted with some viscous gore that had to be old blood. Inside the mouth broken teeth nipped at the air in Ōtoro's direction.

Ōtoro gagged and staggered backward as the Asano guard lurched forward, arms reaching to grab and tear.

Shock may paralyze the mind but it is training that rules the muscles. Ōtoro's hand jerked up and grabbed the handle of his sword just as the thing staggered toward him. There was a silver rasp of metal and then both of the Asano guard's hands went flying off into the brush beside the path. Ōtoro stood poised, his sword raised at the apex of the cut, his body shifted out of line of the natural spray of blood.

But there was no spray of blood, and the man kept coming toward him.

This time the shock nearly froze Ōtoro in place for good, but as the guard took two more lumbering steps toward him, the samurai spun and slashed sideways with a vertical cut that disemboweled the man, spilling his intestines onto the path.

And yet the guard did not stop.

This is madness! thought Ōtoro.

With awkward feet slipping and tripping on his own guts, the Asano guard lumbered forward, relentless in his search for something to quench that awful hunger.

Ōtoro felt the world spin and reel around him. This was truly madness. No plague could do this. Ōtoro had killed a hundred men on battlefields, in duels, and in private feuds. No one could withstand such a body cut. Nothing human could keep coming.

"*Jikininki*," he whispered, backing away.

Hungry ghost.

Hearing Ito talk about it was one thing; Ōtoro had not truly believed it then and could barely accept it now.

The man took another step. One more and he would be close enough to wrap those handless arms around Ōtoro and gather him in toward that snapping mouth.

Hissing with fear, Ōtoro brought his sword around in a heavy lateral cut, higher this time, faster, and the Asano guard's head leapt from his shoulders, landing with a crunch on the gnarled root of a tree.

The body simply collapsed.

No staggering steps, no pause: it just crumpled to the ground.

Ōtoro stood frozen at the end of the cut, the sword blade pointing away from his own pounding heart. This sudden drop was as eerie as the attack. With any ordinary person there was a moment or two when even a headless body tried to function as if life still persisted. Some even took a step, however artless. Severed heads blinked, mouths worked. As grotesque as those things were they were proof of life even at its end.

But this...

The abruptness from which it went from unnatural life to total lifelessness was so completely...*wrong*.

Ōtoro held his blade away from him. The steel was black with blood that was as thick as paste. He snapped the sword downward once, twice, three times before the ichor fell from the oiled steel.

Then Ōtoro turned in a slow, full circle, staring at the murky forest, aware that he had stepped into a new world, some outer ring of hell. Is that what the Spanish Plague was? Could it truly turn men into demons?

All around him the forest seemed suddenly immense, and as he began to move once more down the path he was aware—all too aware—that there were fifty estates here. Each with at least two dozen servants as well as the families of each daimyo. Plus the local militia, the fishermen, the tradesmen. And the samurai from Ito's ship.

If the plague had them all then what chance could he have of completing his mission—of finding Ito's family and restoring their honor through the purification of a clean death?

Ōtoro set his jaw and started to run toward the Ito compound.

-Roku-

Ōtoro met three more of the creatures in the forest.

The first was a skinny old fisherman who lay legless beside the road, his stick-thin arms reaching in vain for Ōtoro as he passed, his toothless gums biting with infinite futility. Ōtoro cut off his head with a deft downward slash, hardly breaking stride. The second was a fat naked woman with a dagger shoved to the hilt between her bloodless breasts. She rushed at Ōtoro and he split her skull from hairline to chin.

He no longer tried disemboweling cuts. He cut the head off and cut the brain in half. Both methods seemed to work and offered him a small cup of comfort. At least he was not fighting something that could never die. That thought was worth holding onto. It seemed to connect these horrors to the physical world rather than allowing them to slide irrevocably into madness and magic.

When he encountered the third creature—a distinguished looking man of about his own age—Ōtoro shook out an iron throwing spike and with a flick of his arm hurled it into the man's forehead. The creature was able to take a single staggering step before it fell. Not as fast as a decapitation, but still effective.

He retrieved the spike. It was coated with a black ichor that no longer resembled blood. Tiny white things wriggled in the goo—threadlike worms almost too small to see. Ōtoro cursed with disgust and wiped the spike on the man's kimono, and slipped it back into its holster under his sash.

These kills had been easy, but Ōtoro did not take much comfort from that. As he ran he wondered what he would do if he encountered a dozen of these creatures.

The path split and in his mind he could see Ito's map. The left-hand path curled around to the gates of the Ito family compound; the right-hand path zigzagged through the trees to the cliff. He went that way.

The forest was not quiet. It never is at night. Crickets and cicadas chirped with an orderliness and constancy of rhythm that seemed to reinforce the truth that their world had little to do with ours. The plague was not a factor for them, and the music of their mating calls was nothing to us.

There were other sounds in the night. Nocturnal predator birds, and even exotic monkeys that had likely escaped from private collections among the estates. Ōtoro moved through shadows, listening for sounds that did not belong. Listening for the ring of steel that might indicate a battle, or for screams.

All he heard was the forest, and its orderly noises seemed to mock the pain and loss of the humans on this island. It made Ōtoro feel angry in a vague way, more so because the notion was fanciful and he was not given to fancy.

He moved along the cliff path and soon the foliage thinned out to reveal nothing but bare gray rocks.

No.

Not *bare*.

The rocks were streaked with something that gleamed like oil in the starlight.

Ōtoro bent close to one smear and even from a foot away he could smear the coppery stink of blood.

He frowned. The copper smell faded quickly as blood dried and thickened, so for the scent to be this strong it must be fresh. A few hours old at most.

The path ahead was too narrow for swordplay, so he sheathed his weapon and instead drew his *tanto*, the short, sturdy fighting knife. On such a narrow path the dead could only come at him in single file, and he was confident that he could dispatch them in single combat. Even so, cold sweat boiled from his pores and ran down his flesh under his clothes.

He crept along the path, following the glistening smears, grateful for the celestial light that turned the rocks from dark gray to smoky silver. The path hugged the face of the cliff and Ōtoro marveled that Ito relied on this route as a passage to safety. In anything but bright moonlight or sunlight this would be a treacherous avenue in any circumstance except the most dire desperation.

The blood spatters increased in frequency and volume. If the gore was all from one person, then that man or woman would have to be bled white.

Ōtoro rounded an outcropping and came to the black mouth of a cave that yawned before him. The light penetrated only a few yards into that dark mouth, but it was enough. The cave was shallow and was mostly taken up by boxes of provisions wrapped in waxed cloth. There were ashes in a fire pit and smoke still curled up from them; a pot of soup was hung from a metal frame above the pit, and the liquid was nearly boiled away. Blood was dottled over everything: boxes, soup pot, the walls and floor.

But there was no one there.

Then he froze as he saw something lying against the back wall. A small, ragged bundle that lay in a pool of dark blood.

Ōtoro had seen every kind of slaughter on his nation's battlefields, including the bodies of his own murdered family...but he had to steel himself to go and investigate that bundle. This would not be the clinical and brutal murder of an enemy child with sword or spear. This would be unspeakable. He steeled himself for the image of tiny limbs gnawed and torn by human teeth.

He crouched and extended the tip of his sword into the outer wrappings of the bundle. Nothing moved.

Ōtoro took a breath and tilted the sword up, using the tip to lift the bloody cloth. There was some resistance, some counter pressure from something slack and heavy within the rags. But he made himself look.

When he saw what it was, he began to exhale a breath of relief, but that breath caught in his chest.

It was not a child.

It was a woman's hand. Delicate, unmarked by the calluses a servant might have. The hand of a noblewoman.

Ito's wife? His daughter-in-law?

If this was the hand of one of Ito's household, and if that hand had belonged to whomever had come here clutching a bundled child to her bosom…then where was the child?

Ōtoro bent to try and read the story told by the scuff of footprints that painted the cave's floor. There was one set of prints overlaid by two others. The first set were small and smudged, a woman's feet in thin stockings. The others were heavier. Men's sandals. Soldiers?

The woman's prints led back the way Ōtoro had come, though they vanished quickly as the blood wore off of the stocking fabric. Partial prints from the sandals overlaid the smaller prints, clear sign that the woman—maimed and dying of blood loss—had managed to wrestle free of her attackers and fled back along the path, and the men had followed.

All of this had happened recently.

Within minutes, perhaps.

Ōtoro turned and ran.

-Shichi-

He slipped once in the blood and very nearly pitched sideways off of the path. Fifty yards below him the ocean threw itself at the rocks, lashing and smashing at the unyielding stone as if venting its fury.

Ōtoro slowed his pace to keep from plunging to a pointless death.

Seconds and then minutes seemed to ignite and burn away around him as he negotiated the devious path. And then he was at the edge of the cliff wall. He stepped away from the sheer drop, feeling his heart hammer within his chest, then he plunged into the woods and ran as fast as he could. Leaves whipped at him, branches plucked at his clothes like skeletal fingers.

Suddenly the compound wall rose out of the darkness in front of him and he stopped and crouched down behind a thick shrub. The wall was in good condition, whitewashed and tall, but gates were smeared with bloody handprints and painted with the wild spattering of arterial wounds. The ground near the gate was littered with torn clothing, bits of broken swords, arrows, a discarded matchlock rifle, and the gnawed ends of bones. Here and there were unidentifiable chunks of bloody meat. Some so fresh that blood gleamed wetly, and some writhing with fat maggots. He found no complete corpses, however. The pall of smoke he'd seen from the coast hung thick in the air. A battle had been fought before this gate, he judged, and the defenders had all died.

All of them.

The main gate was locked, however, and that gave Ōtoro his first flicker of hope. Could the Ito family be locked inside? Hidden behind walls? It seemed unlikely that the creatures could climb. The thought of possibly finding some of Ito's family alive carved a half-smile on Ōtoro's face. Kangyu would love such a tale.

Though, gods help me, thought Ōtoro, *that really would make me a hero. I would kill myself to escape the embarrassment.*

Still smiling, Ōtoro took a grappling line and threw the hook over the wall three times before its spikes caught. He jerked the line to test the set of the spikes and then scaled the wall. Climbing hurt his dying bones and he imagined that he could feel the teeth of the cancer gnaw at him with each grunt of exertion. As soon as he gained the top of the wall and looked over into the courtyard, all hopes of a fanciful last-minute rescue of besieged family members evaporated. His smile died on his lips.

The courtyard below was filled with the dead.

All of them stopped milling and as one turned and looked up at him. Their moans of hunger tore the night.

Ōtoro sighed heavily. He sat down on the tiled walkway and looked out at the creatures as he fished the roll of painted silk from his pocket and spread it out on his thigh. The painted faces of Ito's wife and children looked serene and alive in the moonlight. Ōtoro studied the faces of the dead below, matching several of them to the portraits.

Ito's wife.

His oldest son.

Three of his grand-daughters.

Then he saw the face of Ito's second son, the father of the baby. The samurai had only a single arm, and his throat was a ruin through which tendons and vertebrae could be seen.

Ōtoro cursed softly to himself.

"So much for heroes," he murmured. Now all that was left for him was his original mission. Clean deaths for as many of the family as he could manage before the monsters pulled him down.

He knew that to accomplish his mission he would need to go down into that courtyard. He would need to give closure to each of Ito's family members, granting peace, restoring honor. That meant that he would have to do two things that he didn't want to do. He would have to go down into that courtyard and kill all of those monsters. Twenty-six, by his count. And then he would have to search the darkened house, room by room, looking for the others.

"Shit," he hissed. He was beginning to see the logic in the Emperor's plan. Fire would be faster, surer, much less risky.

Ōtoro rose and began walking quickly around the top of the wall to do a full circuit in case there was something he could use to distract some of the monsters while he killed the others. The dead below moaned hungrily and lumbered along, following his scent.

When he was on the far side he felt a salty breeze and turning saw that the sea was just beyond the compound. The harbor was choked with vessels that had been set ablaze or sunk where they were anchored. The entire harbor area, every pier and wharf, was overrun by the shambling infected.

Frowning, Ōtoro completed his circuit of the wall and braced himself for what was to come. He patted each of his pockets to reassure himself of the number and placement of his weapons, and he loosened his sword in its sheath. The creatures below milled around, their dark eyes and hungry mouths turned toward him as if they knew that he was bringing hot blood and fresh meat to them.

With prayers to demons and gods he'd long ago stopped worshipping Ōtoro prepared to enter hell. He dropped from the walkway to the slanted roof of a stable. The infected reached up for him, but even the tallest of them could barely scrape their finger against the terracotta tiles.

Ōtoro closed his eyes for a few seconds and muttered a prayer to gods he was sure had stopped listening to him decades ago. He prayed to the *kami*—the demons who were tied to this household. He prayed to the ghosts of Ito's ancestors to come and help him restore balance and honor to this family.

Only the cold wind answered him, and it carried within it the stink of rotting flesh, burned hair, and corruption.

The samurai squatted down and reached inside his kimono for a small roll of white paper. He unrolled it and read the words he had written the day after he had learned that he was dying of cancer. His death poem. The words would mean little to anyone else. They would likely never be read by anyone since this place would soon be burned to ash by the Emperor's ships.

All that mattered is that the words meant something to him.

He lifted the corner of one tile and slipped the edge of the paper in, letting the tile drop back into place. The paper fluttered in the breeze but the tile held it fast. Still squatting there, Ōtoro closed his eyes and recited the poem.

Empty-handed I entered
the world
Barefoot I leave it.
My coming, my going —
Two simple happenings
That got entangled.
Like dew drops
on a lotus leaf
I vanish.

A great peace seemed to settle over him as he spoke the last two words.

He opened his eyes and looked down at the milling dead.

"Thank you," he said.

And then the dying began.

-Hachi-

Ōtoro used the throwing spikes first.

He knelt and took careful aim with the first one, cocked his arm, threw, and saw the chunky sliver of steel punch into the back of the skull of Ito's wife. The woman staggered forward under the impact, her legs confused. She dropped to her knees, arms thrashing, fingers clawing at the air.

"Fall," begged Ōtoro, dreading that he had caused her more suffering rather than less. Then the flailing arms flapped to her sides and her body pitched forward without the slightest attempt to catch her fall.

The other infected milled around as before. If they noticed the death of one of their companions, it did not show.

Ōtoro selected a second spike, aimed and threw. This one punched through the eye-socket of Ito's eldest son and the force flung the young man back against the wall.

But he did not fall.

He rebounded clumsily from the impact and growled, low and feral, as he charged toward the stable.

Ōtoro took a breath and threw a second spike. This one hit the man's forehead, but the spike lacked the weight to chunk through the skull. It opened a deep gash and fell uselessly to the ground.

He tried a third spike and succeeded only in blinding the man.

Ōtoro tried to work that out, to make sense of it.

The spike to the back of Ito's wife's skull had killed her as surely as had the decapitation of the guard Ōtoro had met in the forest. He'd also cut off the heads of the next three dead he'd encountered.

Decapitation, it was clear, always worked.

The spike in the back of the skull had worked, too, but not as quickly.

The spikes in the eyes had not worked at all.

So what was he missing? What part of the brain needed to die in order to kill these infected?

He experimented, as grisly a thing as that was. He removed a pouch of six-pointed *shuriken* and hurled the metal stars at the dead. He hit eight of them in the head. Five were unaffected; one fell. That last one had been struck at the very base of the skull, where the spinal cord reaches up to the brain.

And then Ōtoro understood. It was that part of the brain. The big nerve at the top of the spine and the corresponding part of the brain near the bottom. The base of the skull, the neck, and the very top of the spinal column.

A delicate target. Acceptable for a sword, too risky for *tonki*—the throwing items like spikes and stars.

He let out a pent-up breath. He wished he had brought a bow and arrows. He could clear the entire courtyard with a large quiver of arrows. But, he did not have any and that meant that this was sword work. There was even some wry humor in that, a message from the universe reminding him that the samurai's own soul resided within the steel of his sword. How appropriate that was for reclaiming the soul of those who had been lost to the infection.

He rose, feeling his knees pop, and drew his sword. The steel glittered in the moonlight and the sight of him, standing tall above them, drew a deep moan of hunger from the dead.

With a warrior's cry, Ōtoro dropped from the stable roof into the midst of all those dead.

They swarmed around him.

And in his hands the cold steel sang its own death song. The blade hissed and rang and whispered as it cleaved through reaching arms in order to offer its calming kiss to dead necks. The bodies of the dead seemed to fly apart around him. He saw faces that he recognized from the silk portraits fly past him, detached from bodies, which reeled and fell in other directions.

Then there was a searing white-hot explosion of pain on his calf and he whirled and kicked free of something that lay sprawled on the ground.

It was Ito's eldest son, blind and crippled, sprawled on the ground, his mouth smeared with fresh blood. Ōtoro slashed down and the man's head rolled away. But the damage was done. Agony shot up Ōtoro's leg and when he back-pedaled away from the dead he left a trail of bloody footprints.

The bite had been strong, the teeth tearing through cloth and skin and muscle.

The wound burned with strange fires, as if the infection of the bite was already consuming his flesh.

How long did he have before it stole his mind and his life?

How long?

Ōtoro cut and cut, and more of the dead fell before him.

And then something happened that changed the shape of the night and nearly froze Ōtoro's heart in his chest.

It was a wail. High, and sharp, and filled with all of the terror in the world.

Ōtoro looked up, toward the house. Every pair of dead eyes looked up.

A window banged open and there, framed by a strange orange glow, stood a woman. She was as white as a ghost, with black and haunted eyes. She clutched a bundle to her chest. One hand was knotted in the fabric, the other arm ended in a ragged and bloody stump. For a fragmented moment Ōtoro thought that the woman was already dead, that this was one more monster come to the feast. But they he saw the wild panic in her eyes.

She screamed to him. Not in the inarticulate moan of the dead, but in words. Three words.

"*Save my baby!*"

But those words were drowned out by the infant's shrill scream of terror.

Behind mother and child, the orange glow resolved itself into the biting teeth of a fiery blaze. The woman had set the house on fire.

She leaned out through the window and held the bundle toward Ōtoro.

"Please..." she begged.

And she let the bundle fall.

-Kyu-

Ōtoro ran.

He did not remember catching the child.

He knew that he had been in motion before the child fell from his mother's arms, but he did not remember how he had gotten all the way across the compound in time to catch him.

The child screamed all the time he ran.

The courtyard was littered with the dead.

He had managed to accomplish great slaughter, before and after catching the child. But even that was blurred. His arm ached from the swordplay. His body was smeared with gore—red and viscous black. His leg felt as if real fire burned beneath his flesh.

He ran.

Behind him the dead followed.

Ōtoro had killed every member of Ito's family that he could find. Every single one.

The island, however, was filled with the dead. It was a land of the dead, and—drawn by the sounds of battle and the screams of the child—they had come to find a feast. Now they shambled through the woods behind him. Most of them moved slowly, but a few—the more recently dead—were faster. When they caught up, Ōtoro was forced to turn and fight.

Each time there was less of him for that task.

The child struggled and writhed within the bloodstained wrappings.

He did not even have time to check it, to see if it was free from infection.

All he could do was run.

It took ten thousand years to reach the beach. He placed the child in the bottom of the boat and then threw his weight against the craft, sliding it over the rasping sand. The moans of the dead were everywhere. When he dared to turn and look he saw them boil out from between the trees.

Dozens of them.

Hundreds.

The child screamed.

Ōtoro screamed, too.

The boat began drifting, caught by the outrolling surf. Ōtoro ran to catch up, but the dead caught him. Cold hands plucked at his hair, his sleeves, his sash. Teeth sunk into his skin. Blood burst from his flesh.

He bellowed with rage. He kicked and shoved and chopped and bashed.

And somewhere in the mad press of bodies his sword caught in bone and bent and snapped.

Ōtoro staggered backward into the surf, the broken sword in his hand.

He gaped at it for a split second.

The sword was his soul.

Broken now.

With a cry he flung it at the dead and then turned and dove into the waves. The salt water shrieked into every bite.

Ōtoro floundered and slogged and then swam.

He caught up to the boat.

He hung there for a long time as the current pulled them out to sea.

It took another thousand years for him to climb into the boat. Longer still to hoist the small sail.

The breeze was the only kindness. It blew in the right direction and the boat veered off toward the darkness. Toward a ship that lay somewhere out in the night.

When the boat was well out into the current and the sail was guiding them on a true course, Ōtoro slumped down and bent over the tiny, wriggling form. With great delicacy and great fear, he peeled back the layers of cloth. The child was covered in blood. In his mother's blood.

Ōtoro scooped handfuls of seawater up and used them to wash away the gore. He raised the screaming child up into the moonlight, turning him one way and then the other, looking for the slightest bite, the smallest nick.

There was nothing.

The child was untouched.

Pure.

Alive.

Ōtoro removed his kimono and used it to re-wrap the child. After a while the baby's screams faded into an exhausted whimper and then into silence as the rocking of the boat lulled it into fitful dreams.

Ōtoro sat back and rested his arm on the tiller.

He could feel the infection working within him. His skin already felt slack, his limbs leaden and wrong.

How long would it take?

Dawn was three hours away. If he held his course he would come up on Ito's ship as the first rosy light daubed the horizon.

If he *could* hold his course.

As the minutes crawled by sickness began to churn in his stomach.

And with it came a terrible new sensation. Not nausea...no, this was a dreadful, insidious need that burned in his stomach and bloomed like hateful flowers in his mind.

Hunger.

Unlike anything he had ever felt before.

A naked, raw, obscene hunger.

He looked down at the child.

It was a plump little thing. Tender and vulnerable.

Ōtoro set his jaw and locked his hand around the tiller. He would not succumb. Honor would hold him steady. The dawn was coming, the ship was coming. Rescue was coming. Not for him, but for this child. If he trusted to wind and tide, Ōtoro would have pitched himself over the side and left the baby to chance. But that was a foolish dream. That was something out of a storybook.

No, the boat needed a strong hand on the tiller. The sails needed trimming. And this child needed a samurai to see him home.

The hunger grew and grew.

"No," he told himself. "*No.*"

The hunger screamed 'yes.'

And Sensei Ōtoro screamed back at it. In his mind. In his heart. With his dying breath.

No.

The dawn seemed to be forever away.

And the boat sailed on through the night.

Author's Note on "Ink"

Ink is a new story that introduces a new character named Gerald 'Monk' Addison. Like the story that kicked off this book, "*Ink*" is tied to my Fire Zone story cycle. It's the first story set entirely on Boundary Street. Like all of the other Fire Zone stories I've written over the years, this one does not require knowledge of the Zone or exposure to any other story. They're all standalone.

That said, the character of Monk Addison appears in several stories, of which this was the first written but the second to hit print. The first story published was "*Mystic,*" which appeared in the anthology, *Peel Back the Skin* (June 2016, Grey Matter Press). A third, "*Grit,*" will be included in Christopher Golden's upcoming anthology, *Dark Cities* (Titan).

Ink

-1-

"What's this shit?" he said as he held the vial up to the light. "Looks like blood."

"Ink," I said.

He uncapped it and took a sniff. Winced. Gave me the stink-eye. "Fucking *smells* like blood."

I leaned against the doorframe and didn't say a word. This wasn't my usual tattoo parlor. I usually go to see my friend Patty Cakes who has a little skin art place just south of Boundary Street. It's a gritty little storefront tucked in between a leather bar called *Pornstash* and a deli called *Open All Night*, which, as far as anyone I know can tell you, has never been open. Patty never asks questions about where my ink comes from. She probably knows.

This guy, though...? He doesn't know me all that well and I'm not a Chatty Cathy even when I'm in a good mood. Which I wasn't that night. There was a cold late September drizzle falling from a bruise-colored sky. Not actually night but dark enough for the shadow crowd to be out. The neon and back-alley types. The cruisers who want to hit every game in town in the hopes that they can find the luck they misplaced five or ten or twenty years ago.

Like me, I guess.

This parlor was called *Switchblade Charlie's*, but the guy holding my ink wasn't Charlie. His name was Cajun Joe. Probably had a switchblade, though. He looked the type. And there are types, even when it comes to knives. If he was bigger I'd have figured him for a combat vet and that meant he might have a Ka-bar or bayonet in a sheath tucked on the inside of his denim vest. If he was a little guy he'd have a thrown-down. Maybe a .22 or a .25. Something he could palm; something with all the serial numbers filed off. But this guy was medium height, medium weight, medium build, and medium aged. Call it forty and change. Younger than me, but only two thirds as heavy. He had a nervous tic to his left eye and there was gristle around the eye and a cauliflower ear, so he probably picked that up from the ring. Could not have been very good because the good ones can afford the surgery to fix the cartilage damage and they also don't work in shit holes like this one. His hands were steady, though, and his arms weren't overly developed. A guy who likes his speed and doesn't want to get slowed down by bulk. And he had a lot of skin art. Full sleeves, a collar rising to his ears, a burning cross on the back of his neck, and 88 in burning red on the inside of his left wrist. The two eights stand for the eighth letter of the alphabet—H and H. *Heil Hitler.* Cute. He also had '14' on his other wrist, on the arm of the hand holding the vial. That's shorthand for the fourteen-word credo of the white supremacy movement. The whole phrase is 'We *must secure the existence of our people and a future for white children.*'

So, yeah, a dickhead like Cajun Joe would probably carry a switchblade because those knives make a guy like him think he has a big dick, and it makes other people scared. Too many 1950's gang flicks, too many movies since. People see a switchblade and they know they're going to bleed. You don't carry one to help you open packages or cut zip-ties. You carry one when you want to cut someone and you like seeing them get terrified as they realize what's going to happen.

The tattoo artist stared at me, waiting for me to say something. I didn't.

"How do I know this stuff is safe?" he asked.

I shrugged. "The fuck is it to you?"

Cajun Joe thought about that, gave a shrug of his own. "Okay," he said.

"Okay."

"What kind of art you want?"

I was wearing a black hoodie with the sleeves pulled down, the hood pulled up, the zipper halfway to my throat. That hid most of the art I already had.

"Need you to finish a piece," I said. "Someone else started it but I need you to finish it."

"Like doing my own stuff," he said.

"You like getting paid?"

"Well...yeah."

"That mean you'll finish the tat?"

He considered me for a moment, nodded. "What's the art?"

"A girl's face," I said and shoved up my left sleeve. My forearm is covered with faces. Girls and women, but also boys and men. So are my upper arms, chest, thighs, back. A lot of them. Nearly a hundred now, and plenty of room for more.

He grunted and gestured with the vial. "They're all black and white. You thinking about adding color? If so, then I got to use something else than what you brought or they're going to turn out like Indians."

"It's just the outline."

I turned my arm to show him the face. It was three quarters done but there were bits missing. Part of the nose, some of the brow-shape, the corners of the mouth. Enough so that the face as it was looked generic. A woman. Not especially pretty, but female.

"It's all in black," he said. "It'll wind up two-toned."

I smiled. "That ink'll dry dark."

"It won't," he advised.

"It will."

Cajun Joe frowned at the vial then cocked an eye at me. "You sure about that?"

"Dead certain."

"Okay," he said, giving me another and much more elaborate shrug. "It's your skin, brother."

I came real close to killing him right there and then. Some people can call me brother. Some can't. He shouldn't have.

-2-

When I took my hoodie off his eyes bugged at the faces already inked into my skin.

"That's some collection," he said.

"Yeah."

"They all friends of yours?"

"Not really."

"Movie stars…'cause some of them look familiar."

"Do they?" I asked as I hung my hoodie over the back of an empty chair.

"A little familiar. Is that one that chick from the Mad Max film? Charlie Theory?"

"Charlize Theron?"

"Yeah."

"No."

"Oh," he said. "She was hot in that flick, even if she had a robot arm."

"It's not Charlize Theron."

"Looks like her."

"Not really." I touched the tattoo. The woman whose face was inked into the inside curve of my deltoid was named Molly Flanders. A great Irish name for a great Irish-American woman. Mother of two. R.N. at the E.R. over on the other side of Boundary Street. Dead now. Beaten to death by her husband because he wasn't man enough to face losing his job and because Molly got between him and the kids every time he was drunk. Molly died and so did her husband. Two separate but related incidents. Both very violent. I was involved in one of them. I put the husband in the ground and made it hurt all the way. So, Molly was one of my people. One of the pale and quiet ones who come to see if they can hire me. I remember the first time I saw her, standing next to me at my corner booth at Dollar Bill's Tavern. Standing there with her swollen face, smashed lips, broken teeth, and broken neck. I'd tried to talk her out of hiring me. Tried to explain how expensive it was. Not in dollars. In other ways. But...after he'd killed her, Molly's rat-fuck husband had started in on the kids. One was in rehab now, learning to walk all over again. That was Kenny, ten years old and he'd never walk without leg braces. The little one, Lindsay, two, would have to figure out how to make the world work without being able to see it. Doesn't take more than a drunk's fist to do unfixable damage to a kid's face.

Molly didn't want to go into the dark without knowing her husband had paid, and paid hard. Going to jail wasn't enough. Not after what he'd done to the kids.

You see, that's how it usually works. The kind of clients who come looking for me don't want revenge for themselves. The price is way too high for that. Way too fucking high. No, they want me to step in when their killer is hurting—or in Molly's case *has* hurt— others. Sometimes they want me to stop the bad guy before he does something else to someone else. They want me to do what the cops, with all of their limited resources and rules, can't. Or won't.

When a client wants to hire me on those terms, it means that they are willing to pay the price. Not my day-rate, which is what I get paid to find bail-skips or take photos of philandering spouses. No, that kind of work is what I do for greasy lawyers and greasier bail-bondsmen. Like J. Heron Scarebaby and Iver Twitch—real names of a couple of lowlifes who hire me out for conventional gigs.

No, clients like Molly and a hundred others have to pay a higher price but it's not to me. Not sure who they're paying. Who *we're* paying, because I owe something on that tab, too. Each time.

The price is a total bitch.

It's an absolute monster. I'm not sure I'd have the courage to pay it myself if I was in their shoes. And I didn't know about my debt until I took my first client. A village girl in Tibet who'd been gang-raped by Chinese soldiers. The same soldiers who'd raped seventeen other girls and killed six of them. The same soldiers who were garrisoned outside of her village. The village where the murdered girl had four sisters.

You see how it works?

I took that gig and hers was the first face inked onto my flesh. She's there, a few inches from my heart. Half an inch from a bullet wound I got in Iraq.

The girl and I both paid the price. And every single goddamn night we pay a little more of it.

Now I was here at Switchblade Charlie's. I watched Cajun Joe's eyes as he studied the faces on my skin. I usually keep covered up, but enough people have seen me without a shirt for me to have a good read on how they react. Cajun Joe was surprised at the number of tats, confused at the theme, and disapproving of the skill. Patty Cakes is a great tattoo artist but I can't always provide a photo to work from. Sometimes Patty doesn't need one, not when she's totally in the zone. Sometimes she does. The tattoo artist in Tibet didn't. That girl had been his niece. We both wept and we both screamed at different times as he sank the ink onto my chest.

Cajun Joe told me to sit and when I did he moved a light on a flexible arm so that it bathed my arm. He bent and studied the partial tattoo.

"All you want is the lines connected?"

"Pretty much," I said.

"This is nothing. Anyone could have done this shit. Ten, fifteen minutes."

"I know."

Without raising his head he glanced up at me. "But you were in the waiting room for two hours until I was free."

"Sure."

"Why me?"

"I heard you were the man for the job."

He sat back and studied me for a moment, suspicion flickering in his eyes. "Says who?"

I shrugged. "People. I asked around. Your name came up."

"Which people?"

"Hey, I came here for some ink, not to marry you," I said. "I'll pay the rate for a full tat."

The suspicion lingered and he shook his head. "You running a game on me or something?"

"No games," I said, and that was true enough. I wasn't there to play. "Word is that you're good and I don't use second string artists."

He glanced at the simplicity of the faces and maybe that's when he took a longer, better look. They looked simple, but they weren't. Not if you really looked at them. Patty Cakes did a lot of them and she has the touch. So did that guy at the Tibetan village. And Mama Jewel in New Orleans. And each of the artists who have left their mark on me. Maybe not the best fine-artists in the world, but when you look into the eyes of each of those faces and you pay attention, you understand why people say the eyes are the window of the soul.

He made a sound. Not quite a word, not quite a grunt. More like an expression of wonder. Like when you stare at an optical illusion and you suddenly see the hidden message and realize that it was there all the time. Only now you can see it.

"So," I said, "are we good?"

He began nodding while still staring into the eyes of the dead faces on my skin. "Yeah," he said, then he looked up at me. "Yeah, we're good."

-3-

I unwrapped a piece of Juicy-Fruit gum as I watched him pour some of the red juice in the vial into a little pot. He asked if it was okay for him to add some of his own ink and I said sure. The color of the mixture remained dark red, though, even after he mixed it fifty-fifty with black. That surprised him and he commented on it, asking again what was in that vial.

"It's special sauce," I told him as I put the stick of gum into my mouth. "What's it matter?"

It was clear he wanted to object, but in the end the matter was decided by the money he'd make doing half a quick job.

"You paying in cash?" he asked.

And I knew I had him.

"Yeah. Small unmarked bills."

We both had a chuckle over that. But he didn't reach for the tools until I pulled out my wallet and counted out a stack of twenties thick enough to look interesting.

Only then did he set to work.

Most tattoo artists ask to see your I.D. State laws about verifying age and all, but I have a face like an eroded wall and I've been street legal for a lot of years. I look it. Besides, we both knew he was going to pocket whatever I paid him. That's why he didn't have me sign a waiver or provide my address and phone number. He could read enough about me to know that he shouldn't bother.

I settled into the tattoo chair. His workspace was shared but right now we were alone. The place used to be an old-fashioned barbershop and they still had four chairs. Someone had hung tracks for partition curtains, but they were all pulled back. The lights were low except around Cajun Joe's station, and the walls were covered with hundreds of designs. Books with thousands more. Devils and unicorns, pirate chicks and panthers, skulls and snakes. The usual shit. The stuff pinned to the wall behind Cajun Joe tended to have a rougher edge. Zombies with storm trooper helmets—and I'm not talking Star Wars. Swastikas and confederate flags. And all kinds of crosses, some of them on fire.

He swabbed my arm with alcohol and then ran a disposable razor over it to remove any hair stubble. I didn't have much left on my arms.

A lot of tattoo studios use a thermal-fax to make their stencils. This saves the artist the time he'd normally spend tracing a piece of art you bring in. Patty uses one for goofy shit like when people want a celebrity's signature or one of their own drawings. She never used one for the art she did for me, and since Cajun Jack was only finishing a face he didn't have to. That allowed us to skip the step of having the scanned art transferred onto my skin.

Instead he began prepping his tattoo machine. He took the mixed ink and poured it into one of those tiny cups they call an ink cap. He selected his needles and tubes from their sterile pouches and placed them into their slots in the machine. Then he added clean, distilled water into a cup for cleaning the needles during the tattoo process.

Some people pass out during a tattoo job. Not from the pain but from panic. The sight of the needles freaks them out. Not me, though. But I could feel my heartbeat quicken. Soon, I knew, it would begin to race. I could almost feel the sweat lurking inside my pores, ready to pop.

For me it's the actual pain. Not of the needle. Hell, no, that's just skin pain. What the fuck's that to someone like me? Who gives a small, cold shit about that.

No, it was part of the price I had to pay when I took a job. As the face stopped being a collection of lines and became a person, something in that person woke up. And it woke inside of me. It started like a fever and then it turned into a scream.

Hard to explain.

Hard to sit through.

Patty Cakes usually insists I put a leather strap between my teeth. Helps to keep me from screaming. Makes it easier for her to work, though…she's very sensitive, you dig? Sometimes we both end up screaming.

Maybe Cajun Joe would end up screaming, too. Maybe we both would.

"How you want me to do this?" he asked. "You don't have a picture of this broad. How am I supposed to know what she's supposed to look like?"

"Connect the lines."

"Not as easy as that," he protested.

I had to work at it to keep the smile off my face. Not a happy smile. Not a friendly one, either. "I'm sure you'll make it right," I told him.

Cajun Joe took in a deep breath and exhaled through his nose. I was being weird and elusive and it was trying his patience. I saw his eyes click over to the money on the side table and then back to the half-finished face.

He held up the needle and gave me an inquiring uptick of his chin. I gave him a nod.

He began to work.

-4-

The face looked like nobody for a while.

But I could feel her waiting to be seen.

Cajun Joe started with the jaw because that was the easiest to figure out. Most of the lines were done and it was simply a matter of connecting the chin to the jaw. It hurt, but it was still skin pain. I chewed my gum. Salt helps with nausea but for me sugar helps with pain. This kind of pain. I sometimes went through a whole bag of M&M's or a big box of Dots when Patty was doing a face. That sanded maybe ten percent off the top of what I felt. Small mercies, but in this world you got to take what you can get.

"Who is she?" he asked as he connected the jaw to the cheek.

"A woman."

"I know that, but can you tell me something about her? Help me see her?"

Christ I wanted to grab the needle out of his hand and stab him with it. The only reason I didn't is that I was not one hundred percent sure it was Cajun Joe I was looking for. After looking for two weeks he was at the top of my short list. Switchblade Charlie was on the list, too. And Bugsy the Mummy, another skin-jockey over on Shade Street, near that big club, Unlovely's. I had to be sure because otherwise I'm as bad as them. I'm really cool with righteous rage and harsh justice and all that movie vengeance shit, but collateral damage isn't in the game plan. Nor is an unfortunate accident. Making sure, being certain, makes this harder. It increases the risks, it ups the pain, and—for me and my client—it edges us closer to having to pay the whole ticket. If there was any way I could be certain without having the tattoo completed, then it would be a better end to the day. Not for Cajun Joe, mind you. But for my client. And for me.

Life is always a complicated motherfucker. Always, always, always.

So, sure, I decided to tell him something about her. Some of what I knew. But here's the thing...I didn't actually know everything. I wouldn't ever get a full picture until there was...well...a full picture, you dig? All I had to work with was bits of memory. Tastes of it.

"She worked over on the west side," I said. "In one of the clubs."

"Waitress? Some of those bitches over there are hot. And I mean smokin'."

He worked on her eyebrow, matching the missing one to the other.

"Bartender?" he speculated. "She looks a little like this Italian girl who works at Sparky's—"

"She's not Italian."

"Oh."

"Not a bartender."

"Oh."

"Prep cook. Worked in the kitchen," I said.

He finished the eyebrow. It was starting to hurt. A lot. I waited for my comment to catch up with him. "Worked? She's not there anymore?"

"She moved on."

He cut me a quick look. "Ran out on you?"

"She's still around."

He laughed. "Yeah, I guess so. I mean, why else would you ink her onto your arm if she's gone, right?"

I said nothing. All of those faces, female and male, seemed to be looking at him. No, let me change that, they *were* looking at him. I could feel it. Feel them. In a strange way they were all there with me. Like they always are. I'm never really alone except when I go into my special quiet place inside. Meditation is the only thing that works better than sugar. It doesn't stop the pain but it lets me be alone with my own thoughts. Right now, though, we were all watching Cajun Joe work.

He finished the eyebrow, paused, pursed his lips like a jeweler contemplating a cut, then thickened the line a little. He was good, he had moves, at least when it came to ink. He probably thought that he had all sorts of moves.

"What about her cheeks?" he asked. "They as high as they look or do you want me to flatten them down?"

"Cheekbones are fine. Work on the hair."

He nodded. The hair was short and kinky. There was enough there for him to continue the shape and style. With every sting of the needle I felt a knife turn in my heart. There was a big bell ringing, deep and slow, in the back of my head. The echoes hurt like punches. I was sweating now and it took everything I had to keep it off my face and out of my voice.

"So this chick," he said, "she your sweetheart or what?"

He was maybe trying to make conversation, maybe fishing for information.

"Never actually met her," I said.

The needle paused, hovering like a hornet above my skin. "What?"

Instead of answering I said, "Do the lips."

He studied me for a moment, his eyes coming in and out of focus. "Um…" he said, but left it there. Cajun Joe did a last touch on the hair, wiped the blood, and shifted to focus on the mouth. It was almost the last part of the image that would really matter. He started to work, stopped, bent to peer closer.

"Can't tell how they're supposed to be," he said.

"Full."

"What?"

"She had very full lips."

Something about that troubled him, I could see it on his face. But he said nothing as he dipped into the cup for more ink and started to shape the lips.

I wondered if she would scream when they were done. I might.

But I decided, no. The nose was the last thing. After that…well, all bets were off after that.

The lips changed the whole picture, though.

"She looks…" he began, but didn't finish it. His eyes were locked on the image. It was more than a picture. It was becoming the portrait it was meant to be. Dark eyes, short hair, good lines. Not beautiful by Hollywood standards. Beautiful by human being standards, but I doubted Cajun Joe was capable of grasping that.

Something was getting through to him, though.

I smiled through the pain. "Be careful, man, your hands are shaking."

He stopped abruptly, loaded more ink, but was looking at me. Hard. "You fucking with me, man?"

"No," I lied. "Just want to get this done and get on my way."

So many expressions came and went on his face. Doubt, anger, fear, confusion. Mixtures and combinations of those and more. He absolutely knew something was hinky about all this. Knew it. And he knew that I knew he knew it. It was like that, but we hadn't broken through the fourth wall, yet. We were still actors playing out the roles assigned us by our shared participation in the drama of daily, ordinary life.

That wall was crumbling, though. With every drop of ink he drilled into my skin it was crumbling. And with every drop I was getting closer to the truth. Soon I was going to know. Soon it was going to be certain. Either he was the guy or he wasn't.

Right now, though, his doubt was holding that wall in place. He hadn't flipped into an open and obvious knowing. There was no guilt in his eyes. Not yet.

That needed more ink.

So I waited while he thought about it, waited while he decided to go back to the job. Watched and waited while he finished the lips.

"The nose," I said. "That's the last part."

There was very little to the nose. I'd left that part intentionally vague. Patty had understood when she did her part. The nose would clinch it, even in a black and white tat.

"What kind of nose does he have?" he asked. Was there a crack in his voice? Was it a little hoarse?

I couldn't tell.

Almost, but not quite.

"Short nose," I said, touching my arm to indicate where it should end. "Long philtrum. You know what a philtrum is? The gulley under the nose?"

"Yeah," he said softly. "I know."

"Long philtrum. Pretty deep, too."

He cleared his throat. "And her nose?"

"Do the other part first."

He did. It hurt. I bled. We both sweated. The room was cold but we both had lines running crookedly down our faces. He had a drop hanging from the point of his chin.

It seemed to take forever to finish the gulley above those full lips.

"Now the nose," I said, and I traced it on my skin with the tip of my index finger. "This long. Wide. Kind of flat from where she got it broken when her first husband knocked her around. Never set right."

Sweat ran like hot mercury down his face.

"The fuck is this?" he asked.

"It's a tattoo," I said. "Finish the nose and then I'm gone."

He began to work on it, but his hands were shaking pretty bad. It wasn't going to be his best work and I'd have to wear it for the rest of my life. Life sucks in a lot of ways and that part wasn't anything major. I could see the muscles at the corner of his jaw bunching and I knew he was getting mad, too.

Mad was okay. We could work with it.

He worked on the nose, following my directions and suggestions. The more it took form the slower he worked. The nose made the face, you see. It pulled all of the parts together. It made it a very specific kind of face. Even in black and white. Even without the dark brown skin and the darker brown eyes that she had when she was alive. That nose and those lips turned the face from generic woman to black woman.

That's what he realized as he worked.

I watched him to see what that realization would do to him. That he was a racist dickhead was evident from the 88 and 14 tats. But being a racist dickhead isn't enough. Free country, free speech and all that shit. I don't go hunting for everyone whose philosophy pushes my ideological buttons. I'm not a fanatic and I'm not a sociopath.

I'm something else, and that something else needed this guy to be a very specific kind of racist dickhead.

I needed him to look at that face and do more than realize he was inking the features of an African-American woman on a customer's arm. Again, that was nothing. Like me, he probably inked all sorts of shit *he* didn't believe in. Nature of the game in a free country.

I'm not an artist but I've had enough tattoos to know something about it. There is a point when a collection of lines and curves stops being arranged ink and becomes an actual piece of art. I think it's when the subject matter comes into true alignment with the artist's technique. It's a kind of magic. The image becomes real, and when you look at it you're not seeing a painting or a drawing or a tattoo. You're not even seeing the stylized version of it that has been filtered through the artist's talent. You're seeing the actual thing. Look at Van Gogh's *Café Terrace at Night* and tell me you can't hear the sounds of laughter and conversation, of coffee cups clinking on saucers, of cutlery tinking against plates or scraping on teeth, of the gurgle of wine as it's poured into glasses. Tell me you can't smell that wine, and the bread, the cheese, the meats. I can look at that painting, even a copy of it, and smell cigarette smoke, perfume, and fresh-cooked fish. Same goes for when I look at Gauguin's *Tahitian Women on the Beach*. If you can't smell coconut oil on warm skin and hear the soft crash and hiss of the surf then you have no soul.

When Cajun Joe finished the last part of the nose, joining the lines that formed the right nostril, the face on my arm became a person. A woman. Not the representation of a murdered woman, but her. Actually her. Alive. Not in the way she had been before she'd been beaten and raped and slashed to red ruin. And not a ghost version of her. When I looked down at her face I saw the essential woman. The truth of her. The reality of her.

It was so powerful because that acceptance of her kicked open a door in my head and my heart. Kicked it off the hinges and let all of her life pour into me. From the moment she woke up in her mother's womb until they zipped her into a body bag. I saw all of her life. It hit me in a rush and it feels like having forty-eight years of joy, pain, understanding, love, passion, ennui, compassion, dislike, hatred, giddiness, pity, and ten thousand other emotions shoved into me through that five-inch tattoo. I mainlined her entire life and the inrush nearly tore me apart.

All of the seventeen thousand five hundred and twenty days of her life.

How many emotions does a person experience in an average day? How many in each hour? If it was even possible for a person to feel only two different emotions in any given hour that meant that eight-hundred and forty-thousand individual needles of awareness stabbed into me.

In five or ten seconds.

I threw my head back and screamed.

What else could I do?

Cajun Joe staggered backward from his chair, his needles and the pots of ink falling and tumbling, clinking and splashing. I was aware of it but didn't see it. Not really. All I could see was the woman's life. Rushing, whirling, tumbling, kicking, slashing as it whirled around in my head.

And then the images suddenly slowed, crystalized as they do every time I go through this. First it's the tsunami of their life's emotions and then...then...

And then it's the memories of what happened in those last few moments of her life. Those last terrible moments.

The hands grabbing her as she pulled the kitchen door closed and stepped into the darkened parking lot behind the club. Her ring of keys—the bar key, her car key, her house key—tinkled to the blacktop. Hands on her. An arm around her neck to choke off her screams. Another hand reached around, clamped on her stomach to pull her backward from the security light, into the shadows. Turning her, slapping her, a fist driving into her stomach, knocking the air and the hope from her. The hands grabbing cloth, ripping, exposing.

Lips on her flesh. Lips forming words. Hateful words. Calling her a bitch, a whore, a nigger slut as he ripped her clothes and forced her down and swarmed over her like a blanket of hate.

She'd fought him.

She was a woman who worked nights and worked in a club that wasn't in the best part of town. She had pepper spray in her bag, but her bag was gone. She tried to punch, to claw, to bite. She fought to live. For her kids. For her sisters of color who had been consumed by monsters of this kind for hundreds of years. For women of every kind. For her own life.

And the man—if that word even fits—laughed at her and took her over and over again. Hitting her, breaking her. Destroying her.

What was left after the rape was unable to even move. Totally unable to fight.

The knife hadn't been necessary.

Except it had.

In that last moment, while she lay already dying, she had seen the face of the man who had done this. His face. His clothes.

And his tattoos.

88.

The world spun and spun around me but I forced myself back into the moment. Even with her screaming in my head, I returned to who and what I was, and why I was there.

Cajun Joe stared at me and at *her*. I knew he could see her face on my arm, but more importantly he could see her soul in my eyes.

He was sweating and shaking. Equal parts terror and rage. And hate. Let's not forget the hate. Lots of hate in that room.

"What the fuck are you?" he breathed.

I said, "My name is Denita King."

It was my voice but it wasn't me speaking.

Cajun Joe had a switchblade in his hand. I hadn't even seen him pull it. Four-inch blade, glistening with oil. Sturdy, good for fighting.

I smiled at him as I got up out of the chair.

It may have been Mrs. King who'd spoken with my mouth, but that smile was all my own. My hands were my own. My fingers, my fists.

He screamed so loud and he screamed for a long time.

-5-

Back at my place. In my room with all the windows painted black. Lying in bed, praying for sleep, knowing it wouldn't come. Not unless I drank all the lights out.

It's hard to sleep in such a crowded room.

They're always there. Always standing around my bed. Pale faces, gray faces. Most of them are silent. They stand there and stare at me, and sometimes at their own faces on my skin.

Mrs. King was there now. She wasn't silent. She was one of the screamers. She'd loved being alive. She'd loved her kids. And she fought so damn hard.

She screamed.

And she'd scream like that every night for as long as I lived. That was the price and we'd both been willing to pay it.

God damn it.

My name is Gerald Addison. Most people call me Monk.

Tomorrow I'll get up, get washed, and maybe I'll spend the day chasing a bail skip. Or maybe a client will find me.

I lay there at night and listen to the screams.

As the night closes around me like a fist.

JONATHAN MABERRY is a NY Times bestselling novelist, five-time Bram Stoker Award winner, and comic book writer. He writes the Joe Ledger thrillers, the Rot & Ruin series, the Nightsiders series, the Dead of Night series, as well as standalone novels in multiple genres. His novels include KILL SWITCH, the 8th in his best-selling Joe Ledger thriller series; VAULT OF SHADOWS, a middle-grade sf/fantasy mash-up; and MARS ONE, a standalone teen space travel novel. He is the editor of many anthologies including THE X-FILES, SCARY OUT THERE, OUT OF TUNE, and V-WARS. His comic book works include, among others, *CAPTAIN AMERICA,* the Bram Stoker Award-winning *BAD BLOOD, ROT & RUIN, V-WARS,* the NY Times best-selling *MARVEL ZOMBIES RETURN,* and others. His books EXTINCTION MACHINE and V-WARS are in development for TV/film. A board game version of V-WARS was released in early 2016. He is the founder of the Writers Coffeehouse, and the co-founder of The Liars Club. Prior to becoming a full-time novelist, Jonathan spent twenty-five years as a magazine feature writer, martial arts instructor and playwright. He was a featured expert on the History Channel documentary, *Zombies: A Living History* and a regular expert on the TV series, *True Monsters.* He is one third of the very popular and mildly weird Three Guys With Beards pop-culture podcast. Jonathan lives in Del Mar, California with his wife, Sara Jo. www.jonathanmaberry.com

JONATHAN MABERRY,
SEANAN McGUIRE, LAIRD BARRON,
DAVID LISS, and KEITH R.A. DeCANDIDO

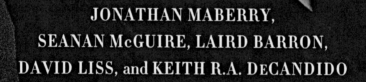

LIMBUS

INC.

──── BOOK III ────

EDITED BY BRETT J. TALLEY

OUT OF TUNE
Book 2
Allison Pang
Cherie M. Priest
Dan Abnett
David Mack
Deborah Grabien
Delilah S. Dawson
Eric J. Guignard
Josh Malerman
Laura Anne Gilman
Nik Vincent-Abnett
Rachel Aukes
Rachael Caine
James A. Moore
David J. Schow
J. C. Koch
Nancy Keim - Comley
EDITED BY
JONATHAN MABERRY
NEW YORK TIMES BESTSELLER

Lightning Source UK Ltd.
Milton Keynes UK
UKOW01f1828020117
291201UK00001B/24/P